PRAISE FOR
Nothing Without Me

"Terrific . . . An absolute humdinger of a thriller!"
—Gytha Lodge, author of *A Killer in the Family*

"Expertly plotted and pulsing with suspense, *Nothing Without Me* plunges readers into the cutthroat world of Hollywood, peeling back the veneer of celebrity and deftly exposing the dark side of fame and ruthless ambition. A twisty and timely read, it kept me guessing right up to the jaw-dropping end."
—Lindsay Cameron, author of *No One Needs to Know*

"A pulse-pounding roller coaster through the shadows of the silver screen, *Nothing Without Me* will leave you questioning the true nature of celebrity and the devastating sacrifices women are forced to make to stay in the spotlight's glow. Helen Monks Takhar lays bare the dark side of Hollywood glitz and glamour in this chilling and intoxicating mystery."
—Jaclyn Goldis, author of *The Chateau*

PRAISE FOR THE WORK OF
Helen Monks Takhar

"An addictive thriller . . . A hypnotic dance . . . that doesn't let up until its final unnerving reveal."

—People

"Delicious."

—New York Post

"Chilling, smart, and brutal . . . A triumph of a debut."

—Harper's Bazaar

"Absolutely haunting . . . I don't believe I will forget these characters, nor their story, anytime soon."

—The Nerd Daily

"Epic."

—CrimeReads

"Enjoyably poisonous."

—The Independent

"Enthralling."

—The Sunday Times

"An impressive, unsettling debut."

—Woman & Home

"Dark and totally gripping."

—Bella

"[A] clever, truly creepy, and uniquely modern tale."

—Woman's Own

"We were hooked from the first page—a brilliant and dark story."

—Closer

"Tightly plotted and gripping."

—*Woman's Weekly*

"Sexy, scary, and satirical, [it's] a cat-and-mouse tale on steroids."

—*The Bookseller*

"Wickedly sharp."

—*Kirkus Reviews* (starred review)

"Fiendishly entertaining . . . A suspenseful and unsettling cautionary tale. Monks Takhar remains a writer to watch."

—*Publishers Weekly*

"Perfect for those . . . looking for psychologically twisty thrillers . . . à la *The Girl on the Train*."

—*Booklist*

"Creepy and unnerving, with observations that are often dead-on. A breathtaking debut by Helen Monks Takhar."

—Samantha Downing, internationally bestselling author of *My Lovely Wife*

"A deliciously dark, addictive, and twisted page-turner."

—Alice Feeney, *New York Times* bestselling author of *Sometimes I Lie*

"I was absolutely transfixed."

—Amanda Eyre Ward, *New York Times* bestselling author of *The Jetsetters*

"If you're looking for smart, suspenseful prose, look no further. Helen Monks Takhar is now on my favorite list of authors."

—Georgina Cross, author of *Nanny Needed*

By Helen Monks Takhar

Nothing Without Me
Such a Good Mother
Precious You

Nothing Without Me

Nothing Without Me

A NOVEL

Helen Monks Takhar

RANDOM HOUSE

NEW YORK

Nothing Without Me is a work of fiction. Names, characters, places, and incidents are the products of the author's imagination or are used fictitiously. Any resemblance to actual events, locales, or persons, living or dead, is entirely coincidental.

A Random House Trade Paperback Original

Copyright © 2024 by Helen Monks Takhar
Book club guide copyright © 2024
by Penguin Random House LLC

All rights reserved.

Published in the United States by Random House, an imprint and division of Penguin Random House LLC, New York.

RANDOM HOUSE and the HOUSE colophon are registered trademarks of Penguin Random House LLC.
RANDOM HOUSE BOOK CLUB and colophon are trademarks of Penguin Random House LLC.

Originally published in paperback in the United Kingdom by HQ, an imprint of HarperCollins Publishers Ltd, in 2024.

ISBN 978-0-593-59618-0
Ebook ISBN 978-0-593-59619-7

Printed in the United States of America on acid-free paper

randomhousebooks.com
randomhousebookclub.com

2 4 6 8 9 7 5 3 1

For Danny, Mohinder and Zora, again and always.

Words—so innocent and powerless as they are, as standing in a dictionary, how potent for good and evil they become in the hands of one who knows how to combine them.

—*Nathaniel Hawthorne*

The entire world feels entitled to know everything about me. . . . If I were just your average twenty-three-year-old girl, and I called the police to say that there were strange men sleeping on my lawn and following me into Starbucks, they would leap into action. But because I am a famous person, well, sorry, ma'am, there's nothing we can do.

—*Jennifer Lawrence*

Nothing Without Me

CAST

April . . . . THE DIRECTOR
Essie . . . . THE ACTRESS
Jags . . . . APRIL'S BOYFRIEND
Janine . . . . ESSIE'S SISTER/MANAGER
Jonathan . . . . ESSIE'S AGENT
Jackson . . . . ESSIE'S EX
Jude . . . . THE TV STAR
Con . . . . ESSIE'S FATHER
Una . . . . ESSIE'S MOTHER
Juniper . . . . THE SUPPORTING ACTRESS

ACT I

'As a director, the best choices you make will often be the hardest won, though to the viewer, these will appear self-evident. Certain scenes, when viewed from the angle and focus you have chosen, feel so intuitive in their design, so obvious in their emotional impact, the person watching will have no idea about the dilemmas you tackled in creating them. They will neither know, nor care, what tortures you endured before arriving at your decisions, purely because you've made that choice feel like the most natural outcome imaginable.'

FILM SCHOOL LECTURE NOTES TRANSCRIPTION

1

Essie, the night of the awards

My body floats facedown in my pool at Lotus Lodge.

My dress is perfect: backless, bright white like the moon. The lapping water sends the hem towards the top of my thighs. Like the rest of me, my legs are spray-tanned nut-brown; my extensions are blonde, snaking across the surface of the water like they want to get away from me; my fingernails, black. My psychiatrist told me I suffer from a dissociative disorder and looking at my body now – its legs, skin, hair, and nails – I believe her. None of these pieces of me feel like they really belong to me now, if they ever did. Maybe that's what happens when everyone from your mother down has their take on every part of you: long-lens beach shots of my legs' 'stubborn cellulite'; newspaper columns on the lines on my face and the procedures I apparently had in a 'desperate bid' to get rid of them; Twitter memes of my damp underarms on set at *Daybreak*. Wouldn't these disconnect even a well-adjusted woman from herself? And with my family, I was never coming at the mad intrusion of fame into my body, into my entire life, from a place where I knew where my boundaries ought to lie.

But none of that matters now. I've crossed a line. I can't

5

come back over it. I don't want to. So, let's pan out and look at the scene.

It looks kind of like the start of *Sunset Boulevard*, only it's me, the star of the screen, who's facedown in the water. No chance I'll be staring into a camera like Norma Desmond tonight, ready for my close-up. And the writer isn't narrating this story from beyond the grave. She is alive, but she's not well, not now she's seen me.

'NO!' April shrieks from my poolside. She's also in a white dress, her grey-blonde hair in its usual braid at her neck. Her palms fly to the sides of her head as she steps closer to the pool, before retreating to the sliding glass doors that divide it from my favourite living space in Lotus. Bent like a drinking straw, her hands against the glass, April hyperventilates as she speaks.

'Oh god, oh god, oh god. No, Essie. Please, no.' She forces herself to turn back to view my body once more. 'What have you done!?'

April immediately assumes I've done this to myself and, in a way, she's right. But millions of people are culpable. Every person who clicked on one of those stories about my body; everyone who piled on to make my name trend on Twitter for no good reason, posted some dark comment on Insta, or picked up a magazine at the checkout because I was on the cover crying over 'my latest heartbreak' or 'the fallout from my shocking scandal'; every single person who shoved a smartphone in my face to steal another image of me, ignoring me when I begged them, 'Please. Not today'; they have their share of blame for pushing me to this point. And if they could see me now, I know what they'd be thinking: *Essie Lay has finally added herself to the rest*: Amy Winehouse, Caroline Flack, Paula Yates, Marilyn

6

Monroe . . . Last year, I fell off my throne as the queen of British light entertainment and into the gutter. Now, I'm one more famous female scalp they picked away at until it seemed there wasn't enough left of Essie Lay worth saving.

April walks shakily back to the pool. She doesn't notice the empty champagne bottle on the tiles until the side of her heel catches it and it rolls into the water with a splash. With her next steps, April grinds some stray pills into the sole of her shoe. Spotting the scattered tablets, she reaches towards the pill bottle on the ground, dropping onto her haunches to pick it up. Teetering now on the edge of the pool, she peers at the label.

'Zolpidem?'

Shaking her head, she places the bottle back down so that she might reach into the water for me, but I'm too far from the side. April strains further. Still, I'm out of reach.

'Hope the head's not too bad – thought I had some ibuprofen in the glove compartment.'

A tall, handsome man calls from far behind April in the entrance atrium in his borrowed black tie. He strides across the marble floor, through to the living room, then to the pool area. Jags, April's boyfriend.

'Maybe Essie's got . . . April?'

Jags comes up behind her, sees me. 'Jesus Christ,' he gasps. Meanwhile, April's fingertips are about to touch the surface of the water near a strand of my extensions.

'Don't!' Jags shouts, rocking her on the spot. She almost falls into the water, but he moves to hold her from behind, retrieving her from the edge. 'Don't,' he repeats more quietly. 'She's obviously . . . oh shit. April, come away, you probably shouldn't disturb the scene.'

7

April snaps her hand back, mouths something inaudible, mystified, like she's having her own out-of-body experience. Jags slips off his dinner jacket and drapes it around her shoulders, his hands firmly on either side of her as he lifts her to her feet and leads her back towards the living room.

'I don't think you need to see this,' he tells her. Still, April can't help but turn her head over her shoulder, unable to take her eyes off me in the water. 'Darling. There's nothing you can do to help her now.' Jags breaks contact only to slide the glass doors closed behind them.

'Oh god, oh god, oh god. Just . . . why?' April slides down the glass doors, unable to stand. They remain in silence for a few moments. April still struggling for breath on the floor, Jags rubbing his mouth and chin with his fingers and thumb.

'Say something. *Please*,' April begs eventually, her voice heightened and strained.

'I'm stunned, obviously. Essie's seemed a bit up and down, I suppose, but I had no idea it was as bad as this. Did you?'

April shakes her head. 'I never thought she'd ever . . .' Does this sentence end with an unspoken . . . *go through with it?*

'I guess she's one of those girls, *women*. You told me once she tried this sort of thing before.'

April blinks away an old memory she doesn't want to recall now. 'You said, *the scene*.' April looks at Jags, bewildered. 'I assumed she'd—'

'I mean, yeah, me too. What else?'

'But *the scene*,' April says, rising panic in her voice. 'You don't think someone else could be involved?' she whispers, looking about in fresh terror, imagining a murderer might still be lurking somewhere in Lotus.

8

'Turn of phrase.' Jags shakes his head dismissively. 'Essie was seeing a psychiatrist, wasn't she? Her mental health must have got the better of her.'

At this, April's head falls, and she seems to swallow the nausea in her mouth.

'But we probably don't want to mess around with anything, not before whoever comes along to do whatever they need to do,' Jags continues.

April half-nods, then blinks herself to a new realisation. 'Who do we call? What do we do?' She swipes her head left to right as though searching for something. 'Is it real? Is she really gone?'

'I'm so sorry. This is . . . just appalling. Here.' Jags holds out his hands. April resists for a second before letting him lift her to her feet and guiding her deeper into the living room to sit. He takes her to a rattan egg chair hanging from the high ceiling, its back turned to the pool.

'I'm so, so sorry, darling. Sorry for her, sorry for you,' Jags says. He is on his knees in front of April.

She swallows and speaks haltingly from a throat tight with tears. 'Tonight was supposed to be about me and her. We were going to show them all we could do things our way and better than they could have ever imagined.' April searches Jags's eyes and finally lets her tears go. But are they for the dead star or for her? Because if everything had gone according to her plan, in approximately two and half hours, April's career, all her life's choices, had a shot of looking like they were all worthwhile.

April is odds-on to win Best Director at the British Film Association Awards tonight, and under April's direction, I'm a sure-fire bet to take Best Actress. She thought winning tonight meant as much to me as it did to her because she hasn't been famous enough for long enough to know this: awards only give you a cheap little break from yourself. Whether you win at the *TV Now* Awards (Best Female Presenter, nine years on the trot thanks to the 'cosy chemistry with screen husband Jude Lancaster') or the goddamn Oscars (where *The Vanished Woman* was carelessly overlooked – your loss, The Academy), it doesn't really change a thing. Because when that ceremony's over, sure, I'd leave with my hunk of metal, maybe even take home a man I've told myself is worth making my whole world for a few stupid months, but I'd also have to leave the after-party with Essie Lay. No prize is big enough to take away that pain.

'It's my fault.' April sobs. 'This is all my fault. How didn't I see this coming?'

'Essie wanted to be back in the public eye,' Jags says soothingly. 'You made that happen for her in the best way possible but, for whatever reason, she couldn't handle it. You couldn't have predicted that. This isn't on you.'

April has stopped listening. 'Oh god. Do we need to call the police? Or should we call an ambulance?'

Jags pauses.

'Jags?'

'April. You were a good friend to Essie.'

She shakes her head. 'No, I wasn't. I couldn't have been.'

'When you cast Essie it was a rescue mission, she'd be nothing without you. You got the very best from her throughout the shoot and now, well, like I said, there's nothing left for you to do.'

'I'm not sure what you're—'

10

'I think we should come back and deal with this in the morning.' Jags rushes it out as though if he says it quickly, it can't be as big and bad as it sounds.

A stunned pause.

'*What?*' April's face is slack in outrage. 'No. This is my best friend . . . This is . . .' She struggles to say the words. 'This is my best friend's body.'

Jags meets her gaze. 'Yes, it probably does sound cruel, but April, I've seen life be pretty cruel to you.'

A tear falls down April's cheek.

'I've seen what trying to get your second film off the ground is doing to you.' April slumps now, shutting her eyes tight, not wanting to acknowledge the struggle Jags has witnessed. 'You're still being lumped with the "rookie female director" label, your brilliant film not much more than a *calling card, a toe in the door.* It isn't fair and it boils my blood, and it is why I'm saying to you: let me get you to the Albert Hall tonight, help you brave-face it, just long enough so you can take the kudos, make your connections and get out of the rut they've put you in, and then, we'll deal with all of this.' Jags gestures back to the pool. 'First thing tomorrow.'

April shakes her head emphatically. 'No, Jagdeep. Absolutely not. There's no way I could do that.'

Jags sighs. 'Darling.' He strokes her cheek with the back of his fingers. 'This is devastating and completely tragic, but for reasons we don't understand, Essie is gone. You're still here, with a life to live. So, for the good of the rest of your career – and your one life – I'm asking you to put your needs first, just for tonight.'

April bites her top lip, takes her phone out of her clutch bag

11

and shows the screen to Jags. 'This is the message she sent me; the reason I wanted us to come here. Essie thought so little of herself, I wanted to convince her she didn't need to anymore.'

April looks away as Jags reads:

Lovely April, I'm so, sorry, I'm not going. Can't face it, THEM! Massive luck to you. Actually, the hell with that, you know you're going to win (and no one wants luck like mine, anyway!). Can I email you my acceptance speech just in case I do get lucky (is that really vain?!?!?!)? You'll go up for me, won't you, in case something good does happen? I'll time it so it doesn't arrive before they announce Best Actress, so it's not sat in your inbox, like a curse. If I do win, April, you know it'll be more yours than it is mine, don't you? *Essie Lay* really doesn't deserve to win, but whatever happens tonight, you definitely deserve it. Exx

'This makes it clear.' Jags flicks the air in front of April's screen. 'Essie wasn't expecting you to come here. She wanted you to go to the awards.' This sends a fresh surge of tears into April's eyes. God, maybe she will actually miss me. 'We could still get there in time if we go right now.'

Another pause.

'No, Jags. I can't leave her. Please, drop that idea and let's call whoever we need to.'

Jags thinks about it for a second before speaking again.

'Janine. Let's get her over here. You can call her on the way, tell her about the message, say you're worried about Essie being on her own, say you think she needs her sister.

12

She'll be here within the hour. Darling, you should let tonight play out exactly how Essie wanted it: you, at the Albert Hall, representing both of you.'

April lets her head fall into her hands. 'I'm in shock, Jags. I can hardly believe this is happening. Essie is dead, for god's sake. I could never act normal tonight.'

But I know if she does lie to Janine, to everyone who asks her why I'm not there, whatever she tells them, they'll all believe her. Because as much as she prefers life behind the camera, April has already shown me she's easily the better actress out of the two of us.

2

April, then and before

The whole show was about to fall apart. It was 4.30 a.m. and the Hollywood B-lister they'd hung that edition of *The Dawn Chorus* on was not in makeup, he was still in a Mayfair club, inebriated, altered, and definitely not coming to the studio.

At twenty-two, in my first job out of university – stuck in light entertainment TV production while I worked out how to get writing work – I watched the usually unflappable producer desperately try to pull in favours with celebrity bookers. But which agents were going to answer the call at that hour? And what did it say about their clients' kudos if they were ready to schlep immediately to Zone 6 for a slot on a breakfast show predominantly watched by students still up from the night before? Senior members of the crew had started to shout; the finger of blame was about to be pointed in numerous directions.

'I know that club; I'll go and get him.'

At first, no one knew who had spoken, the voice was a little unsure and unfamiliar in the cacophony.

'Anyone got a car I could borrow?'

It was a new runner, on her first day in the job, and in amongst the panic that morning, no one had properly noticed her yet. That was about to change. The noise stopped. All eyes turned to her.

She was unmistakably striking, but not in the most immediately obvious way. Her own eyes were darkish, oddly indistinguishable in colour but sparkled brightly. Her teeth were perhaps a little too prominent, and her features a shade lopsided, but rather than detract from her beauty, these imperfections only added to her allure by offering the viewer something different and equally compelling each time you viewed her. I knew instinctively she would look even better on camera than she did in real life. Her face was somehow unknowable and yet instantly recallable. From this moment on, this lowly runner wasn't a woman anyone could ignore, least of all me.

With no better suggestion, the director wordlessly threw his car keys in her direction. She went to snatch them clean out of the air but missed, making a goofy face when she had to scoop them off the floor. Beauty, chutzpah, and clumsiness: an irresistible combination that rendered her simultaneously deeply desirable and somehow available.

'Right,' she said. 'Who wants to come with? I might need backup to bundle his ass into the backseat.' She put her fists up and grinned, a smile that came quickly, drawing people even deeper into her, an expression that made you feel as though she was prepared to give a piece of herself to you, regardless of whether this was true.

'I'm Esther, by the way.'

A dozen hands shot in the air, including mine. Back then, it seemed to me that time in the car with Essie might give me a shot of becoming friends with the most dynamic and charismatic person on set, but more importantly, one who hadn't yet had the chance, like all my other colleagues, to decide I was not friend material. I'd been a runner for a year already; by aligning my stock with her obvious value, she might make mine rise too.

My bid to accompany Essie that morning was ignored. The producer sent her with a big-boned lighting engineer, who later reported how easily she'd entered the club (she either knew someone on the door, or immediately made them feel as though they were well acquainted), found the B-lister who, on seeing Essie, simply obeyed her command. But when they arrived at the studio, there was a further obstacle to overcome: partying all night had rendered him unable to stand, or even sit without slouching into a heap, a major problem given the extended interview he was meant to be doing with Fiona, a veteran newsreader in her sixties whose career was undergoing a nostalgic revival.

But Essie's spark shone through again. 'Why don't they do the interview lying down? It'll be cool; we could make them a little nest,' she said. And from that day on, all Fiona's interviews were performed propped up on a throw and pillows, her loving the sexy undertones of being horizontal with the beautiful people after thirty years buttoned up at the BBC, the Talent delighting in the languid atmosphere.

That first day, I had an idea that would build on what Essie had put in motion: shooting the interview using an old video camera I'd spotted in a storage cupboard. I wondered if there was some way we might use it to capture grainy footage that would create the sense the viewer was watching a home movie, something intimate and that, perhaps, we should not be party to. But when I went to speak, I was shut down by the stressed director, which left me blushing furiously as he sent me away

16

to 'find more cushions' for Fiona's interview cocoon. It was not the first time I had more to offer than anyone was interested in taking. And it made me wonder again, that if I were able to attach myself to the new runner, might I too be seen and heard? Could I finally leave behind the bottom rung of the ladder?

In my spare time, of which there was much, I'd been surreptitiously watching and photographing people since my late teens, quietly writing stories about the imagined lives of myself and others. I savoured many things about doing this, including the specific sense of control it afforded me: how to make a character move through a place or story. Given how compelling I knew Essie would be on camera, it wasn't long after she'd joined *The Dawn Chorus* – and I'd quietly removed the old video camera on unregistered permanent loan – that I decided I would rewrite the play I wrote at university as a short film, imagining one day being brave enough to ask Essie to star in it. (Though for months after she joined we barely swapped little more than pleasantries: a snatched morning greeting when she and I arrived at the same time, earlier than everyone else; a shared eyeroll near the catering station when the Talent moaned about the quality of the coffee, or the temperature of their croissant.)

I believe I must have been the first person to identify the quality in Essie that ultimately led to her ubiquitous presence on our screens for the best part of two decades – on midmorning magazine shows sat on bright sofas, doing earnest pieces to camera; on family-friendly documentaries, putting herself through heart-stopping or cringe-inducing stunts; on wildly popular reality shows, going undercover in spikier journalistic strands. Essie's *It* factor: an inherent tendency to absorb attention, to pull people to her in a way that is neither intended, nor learnt.

17

As well as energising my writing and directing ambitions, the woman who went on to become the nation's sweetheart brought out something else specific and powerful within me. I have never been the least attractive woman in the room; the only thing I truly dislike about my body is my erythrophobia, a potentially debilitating fear of blushing, one so powerful that even the thought of turning scarlet triggers a great and ugly wash of red to flash across my face, neck, and chest. But Essie gave me a specific and ice-cold poke of envy. I didn't think I'd ever persuade anyone to look at me the way every single person she met looked at Essie. Nineteen years on, I'm still not wholly convinced my fears were unjustified.

Essie always seemed to know what was fashionable before anyone else, or maybe things appeared on trend simply by virtue of being chosen by her. When she first joined *The Dawn Chorus*, her hair was her natural tone, a colour not dissimilar to the black coffee she drank in vast cups throughout the day. Soon enough, the set became populated with bottle-fresh brunettes. But a few weeks later, when Essie arrived with a full head of gold and copper highlights – apparently because her mother had described her natural hair as 'dowdy' – most of the other female crew members followed suit. Essie led, people followed, even if she didn't expect or want them to. It was clear to me she was merely waiting in life's departure lounge before soaring to the heights she was destined for, places to which I was not automatically granted passage. Travelling in her slipstream, capturing her magnetism on camera, these were ways someone like me might reach destinations I might never see without the likes of her.

Esther Laycock – or Essie Lay, as she was rapidly re-packaged

18

by Jonathan, her agent, and backed up by her sister Janine, who would cling on to 'manage' her – was fated to be the magazine cover girl, the top story on the sidebar, the woman who would fill your living room with her signature giggle, her loveable manner, and off-centre smile. She was born to variously become the girl next door, the cool older sister, the TV best friend, the 'presenter you definitely would', until the day she became a cautionary tale, an example of how not to be a woman.

I reached out to her after this terrible episode. I wanted to remind Essie of the short but incredibly intense time when she gave me a big role in her life: her cheerleader and confidante. Being with her made me more than I was, gave me access to a better future than I thought I could achieve without her. And then, after she cut me loose and left me out in the cold, sometimes I felt my future might never arrive. Because when I was Essie's friend, some of her stardust seemed to settle on me, making me also fated for success, built for love. And when Essie froze me out only a few short months into our friendship, I felt like nothing, far worse than even before. That entire time left me with a hurt that ran very deeply, a sour flavour I would taste over and over throughout the years that followed.

I believe most of us have an event in our early adulthood that sets us on the trajectory for how the rest of our lives will be; a job you did or did not get, a course you took, a lover lost or never had. For me, my severance from Essie Lay became the touchstone that defined my twenties and the life beyond. It nearly ruined me, until I made it galvanise me into the person I am today.

So, with the distance of the years between then and now,

and with my screenwriting and directing credits, the critical reception for my work so far, I have shown my peers, my family, and more importantly, myself, I am someone who deserved more than being dumped by the cool girl for nothing I had done wrong. And if she had been paying any attention, I would have shown Essie too. I didn't need her to achieve what I have, after all.

Now, as I embark on the biggest career move of my life – directing a film I have written, one with the chance of putting me on Hollywood's radar and of proving my worth once and for all to those who have thought so little of me – I'm about to be reunited with my former friend for the first time since she ghosted me the best part of twenty years ago. And even though as the director of this film, of this scene in my life, I am technically in control, and even though she's here today at my invitation, something inside me wants to run away, scream, and hide from Essie Lay.

3

Essie, before

I wasn't sure what seeing April again would feel like. I haven't let myself think about that whole disastrous time in so long. I nearly didn't come. Twice I asked my driver to turn around, but still I came. So, why am I here? Last week, a rumour I was dead lit up social media. I wanted to post something along the lines of, *Sorry to disappoint you all. Not ready for my dirt nap yet.* I asked Janine if I should, and my sister replied that I should let the rumour 'burn itself out'.

'But they're saying I'm dead. Worse than that, they're dancing on my grave.'

My sister shrugged. I wasn't even allowed to tell the world I was still alive, though there are some days of late, I really wish I wasn't.

April walks towards me. She has the same grey-blonde medium-length hair she had when I first ever met her, plaited at the nape of her neck, and holds herself the same uncomfortable way she always did, like she's borrowed her body from someone who'll want it back soon. She does seem to have ditched a little of her desperate puppy waiting-to-be-kicked vibe, and she looks thinner; small but important now. How things change.

21

'April, you look amazing.' I'm shocked by how ready I am to be nice to her after how it ended between us. I'm also taken aback by how cracked my voice sounds when I speak, even though I managed to stop crying twenty minutes ago. *Oh god, I shouldn't be here. What am I doing here?* While I'm wondering whether we should hug, April goes for it. No one's hugged me, or even been the tiniest bit kind to me, for two weeks now, not since I last saw Jackson. The man who came into my life like an absolute dream come true, the man whom I would have given whatever he asked for. And when I did just that, my whole world imploded. *Don't cry. Don't cry. Don't cry.*

'Essie. You're here. I'm so glad,' April says, her own voice a little shaky. 'Did they get you a drink?' she asks me as she pulls away from the hug without returning my compliment, but then, why should she lie? I look like shit; my extensions are a mess, it's all I can do to pull them into a scraggy ponytail each morning since it all went south. And I've had to start doing my own makeup, my patchy foundation and clumpy mascara reminding me why I've always preferred other people doing it. I think of all the lovely hair and makeup girls on *Daybreak*; all the laughs we had in my dressing room over Jude's latest tantrum before heading into the brutal lights on set. Like a thump in the stomach, I feel the memories of what used to be my life, the people who were around me all the time, who can't get far enough away from me now. I am here because I am a leper to everyone except for a girl I used to be friends with almost twenty years ago.

'Yes, I have a drink, thanks!'

I pick up my big coffee cup from the very long table next

to me and waggle it in the air between April and me, making a splash of coffee fall to the floor.

'Shit.'

I don't know why I did that, why I'm still doing things like that. It feels almost as though I'm doing an impression of the bright and breezy womanchild everyone's known me as for so long. Who else should I be now?

'Still drinking your big black coffees?' April says with a faint smile. I didn't think she'd remember.

'You know me, anything to fill my belly up without actually eating.' I pat my stomach, not nearly as taut as it should be. I don't know why I did that either.

April smiles and flexes a heavy brick of salmon-coloured paper between us. I see she not only has a thinner frame than back then, she has biceps too.

Written on the front page of April's big pink print-off:

THE VANISHED WOMAN
By April Eden

'This is the thing you're directing?' I ask.

'I wrote it too.' It slips out a bit too snappily for her to sound cool about it. I can almost hear the lyrics she's singing in her head: *How you like me now?* Then, a nasty, horrible little thought pops into mine: *I hope she's still single.*

'That's brilliant, April. You always did have a way with words. So exciting you're making your own film.'

She smiles again, a nervous one this time. I wonder if she still does that blushy thing she used to. We move to seats on the extended table, April at the head, me to one side. It seems

23

extra odd to be here, at a huge table in a cavernous converted old church with her. It reminds me so much of the old bank she was living in when I knew her back in the day – echoey, not made for the purpose April was using it for. The years since I last saw her feel like a stretched elastic band going back to its normal size. My head starts to swim in the memories, moments in time where I didn't understand who to believe, who to trust. Just like now.

'I've been thinking about you so much since I saw what happened with your—'

If I didn't want to hear April talk about back then, I definitely don't want to hear her summarise the shame of my professional and personal life now. All I can do is try to keep it light, even as my head starts to fizz on my shoulders. Joking her way past whatever real feeling wants to punch through, it's what Essie Lay would do. 'Oh yeah! I really fucked up there, didn't I?' I rush out before April can finish the sentence.

But what I'm saying is completely true. I did fuck up. And what's worse is that I have to do the next bit of my life almost utterly alone. I've become 'a toxic brand'. All the companies that once begged me to front them have either quietly ended our relationship until further notice or scored points with the public by cutting my contract in full view on social media. Janine's told me that my accountant advised me to sack my glam squad, my publicist, and my PA, as well as my household staff, because in all honesty, we don't know when I'm going to work again and Lotus costs a fortune to run. The whole process of being cancelled – my friends disappearing, having to get rid of my team, my phone only ringing when it's Janine or my parents calling to remind me how stupid I was/am – tells

24

me exactly how alone I am now. Worse than that, it tells me how alone I was all along and didn't even realise.

'I was worried about you,' April tells me. 'I saw that story about you being . . .' She pauses in the spot where she should have said *dead*. 'I know it was a lifetime ago, but I couldn't help but remember . . . how you were that weekend you had me over at your family's place in Kent?'

She says it in a way that suggests there's a chance I might have forgotten what happened. It's pretty ballsy of her to bring that up now like this, straight off the bat. I say nothing. It's all too much, too soon. I can't go into that dark time long ago when today is already so black. I feel the tears hot behind my eyes, where I will them to stay.

'Would you mind if we . . .' *If you never mentioned that time ever again, please?* 'It's been pretty rough recently. I'm happy to let bygones be bygones if you are. That's why I'm here and I'm assuming because you asked me here, you're happy to do that too?'

April smiles again, maybe a shade too wide, but it's there, and the tension is broken again, but only for a moment. Because there's something I have to know now.

'April. Why am I here?'

April nods solemnly. 'Before we get into that, I want you to know I'm here for you. No matter what's gone on between us in the past, no matter what happens after today, I'm here.'

'Right . . . Thank you,' I say. What else am I supposed to say and do with this information? Of all the people in the world I thought I'd ever need to prop me up when times were bad, April would have been close to the last. But unlike just about everyone else I've ever known, she *is* here. She *did* call. I'm

25

not sure anything about my life right now could get any more unsettling. Let's see.

'And about today?' I ask.

April takes a long sip from her own cup and places it very close to her body as if she doesn't want me to see what's inside. The contents: black coffee.

'I'm sorry I was a little cryptic. It's been so long, and I didn't want to scare you off.'

'It takes a lot to scare me these days,' I tell her, even though its completely untrue. Actually, I feel pretty scared right now.

April looks at her script as though it's an animal with a life of its own that's decided to sit quietly for the time being. 'As a director, there are a million options for me to choose from to get it exactly right: how to make my characters move through a scene to convey the story I want to tell, how to be sure I've cast the right people for the two central roles, Antonia and particularly Elena, the woman who vanishes.'

April blinks and a hint of red creeps over a patch of collar bone peeking out from her white T-shirt. I feel as though we might finally be getting somewhere. She stretches a smile across her face in a weird sort of way and looks at her hands for a moment before fixing me right in the eye.

'That's why I invited you here today. We're about to get into rehearsals but I don't think I've found the right Elena.'

'Right. What's that got to do with me? I don't act.'

But could I? God knows I've spent enough years pretending to be someone I'm not – a happy-go-lucky girl, a people person – and I've spent thousands of hours on screen making like being there was my happy place (hence the fits of 'spontaneous giggles' Jude was famous for setting off). On a bad day, it felt like

26

an out-of-body experience. How had I ended up in a situation where my paycheque depended on pretending I was loving every minute? I was like a kind of sex worker who specialised in giggling for cash. I basically monetised my ability to make people think I like them. I know why people might think this was easy money or hate me for not being grateful, but while the career I had might have been somebody else's dream, it was never actually mine. I was forced into being 'Essie Lay' to pay for my dad's money-pit beach mansion before I could work out what my own dreams were.

April looks serious now, and I feel time shrinking again. I'm back there, at Signal House that day twenty years ago, April drinking gin on the lawn with me and my dad. It's not a time or place I want to be.

'Elena,' April says, bringing me back into the room. 'There are secrets she holds within herself. That's until Antonia, a therapist hired by Elena's family, is tasked with unlocking the reason she disappeared and won't say where she's been.' April turns her grey eyes to me like she's about to announce something very important. Her lips tremble for a moment. 'You. You should be Elena.'

I give an involuntary shudder, remembering all the compliments April liked to give me. She was too much. This is too, surely.

'It's amazing you would think that, honey, but you do know I've never acted. Ever.' I think my instincts are telling me to get out of here, but it's been so long since I've been able to follow my gut, make my own decisions, I can hardly hear the voice inside me. I'm like a forty-odd-year-old performing child who needs to be told what to think. On my own, without Janine,

27

Jonathan, my team, I have to react to whatever's happening by myself. It's making me feel wobbly, disorientated.

'I think you can and should do this,' April says.

'Right.' Tears want to cloud my voice. After everything I've been through these last two weeks, in all the darkness, here's a chink of light: someone thinks I might still be good for something, even if it is only April.

The assistant who got me my coffee walks in from the old church's entrance. 'They're starting to arrive.'

I turn to April, panicking, fishing out the fake glasses I always carry with me from my bag and shoving them on my face before pulling my hoodie right over my head.

'Who's arriving? I thought it was just us today.'

'We're doing a table read of the shooting script for *The Vanished Woman*,' April tells me in a way that wouldn't feel strange if she followed up with a *Da-dum-daaah!* 'I thought it made sense for you to see my work this way and see what you make of it all; better than reading the script alone – though, of course, take this home.' She pushes the block of paper to me.

Loud, actorly laughing comes from the vestibule. The cast are about to file in. I'm genuinely scared now. What if I'm seen? What if Janine finds out what I've done today without her sign-off?

'Shit, April. Jonathan and Janine say I need to stay out of the papers for a while. I can't be here.'

'I completely understand. There's a place I've set up for you up there.' April gestures to an upper seating level. 'I've tried to make things comfortable for you and you won't be seen; it will be like you're not here at all.'

'Well,' I grab my cup, looking over my shoulder as the

28

actors' voices grow louder, 'I've got no bloody choice now, have I?' I say, half-jokingly, almost tripping over the straps of my handbag before grabbing that too and heading up the staircase across the room. That unsteady feeling again – I really don't know where I am or what I'm doing. I feel like a balloon someone let go of, floating away from wherever I'm supposed to be.

But what I do know is this: I can't leave here the way I came, and no matter how unqualified I am to take up April on her offer, how weird this whole situation is, the truth is, I've got nothing and no one else to say yes to.

4

April, the night of the awards

'I don't think I'll get the sight of her like she is out of my mind,' I tell Jags.

'I know,' he says. 'Neither will I.'

Jags strokes my arm before getting off his knees and taking a seat at the end of one of Essie's huge cream sofas. The arm looks greyed and dirty. I notice the pale carpet is covered in detritus, with stains between the sofas and the enormous glass coffee table, which itself is coated in dust. It strikes me that like Essie, if you care to look closely, Lotus Lodge is a mess. The only clean-looking thing in the room is the chair I'm sat on. The single domestic task I've seen Essie perform with any regularity is to assiduously wipe down its upholstery with a damp piece of kitchen roll, once, sometimes twice or more a day. She sometimes seemed fixated on keeping what she'd described to me once as her 'safe place' clean, as if by seeing that one part of her world was always in order, she might imagine the rest of it to be the same..

I read Essie bought her neoclassical, three-storey, nine-bedroom mansion in Hampstead on her father's advice soon after she first started making serious money. It's a significant

30

property that needs a lot of upkeep. As well as the shabbiness inside that I'm just noticing, I now recall working out on the veranda last week and registering how the wide pond of lotus flowers that gives the house its name was flecked with dead blooms. The ornamental grass edging its banks was tatty and dry and in need of cutting, while the expanse of the lawn beyond had become overgrown and dotted with patches of yellow weeds. The state of Lotus was a cry for help I not only ignored but I was so wrapped up in my own life – Jags, trying to get my next project *The Longest Road*, off the ground – I did not even hear.

I tip my head back onto the cushion of Essie's chair.

'Essie deserved so much more,' I say to myself.

'I agree.' Jags sighs. 'And now, her legacy isn't ever going to be *award-winning actress*. It'll be . . .' he gestures back to the pool, '. . . *that*. Her award, her work completely overshadowed.'

'That's beyond awful,' I say, a sob breaking through, knowing what Jags is saying is true.

Silence for a couple of moments, as I dry my eyes with the back of my palm, before Jags speaks again.

'There is another scenario, of course; one way to give the way Essie will be remembered a chance.'

I shake my head, close my eyes. Essie's narrative – a hard beast to wrangle at the best of times, including when her casting as Elena was announced – is only going to end up wildly out of control in these very worst of times.

'There's no way I can steer Essie's story now.'

Jags waits a beat before he speaks next.

'You can if you let her, and you, have tonight like she wanted.'

'No, Jags. Not this again. Please, I—'

31

'Hear me out. Please?'

I let out a breath. I'm too overcome to argue with him right now.

'Look, no one has to know anything if we don't tell them yet. But if we call Janine and get her over here, we buy a couple of hours, long enough for Essie to win and tomorrow's headlines to get written. And when Janine gets here, yes, she'll be shocked and devastated, but she'll know what to do, who to call and when and how to best notify the vultures.'

I imagine the horrific headlines if we break the news of her death right now; sickening, cheap, and none of them referring to Essie's talent or accolades.

'I know it won't be how you want it,' Jags continues, 'and I know it will be the hardest thing you've ever had to do, but you *could* do it, and I really think you should.'

'Why are you so desperate for me to leave Essie, Jags?'

He looks at me as though I've said something mad.

'It's my job to look after you. But if you won't go tonight for yourself, then do it for her.'

I don't want to admit it yet, but there is a chance Jags might be right. Not letting the world know what's happened to her before she's had a chance to be awarded Best Actress is the only shot we have at giving Essie anything like the legacy she deserves. She needs to be 'award-winning film star' long enough so this narrative can't be entirely wiped out by tabloids reframing all of who she was using their preferred 'tragic childless woman' lens.

Jags leaves his seat and takes my hand. I feel the pull to Essie, my stomach churning again at the image of her. I move back towards the pool, but Jags gently pulls me in the opposite direction.

'April. Darling. I honestly believe picking up her award, instead of telling the world she's killed herself, is the last thing you can do for Essie. Come.'

And it happens. I nod. My eyes stay closed. I want everything about tonight to be completely different. And now I'm moving away from Essie, telling myself I'm doing this for her, but knowing somewhere this is because I am selfish and I want my moment tonight. And because while I may be fearsome on set, in every other time and place, including now, I am a coward. I don't want to be the one who tells the world Essie is dead.

So, I let Jags lead me out of the living room and back into the atrium, noticing the scruff-marked and grimy marble floor, another neglected element of Lotus; something gritty under my shoe as I walk.

'Wait a second.'

I try to loosen whatever it is I've picked up by scraping my sole against the stone below, steadying myself with my free hand by holding onto the large round table in the centre of the atrium under a circular skylight. On it, an enormous vase of over-bloomed flowers, their dropped petals leaving puffs of dark pollen across the unpolished wood.

'Don't!' Jags says so brusquely I startle.

'There's something on my—' I look down to see rusty scrapings on the grey-veined marble: remnants of Essie's pills. Jags crouches in front of me, taking out the large white handkerchief from his dinner jacket's front pocket and gently wiping away any visible traces of the pills from the floor. Next, he wraps his fingers around my ankle and carefully rubs away the remnants of the pills from my sole. At the feel of his warm fingers on my

33

skin, the tiniest amount of tension leaves my body; in all this horror, some tenderness. Jags places my foot back on the floor.

'Best not to leave obvious evidence we've been here tonight, seen Essie like we have, then left.'

'Oh god,' I say quietly, my blood icing at the notion of *evidence*. 'Is it really better this way?' I ask Jags as I follow him towards the front door.

'Letting Essie have her night as best we can and Janine be the one who stops the whole thing becoming a circus before Essie's had her moment?' Jags says, and it all sounds so plausible, so defendable. But it does not feel right. 'I promise this is the best we can do for Essie right now.' Jags reactivates the burglar alarm, punching the familiar sequence of numbers into a small keypad. The device has just emitted its activation beep when he freezes.

'Wait. Can you hear that?'

'It's the alarm switching back on.'

'No.' He looks back to the pool. 'Essie's phone.'

The sound of a call Essie will never answer pumps fresh dread into my stomach; the ground feels fluid below my feet.

The ringing stops, but only to start again a moment later. I can't breathe.

Jags starts to walk away. 'I'll switch it off.'

'Oh, god, should we? It seems a bit, I don't know . . . next level?' I say to his back.

He stops, half-turns. 'If calls keep ringing out, it could raise suspicions.'

'I'm not sure whether . . .'

Before I can stop him, Jags strides off in the direction of the pool. He seems to do it with an extra confidence, almost as

34

though he's showing me his strength, that he can be resilient enough for both of us in this nightmare. But before he slides the doors into the pool area open, I see him hesitate. He looks over his shoulder, takes a moment to gather himself before heading in. I can't bear to look.

He seems to take forever. I hear water, a faint splashing. Another wait while I cringe by the door, then another soft splash. What on earth is he doing? What am I doing and why couldn't I have stopped Essie tonight? I feel quite weak. I don't know how I will traverse the red carpet without falling. I don't think I can do this. I don't think I *should* do this.

Jags returns with his dinner jacket under his arm, his shirt-sleeves translucent with water. There is chlorine in the air. Essie's crystal-encrusted phone, with its screensaver of a selfie of her and her father, in his hand.

'What did you do?'

Jags looks at Essie's phone. There's something in Jags's expression. I know I won't like whatever he says next.

'Six missed calls. Two voicemails. One long text insisting she come to the Albert Hall, all Janine.'

'How do you . . . Jags, why are your shirtsleeves soaking wet?' My voice trembles.

He pauses.

'I thought it was probably best if we unlocked the phone, listened to the messages before we switch it off.'

'How do you know Essie's PIN? . . . Oh god.' I cover my face with my hands for a second before looking at Jags again, shame creeping into his eyes. 'You used *face ID*? *Jagdeep!*'

'I thought it was best if we knew who'd be trying to reach her. I'm sorry, but it's done now, and at least we know it's only

35

Janine who's been calling. She should definitely come if you call her.'

This started off feeling unreal, but now we're truly entering the horrific.

'How did she—' I begin to ask, but Jags knows me well enough that I don't need to finish the sentence.

'Essie looked like she was asleep. A cliché, I know, and I know you hate clichés, but that's how she seemed. Peaceful.'

I swallow. 'Was she . . . cold? How long do you think—'

'She was the same temperature as the water.'

'And you put her back where she was?'

'I only had to turn her slightly to unlock the screen.'

He regards the phone still in his hand with a grim expression.

'Shit, my hands are soaking, I'm getting water into it.' Jags passes me the phone, at the centre of its screen, a distorting blue cloud blooming over the background image of Essie and her father, Con. Jags wipes his hands on his trousers.

'I don't really want to touch—' I begin just as Essie's phone trills to life. A mangled image of Janine popping up on screen. I look about for somewhere to put down Essie's phone, to be rid of it, but in my panic, accept the call.

'What the fuck?' Janine snarls down the line, I can hear her even without holding the phone to my ear. 'You listening to me? You've not had enough bad press in your life yet? Get your arse here, *now*.'

Jags swipes the air with his hands. *No,* he mouths. *Say no.*

I call on a thousand memories of Essie's voice; so specific, something so warm and inviting about her resonance, even when her voice was ruptured with nerves or fear.

36

'No,' I say to Janine.

A moment of silence.

'So, that's it, is it? After everything you've put us through to get to tonight?'

I can barely believe I've persuaded Janine I'm Essie, or that Janine is framing Essie's unravelling last year as her family's own pain. I do something I've wanted to do so many times since having to deal with Janine but have never been able to as April: I hang up on her. A rush of confidence. The phone goes again, and I switch it off. Jags watches me and nods approvingly.

'Let's go,' I say, hearing a residue of Essie's open, vulnerable cadence in my own usual tone. If I call Janine now she might possibly hear the similarities, call me out for impersonating Essie, and then ask the critical question of why.

'Jags. You need to call Janine for me. I can't do it.'

'OK.'

'In fact, I need you to keep helping me tonight. I don't know what I'm doing. You need to help me do this.'

'I will, of course, starting with calling Janine.'

I realise I still have Essie's phone in my hand and move to put it down on the bureau nearby, just below the alarm keypad, but stop myself.

'I suppose I should wipe our prints from this?' A phrase said by someone mindful of words like *police, investigation, arrest*; words I thought I would never have to say in reference to my life.

'Allow me.'

Jags untucks his shirt, frowning with concentration as he rubs the phone clean, before placing it somewhat gingerly on the bureau. And when he does I feel the rise of panic once more,

37

imagining the keypad, the atrium flower table, and beyond it the glass sliding doors, covered in police-graphite-dusted fingerprints.

'Our fingerprints, they're everywhere.'

'April, this house is filthy, and we've been coming and going from Lotus for months. There'd be nothing unusual about finding evidence of us here.'

'Wouldn't there? I don't know. I don't know what to think anymore. I don't understand anything about what's happening tonight. We should drive around the block, wait for Janine, I don't know,' I fluster.

Jags sighs. 'I *do* know. I know this: the clock is ticking; it's time you went where Essie wanted you to be tonight, collecting your awards.'

I grip onto this truth. I don't say the words, can't bear to hear myself agreeing to leave Essie here for Janine to find once and for all, for Essie's reputation's sake, but for me too. Because if I can't keep making films, if I can't make something indisputably exceptional of my life, then what has any of it been for?

I nod at the door. Jags goes ahead to open it for me. I take one last look behind me at the wavelets of yellow light undulating on the walls of Essie's pool. A chill crosses my shoulders. It feels as though her spirit is watching me. *I'm so very sorry. I should have taken better care of you, I'm going through tonight for you,* I tell her silently.

'Shit.' Jags's voice is now heavy with dread.

'What?'

'Cameras. She's got cameras everywhere.' Jags eyes one just above us, tucked below a corniche, its lens is static, but angled down, as though peering right at us. That powerful sense of

38

being watched, of judgement again, even as a wave of relief washes through me.

'They're not working. Essie was paranoid about them getting hacked after . . .'

I can't bear to talk of the man who wreaked so much pain on Essie's foreshortened life. Jags finishes my sentence for me.

'Since what Jackson did to her?'

I nod. 'There's no red light. They're not recording.'

Jags's shoulders drop as he releases the breath he's been holding, before finally opening the front door for me. My legs are like iron as I go to step over Essie's threshold. I hover in the doorway for a second.

'Ready to do this?' Jags asks.

I make myself remember the many things I have already sacrificed to get Essie into my film and on the precipice of victory at a major awards ceremony which will solidify my reputation and reclaim hers, even if, for Essie, it will only be for one night.

I don't say anything, merely nod before taking a tentative step free of Essie's home, now her mausoleum. I hate everything about this night.

Jags takes one last view inside Lotus, as though double-checking we haven't left anything we shouldn't have, before closing the door behind us.

5

Essie, the day of the table read

As the table read starts, I climb the thin, spiral staircase in the old church rehearsal space, chasing the treads round a stone central column until I'm up in the gallery. Between two pillars sits a leather chair and a small table. On top of it, a fresh cafetiere of coffee, a big clean cup, and three Biros – one red, one black, one blue – that feel squeaky-new when I pick them up. This is such an April move, organised and kind of swotty. In some ways, she's a girl after my own heart. I remember now how she was one of the few people I've ever met who looked like they might graft as much as I do, or did.

Down in the main hall, seven actors – four women, three men – are getting even louder. April perches on the edge of the top of the table as they each come to greet her with air kisses. Two weeks ago, that was me, everywhere I went. Now I'm like a mad woman, hiding in the rafters watching it happen to other people, to April.

I decide to focus on 'the wrong Elena'. I see it's Juniper Jones, an actress known for many completely ridiculous but totally addictive psychological thrillers on Netflix; female-led

40

stories where the big twist leaves you gasping or shouting at the TV, or both.

The way Juniper approaches April is a lot cooler than the rest of the actors. Maybe she knows something is genuinely not quite right with her casting. She's at least ten, maybe even fifteen years younger than me. There's a plainer-looking woman I assume is 'Antonia' who looks like she might be scared of Juniper. Three of the actors, not including 'Elena', are laughing together, while April smiles widely. She isn't in on the joke and is doing her best to style it out. This, I recall, is also a very April kind of move. She's one of those people who's a bit awkward to be around, doesn't make friends too easily. I remember thinking I must have been her only friend back when I knew her.

'Shall we get started?' April says to the assembled actors. There's a clarity in her voice and a confidence in the way she's holding herself, sat ready to assess her actors from the top of the table, that seems completely out of character. A switch seems to have been flipped in April, she's suddenly so powerful. April the Director, in complete control.

The table read gets underway.

*

'The coast's clear now, Essie,' April calls up to me.

It takes more than two hours from start to finish, another half an hour for the actors to leave. I'm stiff and dying for the loo, having been trapped up here for the best part of three hours. And yet the time sped by. April's screenplay. It's brilliant. I wasn't expecting to feel anything in particular, but I find myself moved, touched.

41

The Vanished Woman is the story of a woman who disappears for six months and then comes back into her family's life with no apology or explanation. The screenplay focuses on her father's quest to reveal where she went, what she did, and when Elena refuses to play ball, he recruits his troubled therapist Antonia to both watch Elena so she doesn't vanish again and to finally find out where Elena went and why. It's claustrophobic, disturbing, but unlike the dramas Juniper usually stars in, *The Vanished Woman* feels almost real. Though it doesn't take very much these days, it made me cry. It stirred something inside me. I'm not sure if having been drawn into April's screenplay is making me feel better or worse than I did before, but at least it's taken me out of myself for a while.

April waits for me below, still sitting at the top of the table, scribbling notes onto her own stack of pink paper. April the Director persona has disappeared for now, a tremble in her lips, she's nervous about my reaction; that kicked-puppy vibe that's not always easy to be around has come back. April still seems to send her low self-esteem into the air around her, even though she may be about to become a big-shot film director. I find myself feeling sorry for her, just like I used to.

'That was amazing, April. Incredible. Seriously, you're really so, so talented,' I tell her, and it makes her go fully red, exactly like she used to. My opinion seems to matter to her. Given that everyone else currently thinks I'm trash, I find myself feeling touched again.

'And what did you think of Elena?' she asks me.

'The performance or the character?' The performance, to me, was great. Juniper was so understated and still, but

42

powerful. I have no idea why she'd ever want to replace her, least of all with me.

'The character,' April says carefully.

I think about it for a moment, looking away while I organise my thoughts. 'I really feel the relationships with her parents, and with Antonia. And even though she says very little, I mean she's practically silent, she feels at the centre of everything.' When I look at April, her neck and face are now completely flushed. She brings her lips together again before speaking once more. Her next words seem to fall out of her, a great big gush of truth.

'I think we can take her to the next level if you played her. I think that perhaps I wrote this part for you. I've always thought you could do more than you've been required to do on camera.'

I take a breath, take a moment before I speak. I don't know what I'm getting into here; I don't know if I should be talking myself out of it. 'That's really flattering, April. To be honest, I'm kind of shocked.' Juniper is a pro. And me? I'm like Elena, only everyone knows why I've had to make myself scarce. Maybe *this* is April's real angle? It could be great publicity, though probably for all the wrong reasons.

'Shocked and appalled? Shocked and interested?' April's face remains blood red, her dishwater eyes as needy as I remember them from that summer. I think she meant what she said about writing the part for me.

I focus on the script on the table. 'There's a lot to think about.'

Like, how does she think she's going to sack Juniper Jones and install me instead? How am I going to learn not only the

43

script, but also how to act between now and whenever they're due to start shooting? And why, after I quite deliberately cut April loose just as I was getting famous, does she want so badly to bring the twitching corpse of my public persona back to life again? Maybe she never developed her camera's film after that weekend at Signal House; maybe she genuinely doesn't understand my reasons for not speaking to her for almost twenty years.

6

April, the night of the awards

'What *exactly* did Janine say again? How did she say it?'

We're driving to Kensington, Jags's hands hard around the steering wheel. He notices me looking and instantly makes himself relax his grip. This is what he's like. He's so aware of my feelings, sometimes it seems as though he knows my emotional state before I do.

'I told you already, darling. Janine didn't say much when I told her we were worried about Essie. She didn't sound shocked or unduly concerned, but she definitely took it on board,' Jags tells me.

'And did she say whether she was heading straight to Lotus?'

Jags breathes out audibly, the faintest trace of impatience in the exhalation. 'She sounded like she normally does when she has to do anything to earn her ten per cent: pissed off but nevertheless determined.'

He's clearly trying to draw a line under me questioning him for the tenth time on every beat and nuance of his call with Janine. But I need to know we've not left Essie there on her own and undiscovered for much longer. And I need to brace myself for The Call, what I'll say, how I'll feign the raw,

45

immediate quake of learning Essie is dead while dealing with the aftershocks of what I saw. The image of her floating in her pool, waiting there to be retrieved from the water, turns my stomach. I lower my window and a blast of air hits me just as Jags takes a sharp, unexpected turn down a side road, robbing my breath. He shoots me a quick look before focusing on the road once more. 'Alternate route. If Janine's flooring it to Lotus, we could cross paths if we stick to the main road,' he says.

I nod, my head falling in my hands, part of me is relieved at Jags's good thinking before a surge of something thick and powerful kicks in, guilt. Have I really done this to shield Essie's name, or is the truth of it that despite my shock and grief, a cold ambitious part of me had to go tonight no matter what. Not even Essie's death could prevent me.

We settle into silence while my guilt blooms and blooms inside me like a toxic cloud. Perhaps sensing this, Jags speaks again.

'You're such a good person, a better person than me. A part of me would be so angry with Essie.'

'Angry? No. My head's everywhere, I don't know what I am, but I'm not that,' I tell him, and he quickly drops his hand to my thigh for a split-second before putting it back firmly on the wheel. I love the way it feels when he touches me like that. How much was I hoping tonight would be topped off with Jags coming home with me to my flat after the awards and after-shows, instead of schlepping back to his mother's in Theydon Bois. A rare night together with Jags would have been the absolute cherry on the thickly iced cake after my widely predicted win.

Jags and I didn't have the most conventional start and we're

46

still not a couple who conforms to social norms, not only because he's ten years younger than me. Although we've been together a year all told, our sex life remains infrequent, stolen from nights when his ailing mother finds herself overnight in hospital, or very special occasions when he feels able to allow himself to come to my flat, to choose me over her. He says his mum doesn't know about me yet, though given the frequency of her calls, which only really began when we started to get serious, I strongly suspect she has an inkling. Jags says he wants to keep us under wraps for now because of his mother's health issues and the fact she's always had designs on him marrying a Sikh girl, ideally introduced to him by her. But from what I can glean, she would be devastated her son has any other woman but her in his life. Or maybe it's the fact I'm in my forties and would not be considered anything like the best a gorgeous man like Jags could do for himself. Because, deep down, despite his endless reassurances, that is what I think. Essie doesn't think that; she believes Jags and I are a great match; she always tries to give us more space to be together.

'Tried,' I whisper to myself, correcting my thinking of her in the present tense, hoping it will help me internalise Essie being gone. But it doesn't feel right; it still doesn't feel real, and I still can't really believe it. Is this what the shock of grief does to the human mind; a trick of disbelief to keep us breathing, eating, moving through the world even though the people we love are no longer with us?

Jags pushes through the traffic as we drop from Highgate, down to Archway and past the old bank where I lived in as a property guardian, residing alone there for years while I saved to pay for film school, then my flat. I think about those early

47

days of my friendship with Essie and the one time she came to see me at the bank. Then, my mind quickly moves to the last time I saw her. She was asking me for my take on what she might wear to the awards only last week. We were in her dressing room, me sat on an ottoman while Essie stood before a rail, pulling out a couple of dresses she'd been sent, I assumed by designers' publicists keen to have Essie in their wares for the awards. She seemed a little distracted and not especially convinced by some of her options, including the dress she was wearing tonight.

'What do you think of this? I got sent it yesterday.'

Essie freed a thin strip of structured white satin from the rail. It was so bright as to be luminous, almost like an inversion of the dull white cotton tea dress Elena wears throughout *The Vanished Woman*, and it made me think I should reconsider my dress and also find a white gown. Essie held the dress to her frame. She would look stunning in it.

'Oh Essie, that's perfect. Will you wear it?'

She paused for a moment, the smile that always waited just below her expression, gone.

'I probably shouldn't, but I think I might,' she said.

'Why only might?'

I could have sworn tears came into her eyes, before she chased them away with her asymmetrical smile. 'Cliché alert: it's complicated!'

'Really, why?' I asked, dying to know more.

She spun around and viewed herself in a full-length mirror and ignored my question.

'Do you think it's too slutty? God, I've not had a shag in so long, maybe it's not slutty enough!'

48

'You'll look great in it. You always do,' I told her.

'If you say so,' she said brightly, throwing the dress onto the back of a chaise longue. 'I'd better bounce. My psychiatrist will blab to Janine if I'm late.'

Did she know, had she already planned she would die in that dress? The thought is too horrific. It tears at my heart to remember how she made herself pivot from vulnerable to brassy, her voice masking whatever pain she was holding inside, that neither her psychiatrist, her family nor me, her friend, could access.

I've long collected voices, ever since I was a child and began to write my stories, then my play at university, before focusing on writing for screen. Essie's voice always fascinated me. I can hear her ice-and-fire husk now, ringing deep in my psyche. Essie had the perfect voice for Elena, her throat seemed to hold back the owner's intelligence and vibrate with the possibility of revealing something truthful from within. Tonight would have been brilliant with Essie and me, shoulder-to-shoulder in our white gowns. Now the evening ahead, all the years that wait for me but not for her, make my future – which had only recently felt like a sparkling runway that might take me to the sky – feel like an underground tunnel with all the lights switched off.

'I know you're reeling,' Jags says. 'But it'll be better if you can manage to hold back on crying, for now.'

I hadn't even realised I was again. A grey tear falls on the white of my lap. It will stain and look dreadful on camera. Jags is right, I mustn't let myself cry again tonight. I will grieve for Essie, I will mourn the loss of her for the rest of my life, it's only that I can't start doing so now, not least of all because I need to let Essie Lay have her night too.

We park around the corner from the Albert Hall. It's one of those spaces on someone's drive the owner rents out, and this driveway is extremely smart; smooth, cream-coloured slabs before a grand but empty-looking new-build townhouse in a small, gated development. Jags parks up his ancient Ford Mondeo, which we have dubbed 'The Grey Lady'. He drops the glove compartment open, retrieves our passes for the night, before carefully closing it. I notice something in there, glinting in the gloom.

'What's that?'

Jags pauses.

'You asked me to help you.'

'What is it, Jags?' I say, pulse soaring, because I already know the answer to the question, what I don't understand is what possessed Jags to think storing it in his car was a good idea.

'I thought about the water in Essie's phone. I made a split-second decision, just as we left.'

I look at him, still baffled.

'My thinking was this: when Janine finds Essie, if the phone was wet like it is, she might work out someone had been there. So, I thought I'd take it for tonight, let it dry out, then return it discreetly tomorrow, prints wiped again, screen back to normal. No pointless suspicions if Janine were to see it tonight like it is. No harm done.'

'No harm done!?' I cry.

'Not like that. You know what I mean. You asked me to help; this is me doing the thinking for you. I'm going to protect you from all of this the best way I know how.' Jags reaches for my hand, takes it to his chest. My anger melts, my heart rate slows.

50

'I changed the PIN after I'd . . . after I gained access back at Lotus.'

'Oh god, really?'

'I thought I'd change it to something we'd both remember, just in case.'

'In case of what?'

'I don't know, we needed to access it again?'

I look ahead through the windscreen, as though sense in all this madness is waiting for me on some invisible path ahead while Jugs runs his thumb along mine.

'I changed it to your birthday.'

'*My birthday?*' My heart, which had managed to settle into an almost regular rhythm for a second, leaps in my chest once more. I snatch my hand back from Jags. 'For god's sake, why? If someone was trying to frame me for something tonight, that'd certainly be one way of doing it.'

Jags views me as though I've lost my mind, then looks out of his window, crushed.

'You're her best friend who's enabled one of the most spectacular comebacks in the history of show business. On the night of her life, why wouldn't Essie do something like change her PIN to your birthday, like a good luck charm or something. I'm sorry if I've done the wrong thing.' Jags redirects his gaze to his lap, as though he might be the one now fighting tears.

'It's OK.' I take his hand now with both of mine. 'Thank you. I know you're trying to do everything as best as you can.' I release my seat belt and lean forward to seal my apology with a kiss. He clunks free his belt too and our lips meet. That wash of tenderness again, about to tip into something more urgent.

Jags pulls away for a breath. 'I should have said it earlier:

51

you look stunning tonight, April. And I don't think that tear left a stain.'

I look down at my gown. 'It doesn't look that way,' I say, moving to kiss him again, but just as I do, my mind darkens. How can I be kissing my boyfriend so passionately with Essie how she is? And then, I see her again, floating, so alone, there in her pool. Essie liked to keep the water very warm, like the rest of the house. What will this mean for the state of her body? Will the air be wretched with death even by the time her sister gets to Lotus?

Jags seems to pick up on the nausea now gripping me. 'Breathe through it. Come on, we're late as it is.'

*

The light and the noise coming from the red carpet as we round the corner for the Albert Hall are as terrifying as they are fascinating; a yellow-white halo of pure, sparkling pizazz against the dark orange rotunda behind it. I can see banks and banks of people, mostly middle-aged men, with their lenses trained on some starlet or other at one end near the entrance to the hall. Closer to where we are, camera crews line a walkway I know I must traverse. So much light, there will be nowhere to hide. And once I enter, I can't turn back.

We're nearly there. The shouting, from the photographers, but also the public, squashed up against a row of gridded barriers with film posters tied to them, is almost primal, bringing with it a fresh wave of sickness. I see a poster for *The Vanished Woman*, Essie in Elena's white dress, her face in close-up, looking over her shoulder, one half of her lopsided visage becoming lost, blurring out into the poster's background, over-printed with my name. I can't be here. I need to get back to Essie.

'APRIL! Ap-ril!' At the far end of the barriers for the general public, a woman screams my name, her arms outstretched with a pen and notebook. I think of how Essie encountered people like this at every turn, a heightened marriage of needy and intimidating, and hundreds of them at that. I want to shrink away, protect myself, but I must go over to her, or else be tagged in some post about me being 'a bitch' or 'stuck-up'. I can only imagine what it was like to have this one thousand times a day for nearly twenty years. Little wonder it seemed to chip and chip away at Essie's sense of self, a fragile thing at the best of times. How can you know who you are, identify your needs, when every day you're meeting the expectations of millions of other people?

'And we're on,' Jags says under his breath, leading me to the red carpet, readying our passes for inspection. I don't have a choice now; the hold has descended, I am now strapped into the rollercoaster and cannot get off until the ride is over, no matter how ill I feel along the way. I watch my hands sign the fan's old-fashioned autograph book and feel my body pose for a picture with her.

'I thought you'd be coming with Essie!' she calls after me as I move onto the next person shrieking my name. Thankfully, I'm far away enough and the volume of the other calls are loud enough for me to pretend I haven't heard. I thought she would be by my side too, both of us looking like a dream in white, Essie in her figure-hugging, low-cut dress, me in my flattering goddess gown with far less flesh on display: the demure director with her brassy muse. Perfect. It could have all been so perfect.

53

I'm separated from Jags, then ushered by some assistant types in headsets to be interviewed by a reporter who looks like he's less than twenty and barely knows who I am. Thankfully, I'm quickly directed to a correspondent I recognise from BBC London.

'April Eden, director of one of tonight's favourites, *The Vanished Woman*. How are you feeling?'

'I'm incredibly nervous.' I choose my words carefully, imagining how all this will look if I'm found out. I mustn't seem too joyous, just in case. But over the cameraman's shoulder, in the background, Jags's fingers point to the corners of his mouth. *Smile!* Instinctively, I do as he commands, knowing it won't serve me well to come across as surly or ungrateful. I've only been sort-of famous for five minutes, it's far too early in the game to show any hint of arrogance. 'But I'm just so excited and honoured to be here,' I finish with a grin.

'And of course, Essie Lay's stellar performance is up for a top prize tonight too, as well as you being the hot tip for Best Director – how difficult was it to persuade your backers she was right for the part and to convince Essie this was something she could do after her recent troubles?'

Her recent troubles: the most neutral, BBC way you could refer to what happened to Essie a year ago. 'One was relatively straightforward, the other markedly less so,' I say carefully, thinking back again to the begging I went through to get Juniper recast in the part of Antonia so Essie could be my Elena. My backers thought I was crazy, said the very worst things about Essie. They didn't think I could make Essie Lay into a credible human being in the eyes of the public, let alone an actress capable of holding the entire film together. But I made

54

them come and watch her screen test, knowing the sheer force of her charisma – channelled by me – would persuade them to give her a chance. 'The important thing is that we can all enjoy an—'

My throat closes.

I think of the final scene of the film, and of Essie that day we shot it, how much she finally, fully gave into the part and allowed herself to listen and truly hear the story I was trying to tell. The brilliance of what we'd managed to create together. The memory makes me fear the feeling of my own blood now beating in my chest, across my shoulders, and down my arms; all of it wants to gush into my face. *Please, no. I can't go red now.* I force a smile, take a breath big enough to fight the tide of adrenaline and tears that threaten to engulf me.

'Anyone who loves strong female stories can enjoy an unforgettable performance,' I manage to blurt out.

'Well, the best of luck to yourself and to Essie, who I'm sure we'll be seeing soon.'

I nod my thanks and my make way to the next section as quickly as I can. I cannot blush, not in this white dress, and I cannot cry because I have to face the gauntlet of photographers in a few steps.

'April.'

I look about and see Jags, who has been tracking me a few steps away as I've been moving up the red carpet.

'Go and stand there.' He points to a masking-tape cross in front of the seething rows of men with cameras. They sneer my name; irritated, bordering on hateful.

'Come.' I reach out for Jags's hand.

He shakes his head before putting his hands in his pockets

and looking on with muted pride. And then the braying really starts.

'April! Over here!'

'April? *April!*'

'APRIL, APRIL! To me!'

On and on the flashes go. I put one hand on my hip and try to move my focus left to right, up and down, ensuring each of the photographers gets a usable shot. I try to hold my mouth and my legs still as I move the upper half of my body in small increments to the left and right, like Essie instructed me at the Cannes gala screening of *The Vanished Woman*. She told me how to stand just as she did, anticipating these men demanding she turn this way and that, to do as she was told. I can still see her proffering them her leg through the slit in the dress she wore that day, which was as blue as the Mediterranean and made her shimmer with the pure essence of her *It* factor. I will never have a time like that with her again; never direct her, hear her voice. My best friend and my inspiration is gone.

I feel my obedient smile fall away. Details from the horror of the scene I walked away from now searing themselves afresh in my mind with each blinding flash: her dress, floating around the top of her legs, the incongruous black nail varnish I could see she'd chosen. Now, I feel something under my shoe again; the grit of Essie's pills. I can't help but drag my shoe backwards, a small motion at first, but more pronounced when the traces refuse to shift, the surface I stand on determinedly troubling and uneven. I know someone will use the pictures of me with my jaw hard, my eyes narrow, and my leg in an odd position, and yet I can't seem to stop rubbing my foot on the ground below me.

'April. *April.*'

I turn and Jags looks at me, then at my foot, mouthing: *There's nothing there.*

It's time to move on, the photographers have had their fill. I walk onto the final stretch of carpet up the stairs to the entrance.

'Some of the worst of it's over now,' Jags tells me, but with every step up towards the ceremony ahead, I can feel the soiled, uneven sensation of the pills that killed Essie beneath my shoe. And any minute now, I have to somehow make the most of the fact I'm here, smile over my shock, my broken heart, and pick up her award.

I wish I was in the edit room of my life's film. I would cut and reshoot whole sections of my story to make any other outcome than the one I've now created. Despite what Jags may say, I know the worst is not over. It has only just begun.

7

Essie, before, the day of the table read

I didn't commit to anything before I left the church rehearsal space. I took April's script away with me into my car, having turned down her offer of heading to lunch. I used the excuse I'd already set up that I was under orders not to be seen in public, rather than dabble in anything like the whole truth, which was that I wasn't ready to spend any more time with her yet. Seeing her, hearing her screenplay read, feels like churning up a whole load of stuff from before, when I'm not even on top of what's happening in the here and now; there's only so much I can cope with, and there's too much for me to handle already.

But I am desperate to work. I don't know who I am when I have to sit still and alone. I miss all the daily routines I used to have, the little rituals that meant I was never flying solo. I was with other people from the minute I got out of bed and my housekeeper made me my coffee for the car, to the *Daybreak* studio where everyone knew how to whip me up into being Essie Lay ahead of meeting guests and rehearsing, all the way up to the music of the title credits, my heart racing in anticipation of Jude's cues to lose myself in a trademark fit of giggles. I don't miss doing that, but I do miss the comradery with the floor managers, home economists, and everyone in between. They had seemed like they would always be by my side because they knew what a true arsehole Jude was. I was so wrong.

I keep remembering the way the cast at the table read seemed to genuinely like each other, how they felt like a real team gathering around April. Then it makes me think how no one from *Daybreak, Don't Go Out, Eat Yourself Thin, Sunday with Essie Lay*, in fact any of the shows I've worked on since I was twenty-one, have picked up the phone these last two weeks. Maybe I could be part of a team, one that might genuinely have my back, if I said yes to April.

My driver is taking me back to Hampstead, to Lotus Lodge, the safe place no one can take away from me. I might not have wanted to buy it so much as my dad wanted me to, but he was right, though not only because it proved to be a great financial investment. This property isn't just another show of Laycock good fortune. To me, Lotus is a symbol of the graft I put in; my crazy work rate, that and endorsing shampoo, moisturiser, cruises, cars, high-street fashion brands, a travel website, anything Janine could organise that paid enough. We're through Highgate Village now. Not long until I can close the door and be alone, inside my egg chair with April's script.

My phone goes. Janine. 'Hey,' I say.

'Sent you something. Didn't think about telling me?'

I put my sister on speaker and open the link that's just appeared in my messages:

59

ACTING UP: SAD ESSIE SETS
SIGHTS ON SILVER SCREEN

In a desperate bid to revive her career, cancelled TV star Essie Lay, 40, is set to try her hand at acting. A grim-faced Lay, recently sacked from a spate of lucrative TV and brand contracts, was spotted leaving a well-known London rehearsal venue where it's thought actors were reading through the latest script of critically acclaimed screenwriter April Eden, 41.

The image of me was clearly taken on someone's phone, the speed of the story getting out there tells me it was an inside job. I wonder if Juniper might have somehow got wind I was there and, sensing trouble ahead, has tried to sabotage me.

'I thought April wanted to meet up, I didn't know—'

'Sorry, you lost me at *meeting up with April*. What the fuck were you thinking?'

'I don't exactly know, Janine. OK?'

'Besides which, you've never acted in your life. You can't just switch it on, you know.' Janine, the nearly child-star who's not acted since she was fourteen, twenty-eight years ago. 'She's setting you up to make a fool of yourself.' Janine, who insisted Jonathan put me forward for a stint in *Celebrity Hell* last year, where I had to live with ten of the most desperado fans for a week, share a room with them, a bathroom, my every moment recorded. I couldn't even get that god-awful gig now.

'How do you know that?' I speak.

'What, that whatever April wants with you, it's no good, or that you can't act? You really need me to present you with evidence for either?'

60

My thumbnail, or what's left of it, finds my teeth. 'All right then, what's the plan? What's your strategy to get me out of where I am now, doing something useful again? Help me turn this around, Janine.' I want to weep so badly, but my sister shouted at me the last time I did, so I hold back.

A pause down the end of the line.

'Jonathan and I think it's best if you disappear for a bit.'

'I've not exactly been sat outside Scott's waiting to get papped for the last fortnight, have I? What do you mean, *disappear*?'

'We've agreed you need to look like you know you shouldn't be here – show the public you hear and respect the need for you to be exiled.'

I shake my head. 'For god's sake, Janine! I'm not a criminal. Jackson is, for filming that video without my consent and editing it so it was guaranteed to finish me off.' I give up trying to stop myself and I sob.

Janine waits quietly on the other end until I've calmed down enough for me to hear her. 'It's all sorted. You'll get flights and an itinerary later today. You're leaving at the end of the week. This could be really good for you.'

'And you?' Easier-to-ignore calls in the middle of the night when I don't think I can go on; far fewer demands on Janine's time.

'That's not what this is about. Es, if you want a career like you had again, it starts by you getting out of peoples' faces long enough to make someone else their target.'

'Don't . . . please don't say it like that.'

'Why not? We both know it's true, you more than most.'

61

*

A week later, I find myself on Hamilton Island, Australia, trying to make the best of my time. In the potential wasteland of the next three weeks, I've decided to work on getting back to who I was not just before Jackson did what he did to me, but a long time ago, in the days before I was famous, the time I first knew April, in fact. Who was I before I got sucked into the fame game? I struggle to remember the differences between who I am and who I was. I still went for the worst men out there, still found meeting people hard, which is why I worked at making it so easy for people to like me. That's what I always did; I worked at whatever I wasn't very good at, and I didn't think I was much good at anything. Still don't.

I've signed myself up for all sorts of courses and activities, including some experimental one-to-one online acting courses run by esteemed drama schools back home. These are reassuringly expensive even though they claim to only cover 'the basics' of screen acting, script analysis, movement, and breathing. I pay for it out of my secret stash of savings, so Janine won't know. I'm going to cram as much as possible into myself between now and getting back to the UK. With Janine's comments jangling inside me since our call, I'm going to see if there's an outside chance my on-screen future is through acting, though I'm still unsure whether kicking off any new career with April is a good idea if I want to look after my mental health.

I leave my hotel room praying to god I won't bump into any paps today. My body is a mess; loose and squashy from little food and no training; my mind isn't much better. I hope the activity I've booked, snorkelling on the Great Barrier Reef, might make me feel better inside and out. I signed up to this afternoon's private charter under my own name. Re-introducing Esther Laycock to the world feels like a healthy new start. And the destination feels suddenly important too: the Great Barrier Reef; because I have some pretty massive barriers to clear if I want to have some kind of life again.

The boat seems to skip on the waves while the sun toasts my skin. Being able to enjoy sailing without Janine bossing me about, I feel free. And the captain is a woman, one who pointedly called me 'Esther' when she welcomed me on board, even after it was clear she knew me as Essie (the details of my nasty little life have shifted magazines and driven hate traffic to social media in both hemispheres – go me!).

I've been made to feel safe, just for a moment. Then, when I slide my body tentatively into the ocean, it takes all my strength not to go to a place where I hear myself thinking: *I don't want to be safe.* As I drop further into the water, I imagine what it would be like to get caught on the spiked coral below, and never surface again. The captain watches me as I prepare to swim over to join my snorkelling guide.

'I've heard there are sharks, lots of sharks,' I say to her, not knowing if I'll be reassured or disappointed by whatever her answer is.

She smiles softly, catching the eye of my guide. 'There are black-tip reefs, grey whaler reefs, leopard sharks, epaulettes, and wob-begongs. Esther, if you knew how many sharks could see you once you're in there, you most likely wouldn't get in.'

'Right.'

And if I'd have known how permanently watched I would be – on screen and in my daily life – would I have let myself be

63

pushed into the shark-infested waters of showbiz, like my dad and Janine did to me?

I swim away from the boat to follow my guide into the blue, peering through my goggles to the deep, taking in the pink, greens, and bleached patches of coral and schools of bright striped fish, while looking out for the dark shadows of bigger animals that might want to eat me. I can't help but think if that's how it all ended, maybe then there was half a chance when you type 'Essie' into any search engine, the predictive search terms would complete as 'got eaten by sharks' rather than the horrible things they suggest now. It would be better for my family that way. Everybody would be happier, me included, if I simply took myself out of living.

'They're all harmless to humans,' the captain calls to me when I surface, a smile still in her voice. 'And anyway, if anything *was* going to attack you, the truth is, Esther, you never see the shark that bites you.'

'Don't I just know it, honey,' I tell the water. I didn't know Jackson was a shark, but he was. And he bit me hardest of anyone.

As I keep swimming, I do see sharks, small ones, but my heart nevertheless beats harder every time they zip over the rocks and plants below me. But I never feel properly afraid. In fact, the afternoon is bliss. Maybe it's being submerged more than me recovering from what I've gone through, but it's the longest I've gone without crying since I found out what Jackson has done. I feel something like calm.

Back on the boat, I see Jonathan has forwarded me news from the trades about not one but two cheap 'documentaries' on my downfall being commissioned by rival networks. But even that can't completely bring me down. I get to thinking about how one

64

day, I should tell my own story. Better than that, I start to have the first inkling that maybe I *could*.

As I disembark onto the jetty, though, I'm right back to where I was before. Because waiting to capture every dimpled, out-of-condition surface of me are two paparazzi. They snap at me and sneer my name as I try to slip past them to my car.

The good captain had clearly tipped them off. Just like Jackson, just like so many friends and colleagues I've allowed myself to trust, she let me down when I least expected her to.

OK, world, lesson learnt once and for all: make sure you see the shark that wants to bite by the time they see you. I get back to my room, lock the door and message April:

If you can make it happen, I will be your Vanished Woman. Exx

8

April, the night of the awards

Jags and I are chaperoned to our seats. I feel a small pulse of justification when I see they're located just one row back from the stage, suggesting victory is more than possible. It adds to the sense I was right coming here, to take Essie's award, and mine. But my modicum of relief is short-lived when I spot Jonathan. Four empty seats stretch between him and the aisle: one for Janine, one for Jags, one for me, and one for Essie, making me realise once again how I don't know if I can or should do this anymore. As the house lights dim, I turn from our row, unable to breathe, ready to walk right back the way I came. How can I look Jonathan or anyone else in the eye tonight, knowing what I know?

Jags stops my retreat with a light touch on the arm, whispering into my ear, 'I'll go first, OK?'

I swallow, mouth my thanks, and press my hand on my stomach, coiling with adrenaline. As we take our seats, Jonathan doesn't bother looking up from his phone, only offers Jags a disinterested, 'Hey.'

'How we feeling?' Jags asks him as I take the seat closest to the aisle, farthest away from Jonathan.

'Royally pissed off at Madame No-Show,' Jonathan says, still fixed on his screen. 'She's been put under a lot of pressure, hasn't she?'

'I guess she has been doing a lot of press,' I say, referring to the gruelling schedule of interviews, podcasts, and TV appearances Jonathan and Janine fielded Essie for these past weeks.

'The movie, April,' Jonathan says, sounding bored. 'Whatever it is you made her do to get that performance out of her, it was too much.' He finally drops his phone into his lap and stares straight ahead for a second, narrows his eyes, his thin mouth twisting in indignation. 'Why do I get the flavour you knew exactly what it would do to her?' He tilts his head, then angles his face to look straight past Jags and directly at me again. 'You did. Didn't you?'

I falter, while Jags takes his cue to lean forward, blocking Jonathan's view of me while he returns to his phone. 'Has Janine called?' he asks, saving me from further accusations. 'We haven't heard back since we called her about Essie.'

Jonathan ignores Jags and speaks to whoever it is now on the end of the line. 'Hel-lo legend . . .'

Jags catches my eye, gives the tiniest of shrugs, before looking around us, putting a hand onto my knee, then taking it back again. He's fidgety, nervous.

'How are we going to get through this?' I ask quietly.

Jags whispers into my ear, the warmth of his breath sweet on my neck. 'We'll do it by acting as we would do in any other circumstances. We'd be super-nervous. We'd be sticking together.' He nods. I nod back. *We've got this.*

Taking Jags's lead, I think about what I would have done in 'normal' circumstances. I turn around in my seat to cast about the darkness to see who I know, or who might want a word in my ear at the after-shows, anything to make my being here worthwhile. Then, I wonder, for one horrific moment if Con and Una, Essie's parents, are nearby. The chances of those two not dining out on Essie's success, not securing the opportunity to flaunt themselves, thinking their apparent wealth means they can hold their own with the stars of silver screen, are almost non-existent.

I'm turning back to face the front when I catch the eye of a senior commissioner at a big streamer. He immediately gives me a thumbs-up before leaving his seat to walk over. He's typical of his kind; a bit younger than me but has nevertheless been in a commanding position for years having got off to an accelerated start through his mum, an establishment producer. He's the kind of man who's not exactly terrible, but not that talented either. He's good at picking projects that take well, or win awards, sometimes both, but is almost completely creatively dead inside. Either way, he gets to tell people like me that he only knows what he wants when we give him something he does not. He's the kind who'll string you along forever, only to strike you off his 'slate' of projects because he realises he's 'already greenlit a female-led drama'. And that's the last eighteen months of your work down the drain. Again. Then he dangles another prize, but only to keep you from getting too close to any other commissioners just in case it's them who ends up backing a stone-cold hit. It suits men like him very well if women like me never get to make anything at all.

I give him a wide smile as he crouches next to my aisle seat. 'Ed. Hi.'

'We need to talk.' He sounds so serious, looks so threatening

68

as the house lights die and blackness fills the hall. Oh god. Has he heard something? Has Janine already put out a post on social media?

'First-look deal. It's time. It's yours. Let's seal it.'

'This is serious, as in . . . really?'

Of all the wins I was expecting from tonight, this comes a close second. This deal would fund the torturous, morally, and sometimes financially ruinous film development process. It could turn my luck on *The Longest Road* and make it so much easier to consolidate my success with films three and four. I should be well into making *The Longest Road* by now, but I haven't been able to get anything going. Three versions of the script, all with Essie attached to star in the supporting role which I'll have to unwind now; the latest draft was fully developed with the financiers of *The Vanished Woman* but who ultimately didn't believe they 'could find a home' for it. They're now starting to see me, despite my nomination tonight, as a cost-generator, not profit-maker. In this industry once you start to fly, you have to beat your wings twice as hard to stop yourself from falling, eight times as strenuous and just as fast if you're female; multiply all those numbers again if you're not white.

'Yup. I hear you've got Essie Lay on board, but attach some balls-out Hollywood talent, and we'd really be away.'

I have had some dealings with Hollywood stars in trying to cast the male lead for *The Longest Road*, but only character actors and Best Supporting nominees, no one you could really see holding the project together, and nobody who was ready to ringfence their schedule for me anyway until I'd secured backing.

69

'I can do that,' I tell Ed.

'Let's get this in the bag. I want that *Deadline* announcement about you and me getting into bed together.' He gives my shoulder a proprietorial squeeze as he uses me to prop him up as he stands. 'Oh, and this isn't about the report, by the way, the *quotas*.' He puts the word between his fingers, tweaking the air with quote marks. 'We'd be having this conversation anyway. Best of luck for later.'

And with that, he's gone. I get my phone out and google Ed: a rash of headlines calling out the paucity of diversity on his slate, despite promises to shareholders and a directive from the board. Then, a rush of stories about shareholder activists looking to protest at a board meeting if he can't show he's taking his gender diversity 'quotas' seriously. This makes the reality of what he's offering more likely than I might be inclined to believe, but I would have hoped I'd be on the cusp of being anointed with a first-look deal because Ed could finally understand my long-term potential. What's more likely is that he knows all is not well between me and my existing backers and has identified me as female director low-hanging fruit.

Resentment simmers my blood. Since I was a young woman, I've managed my existence by fostering my gift for generating stories that mean something, that reach people in the way my personality alone cannot, stories that move people, that stay with them. But here I am, faced with crawling my way closer to longer-term success and Hollywood on a diversity card. On a better day, I would tell men like Ed where to put their half-baked quotas, but this is the worst of days and the truth is, if there is a first-look deal to be had, I need it. I'm desperate to have Essie here to vent to, to share my rage about

70

the unfairness of it all, but also the excitement of a first-look deal with Ed's streamer. Only she would understand the many flavours of shit we have to eat to fill our bellies in this industry.

Now, three seat fillers in the row in front of us rise and depart quickly, leaving no one between me and the lectern. And suddenly the idea of having to get up there, having to smile, performing the role of the overwhelmed winner, not the person who's just lost their very best friend, their muse, is overwhelming. I need to get out of here, maybe just for a moment, possibly for the rest of the night.

'Jags. I think I need to—'

A minor commotion as the Talent and his confidently tight entourage of two arrive to take their seats, and for a second, I forget to breathe. Because this is not just any rising hope, or even any established face – this is the absolute ultimate of every glittering star here.

Martin Russo.

Arguably the most famous man in the world, King of Hollywood. He's well into his fifties but no less stupefyingly beautiful than he was when he started. He's recently divorced, dried out, and up for Best Actor for his role as a recovering alcoholic who washes up in a Native American reservation. If it sounds like semiautobiographical Oscar bait, that's because it is; tonight is merely a warm-up for the Academy Awards next month. My god, he's even more gorgeous up close, the unmistakable shadows cast by his fine cheekbones, the inimitable post-coital sleepiness of those famous blue eyes. His hair, so thick and showy for an older man. I love it. He's sat down right in front of me. Jags shifts uncomfortably in

71

his seat, as touched by the sheer charisma radiating off him as every other person in a one hundred metre radius.

Someone is now blocking my view, and I wish they would hurry up and sit down. 'Put your tongue in, April.'

Oh god. Janine. What is she doing here? Why isn't she at Lotus?

I'm about to say something to her, I don't know what, because now someone else is speaking to me.

'Excuse me.'

Martin Russo has turned around and appears to be talking to me, the fullness of his lips, the tiny muscles in the cheeks by the side of his mouth, heart-stopping.

'Yes?'

'I wanted to say to you . . .' Martin Russo's eyes race across my face; this may be the single most erotic moment of my entire life. 'I loved *The Vanished Woman* and, you know, if you ever find yourself writing an incredible part for an open-minded guy with a lot of experience . . .' Now he looks to the floor in a loaded moment of faux modesty before the startling blue of his gaze swoops up to land on me again. 'You be sure to give me a call now. I love working with strong, visionary female writer-directors.'

A cough. Jags wants an introduction or, perhaps, for me *to put my tongue in*. I allow myself to think a little jealousy might prove to be no bad thing given the context of the stuttering status of our relationship. Maybe this would speed up my meeting his mother, and his friends, for that matter.

'I'd love that. I'm working on something you'd be perfect for.' My first-look deal, and *The Longest Road* and with Martin Russo attached as the lead? It would be the dream casting,

72

the optimal way to dispel any idea I was a one-movie wonder. Forgetting for one sweet moment that I'll have to recast Essie's part, I feel, just for a second, as though my professional life is racing towards a brilliant new chapter.

'You're with Global?' I say it like I don't know who his agents are. I do, everyone does. Everyone knows everything about Martin Russo.

He nods, his lids falling, a suggestion that I shouldn't really have to ask. 'Yup. And I'm in London for a coupla weeks. Give me something smart to read.'

'I'll get my agent to send it to you now.'

'And I look forward to seeing a lot more of you later.' Martin's head tips back towards the stage. 'I'm reading the nominations for Best Director.' He taps the side of his nose with his finger conspiratorially before turning back to face the stage. I feel like my heart might burst, until I tune into Jonathan and Janine's conversation.

'Better late than never,' mutters Jonathan as Janine settles into her seat. 'Thought you might have mounted a damage limitation exercise *Chez Lay*.'

'I got held back by the hacks on the red carpet. If my sister wants to miss the night of her life, that's her choice. As her manager, I have to show up, get ready to wipe up another public mess she's making,' Janine huffs.

'What will we tell the press?' Jonathan asks.

'We can play the anxiety card, for now.'

'You're not worried at all, then?' Jonathan says this with some care, apparently afraid, like the rest of us, of crossing Janine.

'I called her after I saw the text telling me she wasn't coming.

73

She sounded weird, but fine, before she bloody hung up on me. I've just seen I've got an email from her. This whole thing is so her, her normal, flappy, attention-seeking self. I don't know why she has to make so much bloody hard work out of everything. There's something seriously wrong with that girl.'

I think back to hanging up on Janine back at Lotus when I mistakenly answered her call and she thought I was Essie. How could Essie have emailed her after that?

'When did Essie send the email?' I ask Janine as neutrally as I can.

'I don't know,' Janine says, her brusque tone telling me that, as always, she's keen not to waste her precious seconds talking to me. 'It's only just come through. The reception's shit here.'

'I'm pretty worried about her, Janine,' I say, heart racing.

Janine puts down her phone for a moment to view me with a sudden interest that startles me. 'You are? Well, join the club, there are good reasons we all are; very worried. Essie needs more than a mercy dash to Lotus tonight to address her needs in the longer term. Sounds like you would agree?'

'I . . .' I hesitate. I don't know what Janine is asking me to concur with. I also feel like this conversation, anything centred on Essie's wellbeing this evening, is too dangerous to prolong.

Because Essie is dead.

Essie is dead and alone because I left her in the overheated waters of her swimming pool, and a family member I should have known didn't care enough about her has abandoned her too. All so I could be here with people like Martin Russo, so the industry would finally start giving me my due.

Essie is still floating facedown in her pool.

Essie's face, bloating in the water.

74

Essie's flesh, mottling in the heat overnight, because I left her there.

I so deeply want to exist in another world, a brighter one, with Essie still living in it.

Essie, next to me instead of the horrid, empty seat in between Jags and Janine; Essie's sister sat gossiping with Jonathan as though she hasn't been informed someone she loved is in the midst of a crisis. But then who am I to criticise? I am sat here too, and I know far more about Essie's terrible fate than anyone.

*

Finally, we're minutes away from Best Actress being announced. I've coached myself into a state of relative calm. I've decided when I get up there, focusing on Martin will get me through. And if I do colour up or cry when I speak of Essie – the courage it took her to accept the part of Elena, the places she went to in order to access being her – there will be nothing surprising about this, nothing at all to suggest I know what I know. Tears and blushing could, in fact, be enormously beneficial to demonstrating my benign intentions should my walking away from her ever be outed.

'Any nerves about giving Essie's acceptance speech if she wins?' I hear Jonathan say, but he's not asking me.

Janine puffs her cheeks out. 'I've not even looked at it yet, I very much doubt she'll win. I'm only here so it doesn't look like sour grapes and we have to dig her out of another reputational crisis.'

I open Essie's text on my phone, ready to show Janine my

75

screen with proof of her sister's plan that I should be the one to go up.

'You can do it on the night if she does win anyhow, what with your years treading the boards, *darling*,' Jonathan says to Janine. 'It'll be like riding a bike.'

'I'm really sorry, Essie wanted—' I falter, 'Essie wants me to go up for her.' I lean past Jags and show Janine my phone. 'See?'

Janine begins to read, frowning deeply, her small, uneven mouth pursing. 'Er, nope. In the unlikely event of her winning, I have her speech already, thanks very much.'

'And the nominations for Best Actress are . . .' The announcer has begun.

'Janine. If it weren't for me, there wouldn't be a nomination.'

Janine's jaw hardens. She tries to act as though she hasn't heard me.

'Sarah Cushing, *In Our Time*.'

'Janine?'

'Nadine Braithwaite, *A British Marriage*.'

'*You* do *not* get to take what's hers.' Janine stares hard at the big screens where the nominated actresses are being shown, all of them here in the Albert Hall, it seems, besides Essie.

'Essie Lay, *The Vanished Woman*.'

'And you do?' I dare to say. It seems to strike a chord. Janine averts her gaze to the stage where, on the big screen, they briefly cut to the empty seat where Essie should be, before flashing an archive image of Essie's face. There she is. Stunning. Alive. Overwhelming. I turn back to Janine.

'You had nothing to with Essie's performance, nothing to do with the film,' I say.

76

'And Serena Cheung, *Fragments of the Things We Broke*. Let's take a look at all of the nominations . . .'

Snippets of the actresses in action begin to play.

'Didn't I, April? I know what you were saying about my family with your little movie,' Janine sneers.

I open my mouth to defend myself but can't reach for the words I need.

'Yeah, don't think I didn't put it together, it wasn't exactly subtle, was it? So, you owe it to us to step aside if this plays out in Essie's favour.' Janine gestures towards the stage.

'And the winner is . . .'

'Your way of saying sorry for all the damage you've caused,' says Janine.

'Essie didn't think I had anything to apologise for. She relished her part. You didn't want her to take it.'

'It wasn't the part that was the problem, *April*.' Janine seems to be daring me to ask her what powers the bile behind her words.

'Essie Lay, *The Vanished Woman*!'

Both Janine and I look to the stage; Essie's uneven smile, wide and dazzling on the big screens either side of the lectern.

'Don't you dare get up, April, I swear to god,' Janine says through gritted teeth.

The cameras are fully trained on us now. I'm at the end of the aisle, so there's no way Janine can stop me, but I can't block her either when I leave my seat.

'Let's both get up there. It's clearly what Essie wanted,' I whisper.

'Well done, April.' Jags takes my hand, webs his fingers with mine, and gives it the briefest of kisses. I'd almost forgotten about him, and he knows it.

'Thank you, darling. Thank you for absolutely everything.'

I kiss him on the lips, noticing a slight reticence. Perhaps because he knows the camera is on us and doesn't want to risk his mum finding out about us this way. I get up and wait for Janine to shuffle after me. Barely disguising a face like thunder, Janine makes it to the aisle, the applause loud and emphatic over Essie's victory.

I realise my phone is still in my hand when it buzzes.

Email from Essie

Relief races through me for half a second – *Thank god! She's not dead, she was only playing with me somehow! It was all an elaborate prank to get her out of going tonight* – until I remember her plan to send her speech to me on a delay. What 'curse' did Essie suppose she might avoid in doing this when she hexed her own fate tonight? I begin to quickly scan Essie's message.

As I take the last few steps to the award presenter – a smooth-skinned eighty-year-old Hollywood icon in a plunging diamante dress – my mind swirls; I would usually be thrilled and wholly absorbed in being in her presence but instead, as I walk to her open arms, I'm deploying my speed-reading skills to see if Essie's speech might give me any clues on what she did tonight. It does. And there is absolutely no way I can read it out loud.

I grasp the award, a heavy bronze rendering of an old-fashioned film projector on a silvered base, before Janine can take it. The weight of it in my hand steadies me somehow after the heartbreaking power of Essie's acceptance speech. I have in my hand a real thing, tangible recognition for the performance I managed to coax free from Essie. *This* is what they'll be talking about tomorrow morning: her laudable talent, not her sordid death.

'Congratulations,' the icon purrs, 'I just loved your movie. You're going to be huge, your girl Essie too.'

I smile at her feebly, the threat of tears around my throat.

'Unfortunately, Essie felt unable to be here tonight . . .' As I've been talking with the veteran actress, Janine has installed herself at the mic. The applause calms. 'But my sister has sent me the message she wanted you to hear.'

Oh god. No.

Janine clears her throat, views her phone's screen.

'Elena: a woman who felt she had to vanish. What a part. What an absolutely perfect role for me. Because I'm an expert at vanishing. You all made me into one.'

A quiver of confusion in Janine's voice.

'I was just a normal girl. I never wanted to be famous. But she wasn't good enough for certain people, so she had to disappear.'

Janine coughs now, her hand in front of her face. She swallows and continues. She speaks quietly, caught between not wanting to read on, but not having any other words in her mind to replace the ones in front of her. 'Esther Laycock had to vanish to make way for the clean living, always-smiling kids TV presenter *Essie*. And when she started to run out of juice, we had to make her go away and replace her with the edgy, cool version of Essie, one who had to date pop stars and fall out of clubs. But then you grew tired of her and,' Janine reads the next bit very quickly, 'people needed me to keep earning, so *that* Essie Lay had to disappear so the next Essie could do

79

whatever it took to be on your TVs morning, noon, and night until you were all probably sick of me. I was completely sick of myself too, so much so that I wanted someone to take it all away. I wanted to disappear into love, into marriage, into being a mum, maybe. But together the man I loved, and you, made that Essie vanish too.'

Janine pauses for a few, painful seconds, scans to the end of the message, seems to recalibrate herself somehow before staring at the audience.

Finally, and with a sigh, Janine speaks again. 'I'm going to read to the end of my sister's speech. But I hope you can remember how much she's been through. So, as well as this award, Essie deserves your understanding and your kindness.'

The entire Albert Hall falls still and silent. Sickness surges through me, bringing with it a full-throttle wave of blood from my arms to my hairline. And Janine hasn't even got to the worst part yet. Why does she want to keep reading?

'The woman you keep making disappear whenever you want her to is doing one better. I've decided it's time I disappeared on my own terms and this time . . .' Janine pauses before delivering the final words of Essie's speech. 'Essie Lay is going to vanish forever.'

9

Essie, before, the screen test for The Vanished Woman

THE VANISHED WOMAN

[TEASER]

OVER BLACK:

FEMALE VOICEOVER

What does the truth look like? How does it feel?

[FADE UP]

INT. DAY

A well-appointed kitchen, in the background, through a window, a bright courtyard garden. A woman, late thirties, ELENA, slight, and wearing a SIMPLE WHITE DRESS circles her finger in the air above the jagged rim of a tall, BROKEN GLASS on a LONG KITCHEN TABLE.

ANTONIA, 40S, not more than a shadow in the middle distance behind Elena at first, walks towards her. Now directly behind Elena, we

```
see only Antonia's hand, reaching down to
the table to . . .
. . . snatch the broken glass away from
  Elena by its stem.


                  ANTONIA
You know your father won't let me go
until you give me what he wants: the
truth.


Elena turns to face Antonia. She appears
even smaller when she stands next to her.
Elena takes a step closer to Antonia, who
senses danger. Dread.
Close on Elena's face. A hand comes in
from the right. To slap her. Hard.
Her own.
Elena appears to register no pain.
```

I'm re-reading the first page of April's script in the reception of her financiers' offices in Soho. It's the teaser, which is based on one of the set pieces before the climax of the movie, one of the scenes I have to read at my screen test today. I need to think only as Elena, not Essie, while still giving something real from inside me. It's all so intense and surreal, I don't know if I can do this. I should be back home, out of sight, away from any kind of scrutiny; safe.

I coach myself to stay in my seat, reminding myself I know my lines inside and out, after recording and rerecording myself, internalising everything my acting tutors taught me over the past couple of months, and then recalling my track record of whenever people are inclined to think I can't do something, the harder I try to prove them wrong, a mindset probably forged in the friendly fire of family criticism.

At my first job, the kids' magazine show *All Aboard*, when they thought I wasn't much more than a pretty, ditzy face, I encouraged them to throw me out of planes, make me climb mountains. They soon caught on to my willingness to be tested. I hold world records in raw-egg eating, window cleaning, but also solo kayaking. I've faked being a chef, fashion buyer, hospital porter; I passed every test. I can pass now. I have to, because if something good doesn't happen soon, I'll stay like I am now, *who* I am now, a person I don't know. I can't switch back to being Esther Laycock overnight; I need to be Elena first. Because I don't know who Esther Laycock is anymore and I've got no one to be her with anyway.

'Essie?' April's head finally pokes out of the room where she waits with her backers.

I give her one of my shiniest smiles, then tell myself not to fake it, to hear in my head my acting tutors' voices, not Jackson's, not Jude's and all the people who enabled him, not my father's, Janine's or my mother's. Actually, the only voice I need to think about right now belongs to the only person who always seemed to start from a position of believing I'm capable of doing something good. April.

'We're ready for you,' she says.

I grin over the sickness inside and get ready to prove she's right to always have faith in me.

*

83

Even though I almost dropped my script when I first went in, I was indeed tested and feel as though I may very well have passed. An hour and a half of being Elena at her most vulnerable, then discussing it in detail with April and her financiers, was draining. And, of course, I had to hit myself. Three times April made me shoot the slap scene. I think she was watching to see if I was going to hold back. She has no idea how easy I made it for myself not to.

I whacked myself, hard, then again. And when she asked for one last go, I hit myself so forcefully my cheek's blown up. I slapped myself first for being so stupid as to fall for Jackson the second he came into my life, then for wanting to trust him so deeply, and finally, because I don't believe anyone good will ever love me again. And even if they did come along, would I know how to spot them anyway?

When I started to become famous, Janine decided she and Jonathan would broker my relationships. They worked with other agents to pair me with men who would boost my career and vice versa. This meant I dated wholesome and non-threatening men when I was in *All Aboard*, then DJs and drummers when my career moved on. I wasn't forced to do anything with anyone I didn't want to, not really. And if I didn't like the guy, it didn't go anywhere at all. I got used to other people arranging my dating life for me. Every now and then, I'd fall for someone because I never feel more in my body as when I'm giving it to someone else. And now, I'm trying to start earning again by giving my body over to being someone else, hurting that body in the name of doing this. What a weird life Essie Lay's been given.

We're wrapping up. I want to go home, to lose myself in the warmth of Lotus, cry over all the memories I've been made to

84

relive. I'm preparing to say goodbye to April and the money-men, pulling on my hoodie and fishing out my fake glasses, when one of the men holds out a beer bottle, the kind that sits in an underpowered fridge in a Soho office to suggest to all the interns they don't pay that they're really great blokes. Now, it's being offered to me.

'Oh, thanks, I'm not really—' I look to April for backup, but on seeing me about to refuse her backer's bottle, she looks as though she might colour up or cry, or both, '. . . a beer drinker but', I hold the not especially cold glass to the heat of my slapped cheek, 'today, I make an exception!'

April lets out a laugh that's a bit loud and I take a long swig of the stale beer. How else am I going to get through this?

'There's a screening on Dean Street, now; the last feature we produced,' the man says. 'It'd be great if you came, see what we're about, get to know you better.' His gaze starts on my face before swallowing the rest of me, piece by piece. This. Always this. I see the ring on his finger and think of the lovely wife and toddler waiting for him in a nice house in Dulwich or similar and I hate him and the millions of men like him; all of them expecting me to love their tweets and comments about what bit of me they'd like to fuck first. Meanwhile, April seems to have found something fascinating in the street beyond the window. She can't stand to watch either him flirting with me, or me turning him down. If I do, will they still hire me? And what will I do if the financiers say no? What will I do with the next week and the one after that? I don't know how I can survive here in no-man's land for much longer.

I take another long gulp of beer into my empty stomach. April smiles apologetically over the moneyman's shoulder, but

85

she doesn't do anything to suggest I shouldn't go along with his invite.

'Screening sounds great.'

*

I call Jonathan from a doorway near the screening house, my back to the street to avoid being spotted or having to talk to anyone before the film starts.

'How was it?' he asks about the screen test, but only because he feels he has to, not because he or Janine want me to do it. They both think it's a terrible idea, not least because I've decided if I get the part, I'll take only a nominal fee upfront and share in a cut of the profits instead. This way I make buttons if *The Vanished Woman* tanks, a small fortune on the outside chance it achieves the global domination and awards recognition April is definitely longing for. Jonathan and Janine have made it clear they want me waiting it out in the shallows before they can push me back into the guaranteed income mainstream, a place comfortably far away from April for Janine.

'It went well,' I tell Jonathan.

'So great. Call holding. More soon.'

'More what? You haven't had anything for me since—'

'Gotta go, queen.'

I wait another ten minutes before I go in. It's freezing for October, or maybe the papers are right, maybe my body fat is becoming 'dangerously low', that's why the wind feels so brutal on my self-inflicted injuries.

I slip into the screening once the lights are down. April has kept a spot for me between her and the financier who invited

86

me. He leans into my space a few seconds after I've taken my seat. 'I hope this doesn't make you feel uncomfortable.' Whenever they say this, the next thing they say is guaranteed to leave me squirming. 'But I think you're such a special talent.' He drops his eyes from my red cheek to take in the rest of my body, hiding underneath my defensive hoodie and straight-legged jeans. I'm not advertising any bit of me, yet still he thinks he can have me; bag a night with me to add to his canon of showbiz anecdotes. 'Drinks after this. Stick around?'

It's said as a question, but it really isn't. He knows he owns my ass. My body has always belonged to other people who want it to do what they need, not just the bad men in my life, but the brands I was told to work with too; I didn't even have a choice over what to wear on my body, what products to use on my hair and skin. And even before I was famous, it sometimes felt my body existed only for my dad, mum, and Janine to point out all the things wrong with it, before they put it to work so I could pour money into Signal House.

'I'd love to get a drink afterwards,' I tell the producer, forcing a smile onto my mouth that makes my face feel as though it is being torched.

*

The drinks reception after the screening is full of very shouty people on the hustle. The man who asked me here is enjoying being worked by a pod of much younger people, so I'm already forgotten. If anyone here has recognised me, they're too cool to show any excitement over the Troubled Former TV Star. It's not that I especially mind this, or the fact the sleazy financier

87

has found younger bodies to make him feel like The Man, it's only that I've put myself in a public place in the UK for the first time in a while and there must be a part of me that's unused to not getting any attention. The sad fact is after nearly twenty years of being at the centre of things, I'm hard-wired to it, and now I'm in a room where no one is pawing at me, trying to get something out of me, I get that feeling again: I'm not totally sure who I am.

April is stood next to me and also appears uncomfortable, though to be fair, she looks uneasy in most settings. Right now, she keeps looking at the door, clinging near the side of the buffet table like it's a life raft, and because I can't face anyone else, I've ended up holding my spot by her side; a pair of spinsters at a family wedding, two maiden aunts who haven't quite worked out how to live. God, what have I come to? I want to go home very badly now. I decide I'll finish my drink, then slip back to the safety of Lotus.

'OK. I'm going to do something really cheesy.'

An extremely good-looking Indian guy in his early thirties has come up to us. He's wearing a sensationally well-fitted navy pea coat that showcases his height and the breadth of his pecs and shoulders, but all I can do is look at the floor and think: *Here we go, another man who thinks he can chuck me a compliment and have all of me.*

'I noticed you the second I walked in here and now, I have to go, and I've had a drink, but I'd never forgive myself if I didn't come over here and tell you . . .'

That you're my biggest fan? That I'm still gorgeous? That any man would be the luckiest guy in the world to be with me, even now?

88

'That you have such a nice face. Sorry, that's such a rubbish word and I bet you're really clever, as well as beautiful.'

Please. I've heard enough. 'Thanks, but—'

I finally look up at him. He seems a bit shocked at me speaking, not because he's just realised I'm Essie Lay, but because he wasn't speaking to me at all.

'Sorry, I was just . . .' His deep-brown eyes dart away from April to me, but only for a second, because the only person who exists to him in this whole room is her.

'That's OK.' I look deep into my cocktail glass.

'Would you tell me your name?' the hot guy asks April. She's as red as I've ever seen her.

'April.'

'I'm Jagdeep. You can call me Jags, if you'd like to call me at all.'

He hands April his card. An ancient memory springs to the front of my mind that makes me think she'll love this move. He gives me a business card too. It describes him as a business affairs specialist for film and TV.

'I'm sorry for being so in-your-face. I wouldn't normally, I just . . . well, I've had it with waiting for something good to happen. Because maybe it won't unless you meet it halfway, take a chance.' He screws his eyes up, pushes his fingers into them with a wide but shy smile that would have most women on their knees. 'Sorry, I'll shut up now. I'll go.' He looks mystified at his own uselessness, an adorable contrast to the cover-of-*GQ* face and body. 'Wait! I've not asked you anything! What is it do you do?'

'I'm a writer,' April says meekly.

'Oh, yeah? What do you write? Anything I would know?' he asks.

'Have you seen *Encounters*?'

Encounters was a series of female monologues April asked me to watch in preparation to join her production. It was widely acclaimed, particularly the two episodes she directed which helped secure her shot at making her film. I feel a burn of jealousy that I'm not at all used to and don't like one bit.

'I *loved Encounters*!' The glee on Jags's flawless face turns up another notch.

'Well,' April says quietly, looking at the drink in her hands, embarrassed, 'that was me.'

He seems so impressed with her, and her modesty. God, he could love her. Another thump of envy hits my chest. Meanwhile, Jags can't stop staring at April, who feels it and gives a nervous little laugh. Then, they both sort of stand there for a moment, like they have no idea what to do.

'Allow me to help,' I say, grabbing a pen from my bag. I scribble down April's number on the card Jags gave me and give it back to him. 'You call her, OK?'

He doesn't look at me, only keeps his eyes fixed on April the whole time.

'I will. I *will* call you. Goodbye, April.'

'Bye,' she says almost inaudibly.

He nods and turns to me. 'Oh, and bye . . .'

He waves the card, caught between his two fingers. 'Thank you.'

Once he leaves, April doesn't seem to want to talk about what just happened. Maybe she feels guilty, given what went down with me and Jackson, but that wasn't her fault. Just because I've had my happiness, the family I thought I'd have with him, my whole future, robbed from me, doesn't mean

I want to hold everyone else down with me, least of all April, who, from what I can tell, hasn't been in any kind of serious relationship for some time, if she ever has.

'Wow. He's a bit gorgeous. And so sweet,' I say to her.

April shrugs.

'Tell me you'll go out with him if he calls.'

'I don't know. I'm going to be so busy with the shoot soon, it's not really the right time.' She bites her lip. She looks almost scared about the idea of starting something with that guy, with anyone. I don't think it's been easy at all for her on the men-front over the years. I feel a low stab of guilt I don't want to acknowledge.

'Oh, April,' I say, swinging my arm around her shoulder. 'You're forty-one and a really lovely, seriously hot guy has just practically fallen for you on the spot. Trust me, honey, it's the perfect time.'

April's phone goes. It doesn't look like she recognises the number, but she accepts the call anyway. The person on the other end speaks so loudly, I can hear his every word.

'It's Jags. I'm in the car, sorry if I'm shouting. Can you hear me?'

'Yes,' April says.

'What's that? *Yes,* you'll come for dinner with me tomorrow?'

She tuts through an awkward smile.

'That wasn't a no, so can I take it as a yes?'

I roll my eyes and mouth the word for her to say.

'Yes.'

10

April, the night of the awards

Janine and I are backstage, posing awkwardly for pictures with Essie's award. When someone from BBC News asks for an interview, Janine refuses for both of us, instead, dragging me into a quiet corner.

'*Essie Lay is going to vanish forever*? You wouldn't happen to know what she's talking about?'

'I—'

'She scuttled back to Australia? What if I need to see her about work?'

'I really don't—'

'What've I ever done to deserve this?' Janine holds her phone out as if the device itself is somehow to blame for her reading out Essie's anger-fuelled message to a full Royal Albert Hall. 'She's fully deluded. If she's fucked off to Oz without consulting me first, that just goes to show . . .' I see Janine calling Essie's number. 'It's fucking switched off. She's probably in the air now. What have you said to her now?' she asks me.

'Nothing, Janine,' I tell her truthfully.

Jonathan has found his way to us.

'Essie. Australia. I'll put money on it,' Janine tells him.

'Yeah. That *is* a possibility. You didn't think it maybe sounded a little *darker* than that? The film really did seem to make her feel like she wasn't in the driving seat?' He peers over his lenses to look right at me for a second. He and Janine make their money from controlling everything Essie does, and now he's trying to suggest it was I who disempowered her, despite the fact my film has given her the accolade of her career and more control over her image than she's ever had. Jonathan has never forgiven me for negotiating Essie's deal for *The Vanished Woman* without him and for almost no fee, though he did, of course, extract his ten per cent from the token amount anyway.

'Her phone still switched off?' Jonathan asks Janine, who nods. 'Fine. Let's give the press the slip and play the anxiety card until further notice.'

Janine and Jonathan get back to their phones and leave without saying either goodbye or good luck to me. Part of me is relieved Janine has left, another worries the situation is more dangerous now I can't see what she's doing. I retake my seat in the auditorium only just in time for Best Director. Jags gives my hand a quick squeeze, which does nothing to calm my stomach, already roiling even before Martin Russo arrives onstage to read the nominations.

He does a brief, self-deprecating monologue, even though he took Best Actor while I was backstage and the entire Albert Hall is eating out of his hand. He reads the other nominees, meaning he'll say my name last. The cameras cut to me in preparation. I work to remain neutral, completely still in my seat, determined to display neither my desperation to win, nor my guilt for leaving Essie.

'April Eden, *The Vanished Woman*.'

My name filling Martin Russo's mouth gives me a snatched

second of delight, a tiny portal through which I can glimpse how incredible this night would have been; the way his muscular lips seem to kiss the *pr* sound in the middle of my name into the air. I wonder whether my parents are watching, if they're showing any interest in my achievements for the first time in their lives. Perhaps all of the people I couldn't make love me – my family, my peers at Oxford and film school, the crew at *The Dawn Chorus* – all of them are seeing me, hearing my name on Martin Russo's lips. Perhaps my parents are pretending that they do, in fact, care, and all the people who left rooms whenever I came in are telling their friends they thought me 'lovely' after all, and never did understand why we weren't close. And perhaps, somewhere, Essie is watching too.

'Best Director goes to – I loved this movie so much – yes!'

Martin Russo beams as if my movie is his own. I cannot wait to be embraced, to be kissed on both cheeks by him, to inhale his cologne, to take the award in my hand and convince the world every choice I made to get to this point was justified, even if, with Essie gone, I cannot believe it myself. My whole life seems to pour into the elongated pause before Martin Russo announces the winner.

'Roberta Wang, *Fragments of the Things We Broke*.'

For a moment, I can't exhale. It's as though I am hoping to freeze the moment before this one and the one before it, the last second I had a chance, the closing nanoseconds of hope. I breathe out. I have lost. I am a loser, of the award and of so much else this evening: my morality, my dignity, and Essie.

I clap, forcing myself up off my seat as Roberta Wang, a thirty-two-year-old American with an Oscar nomination under her belt already, goes to accept her award against a backdrop of a standing ovation so adoring, I feel the applause rumbling in my ribcage, knocking my heart out of its rhythm again. As soon as I know the cameras won't return to me, I slump in my seat.

'I'm so sorry, darling,' Jags says into my ear.

I wait until Roberta finishes her speech before, without words, I leave my seat, leading Jags by the hand to follow me out towards the exit, out of the auditorium and onto a wide stairway. Jags leaves me to go to the bathroom and I linger, desperately hoping I don't have to see anyone, so I can avoid dealing not only with questions about Essie, but also commiserations on my losing.

'Alright there.'

A voice I could never forget. One that makes me burn and freeze all at once. I can barely make myself raise my eyes to look at him.

Essie's father, Con, greyer than he was twenty years ago, but still solid, still immaculately clean-shaven, a golden molar finding the light as he smiles at me open-mouthed. He walks up the stairs before waiting half a beat to appraise me, then leans forward to plant a kiss on one side of my face, saying under his breath, 'You're not in too bad nick . . .' He moves to kiss the other cheek, '. . . for an old girl,' before taking a step back.

Una, Essie's mother, in a close-fitted pink dress with a deep-V neckline, not dissimilar to the style of what Essie was supposed to be wearing to the awards tonight, appears at his side. She moves two steps above me and takes Con's hand to make him ascend with her.

'April.' She says my name with as much civility as she can muster, though she clearly wants to walk past and up the stairs

95

without saying anything further. I nod a greeting and will the pair of them to get as far away from me as they can.

'I was just saying, it was a shame April's lost,' Con says, rooting himself to the spot, enjoying prolonging the agony of this interaction.

'Well, it was never going to be everyone's cup of tea,' Una says coldly and to the carpet. 'It was all rather melodramatic for me.' She glimpses at me. 'Seems like the histrionics must really have got to Essie.'

I swallow. 'It's such a shame she couldn't be here in person tonight.'

'It's hardly a surprise, is it?' Una's face is possibly even more naturally beguiling than Essie's, but soured by the distaste she clearly still has for me, twenty years since I last saw her. She looks to Con. 'We're all at a loss with her since the filming. She's barely been speaking to us.' Una's lips harden, and now she looks less like Essie, more like Janine. 'Tonight's little outburst is par for the course.'

Con nods. 'She needs to take better care of herself, eh?' he says to Una, who sighs with a strange sort of stoicism and a pervading sense that whatever ills have beset Essie's mental wellbeing, they have nothing to do with them and everything to do with me. I can't bear another second with them. I move to the next step down, mutter a goodbye, Una doing the same, sashaying away from me up the stairs. But Con still isn't done with me. His hand reaches down to find the skin on the side of my arm. Now, with Essie's father touching me, I find I can no longer move, my next breath freezes in my lungs too. 'Come back to Signal one day, you and Esther. Draw a line under the past; be like old times.' I view his hand on me, then his face as he gives me a wink before

96

bounding up the stairs to catch up with his wife, passing Jags on his way to join me.

'Was that who I think it was?' Jags asks.

'He's no one,' I breathe, before rushing out my next words. 'Stay with me tonight. Please.' I'm as desperate as I sound. I want to go home, take a scalding bath, and wash off Con's touch, as well as every bad choice I've made to get to this exact point in my life. And then I want to climb into bed and give in to my grief and shame with Jags holding me tight.

'I can't, April. I'm so sorry. There's no one else to take care of Mum.'

Despite my efforts, I feel a heavy tear leave my cheek and fall to the front of my white dress; clouded black with mascara, this one will definitely stain.

*

We get back to Jags's car, parked in the driveway of the house in Kensington. Jags is about to open the door for me when he spots something. 'Shit,' he says, squatting down to view what I can now see too: a grey-black oil patch peeking out from under his car.

'Is it dangerous?' I ask.

'Dangerously expensive.'

'I'll pay – for the clean-up, to get it fixed.'

'I don't want you to pay for anything,' he says, opening my door. 'I'll sort it myself.'

'I don't mind. It's just until you find more work, or I can give you some,' I say, climbing in. Jags joins me in the car, leans towards me from the driver's seat to kiss me gently on the forehead, before tilting his head, so our brows are touching.

'If I ever get the chance, I will work so hard for you.'

'I know you will. Hopefully, one day soon, if I get that deal Ed's promising, possibly on *The Longest Road*, but definitely by film three when I should have more say over hires.'

Jags nods before kissing me deeply and while I want to disappear into him, I pull back after a couple of seconds. Being intimate with Jags while Essie still floats in her pool would be in sickeningly poor taste. 'I can't,' I say, sitting back in my seat.

'That's OK,' he says, immediately starting the engine.

We're largely silent throughout the drive back north. I can find no words to describe anything of what I'm feeling; my grief, regret, dread, all too dense and primal to be converted into language. If my cameras were the only way I could connect with others, writing was my retreat. The empty page has long been a very specific type of friend to me, one that would always listen, ever-ready to help process my pain. Not even having words available to me tonight leaves me feeling more alone and weak. By the time we reach my building, I feel as though I can barely put one foot in front of the other, yet I already know I will not be able to sleep.

'I wish I could stay,' Jags tells me as I leave his car. 'I promise tomorrow, I'll try to make everything as easy as I can for you. I'll be back here at eight.'

I watch him drive away from me, then drag myself into my building and the long night ahead.

*

The wait for morning is excruciating. Many times, I consider rushing over to Lotus, but the idea of returning there in the dark leaves me stiff with terror. I resolve to go as soon as the sun rises.

As the night passes, I can't help myself, I want to understand Essie's last moments. I read the NHS webpages on zolpidem, the pills I saw on Essie's poolside, a potent sleeping pill that should not be taken with alcohol. The champagne bottle I knocked over was empty, but what did Essie care if it was going to be her last drink? Perhaps the champagne would have made going through with it all a little easier. Next, I learn that zolpidem is what's known as Ambien in the US.

After this, my clicking and scrolling become fevered.

There are pages and pages about accidental deaths due to Ambien, particularly when the user combines it with alcohol. A thought cleaves my mind: what if she'd fallen into her pool in a stupor, or had 'irrational thoughts' – one of the side effects of the medication – but never really intended to kill herself? Why didn't I check to see if she was still breathing? She may not have been in the water long; I may have been able to revive her. I didn't even investigate what state she was in, only left her there for a sister I should have known didn't care enough to go to her. But by this logic, I must not have cared enough about Essie either.

99

11

April, the morning after the awards

I get the bus up to Hampstead just after six, the night draining away from the sky as I trudge to Essie's home.

My hand quakes as I enter the security code for the electric gate blocking the view of Lotus from the street, the gravel of her driveway uneven under my boots as I make my unsteady approach to the dark wood of her door. I turn my keys in its three locks, recalling Essie's kindness when she told me she wanted me to have keys to her home so I could have somewhere else to write – my preferred spot became at the kitchen table, looking out to the lotus pond – as well as a place Jags and I could come to swim or sit on the veranda to talk while enjoying the view of the garden. The final lock gives with a heavy clunk.

I push the door ajar, pulling my jumper up to cover half my face to protect my senses from some unfamiliar tang. I step inside and deactivate the burglar alarm, then dare to sniff the air. The only thing I can smell are the rotting flowers on the table below the atrium's skylight, but Essie's house remains so overheated, I remain very afraid of what I must face in the pool.

I reach the dirtied cream tones of her living room, breathing heavily as I approach the aquamarine and white of the pool through the sliding glass doors. At Essie's egg chair I pause, allowing my hand to run over its stiff, woven lip as I pass, woefully imagining a world where Essie is nestled inside it, remembering how she'd often be sat in here, watching her boxsets, painting her toenails, or quite often, brushing her hair. There are no traces of her on the chair now.

Behind me, a white smear catches the corner of my eye.

Someone is moving through the atrium and in the direction of the kitchen.

I freeze.

A clink: porcelain being moved, or a pan, one that might be used to deal a blow to the head.

'Hello?!' I call.

No response. Have I walked in on an intruder, breaking into Lotus now Essie is gone? My heart thumps against my ribcage.

'This is April! I'm with a group of Essie's friends here to see if she's OK!' I call out, voice cracking with obvious fear.

Silence.

Then steps, determined and quick. All I hear now is the blood pounding in my ears.

'Hey.'

It's Jags. I crumple into Essie's chair. I can't speak, can't make sense of what I'm seeing. Jags looks to be wearing night clothes: a loose-fitting white T-shirt and navy jogging pants, sliders on his feet.

'What are you doing here?' I ask him.

'I've been tossing and turning all night. Thought I'd check out the house first before you had to face it too, and get this . . .' He pulls Essie's incongruously sparkly phone from the pocket of his joggers, '. . . down the back of her chair or someplace – I'm pretty sure it's dried out now, thank god – then, I was going to collect you at eight, like we said.'

'You look like you just got out of bed.'

He looks down at himself as if he's only just realised what he's wearing. 'I kind of have, not that I slept.'

I nod. But still, something isn't right.

'How did you get in?'

'You left the door open. Don't worry, I closed it.'

Did I leave it open, for ventilation, a quick escape, or both? Yes, maybe.

'Why did you go to the kitchen, not come straight to the pool?'

Jags shakes his head. 'I was just double-checking the coast was clear, I guess.' He looks down once more. 'Or maybe I was stalling. I might be more scared of this morning than you are.' He smiles faintly and apologetically. 'Sorry.'

I play through Jags's choreography in my mind as if I'm planning a scene: he walks into Lotus Lodge behind me; decides to quickly check in the kitchen first, to gather himself as much as to check that Janine, or anyone else for that matter, isn't lurking here already; I call out and he comes straight to me. OK. Nearly.

'I could have sworn I heard something like someone getting some crockery, maybe moving a pan?'

'The kitchen's a pigsty, like everywhere else.' He looks to the detritus around us, and I do the same, noticing a ball of screwed-up notepaper on the table next to Essie's chair. 'You sounded scared. I must have clipped something when I ran to you.' Jags comes over to me. 'God, state of me.' He pulls at the sides of his joggers, giving me a glimpse of the hardness of the stomach in between his hip bones. 'A bit of a comedown from black tie,' he says, but even in what could easily pass for pyjamas, Jags looks better than most men on their wedding day. He wraps his arms around my shoulders and the warmth and solidity of his body provoke some primal need in me. I want to melt into him, I want every piece of our bodies to come together. I know it's wrong to feel this urge here, now, but it's something beyond rationality. His fingers, soft under my jaw, bring my eyes to his.

'I'm happy to go first, go alone, whatever you want.' He eyes the pool area behind me. I'm so grateful he's here, I could weep; so relieved to not have to do this, as I have done so many things in my life, alone.

'Let's do it together,' I say.

'Together,' Jags says, giving me the gentlest of smiles, and with it that curious feeling once more, that going through this awful series of events is bringing us closer than perhaps I'd ever dared hope.

'Should we . . . ?' I break from our embrace and pull my jumper up to cover my nose, motioning for Jags to do the same with his T-shirt. Both of us take an audible breath behind our makeshift face masks and take our first step together towards the pool.

A series of metallic clunks from the atrium. Someone else is entering Lotus.

Breath leaves both of us.

'Who's in there?!'

Oh god, no.

Janine is walking through the door.

I grip Jags's hand and we both rip the clothes down from our faces. I look to him, wide-eyed in panic. He blinks slowly, pats the air either side of him and mouths: *It's OK.*

'It's us!' An unnatural lightness in Jags's voice as he tugs me back from the pool's sliding doors. Janine stomps through the atrium and joins us in the living room, viewing us with unhidden suspicion.

'Essie's phone's still switched off,' Jags says. 'We were worried, we couldn't sleep, so thought we'd come and check on her.'

'Oh, we did, did we?' Janine takes Essie's award out of the holdall she's carrying and places it on the side table by Essie's chair, all the while appearing like she's mentally cataloguing the mess of the place. 'She up yet?'

'I don't think so, but we've only just got here,' I say, trying to keep the adrenaline powering my pulse away from my tone.

Janine turns on her heels and makes her way back through the atrium. We follow her.

'ESTHER!' she calls up the staircase. 'We need to talk about last night, like, now!' Janine starts to climb, muttering, 'She's probably out of it on her *little helpers*.'

So, Janine knows about the pills.

She doesn't invite me to follow her, but I do anyway, gesturing to Jags to stay behind in the atrium. Janine reaches Essie's room, casts a disparaging look my way as she yanks open the door. 'I shouldn't think she'd want you to be . . . *fuck*. Oh, my fucking god.'

My blood does not rush to my face, some cold force is chasing it out of me through my feet.

'*No*. No. Nooooo.'

'Janine?' I ask feebly.

She doesn't answer but walks slowly into the room. 'She's fucking gone and done it.'

Essie's room is a mess of open drawers, strewn clothes, her bed

104

unmade. I peer through to her dressing room. The shelves are lit, but her designer shoes and bags are missing. The rail of Essie's shortlist of dresses for the awards is bare and on Essie's dressing table, empty jewellery boxes of various sizes. Where would Essie have moved her things before she did what she did? And why?

I examine the chaos of the scene again. What if Essie didn't take her things? What if someone else was involved in what happened to her? What if someone got her drunk then smuggled the pills into her champagne, or worse, forced them down her throat? My mouth sags with sudden nausea while Janine continues her examination, walking over to one of Essie's bedside tables and yanking out the drawer.

'Fucking idiot. Passport. Gone. Knew it.' She looks to me. 'Did you know she was about to do a runner? I need to speak with her urgently after last night's little outburst.'

'I don't know where she is,' I tell her, hearing the strain of underlying panic in my voice. Janine hitches her holdall on her shoulder and pushes past me to leave the room. I follow her down the stairs, allowing one last look at Essie's ransacked quarters, trying to piece together what may have happened, thinking again about exactly what I saw yesterday and whether there was any indication anyone else was there. I draw a blank, but that doesn't mean to say someone couldn't have been hiding in one of Lotus's many rooms.

As Janine races back downstairs, I assume she's about to leave, or call Jonathan and work out how they're going to bring their volatile asset back into line. I don't know if that's a good thing or not; if she's halfway to Highgate the moment we 'discover the body' or if it's best we rip the Band-Aid off now and I'm forced to witness the whole, awful truth side by side with Janine. There's no time to choreograph either scenario in my mind first; Janine has turned away from the direction of the front door and is heading back towards the living room.

'What are you doing?' I ask.

'Having an early swim; getting my head together before fielding another thousand calls on Esther's to-be-continued shitshow, if that's all right with you?' Janine strides away from me, not turning around as she tells me, 'Do see yourself out.'

From the atrium, Jags and I watch Janine head to the pool. I've got so much wrong about dealing with Essie, but I do know it's the right thing to not let her sister see what she's about to on her own.

'I need to be with Janine,' I whisper to Jags.

'We should go,' he whispers back.

'No. I can't.'

I leave him, following Janine until I'm almost behind her as she slides open the glass doors to the pool.

A blast of sweltering air hits me. I brace myself for her shrieks of horror.

The seconds stretch.

'Fuck,' Janine breathes.

I focus on the white tiles just ahead of my boots, knowing I need not speak, understanding that Janine won't hear me anyway if I do.

'Why does she keep this place so fucking hot?'

I look up, take a step closer to the edge of the pool.

There is no champagne bottle in the water.

No rust-coloured pills.

No body in the pool.

Essie has vanished.

ACT II

'Directing is about creating emotional reality where none exists. For example, the way you frame a shot can make the smallest gesture feel sentimental, sinister, or seismic. Or, if the lens is long enough, and if this is the reality the director wants the viewer to experience, the lead actor in the foreground can almost disappear.'

FILM SCHOOL LECTURE NOTES TRANSCRIPTION

12

April, the morning after the awards

'Something you needed?' Janine kicks off her shoes, pulls off her clothes, her swimsuit already on underneath them, and throws her trousers and sweater onto one of the loungers by the side of the door.

'I wanted you to know . . . I'll do what I can to get in contact with Essie.'

Janine gives a sarcastic thumbs-up before diving into the exact stretch of water where her sister's body floated not twelve hours ago.

I take myself back through the living room. On the way, I spy the screwed-up ball of paper again, now next to Essie's award on the side table by her chair. In desperation for any clue on what might have happened to her, I scoop it up and press it into my palm.

Jags is waiting for me in the atrium with a frown of pure bewilderment.

'Go,' I whisper.

'What's happening? What about this? Is Janine—' he whispers, gesturing to Essie's phone, now in his hand within his pocket. I glance back to see Janine, treading water, watching us, ensuring we're not hanging around.

'Not now!' I grab Jags's hand and usher him to the door.

'April. Wait a second.'

'We have to go.' I all but pull Jags behind me. Once we're outside, the door closed behind us, I quickly unfurl the notepaper as we cross the gravel:

I hope you love this dress, as white as the moon, because you deserve the moon and stars. Send me a sign. Wear it to the awards. Because no matter what else has gone on, I love you. To me, you'll always be the most beautiful girl alive.
Jxxx

Someone chose Essie's white dress for her, someone she apparently had a close or intimate relationship with, one that Essie described as 'complicated' and did not want me to know about. Did *J* pass where I'm walking right now last night? I examine the dimples in the stones below me, not knowing what I'm looking for. I thought yesterday was the most shocking, incomprehensible day of my life, but things have been pushed to a whole other level now, one I do not want to inhabit. I don't understand anything about Essie's life; maybe I never did, even though I've had a front-row seat to it.

Jags and I have been spending time with her for months, how could I have not realised if she was in contact with a 'complicated' lover, someone Essie never mentioned and I never picked up on until that day she showed me the gown they gave her? While Essie seemed privately upset about the sender, she didn't seem as though she was living in fear of whoever sent it. But then, isn't *You only hurt the ones you love* the truest of clichés?

Perhaps J or another person had access to Lotus like I do, and this individual did her harm, or removed her body once that harm was done? Was this person, as I suspected for a moment yesterday, also at Lotus last night? Are they now seeking to frame us somehow? Or is this whole thing the sickest of jokes? Might Essie just return from Australia in a few weeks with some bizarre explanation? No. I know what I saw. Essie was dead or as good as, and now someone has removed her for what can only be nefarious purposes.

Or is there a chance J could be Janine? But there's no way she'd ever be that effusive over Essie and the note is too romantic to sound anything like something a sister would send. Jackson? He wouldn't risk it and Essie, surely, would never have worn a dress from him no matter how sorry he said he was for what he'd done. *Jonathan?* Maybe he was using a grand gesture to boost Essie's fragile confidence, apologising for not being more supportive just in time for his client to be globally recognised for her fresh acting income stream.

My mind is in overdrive as Jags and I cross the gravel away from the house.

'What's happening?' Jags asks. 'I don't understand. Why isn't Janine—'

'Essie's gone,' I whisper as we continue to walk.

'*Gone? What?*'

'Her body's vanished.'

Jags halts.

'Vanished? How? Where?' His hands press the sides of his head, as though trying to contain an explosion within.

'I don't know. I don't know *anything* right now,' I say, gazing around, desperately searching for any more clues on J or anyone else who might have come here last night to hurt and take Essie away. I see Essie's SUV parked in its usual spot and notice the tracks another car has left in the gravel, but that could have been The Grey Lady, getting us here last night. Then, I realise, Jags's car is nowhere to be seen.

'How did you get here?' I ask.

'I . . . Wait, what have you got there?' Jags goes to take J's note from my hand. I shove it in my pocket before he can touch it.

'Jags, why isn't your car here?' And now I notice something else. It's cool and yet he's wearing no other layer besides his T-shirt. And while I can see the outline of Essie's phone in one pocket, he has no other phone on him, nor wallet.

'April?'

'Yes?'

'Is there . . . Do you think there's something weird going on with me and whatever the hell's going on here?' Jags asks me quickly, his deep-brown eyes begging for understanding.

'*Weird?* No. Why?' I ask; an image of Jags in bed with Essie flies into my mind, turning my stomach, making my eyes squeeze tight against the horror of it. When I open them again, I see Jags's face, fallen.

'I know even less than you do. This is a total mind melt.' He shakes his head.

'Yes, of course,' I say. I can't find the words, any phrase to describe any of it. Essie, here, in the house last night, dead or dying; Essie's body, now missing, and her things too. A fight, or maybe robbery gone wrong, but why hide the body? J is Jude Lancaster perhaps, trying to worm his way back into Essie's world as her star rose again, angry when he couldn't

112

make her do as he wanted? Maybe this was why Essie seemingly crumpled up the note about the dress in a drunken, or pill-induced, rage.

A skitter of gravel. While my mind has been flustering through another scenario that's led to Essie being dead and gone, Jags has started walking back to the house.

'Where are you—'

'You rushed me out of there. I didn't have time to get my stuff from the kitchen,' Jags calls out without turning around. 'I got an Uber, by the way.' He stops and faces me now, his eyes on the ground. 'The Grey Lady's still leaking. I didn't want to leave a fresh load of oil on the gravel in case . . . I don't even know.'

Jags presses the doorbell. After a few moments, a dripping Janine answers in a towel, clearly fuming. I hear Jags apologise, say he left without taking his things, then tell Janine to get back to her swim. He returns soon after wearing a tracksuit top, the pockets of his pants clearly heavy with his phone and wallet. I feel I need to do something to show I do trust him.

'Read this.' I hold J's note.

Jags takes it and scans it quickly. 'J. Jonathan? Do you think he's involved in whatever's happening? I know he's mostly into boys, but I always wondered if they'd ever . . .'

'Essie never mentioned anything to me.'

'Just because she didn't confide in you, doesn't mean it never happened. Haven't you begun to wonder whether you knew Essie as well as you thought you did?'

'I have. I *am*,' I say, just as Jags's phone starts to ring.

He answers it quickly and greets the caller in a now-familiar rat-tat stream of Punjabi before breaking into English. It's his mother. He says the same thing each time she phones. I've been trying to commit a few key phrases I've heard repeatedly over the past months to my memory in the hope one day soon I may get to use them in conversation with her.

'Listen, Mum, can I call you later if everything's OK?'

Jags turns his back to me, hunches over the phone. 'Have you had your pills this morning? . . . I'll be back home later, OK? We can talk then.'

I can hear his mother's voice, faint but terse on the end of the line. Something changes in Jags's body language before he turns around; he stands taller and looks me dead in the eye.

'I'll tell you all about it, later, but right now I'm with April. April, my girlfriend. I'm going now.'

I've wanted him to tell her about us for so long, but why did it have to happen now, here? Under these circumstances, I can't take even a sliver of joy from us finally going somewhere as a couple. Nevertheless, when he hangs up, I take his hand.

'Did she sound OK?' I ask Jags and he shrugs his answer, looking at the gravel. 'Are *you* OK?'

'Yeah . . . No.' He puffs out a breath and looks about him, as though disorientated. 'Essie's not there?' He says it to himself, trying to stamp this reality into his brain. 'Let's go back to your place, try to get our heads round whatever the fuck's going on.'

'OK.'

Yes, let's get away from Essie's home, Janine, and try to process this whole awful mystery – who J is, where Essie is, who is to blame – and perhaps snatch a few moments of being the couple we appear to be blooming into under the strangest of conditions.

'Before we do, can I say something?' Jags asks me.

'Of course.'

114

'Everything's crazy right now, and I'm guessing there's some people you probably shouldn't trust, but I hope you know, I don't need to be one of them.'

I rest my head on the sturdiness of his chest. I want him to hold me close, hold me to the earth. My spinning head slows.

'You aren't.'

13

April, the day after the awards

Jags doesn't usually spend much time with me at home; we mostly go for walks, or meals, or to the theatre or cinema. So many long days shooting or in post-production for *The Vanished Woman,* I'd be desperate to just go home, have a takeaway and some alone time with Jags, but he'd want us to eat out, or head to Lotus to watch the sun go down on the veranda while Essie was inside, watching one of her boxsets, brushing her hair like a mermaid in her egg chair near the pool.

I'd always assumed it was mum-guilt that kept Jags away from my place – a flat in a 1930s art deco block I bought after seven years of living in an abandoned bank as a property guardian – but when I look about the place now, I wonder whether there's something about my flat that makes him uncomfortable. Perhaps given his somewhat stalled career, my flat wears my industry successes on its sleeve a little too obviously. In the absence of pictures of me and my parents, it's filled with evidence of my proxy families and avatars, with stills and props from the various shows I've either written on or directed. This includes an oversized promo poster of *The Vanished Woman,* with Essie's eyes blown up in huge detail so you can see the stitches of green, brown, and golden pigment in her irises. Jags takes a seat on the end of the sofa, right next to it. She is watching us. A squeeze of sickness takes my breath away.

'It's a picture, babe. Wherever she is, she's not here,' Jags says.

I merely nod my agreement and the nausea subsides, quietly relishing how I didn't need words to tell him my thoughts, this beautiful man on my sofa. How deeply do I not want to take things slowly with him. I want, I need, things to go faster, accelerate us into a future where we are bonded forever, where I will never have to feel alone again, and I certainly won't have to unravel whatever's become of Essie on my own.

'Tea?' I ask.

'Have you . . . I think I might need something a bit stronger this morning.'

'Oh, OK.' This isn't like Jags, but maybe this is his way of coping. 'I'll see what I can find.'

I leave Jags as he frees his phone from his tracksuit pocket while I head to my kitchen to dig out the bottle of rare whiskey the cast of *Encounters* bought for me when we wrapped. They said they chose it because they had no idea what I might like as a gift. I was struck by how little they all felt they knew me but treasured the gesture regardless. I never intended to open the bottle, but after everything we've been through in the last twelve hours, and with Jags finally telling his mother about me, now feels like the moment. I return to him with the bottle and two tumblers, sit next to him on the sofa, and break the seal.

'I'd love to meet your mum, you know.' I pour two measures of whiskey. 'I've told you, I'm no longer in meaningful contact with my family so—'

'You'll meet her, soon. Trust me.'

'I do.'

A beat.

'Do you really?'

'I do, Jags.' I lean into his space, bringing my face to his. I kiss him. It's not fully returned at first but then, he kisses me with a forcefulness that makes me gasp. I've read about this: how death so often leads to sex so profound it feels like an affront, an act of aggression against the possibility of the end of life. I'm so ready to be part of that, but as soon as things heat up another degree between us, he pulls away.

When I was younger, my self-esteem was such I would tell each man I slept with, apart from the unexceptional first, that I was a virgin. My maladjusted objective was to make me potentially more alluring and to manage expectations around my aptitude in bed. It seemed to make the sex at first tender and then rough, as though those men believed they were claiming an independent, if apparently, innocent, young woman's body for their own. I relished the initial softness some of them showed me, then sensed the misogyny strongly as they abandoned their care for my apparent naivety and gave in to their desire to overpower. I grew accustomed to the specific soreness of the kind of sex this dynamic delivered. Of course, I was too old to spin my virginal patter when Jags came along, and these days, I'm less concerned with my performance than increasing the frequency of our intimacy. I crave to know his body better, even now, *especially* now. I consider a new tactic.

'I think if you let your mum see I'm no threat, you wouldn't feel so guilty. You could let us be us without worrying.'

'I'm not worried about my mum right now.' He leans forward

to turn his phone over, revealing its screen. 'I'm worried about this.'

FEARS GROW FOR TROUBLED ESSIE

Following a bizarre acceptance speech at the glittering British Film Association Awards last night, Essie Lay's manager – sister Janine Laycock, 42, who was forced to give the speech after her sister refused to show up – has expressed concerns for the star.

The one-time disgraced TV presenter made her sister tell the starry audience, which included Hollywood A-lister Martin Russo, she intended to 'vanish forever'.

'Not mentally strong'
Speaking exclusively to EyeNeedNews, Janine said her sister's no-show was only the latest downturn in her mental health. 'Essie's troubles are no secret. It's everyone's hope she can break the cycle of erratic behaviour. The fact she's now taken herself out of public life sadly confirms she's not as mentally strong as we'd all hoped.'

Harm TV star has 'brought on herself'
Janine added how all steps necessary would be taken to protect Essie's mental health, and her fortune, from what she described as 'Essie's worst instincts'.

Rumours about the one-time TV darling yet again began to swirl last night following the shocking speech, with #RIPEssie trending on most social media platforms.

Asked if she believed Essie had come to harm, Janine responded, 'I dearly hope not, but I'm sad to say that if she had, it would be nothing she hasn't helped bring on to herself. Unfortunately, there are some people who, when they are not able to make sound decisions, prove to be their own worst enemy.'

READ MORE: Shamed Essie's 'screen husband' Jude Lancaster refuses to comment on 'vanish forever' rumours.

'Even if it suits Janine to believe Essie's learning to surf in Oz, or whatever, this isn't going away,' Jags says. 'People already think she's dead. We *know* she is because we walked away from her body, didn't we?'

I feel the coldness of this reality biting anew. 'It was the wrong thing to do, I know that now.'

'So, you shouldn't have made out to everyone last night you *hadn't* left Essie's body?'

I look at Jags, perplexed. He sounds strange, not at all like himself.

'We could be facing time inside, you know. It might be better for us to confess now.'

'Confess? What to?' I say panicked. 'We may have walked away and hoped her sister would be responsible for Essie, but we didn't commit a crime.'

'I don't know that we didn't. Aren't there criminal offences about not reporting something like we saw, or getting in the way of decent disposal of a body?'

I hold my head in my hands, then take a sip of my whiskey. 'I never meant for any of this to happen. How does anyone prepare for a night like last night?'

'You can't.' Jags lets the next words into the air almost

tentatively. 'Now you can't change how you walked us away from Essie's dead body.'

'Darling. You were the one who encouraged me.' I put down my drink and turn to him. 'Leaving Essie and getting Janine to deal with things was your idea.'

My gaze rests on his phone, still on the table in front of me. I notice something strange about the way the tiny lozenge showing the time is displaying in the top left-hand corner. It's red, alternately fading then becoming more intense.

'Are you . . .' I snatch his phone, collapse the news story on Essie, and see a voice memo in process. 'You're recording me? You've wanted to get me to confess to going along with something that was your idea?' Jags looks at his lap, shame-faced and silent. 'Jagdeep?'

'I'm sorry, OK? But you treated me so suspiciously at Lotus, like you thought I'd done something very wrong, even though we found Essie together; even after everything we've been through. It felt like maybe I needed an insurance policy, because you were turning against me, against us.' He looks to me now. 'I couldn't bear that, couldn't take how you've been looking at me, how you're looking at me right now.' He rubs his eyes with his thumb and index finger as though dealing with tears he doesn't want me to see. 'Because I was beginning to think you and me could really start being . . .' Jags swallows, '. . . proper partners. I'd started to let myself believe that despite everything that's happened, we were onto something real.'

I wait a moment, choosing my next words with care.

'You don't always make it easy for me . . .' The way he shifts where he sits and pours himself another measure of whiskey seems to suggest he knows where I'm taking this conversation, '. . . believing we're a real team, a proper couple.'

He puts his glass down now to take both my hands in his. 'April, I'm going to help you. I'll prove to you we're really together. I'll help you stay on the right side of everything as far as what's happened to Essie. If you let me, we'll do it together.'

'I'm going to forgive myself for using a cliché, now: actions speak louder than words, Jags.'

His phone rings, 'Mum' lighting up on the screen. As Jags rushes to answer it, another cliché springs to mind: *saved by the bell*. The syllables of his familiar Punjabi greeting are at turns soft and harsh, before he breaks into English. 'Right now, I'm with April.'

I hear nothing on the end of the phone.

'Yes, I'm with my girlfriend.'

Jags pushes himself off the sofa with obvious resentment before taking himself into the hallway, knowing I'll keep listening but perhaps wishing to spare me the indignity of hearing his mother say something hurtful about me.

'You're threatening to throw me out?' he asks her.

I'm familiar with parental love being only granted with strict terms and conditions attached. The defining incident of my experience of this was probably when I was nineteen. I had begun writing in the long and lonely evenings at college. Without ever expecting anyone to stage it, I'd nevertheless tried my hand at writing a play, channelling my loneliness into a tale of female disaffection and vengeful sex. I heard about a competition for new playwrights, dared to enter my effort and won. The prize money would be awarded at a finalists' dinner held just before we broke for Easter. I sent the invitation to

122

my parents, which included a description of my play, written under the name I was born with, one I changed when the right moment came, not long after I'd met Essie:

Singular
By April Eisdale

Cut off from her family, abandoned by her friends, a nameless young woman searches for meaning and love in the wrong places. Eisdale's impressive and darkly brooding exploration of deep-seated needs and thin gratification makes her a talent to watch.

I had dreamt that, despite their long track record of disinterest in my achievements, my parents might want to join me at the dinner. It could have been the subject matter or merely the fact I was being recognised for my potential that led them to tell me they would not be coming to the dinner, and that I could make my own way home for the holidays if I wanted to, but my father had turned my room into a store room for the surplus office supplies it was his job to sell.

'You don't really want me out of the way, do you, Mum?' Jags says calmly now, though anger tightens the end of the question.

My parents found my intelligence and my aspirations to extract all I could from the mind I'd been given at first confusing, then inconvenient. When I insisted on spurning the local comprehensive for a grammar school on the other side of town, my parents made it clear they resented being deprived both of a further hour in bed and the cost of the extra petrol. As I matured and my academic achievements accumulated, they told me I was getting

123

'ideas above myself', translated easily into 'ideas above them'. Their failure to not be proud of me and my first writing success, and the way they made it clear I was not particularly welcome at home at the end of Easter term, only confirmed this.

That holiday, I secured a job on the college waiting staff for the conferences held there in between terms. The role gave me a subsidised room, money, and a ready supply of sexually available middle-aged men who believed they were deflowering me. I rarely came home from then on in, though I remained friendless at college. No one was specifically nasty to me. It was, I realised, something to do with me finding it hard to connect with others in the moment. I do not always know what to say to appear appealing, and I cannot easily mask the poor self-esteem bequeathed to me by the unfortunate alchemy of my own mind and my parents' desperately low expectations.

With the prize money from my play, I bought my Canon camera, and with it round my neck I never had to be truly alone again. I began to steal images of the lives of other people and to write about them too. It made me feel as though I was participating, even vicariously, in the world of normal human connections. Developing my writing, never being without my camera, was the beginning of me being able to tell myself that even if I couldn't bond particularly well with people in the flesh, I could create stories capable of reaching their hearts. Some days this feels like enough consolation; many days it does not.

'You can't just tell me what to do, you know.' Jags finishes this statement to his mother through gritted teeth. I silently root for him to break away from his mother the way I had to from my parents. Just as my parents should have been delighted, rather than disgusted, by their bright child, Jags's mother

124

should be grateful for his care and indulgence, not constantly seeking to guilt or blackmail him into giving more. And Jags should sever the connection, just as I did. Good things can happen when you show the people who failed to cherish you that you care even less for them than they do for you, even if, in your heart, you know this not to be true.

Jags hangs up. Then yells down the dead phone, 'Fuck you. Fuck you!'

I take a mouthful of whiskey, savouring his filial fury as he stomps back into my sitting room and stands over me.

We need no words.

I put down my drink and stand up so our bodies touch from our toes to our chests. He takes my face in his two hands and he kisses me with the most exquisite violence, then tugs down my jeans and his own, and all but throws me over the arm of the sofa.

For a few minutes of animalistic abandon everything is just as I want it to be. I forget about all that's happened in the last twelve terrible hours. I put aside the memories of my loveless childhood, the loneliness of my youth, until I could assemble temporary families around me, rediscover Essie, and find Jags. But the second we're finished, as Jags and I pull our clothes back on, the dread descends, the roaring of the hurricane after the false comfort of the eye of the storm.

On paper, my life has never looked brighter; a post-awards gala screening of *The Vanished Woman* is in two days, and my meeting with Ed to discuss my first-look deal is now confirmed for the day after. But I made a terrible mistake yesterday, and like my life's other missteps, I fear this too will darken and taint anything I may achieve from here.

125

14

Essie, before, the day her casting is announced

The latest bouquet is probably the biggest one of about twenty that have been turning up all day since my turn as Elena in *The Vanished Woman* was announced. It's amazing who crawls out of the woodwork when things are looking good for you again. Each new bunch arrives with a completely fake message that makes me feel more and more confused. There are words that look kind and supportive on the cards but come after weeks of being ignored and sometimes openly abused by the sender. If I was rubbish about knowing who to trust before, this sort of thing is making it so much worse.

Well done, you. Can't wait to watch. No hard feelings, Yours ever, Craig xxxx

This from the chat show host who I thought was an actual mate, someone who was a regular at my parties, a man who'd interviewed me about twenty times over the years but who only two weeks ago used my name as a punchline when he compered the *TV Now* Awards, the only time my name was mentioned on camera all night.

*We are all so very thrilled for you at Beteille HQ. We cannot
wait for your inner beauty to shine through the outer you on the
silver screen. Jo, Pascal & Benoit x*

The big cheeses at the shampoo and skincare brand I had
a fifteen-year relationship with; the company that practically
paid for Lotus Lodge but sacked me via Insta when it all went
down after Jackson's little home video.

I read the card from the latest and largest bouquet, an almost
ghostly sheaf of white flowers, which feels kind of appropriate:

*Total congratulations from the bottom of my heart, you're
still amazing to me, still the most beautiful girl alive even if
I know why you hate me Jxxx*

This note threatens to tip me over the edge. I call Janine to
vent, cry a bit, and afterwards rip the card down the middle
before shoving the flowers head-down into the outside bin.
I have to wash my hands over and over when I get inside; one
of the flowers has the type of pollen that stains your skin. Even
though I spend forever scrubbing, I know I'll have to look at
the faint shit-brown dots along the side of my fingers until
they wear away.

By the time I get the flowers from my parents, I'm on high
alert. A simple bunch of pink lotus blooms, the big, heavy heads
drooping on their stems, too weighty to be supported by their
stalks once they've been taken out of the water they grow in.

*We hope this is what you want, Esther. Watch yourself and
don't fuck it up. All our love, Dad and Mum xx*

Janine and Jonathan don't send me flowers but keep forwarding me the latest media reactions to my casting, which pushes and pulls me up and down from minute to minute. One broadsheet says it's a gamble that may well pay off, while a tabloid describes the move as my 'last-gasp attempt to crack America', which, at my age, is both desperate and unlikely. But the tabloids and gossip sites being nicest about my move into acting are the ones that make me most petrified, because this is what they always do: build me up, make the public love me only so that when they cut me down again, the shock is all the harder, the drama stronger and more saleable. The worst stories of the bunch are always written by women. They don't think I should ever be forgiven for what they think I did. Even if they believed everything they saw on that video, I don't know how this makes them better feminists. These women saying I'm living on borrowed time, that it won't be long before I'm on the edge again, have given me the first palpitations of the day, a thudding in my chest, then a fluttering, like my heart has forgotten how to do its job.

This debilitating anxiety started six months ago, the day the story broke. I was on my way to the *Daybreak* studio at the usual ungodly hour when I got the call from Jonathan. It had been an OK morning until then, my notifications were calm, but better than that, I'd been out with Jackson for an early dinner the night before, and it had been the most beautiful evening in a rollcall of wonderful evenings together since he came into my life.

When I was with him, for the first time in my life, it was like I always said and did all the right things. I could always make him smile, make him say something perfect back. It felt so different with him than with all the other men before. He showed those 'relationships' set up by Janine and Jonathan for what they were: brand partnerships, pretend play. I didn't have to hide anything: how I was feeling more and more uncomfortable at Janine and Dad and Mum telling me what to do with my career; how I sometimes wondered if I'd struggled with relationships because I'm too needy, demanding constant reassurance. I didn't have to laugh over or cover anything up anymore. Whatever I threw at Jackson, he held in his heart and transformed it into something amazing.

Over dinner that night I had told him, 'My family think if I was left to look after my life on my own, I wouldn't have anything, no career, not my home. But maybe I *would* be nothing without them telling me what to do.'

'And what do you think?' Jackson asked me, so gently, so without drama. He never ran out of patience, always let me get to conclusions that were my own and in my own time. He never once told me what to think. OK, physically, he was gorgeous, but the most irresistible thing for me was how after only three months, he made me feel as though I could be at home with myself, because being with him felt like coming home.

'What do I think?' I said to him. 'I think I found you on my own and that's working out better than anything I've ever done in my life that someone else has done for me.'

Jackson and I were not introduced by Jonathan, nor was our relationship brokered by Janine as most of my dates and public couplings were. Jackson manifested one day at my favourite coffee place in Highgate village. I bumped into him as I rushed out before anyone could recognise me, making him spill his smoothie down himself where he stood. It was like a meet-cute

129

from a rom-com. As I apologised and started to throw napkins in his general direction, he spoke to me so calmly and with such kindness that the fact he looked like a god was only the second thing I noticed about him. He had no idea who I was, he didn't really watch TV, that's what he told me. I replaced his smoothie and we began to talk. He made everything unbelievably easy from the get-go; talking to him, being myself, not holding back or saying what I thought he wanted to hear. He made me unafraid, and this is what made him so dangerous. It meant I didn't hold back telling him how much I liked him, then that I loved him. I never felt embarrassed because everything I said was always returned to me three times bigger than I gave it to him. He brought down all the pretences I realised I had with everyone else, destroyed all my defences.

'You're the best thing in my life. Ever,' he said to me the night before the story broke, and when he did, I felt no shyness about saying what I said next, even though it had only been a few months: 'I want you to think about moving in with me.' He didn't flinch.

'And I . . .' he said, taking my hand, '. . . would like you to marry me first.'

I gulped the air. Joy, shock, and maybe the tiniest trace of queasiness that this was happening even faster than I was ready for.

'Don't say yes now,' he said. 'But don't say no. Don't say anything. Put it in your pocket for whenever you're ready but know it's yours if you want it.'

I did want it; being with him, a whole life with the right person. And children. It wasn't too late for me; it was only the beginning. And yet I couldn't say yes that night. *This* was the only thing that let me keep body and soul together after things fell apart: if I didn't say yes then I couldn't have been quite as dumb as I must have looked to him.

We finished dinner, went back to his for a couple of wonderful hours before saying goodbye on the happiest and most loving of terms. I had to get back to Lotus for the night because I needed to be out of the door by five the next day for another edition of *Daybreak*.

We had some regular contributors lined up for the show that day, and no difficult reality stars who'd been famous for five minutes and didn't know how not to be an arsehole yet. Also, with Jackson's open conversation, I'd made a big decision that had been on my mind for a while. With this, and Jackson's proposal, my future felt like it belonged to me and no one else for the first time since I could remember. And then my phone rang.

'Hey babe, you sitting down?' Jonathan asked.

'I'm in the car. What's up?'

'Jackson. There's a video.'

'A video? . . . What, like a sex tape?' Had someone hacked my phone after he and I were messing around one night? Last night? I felt immediately violated.

'Worse,' said Jonathan. My car felt as though it was speeding on grease, slipping and sliding down Highgate Hill as Jonathan described the tape.

'I don't believe this. Only last night he said . . . Why has he done this?'

Jonathan, who together with Janine made no secret of the fact they disliked me going 'off-piste' with someone they hadn't pre-vetted or approved, did not answer. I cleared my throat

131

and switched into professional mode, trying to win a bit of respect back.

'When is this coming out?'

'By the time we finish this call, the first story will be live. I've drafted a statement.'

'You want me to approve it?'

'It's already out. With you now.'

I read it, horrified. It was like I'd been attacked, assaulted by Jackson, then offered to stab myself in the heart to finish the job. My chest began to ache, my heart stutter.

'Why am *I* apologising? Wait, is Jude going on today?'

'Jude is starting the show with a monologue to camera, an apology to his wife, to any women he's ever offended, then, he'll be going straight into rehab for sex addiction.'

'Right. So, he'll be back on the sofa in about a month. What about me?'

'You've got a Zoom with the station later this morning. I'll be there, and Janine. Go home, don't read the papers and don't go out until I give you the say-so.'

And just like that, it was over. My whole adult life and the future I thought I'd have, the babies I'd begun to see in my mind's eye at night, all of it, dead. Britain's sweetheart had been cancelled because of the actions of the love of her life. In one phone call, I knew I'd lost my job, what little respect I might have had from my family, and the man whom I believed to be my soul mate. And with it, I'd lost any idea of trusting my own instincts. I'd also lost the public, who asked so much of me every day and been given it by me for twenty years. Now, they were telling me to die.

The hate exploded immediately once the story was out

with #EssieCancelled #BinEssie and #RIPEssie all trending. Then, the actual cancellations, people who I thought were friends, commercial relationships I'd mistaken for something else withdrawn, as well as years' worth of jobs already booked and in the diary, all of it, scrubbed out. And all the while, my heart was breaking and the future, the family I thought I was in touching distance of, evaporated.

Even though today's casting news in *The Vanished Woman* is exactly what I wanted, being thrust back into the public eye, having my house, my sanctuary, filled with messages from people who left me for dead, is taking me right back to that morning when Jonathan called to tell me it was all over. My heart lost its rhythm that day; it's happening again now. I'm scared and I have no one I can call. Everyone has let me down or shown just how little they ever thought of me.

Except for April.

Despite what she may have done in the past, it's her I can trust most in the entire world. There was no way I could have kept her in my life all those years ago, when we were little more than kids. But present-day, adult April has moved past that time and invested in me. She genuinely thinks more of me than anyone else, even myself. She wants me to succeed. She wants to be my friend again, and there don't seem to be many people she trusts or wants to spend much time with either. How crazy that after having completely different paths, after deliberately keeping myself away from her, April Eden is the person I'm starting to need the most.

I call her to catch up on the reaction to the announcement of my casting, thinking she'll give me the boost I need to shake my palpitations. Her phone rings. And rings. With every

133

unanswered beat, I realise how desperately I need her to pick up. If I don't get to have a positive conversation with her, I'll be completely on my own. She doesn't pick up, so I try again. Eventually, she answers.

'Hi, Essie. Everything OK?'

'Yes! Everything's great, just thought you might want to catch up on all the press today.'

'One of my team will put something together shortly. I'll make sure you get the roundup.'

'Great. Thanks.'

There's a pause and I feel like April can hear my hurt and all my worries rushing into the silence. 'Are you OK?' she asks me, and I realise no one's asked me that simple question for so long.

'I'm fine. It's just . . .' The tears come. I can hardly speak through them.

'I don't need any press report to tell me we made the right decision casting you,' April says in a firm but gentle voice. 'You should take a lot of confidence from so many people being so receptive to you as an actress. And you should be so proud of yourself too, Essie. The shoot is going to be amazing; you're going to be brilliant.'

'Two weeks!' I can talk again, and I'm smiling now, relieved at April's kindness and thinking that in just a fortnight's time, I'll be properly working again. 'I can't wait.'

'Absolutely. Me too.' April sounds unusually distracted.

'You out somewhere?'

'I am. Shall I call you later perhaps? Tomorrow?'

'Who are you with?'

A pause.

'I'm with . . . Do you remember Jags?'

'Oh yeah. Are you dating?' I feel a poke of jealousy.

'I heard that! Yes, we are!' I hear Jags, calling out from the background. April giggles and does a kind of tut. I can see them, hand in hand, walking through Regent's Park or whatever it is they're doing as we speak. A normal couple, having a normal day. The idea of it leaves me sick with envy and loneliness. I can't be frozen out of April's life now, not when I've just let her back into mine.

'Come here, to Lotus; tonight, both of you. I've been meaning to invite you round for ages and I'd love to meet Jags properly. I'll order some dinner in.'

'Oh, I don't know, we did have a loose arrangement to—'

'Please?' I can't be on my own tonight and there's no one else I can ask.

'Sure. Of course, Essie, we'd love to come over, wouldn't we, Jags?'

I want to tell her thank you and I'm sorry for hijacking her romantic evening, but I'm too ashamed. 'Sevenish? Shall I send a car to you?'

'That's OK, Jags can drive us.'

I'm not sure why, but it's these words, more than hearing Jags's declaring they are dating, April's girly little giggle, or her slight guardedness about what she was doing, that irk me the most. April has a man she can rely on and who cares about her, a brilliant reputation, and an impeccable career. She's kind of got it all. As I hang up, despite everything, there's still a tiny part of me that's struggling to feel she really deserves it.

*

135

I try to hoover before they get here, but it doesn't go well. I haven't done it for myself for years, and the machine sucks up the fringe of one of my rugs, then gobbles up my phone charger wire so the whole lounge smells like it's about to go up in flames. I give up.

I don't bother trying to cook but order a ton of things from Supper to make sure at least some of the food caters to whatever it is Jags and April eat. I don't want April to think I live in some dusty old pile with nothing in the fridge like the dried-up old spinster I probably am. I want tonight to be happy, warm and fun. I want April to see I'm in control.

Waiting for April and Jags, I hold myself back from falling into the twin rabbit holes of online love from my diehard fans, and stomach-turning hate from the shocking number of people who think I deserve to die for attempting to un-cancel myself through acting. The old days, when I was starting out, were terrible in many ways – upskirting, phone hacking – but at least we didn't have Twitter.

I hear a car pull into my drive. They're here. I'm so nervous.

'Hello! Come in, come in. Thanks so much for coming.'

April steps inside, followed by Jags. She's bright red and he looks slightly sweaty as her eyes dart up and down my atrium, from the marble floor to my skylight. God, did they just have sex or something? Then, I remember how big my house is, how it might be a lot to take in if you're someone like April. It's been so long since my life was what most people would think was normal, I realise I've forgotten what might be surprising or impressive about how I get to live.

'Nice to see you again, Jags,' I say over a growing sense of shakiness at having both of them inside Lotus. Jags hands me

136

a bottle of white wine and doesn't bother hiding the fact he's checking out the size of my home, his head craning to scope out the formal living room which I've never really used, and then the grand dining room I used to have guests in all the time but haven't even been in for months. The glass on the neck of Jags's bottle is warm from being in his hands in a way that makes me feel slightly icky as I take it.

'Thank so much, I'll just put this in the kitchen. Go ahead to the pool room straight ahead. Let me bring a few things in.'

I leave them gasping their way into my poolside living room and eavesdrop on them as I walk slowly to the kitchen.

'Wow. This place is huge,' Jags says.

'I wonder if you would ever get used to it,' April replies.

I leave them to it. When I join them again, it's with a hostess trolley full of various bottles of alcohol and soft drinks, Jags's clammy white wine in a silver ice bucket.

'What can I get you?' I say to Jags and April, who are mid-embrace when I return. I feel like such a third wheel and decide I'll fix myself a very strong sidecar. It was probably one of my stupidest ideas ever to invite the pair of them over tonight. Their togetherness was only ever going to leave me feeling even more alone.

'Is everything all right, Essie?' April asks and Jags immediately looks at her, then me, concerned.

'I saw all the press today. Congratulations,' Jags says, and April reaches for his hand and gives it a grateful little squeeze. They're coming across like an old married couple speaking to a troubled daughter. I bristle, but there's something weirdly comforting about it too. It was nice of Jags to say that, and sweet how April is so grateful he's being so kind around me.

137

Given how difficult my own family are, maybe this is the start of what normal people do, make family from their friends, not from people on the payroll, like I did.

'Not everyone was nice,' I say.

'Most were,' April says softly.

'Here, let me fix you girls your drink. Why don't you two get yourself comfy and have a bit of a chinwag while I do.' Jags looks so unbelievably earnest, I could cry.

'Do you know how to make a sidecar?' I ask him.

'Sure,' he says in a funny sort of way that tells me he'll google it the second my back's turned.

'Make that two, please.' April takes my hand now and leads me over to my egg chair, her sliding over a nearby ottoman to place herself right next to me.

By the time Jags comes over with our cocktails, I've unloaded everything; in fact, I'm crying my eyes out on April's shoulder.

'God, Jags. What must you think of me,' I say, doing all I can to smile over the ongoing flutter of heartbeats. 'I didn't used to be like this.'

'That's all right, Essie. I'm sure April will tell you, I'm an emotional wreck most of the time.'

I laugh again as he hands April and me our glasses. 'Let me find you some tissues. And tell me how I did with your sidecar. Be kind, unless you actually want to see a grown man cry.'

We all share a little laugh before April and I watch him leave the room.

'There's a bathroom next to the kitchen on the left there!' I call, and Jags makes a thumbs-up above his head without looking back. Once he's out of sight, I turn and whisper to April, 'He's so lovely. How's it going with you guys?'

'It's . . . good.'

'Oh, come on, it's more than good, I can tell. You two look like you've been together forever.'

'We *have* been spending a lot of time together since the screening.' She looks at her hands around her glass.

'Right.' I swallow the sip of cocktail in my mouth as quickly as I can. Jags has underplayed the lemon juice, overplayed the triple sec; the result is syrupy and saccharine, cloying in my throat. 'Good for you.'

April takes a sip of her drink, her eyes close in pleasure. 'Oh my god, this is delicious, isn't it?'

I don't answer. I'm distracted by the sight of Jags coming back from the downstairs bathroom with a box of tissues, his face slack, his expression strangely resentful, but he completely changes it before he reaches the doorway. With the flick of a switch, he's his normal sweet self again. I quickly look away so he doesn't know I've seen this.

'Here you go, Essie,' he says, handing me the box.

'Thank you,' I say, but my tears have already dried on my face.

15

April, one day before the London gala screening

One day has passed since I discovered Essie's body has gone missing, and only one day to go until the gala screening of *The Vanished Woman*. Every waking minute is torture, my mind swirling with what-ifs, alternative realities where everything is different, and a thousand scenarios I play through to try to get me closer to what happened to Essie and at whose hand.

If it weren't so incriminating, I might apply my plotting techniques to unravel Essie's mystery; get out my whiteboard, divide it into five or six sections, and start to think about what happens in each act and to which players. We've had the first act and the inciting incident of Essie's body, then the act break when it disappeared. The second act happening now would be about rising tension and letting the seeds of suspicion sprout over J and who could have this done to Essie. If I was plotting this story, there's a version of it where by Act III, I am the prime suspect; me who saw Essie dead and did nothing but remove her phone, me who has seen her body. With each passing hour, the potentially serious consequences of my silence must surely be growing. Meanwhile, the social media rumour mill is in overdrive about whether Essie will show up at the screening tomorrow and where she might be in the meantime, with #WhereisEssie and #FindEssieLay both trending.

I'm desperate to at least get Essie's phone back to Lotus and neutralise this threat to being viewed as innocent. With Janine potentially lurking about Lotus after her swim, we dared not return yesterday. To see if the coast might be clear today, I asked my agent to ask Janine what her plans for today were in light of all the social media noise about Essie. My agent informed me Janine is spending the morning at Lotus to 'go through some of Essie's paperwork' and she'll be meeting with Jonathan in Soho later to 'discuss strategy'. I decide I'll go to Lotus, too, under the guise of working, as I typically would, as soon as I've finished at the hairdressers where I'm headed this afternoon.

*

I made the appointment at Essie's salon a couple of weeks ago. That was back in another era of my life when I felt now would be the right time to move on from the plait I've worn my hair in for years. I asked Essie to tell me where she got her hair done so I might consult the experts on red-carpet looks. I imagined I would be victorious at the film awards and hoped I could mark a fresh beginning with the London gala screening – my financiers' idea to capitalise on the revived focus on *The Vanished Woman* post-awards and in light of the actual UK premiere being a low-key affair at an indie film festival a month ago. I had wanted my new hair to signify to the industry that April Eden, award-winning director, had arrived.

Now, instead of victories, new beginnings, and my arrival, all I'm stuck with are loss, endings, and goodbyes: the directing award gone to someone else, and the end of the good things my future promised should I become incriminated in Essie's death and disappearance: goodbye first-look-deal, goodbye casting Martin Russo, goodbye a future with Jags, goodbye freedom. Once the police are involved, I can surely kiss farewell to everything I've ever cherished, all the future I've worked so hard to create. But I've already lost the very worst thing: Essie and the chance to ever be close to her again, my best and only friend, the thorn in my side but also, my long-held inspiration.

As I wait for the hair stylist to return with my coffee, instead of looking at potential new styles, I'm riding out another adrenaline wave, thinking again about The Phone Call, The Knock on the Door, an image of me with a police officer throwing a blanket over my head as they escort me between custodial settings; they're all waiting to happen to me because I was not honest, because I did not do right by my best friend. Each minute without incrimination feels like it might be the last. I can't spend another one of them alone.

I call Jags, letting all my concerns rush out of me in one long whisper between my cupped hand and my phone.

'Come over this afternoon, once I'm done here? Please, come to my place, come with me to Lotus.'

'I really can't today, April. But call me, call me every step of the way. Even if I can't be by your side, you're in my thoughts, in my heart. Even if I'm not physically there right next to you, you're not doing this alone, OK?'

'OK, darling.' Hearing his voice, his gentle words for me slows my pulse. 'Thank you. I love you.'

I could not help it. It slipped out before I could stop it. And now I fear I will go as red as it's possible for me to be.

Silence on the line and now I'm beginning to feel an utter fool, heat sweeping from my scalp to my shoulders. 'I understand if you're not there yet.'

Jags sighs. 'I don't know what to say, I feel like if I say it now, you won't believe me.'

'If it's true, then I will,' I say quietly.

A pause. I look at my blotchy reflection in the mirror, wondering whether the lights are specifically designed to make the person sat here look as breathtakingly ugly as possible, or whether this really is the face Jags sees when he looks at me; sees and cannot love.

'Don't say anything,' I say, noticing the hair stylist in the mirror behind me, finally returning with my coffee. 'I have to go. Bye.'

I hang up and the stylist gives me my coffee before pulling the plait out of my hair and untangling its lengths with her fingers. I can't look at myself a second longer, so I divert my attention to the bound file showcasing the hairstyles I might choose from in my lap. The next leaf of the file falls open on a double-page spread.

'You would *so* suit that,' the stylist says.

The image on my lap is of Essie. Her mint-and-bark eyes smiling directly at me, her blonde extensions resplendent across the pages.

'Is that what we're going for today?' the stylist asks.

The chance to look more like Essie, to feel less like me, more like the woman in the photo.

'Yes.'

*

143

The colour, the condition, the length: my hair is not my own anymore. The streets feel different when viewed from behind my new choppy blonde fringe, my golden extensions swishing down my back. Heads turn when I walk by. Might my Essie-esque hair make me more capable of being desired, of maybe even loved by Jags, because I look and feel so unlike myself? When I get back to my flat, I can't help but stare at myself in the full-length mirror in my bedroom, transfixed. When my buzzer sounds I jump, my mind immediately pivoting to the very worst.

Oh god. Oh god. It's happening. The police have come for me.

I take a faltering breath and leave my bedroom.

'Hello?' I say into the intercom, somehow trying to inject the word with an innocence I wish I had, wondering, for a flash, if it's too late to throw Essie's phone from my back window into the brambles of the poorly tended garden flat two floors below.

'Delivery for April Eisdale,' a man's voice says.

A punch of relief deadened immediately by confusion. 'Sorry, what name was that?'

'April Eisdale, Flat C, Mendax Mansions. Delivery.' The accent is rough and there's something put on about its tone: someone is trying to sound unlike themselves. More than that: I haven't used my family's name for getting on for forty years.

'Are you April Eisdale?'

I pause. Swallow. 'Where are you from? Do I need to sign for whatever it is? . . . Hello?'

Nothing.

I run to the hallway window, open it to lean precariously

over the ledge so I might steal a glimpse of the deliverer. I see nothing.

I grip the banister as I make my way down the stairs, shaking. When I get to the shared hallway, I can see it waiting for me on the other side of the glass double doors: a large black square box on the wide stone front steps into my building. I release the entrance door and view the dark shape, knowing I have to reconcile my desire not to touch it with my instinctive need to take it and myself away from public view as soon as possible. I grab the box – neither light nor heavy, no obvious smell, no visible markings, not even my own address, simply uninterrupted black – and run back up the stairs. I slam my front door shut behind me, then awkwardly turn the lock so it's left on the latch, should I feel the need to run away from whatever is inside.

I place the black box carefully on my dining table, then decide I want it nowhere near any of my things; I instinctively know there is something dirty, something soiled about whatever is inside. I leave it on the floor by the table, then find my kitchen scissors to sever the thin black tape that covers the entire seam where the lid meets the box. I'm about to lift the lid, my hands either side of it, when I decide I don't want to come into direct contact with the contents. I run back to my kitchen to pull on some rubber gloves, before squatting down to the box once more.

I raise the lid and set it aside, my eyes half-closed, not wanting to fully face the reality of what lies within.

A quiet whimper leaves my throat.

Tissue paper; white, pure, ephemeral. I pull the sheets apart with my rubber-gloved fingertips.

I'm no longer whimpering now. I hear a shriek leave me.

Essie's dress. The one she died in.

Lunar white and as clean and dry as could be.

The garment is startling in its unexpected beauty and sheer, obvious luxury. I can't help but throw my rubber gloves to the floor and pull the swathes of fabric free. I stand up to reveal its full length against me, the satin seemingly reaching out to cling to my legs and torso; the same fabric that would have surrounded Essie's skin in her pool. Oh, Essie, what did they do to you? And what are they trying to do to me?

I catch my reflection in the glass of a framed *Encounters* still, gasping when I do. For a fleeting moment, it was as though she was here. With the dress and my hair, I look just like her. I have long imagined, in my work, in my daydreams, how it would feel to move about in her skin, within her aura. I don't think, I act. Almost before I know what's happened, my jeans and T-shirt are on the floor, my bra too. I squeeze into Essie's dress, pulling the lengths of my newly blond hair free, reviving it afresh with my fingertips before clasping the dress to a close at the back of my neck. I go to the bedroom to inspect myself in the full-length mirror.

The dress is a wonder of tailoring, of engineering. It has transformed my distinctly average body into something altogether starry. I run my hands over my hips, letting them rest now around the structured narrowness of my waist, then sliding them back down to the sudden curves of my thighs. I smooth my hands over my breasts next, held round and high on either side of the slash of skin exposed down to my stomach. Just enough is on show to persuade the viewer the

146

unseen parts are perfectly trim and firm. My body doesn't look like mine. When I squint at myself in the mirror, I feel truly beautiful. I feel like her.

A sound behind me. The click of the hinge of my door. Movement.

Someone is in my flat.

I go to gasp, then press my hand hard over my mouth. The police would announce themselves. This could be someone far worse, the person with the fake voice who sent the dress. This could be J. The person who surely harmed Essie.

I stare at myself in the mirror again; willing my breath to stay quieter than it is, huffing through my nose onto my fingers, trying to remain still and silent, give me half a chance of escaping whoever has entered my home.

The sound of shoes on parquet.

The creaking of the floorboards outside my bedroom.

They are coming for me.

I watch the doorway in the mirror, my lungs heaving against my ribcage, my panicked breaths loud enough be heard. I await my fate.

A face behind me in the doorway. One so familiar in my mirror, so beautiful, I could cry.

My Jagdeep.

He startles, then seems to check for someone else over his shoulder before returning his attention to me.

'What the hell are you thinking?' He speaks through gritted teeth.

I try to speak, but he interrupts me.

'Esther, seriously, what the fuck do you think you're doing?'

147

16

April, back then

At least once a month, Essie's father and mother and Janine would pick her up from the studio where we shot *The Dawn Chorus* and together they would go to stay for the weekend at Signal House, which was, I understood by eavesdropping, the sprawling beachside mansion they owned near Whitstable on the shimmering Kent coast.

I'd always know it was a Signal weekend by Essie's behaviour. She'd change her outfit, once or perhaps twice, and when she put on her clothes, she'd pull at them on her skin, tuck, untuck, and retuck her top. She would always get some girl on set to do her makeup. It clearly mattered to her to look good for her family for reasons I did not understand. My family had no interest in what I did, never mind what I looked like. In fact, whenever I caught glimpses of the Laycocks they seemed to me everything my parents weren't: wholly engaged with their daughter, and rich with self-made money; wealth signifying an ambition to which they attached not a speck of shame. I became almost as interested in the people who had created Essie as I was with the woman herself.

If I knew it was a Signal weekend, towards the end of the

day, I'd ensure I positioned myself at the far edge of the studio, close enough to the big exit onto the car park. I wanted to see her family arrive and hear the seemingly good-hearted bickering from inside the vehicle as Janine pushed open the passenger door and Essie joined them. I'd feel a thud of jealousy whenever I heard them greeting Essie as she climbed into the big black vehicle. I imagined I could hear the love ricocheting among those four happy, confident, lucky, moneyed individuals who formed Essie's family, so different from the don't-get-ideas-above-yourself dreariness of my parents, whom I'd not seen since arriving in London.

That Friday, Essie had changed her outfit once already as we readied the set for Monday's broadcast. I had been asked to clear the output of a confetti canon. Essie was by now already deemed above such lowly tasks. When she returned from the toilets in yet another fresh outfit, I was the only person left on set.

'Oh fuck, my dad'll be here in a sec,' she muttered, almost to herself, then to me, 'Hey, Avril.'

Avril? I'd been working with her for months and she didn't know my name? I felt my blood churning in my chest, from outrage, from shame, from not knowing how or if I should correct her.

'Yes?'

'You any good at mascara?'

'I have a steady hand.'

'That'll do. Here.' She passed me the black elongated bullet in her fingers. 'You're a bloody lifesaver. I'm so clumsy, I can't do shit.'

'That's the opposite of true,' I said, leaving the confetti and

149

smiling as I unscrewed the mascara's cap, confident I was past the threat of blushing. By the time I met Essie, I was finding ways to keep on top of the worst of it. Smiling was one of them. In my first term at Oxford, I found if I sent my face into a broad smile, no matter what, it would provoke a temporarily friendlier reaction in others, enough that I could get past the peak of a reddening more quickly.

I directed Essie to a nearby stool, not far from the catering station. She sat while I stood and swept the mascara brush over her lashes. I was so keen to impress her by doing it perfectly.

'You have such long lashes. You hardly need mascara,' I steeled myself to tell Essie.

'Ah, that's sweet of you to say. My eyes practically don't exist if I don't wear makeup.'

'You have lovely eyes. They're very unusual.'

'Ha! They're weird, aren't they? Are they brown? Are they green? What are they? I never know what properly suits me because of them.'

'Everything seems to suit you. Bright colours,' I twisted the brush delicately over the tips of her lashes, 'dark colours. Black. White.'

'You're too much! I'll pay you later!' She laughed, her breath on my chin. 'We about done?'

'One last—'

An already impatient honk droned into the air outside the exit. The Laycocks were here. Essie gasped at the familiar horn's sound, which made me jump and the mascara wand jab into her eye. I could see a great smudge of brownish black on her lid and her eyes immediately began to water, ringing both of them with wet blobs of makeup.

150

'Shit! Shit, shit, shit.' With one hand, Essie attempted to wipe away the mess with the back of her palm, while clicking her fingers with the other. 'Tissue!'

I grabbed the nearest thing I could, a wad of the cheap square paper napkins from the catering station. They smelt distinctly of the sausages that had been on the menu that Friday, but it was all I had. I pressed them into her hand, aware by now my face would be on fire, signalling to all the world how needy of her approval, how pathetic, I was.

'Esther, I am so sorry.'

'No, no, it's fine. No permanent damage or anyth – urgh! What's wrong with these tissues?' Essie hesitantly sniffed the tissue in her fingers.

'It was all I could find. I'm not normally this—'

'It's OK,' she said, not yet smiling, but then looking back to me for the first time, and offering me a quick, kindly flash of a grin. 'Hey, it's OK. An accident. I'm a complete klutz. I can't be trusted with one of these either. That's why I asked you!' She waved the mascara in the air before twisting the lid back on and dropping it in her handbag. A series of quick, demanding honks came from the car.

'Better go. See you Monday!' She was about to turn to leave, still dabbing her eyes with the offensive napkins.

'I really am very sorry. I know you like to look smart when your family arrive.'

'Yeah, well . . . that's them, then.' A pause where some strange discomfort over someone else noticing the extra efforts she made to look pretty in front of her family seeped through. 'Hey, don't look so worried. You were only trying to help.'

'Thank you for being so good about it,' I said.

151

Essie gave a quick nod and one of her beloved wonky smiles. She was almost at the door when she paused and turned back to me.

'It's not for my family, you know. I mean, maybe my sister and Mum, and Dad, would probably say something if I looked completely rubbish. My dad's only looking out for me though, like, all the time. He's the only man a girl can really rely on, right!' She looked to the floor with a gooey smile on her face. I felt the unmistakable ice-poke of jealousy of someone having such closeness to their father. 'Anyway,' Essie continued, 'there's a boy, in the village near our house. He's absolutely and completely gorgeous and I totally want his babies. It's on the off-chance he sees me arriving that I doll myself up, it's not to keep my family off my back, or anything.' At this stage in her life, Essie was wholly unaware of her duty to be permanently physically pleasing, even to her own flesh and blood.

'Well, I hope it all goes well for you,' I said.

Essie put her hands by the side of her head, rolled her eyes to the sky, and waggled her crossed fingers with a physical wackiness TV viewers would soon fall for. She went to turn away again.

'I'd love to know how it goes, reassure me I didn't ruin your chances with the boy from the village,' I called after her. 'Take my number.' I followed her out of the exit, thinking on my feet.

'Oh, I really don't have time to—'

'Here.' I ran over to my backpack and took out one of the business cards I'd had printed on my father's advice when I knew I'd secured the runner's job. Before I left home for London, he told me I may have my 'fancy degree', but I had to be ready to 'make people remember me' like he had to in his

152

role selling office supplies. I don't know why I believed him, perhaps it was partly because my real second name, which I was still using at the time was, while drab, tricky for people to spell correctly on their first attempts.

Essie took the card off me and laughed without reading it. 'A business card! For a runner! Wow, Avril, that's some old-school move you've got going on!' She shoved it carelessly into her handbag, the thin, bone-coloured card creasing in the middle as it disappeared into a side pocket. I was relieved when someone started to shout from outside.

'Fucking get a wriggle on, Fat Arse!'

I watched Essie head to the exit and saw Janine, now standing, waiting next to the car. There she was: Essie but thinner, taller, more tanned, a few years older but clearly nowhere near as attractive, sulking behind bug-like sunglasses and wearing a pink jersey dress that was little more than a vest. Essie was wearing something similar but in bottle green and looked stunning. I watched Janine take Essie in, from her flip-flops to the thick layers of hair which fell about her shoulders. Janine, the practice run; the clearing of the pipes before her parents created something altogether better in their second born, Esther. Essie ran out without giving me another thought. I watched as she and Janine shared a glamorous sort of double kiss before Essie ran to the other side of the car.

Janine seemed to blanch as Essie moved away. Picking up on this, Essie, about to open her car door, also stopped in her tracks.

'Esther,' I heard Janine say sternly.

'What?'

'You smell like bacon. And what's wrong with your face?'

153

'An accident,' Essie said, trying to smile and shake off the criticism.

'Tell me you accidentally chose that green for yourself too?'

Essie muttered something along the lines of it being the only thing she had clean and slid into her side of the car. I watched them leave together, still thinking despite Janine's comments, how lucky Essie was to be disappearing with family, people who were interested in her, invested in her. I would only learn the truth about life inside Signal House and within the Laycock family by finding my way into both.

*

The derelict bank where I lived when I first moved to London was cold, lonely, and not especially safe, the walls being held up by great steel devices and rises of scaffolding. The odd piece of Victorian masonry would fall when the roof became sodden with rain, and at night, I would lie awake listening to the dreadful scuttling of rats, whose population I was responsible for managing in my role as property guardian. When my phone trilled at midnight, it was not interrupting any dream, but arrived soon after the sound of a trap somewhere in my cavernous dwelling snapped shut on one of the rodents' necks.

'Av . . . April?' said Essie when I answered.

'Esther . . . Are you OK?'

'He's a fucking wanker!' she slurred.

'The boy in the village? What happened?' I said, employing the kind of concerned strain I knew girls used when they wanted to show they were absolutely on your side.

'He's a twat! A complete and total wanker . . . No one else

154

was up. No one else picked up. You picked up when I called. *You* picked up.'

'Where are you?' Was she calling me from within Signal House, the place I'd been constructing in my daydreams? In that moment, I imagined a sea breeze drying the tears on Essie's face from a huge bedroom window looking out over the ocean.

'I'm in the kitchen. Janine's ignoring me and Mum's told me to get a hold of myself. Dad gave me another drink; told me I should get dolled up tomorrow and find another boy to show I'm *worth ten of him*. Why can't all men be like my dad?'

'It sounds like that boy really upset you.' I spoke carefully, bringing to mind all of the conversations I had listened to between other girls about their bad boyfriends. It did not come naturally, but I was determined to make a good job of being Essie's friend now that she'd chosen me to confide in. Yes, I felt being aligned with Essie would do my professional and creative life no harm, but more than that, I needed a friend. I had so much to offer Essie if she'd only let me in. 'What a complete arsehole.'

'Arsehole,' Essie slurred back, and I was pleased I appeared to have hit the nail on the head. 'He called me a bunny boiler in front of the whole pub! *Him!?*' I loved the sound of her voice in my ear, I always thought she had a terrific cadence and it felt incredibly special it was only me getting to hear it in that moment. I looked at the latest draft of my film short version of *Singular* on the floor next to my futon and imagined, for the thousandth time, Essie saying my words, being my avatar, something like Robert De Niro to my Scorsese, only the first female version. 'I'm so stupid,' she said through a sob.

'No, you're not, and if that boy isn't completely in love

155

with you, he's about the only man who isn't.' A snuffle, the blowing of her nose, the wordless permission to continue my compliments. 'You're an amazing, beautiful person, Esther. Everyone knows it.'

'Do they? I'm stupid and I'm ugly and I'm crap and I'm pointless.'

'You're the absolute opposite,' I told her, and I meant it. I wanted to one day involve her in my work so she could see that.

'I shouldn't have called you, should I? I don't know why I called you. Forget everything I said. I'm gonna feel like a total dick tomorrow.'

'Why? You've not done anything wrong.'

'I need to lie down now. I feel sick.'

'Make sure you drink some water. And wash your face, you'll feel so much better for that in the morning.'

'Yep.'

I wanted very much to carry on the conversation with Essie but didn't want her to think I had nothing better to do than to listen to her drunken ramblings. Better for me to set up a way for us to speak when she was sober.

'I'll call you in the morning, make sure you're all right.'

'Oh, I'll be fine. I always am, until the next wanker.'

'Good night, Esther. I'll check on you tomorrow.'

In the end, Essie called me first, having seen she'd called a number she didn't recognise the night before, terrified she'd drunkenly dialled some boy she shouldn't have.

'I don't remember a thing. Did I sound horribly, dribblingly rat-arsed?'

'You were fine. Upset, but fine.'

'Hope you got back to sleep OK. Well, enjoy your weekend. Bye.'

I swallowed. 'Will do, you too. Oh, and does Friday still work?'

'Friday?'

'You said we should go for a drink this week. You thought you were free Friday?' Adrenaline crept across my chest as I made the most of the opportunity fate had given me.

'Oh no, I'm not around. I must have been well drunk. Sorry.'

'You must have meant another day then.'

'Right.'

'Is there another better day for you?' My breath was hot in my mouth. I pulled my cardigan off me and flapped my T-shirt against my body to send puffs of cooler air to my face, scared Essie might somehow sense the heat of my cheeks down the line.

'I could pop out for a quick one on Wednesday maybe?'

'Wednesday it is,' I said, punching the air.

A voice in the background, Janine's, wanting to know who Essie was on the phone to.

'A friend from work. Gotta go. Speak next week.'

A friend from work. Speak next week. Yes, I am. Yes, we would.

*

I remember the Monday morning that followed so vividly. It was one of those days when you are young when all the colours are in high contrast, every bit of the world illuminated to the point of shining, your life moving in tones and a rhythm you've not yet known. Essie arrived as she always did following her

157

Kent weekends, dropped off by Una and Con with a shouty chorus of goodbyes.

I watched Una lower her window as Essie walked into the studio; she seemed to be checking, or assessing her. It was difficult for me to understand why she was so over-invested in her daughter's appearance, though looking back it was almost certainly about living vicariously through Essie, and with a level of vigilance she was no longer able to apply to her own life. Una was once a dancer. I had gleaned that this was how she had met Con, who owned several nightclubs, among his other businesses. Una had let herself get married very young, when she was just twenty, and had Janine soon after, with Essie arriving a few years later. It was as though the care she failed to deploy on her own body needed somewhere to go, and poor Essie had ended up being the unwitting receptacle.

It's somewhat disorientating to realise that back then, Una was around the age I am now. That morning, we watched each other for a moment, she in her black shining SUV, me standing by the side of the car park. Essie was oblivious, looking at the tarmac as she strode with her cabin case trailing behind her. I could sense Una was silently assessing my own fascination with Essie, while I did the same to her.

'Oh, hello, Esther,' I said, my eyes still on Una, who finally raised her window and stopped watching her daughter, and me.

Essie seemed slightly shocked to see me there as she walked in, even though she must have realised, surely, that I always got to the studio early and left late, just like her.

'Hey, April. Not late, am I?'

'No and yes, thank you, I'm very well. How was the rest of your weekend?'

158

'All right, I guess,' she hung her denim jacket up, 'normal, for us.'

How deeply I wanted to understand what 'normal for us' meant to Essie's family.

'Ha!' I laughed at Essie's quip, and watched as she walked over to the catering station to pour herself a huge black coffee in preparation for her morning.

'My family are completely weird,' I told her, hoping she might follow up with a question for me.

'Right,' she replied, clearly looking about for the floor manager we both reported to.

The show that day went according to expectations. I had, as usual, the task of keeping the set tidy and the catering station in an acceptable state, while Essie ran around distributing call sheets, assisting on wardrobe, and, on this day, co-ordinating a crowd of extras we had in for an item with a footballer whom Fiona was interviewing. Of course, the footballer wanted Essie's number and I was unsurprised when she acquiesced.

He seemed to me to be her type: flash with his cash and a little rough around the edges, much like how I imagined her father was. I watched them flirt and 'banter' and while I didn't like it, worried Essie was vulnerable and clearly on the rebound from her romantically painful weekend, I left them to it until I overheard them saying goodbye to each other.

'I'll see *you* on Wednesday.' The footballer leant deep into Essie's space and took her hand, his face attempting to reach hers. She took a step back; aware that neither the floor manager nor the footballer's handlers, who were waiting in the wings, would approve.

'Right,' she told him.

I could see he held her hands quite tightly now, gently tugging her towards him, apparently intending to whisper something into her ear.

'Excuse me, Esther?'

Essie startled to see me standing there. The footballer, meanwhile, scowled for a second.

'Sorry, you said we were going out on Wednesday?'

Essie's face washed through first with horror, then something even worse: sympathy. 'Oh yeah, sorry. Wednesday. Right.'

'It's cool. I'll bring one of my boys,' he looked me up and down. 'I know someone who's gonna *love* you.'

*

The footballer and his friend were meeting us at a fashionable nightclub in Camden. Essie invited herself round to mine to get ready as it was on the way. I'd tidied up the old bank as best I could, but there was no hiding the reality of my quarters.

'What is this place? Is it even safe?' She took in the scaffold at the end of my bed. 'You live here alone?'

'Yes. I'm the building's guardian. I barely pay rent. I should be able to afford a flat of my own in few years. Where do you rent?'

'I don't. My dad bought a place for me in St Katharine Docks.' She immediately sensed my surprise, my jealousy, perhaps. 'You'd think that makes me really lucky but even though it's in my name, my dad *owns* the place. I can't do anything to it, put any of my shit on the walls.' She walked past a bare expanse of flaking plaster. 'I can't make it my own.'

'My parents hate me,' I blurted out, turning to Essie who

was watching me with a mixture of shock and a kind of horror at my sudden outburst of honesty. 'I feel like a completely different species to them. They're not nice, not happy like your family seems. I don't think they even like me. It's why there are no pictures up of them. I'm actually thinking of changing my name, because I definitively don't want to be like them, or part of them.'

Essie glanced about the empty walls again.

'Right.' She wrapped her arms around herself and rubbed them as if she were cold, though the season had all but tipped into summer. Essie's eyes took in the four corners of the damp cavern I was forced to call home. 'Shall we get out of here? Get a few drinks in before they arrive?'

'Sure. Would you like me to touch up your makeup before we go?'

'I think I can manage myself tonight, thanks.'

*

Essie and I waited in the VIP area of paparazzi favourite The Albion Club for Boys and Girls for her footballer and his friend. It was my first ever experience of paparazzi, though they ignored Essie and me on our way in.

The booth that the footballer had booked was made of the whitest leather that glowed under the UV lights. The crowd were as noisy as the music, the air-conditioning aggressive. We were both trying to act as though we weren't nervous, or freezing; Essie in a stunning, very short silver dress that had no back, and barely any front for that matter, me in a short black skirt and a black vest I had hoped would work with it. I'd

161

been hoping I might somehow look preppy but contemporary, but the increasingly familiar swill of sympathy through Essie's eyes after I'd got changed back at the bank told me my outfit was neither.

By nine the footballer and his friend were an hour late and Essie was clearly becoming nervous to the point of quiet hysteria. Our conversation had stalled. I wonder if it was, perhaps, that I asked too many questions. It was something I tended to do, as well as spray people with bald compliments and smile over my redness. Eventually, powered by several orange-flavoured cocktails, she stood up without warning.

'Sod this for a laugh.'

And with that, Essie disappeared into the crowds in the sunken level below. She emerged a moment later, in the centre of the underlit dancefloor. She was alone, the first and only person on there, and immediately lost herself in the bass and in the lyrics.

'Fuck me.' The footballer announced his arrival in the booth. A less good-looking, heavier-set man was with him. Neither acknowledged me. 'She is *mad* for it!'

Essie, on noticing him, pointed two fingers at him, then dropped her arm with a flourish behind her. She stuck her behind out before spinning around and sliding her hips in time to the bass, her hair seeming to catch a gust of air that charged the entire sequence with a sexuality that was almost epic. The footballer disappeared. His friend looked at me, a disappointment that turned to a kind of resignation as he lowered himself into the spot next to me.

'I'm April. I like your arms,' I told him. A smile men have

162

when women like me say things like that to them advanced over his lips like a lump of butter sliding across a hot pan.

'I think it's time I got you some champagne, *April*.' He took in my hips, my breasts. '*April Showers*.' This made no sense whatsoever and it wasn't funny but was said in a way that was supposed to sound witty and sexual. I let him slide in close to me and told him I would drink his champagne.

As I became more and more drunk, I continued to watch Essie, controlling her footballer, the crowd amassing on their periphery, as she ground her hips against him and mouthed lyrics. I knew in my heart that I would not be speaking to her again about anything important that night. I staggered free of our VIP booth to leave, my night over.

Before I reached the cloakroom, I found I'd been followed by the footballer's teammate and had let him bundle me into the men's toilets. I knew, I suppose, what was happening, but not specifically, what I was doing. I remember my knickers on the damp floor, the underwire of my bra digging into me as he accessed my breasts. I did not particularly want what was happening to happen, but I was drunk enough not to stop him, maybe even to want the sour comfort of a man's body, the physical warmth of another human being near me.

Afterwards, I went next door to the women's toilets where I cleaned myself with a cold wet tissue and did my best to wash off the blotches of semen on my vest where he'd pulled out of me and pushed me down on my knees to catch me on my face and neck. I took some thin solace from the fact the teammate had told me he would call me in the week, even though I had no interest in seeing him again.

I'd managed to forget my bag in my inebriation, so I headed

back to the VIP area. Essie caught my eye as she danced; the footballer had his legs apart, pelvis angled to her hips, but it was as though he wasn't there. Essie pointed two fingers at me, summoning me. I pushed my way through the other dancers. When I reached her, she hugged me around the neck and for one perfect moment, it was me and her effectively alone on the dancefloor. I wanted to tell her everything; not just what had happened with the footballer's friend, but all of it, my whole dreadful, pathetic life, and how I had ideas, stories, a project I wanted her to be part of.

When the song finished, we left the club with Essie's footballer. As we reached the doors, I was temporarily blinded. The paparazzi. The photographer who asked me who we were and for our names was no more than a black shadow as I waved goodbye to Essie who was climbing into a waiting car with her man.

'We work in TV. She's Esther Laycock and I'm April . . .' I stopped myself, thinking now would be an ideal time to make the move I'd been thinking about for some time. The moment had come for my rebirth. 'My name is April Eden.'

*

In the morning, a picture appeared, a small black-and-white image in a tabloid newspaper. In it, the footballer, Essie, and me. The subject of the story, little more than an elongated caption detailing how the footballer had left The Boys and Girls with 'two mystery blondes' said to be 'TV girls Esther Laycock and April Eden'. Nevertheless, it was clear the small story had found some readers. A few days later, I received a letter from my parents.

164

Dear April,

This letter is to say we hope whoever you think or want April Eden to be, her life is sufficiently happy that it's worth all the pain you have given us over the years. Seeing as how you are now fully committing to not being part of this family, allow us to make it easier for you. Your mother and I would prefer it if you did not contact us for the foreseeable future.

Reluctantly your father and mother

I was outraged. It wasn't only that he must have surely missed a comma after the word *reluctantly*, which made the letter even more hateful, it was that cutting all contact with them had been *my* endgame, which they'd now cheated me out of. *I* was going to let *them* know I no longer wanted contact when I was ready. I liked to imagine it would have been once I felt strong enough to rebuff any attempts to get me to change my mind. I fancied I'd do it a year or two down the line, once I'd got my creative career going, a place of my own in London and, of course, a serious boyfriend.

But with this letter, with my mother and father effectively ending their parenthood, there was a relief too. My family now completely out of the picture, I could fully concentrate on building the life I wanted. And I could begin to devote my time to the people who really mattered, those who would take my life forward, not hold it back. I had no more distractions from being the friend Essie needed, and I wanted, to be.

*

165

As weeks passed, Essie and I talked much more on set, but I hadn't yet seen her again outside of work. Whenever I asked, she always seemed to have something else on.

'I can't come out tonight, sorry,' Essie told me one summer afternoon for what felt like the hundredth time. 'We're going for dinner,' she said, referring to the footballer who had become a permanent fixture in her life. She happened to look up at the end of her statement which enabled her to register the rejection on my face. I cursed my transparency, especially when I saw that specific type of sympathy running through her eyes. 'I promise, we'll go out soon,' she said.

I nodded, clearly unconvinced.

'Tomorrow,' Essie said, clearly unable to bear the sight of me so obviously let down. 'We could try tomorrow?'

'Whatever works,' I said, hoping to dial down my desperation by not moving to lock it down to time, venue, and the like. 'Where are you going tonight?' I asked.

Essie looked at the call sheets in her hands distractedly. 'Not sure, he's booked it. A new Chinese place near Piccadilly?'

'Oh, I'm meeting some friends in Soho later,' I said, keen to look less weird.

'Right.' She looked up from her papers, a trace of confusion about her. 'I thought you said you were hoping to catch up with me?'

I blinked and smiled through the rising tide of redness. 'I meant a quick drink after work. I'm supposed to be meeting my friends at eight. It was only if you were free for a couple of hours.'

Essie appeared poised to ask me another question when the floor manager called her over. We didn't speak again for the rest of the day. That may have been because Essie was so busy with the elevated tasks on set, but I grew worried she had become fully aware of my oddness, my loneliness. I needed to do something to show her I was more normal than she might have been imagining.

After I finished my work, I went home, grabbed my Canon camera, and headed into Soho, the camera reliably transforming me from sad misfit into someone creative, an artist, even. I'd discovered the latest restaurant to be seen at was indeed a recently opened, very expensive Chinese place just off Piccadilly. I walked past it a few times and managed to spot Essie and the footballer inside towards the back of the room. I packed away my camera and waited on the other side of the road, my plan being to casually bump into Essie and the footballer as they left, me apparently heading home after a brilliant night with my pals. I wanted Essie to believe if other people had made me their friend, there was no reason she shouldn't.

The night wore on. Every so often a drunk girl or two would go by, sometimes singing, often giving me the thumbs-up or making a comment on some imagined man I was watching not being worth it. An idea came to me. I slipped to a nearby cashpoint, took out twenty pounds, and began to assess the drifts of single girls anew. My first casting.

Eventually I saw her; inebriated and jolly, wearing a short skirt. She began singing in my direction as she moved to the bus stop and had the air of someone who could be tipped towards the mawkish, the smile falling from her face as she searched for her travel pass in her purse.

'My name's April. I like your skirt.'

167

She glanced down at herself as though realising she had legs for the first time.

'Can I ask you something a bit mad? I'll give you twenty pounds if you stick around for a couple of minutes and when I say, pretend to cry, I'll give you a hug and we'll say goodbye. That's all you have to do.'

She scanned the street around us. 'Is this some sort of secret camera . . . *prank* show?'

'No. Here.' I gave her the twenty.

She appraised the bill in her hand. 'Easiest twenty quid I ever earnt.'

The timing was perfect. Essie and the footballer emerged from the restaurant over the quiet road. 'Quick. Start crying.'

My casting instincts were solid. The girl cried, she near-howled, so much so, I had to ask her to tone it down a little, whispering in her ear, 'You've been dumped by your boyfriend, but the truth is, you always knew, deep down he was no good. You're distraught, but relieved.' My first direction.

Over my shoulder, Essie had noticed the commotion.

'It's going to be OK,' I told my new friend clearly and firmly, 'I'm here for you, all right?'

Essie was in a short red dress and a pale pashmina, her hands on her hips as she watched me and the girl for a moment. The footballer, meanwhile, scanned the street for their ride back to his place.

'April?' Essie said as she walked across the road, the footballer following her.

'Is that your bus?' I whispered to the girl, gesturing to the double-decker that had just pulled up behind her.

'Er . . .'

'Get on it,' I told her. 'You can get off at the next stop if you need to.'

She shrugged and left me for the bus. I waved her off and, as the bus pulled away, called out some words of comfort: 'It's going to be OK! Love you!'

'April!' Essie was now at my side.

I continued to wave off my actress until Essie reached me.

'Essie? Hi!' I rolled my eyes at the back of the bus, telling Essie, 'God, what a nightmare. I've been walking with her for hours. Did you have dinner round here?'

Essie and I were soon joined by the footballer. 'What's she doing here?' he said to the ground.

'April's just been looking after her friend.'

The footballer viewed me. 'Yeah?'

Ignoring the barb of his tone, Essie focused on me. 'Is she OK? She sounded in a right state.'

I sighed and watched the bus swing round the corner and safely away from us. 'Hopefully she will be. We had a good old pep talk. Anyway, I'll leave you to it. See you tomorrow.'

'It's Saturday, silly. No work!' Essie waved a softly clenched fist in the air in celebration.

'Not work. We're going out tomorrow? I just told my friend I couldn't see her because we had plans,' I said, smiling through the threat of colouring.

'Right.' Essie looked disorientated for a second, then shook herself out of it. 'Sorry, April, I said we should go out tomorrow without thinking. Dad's taking me to dinner.' Essie must have seen how disappointed I was to have the chance of an evening with her taken away from me. 'But you must come along.' She leant forward into my space and squeezed my arm. 'Please.

You'll be doing me favour, making me look so clever to have such a smart friend.' She wedged herself to my side, as if to drive the offer home.

'Sounds lovely,' I said to her, almost forgetting the footballer was still there, until he spoke up.

'Let's head then, yeah?' he said to Essie.

I didn't say goodbye to the footballer, but dared to give Essie a hug, just as I had my drunken actress. 'Good night, Esther. Can't wait to meet your father tomorrow.'

Essie smiled, before blinking quickly, as though she was bringing herself out of another state of disorientation, only just realising what she'd been blindsided into doing by my desperation to be friends with her.

Eager to escape that look, and the way it reminded me of the unlikability that seemed to have attached itself to me the day I was born, I turned around and jumped jauntily onto the next bus that pulled up, even though I had tears in my eyes and it was going nowhere near where I needed to be.

*

The next evening, I met Essie in a French restaurant in Chelsea. It was an old-fashioned sort of place that had been there for years, with yellowed silver cutlery and thick white tablecloths. Essie was nervous. She'd been pulling at her clothes, tucking her top into her tight denim skirt and bagging it out again repeatedly. We were awaiting Con's arrival. Essie spoke to me from behind the thumbnail she kept chewing on.

'I've been thinking a bit about what you said about your family back at your place the last time we went out; about

170

you getting away from your folks. I don't want to get away from mine as such, but I think I'd like to start making some decisions for myself.' She stopped biting her nail for a second and scrunched her large lips into a troubled pout.

'Go on,' I said, feeling as though she was about to reveal the darkest contents of her heart to me, like I knew true friends did but had never experienced first-hand. It was by having these sorts of conversations I would get close to her, gain her trust, ask her to join me on my creative adventures.

'Sometimes,' Essie continued, 'I guess, I'd like to make my own choices, instead of doing what my family think is best. I mean, I know they're pretty much always right, but one day I would like to do something that's not their idea, something that's just for me, that'll give me . . .' She took a great big breath in, then breathed it out through one of her smiles, '. . . a bit more breathing space.'

She went on to reveal that Janine had found Essie her job, her father made her live in a flat he had bought for some kind of tax purposes, even though she was often bored and lonely there, but that she would never do anything to disappoint him or appear ungrateful. She detailed the way her mother constantly told her how to look, how to behave, what to wear, what not to eat.

'I know they all want what's best for me,' Essie said, appearing almost tearful. 'But how do I start to have a bit more control of my life?'

I thought about it a moment. How did it start for me?

'You have to get used to telling your family no to everything they think is "best" for you and eventually they'll get it.' My parents denied me so many times, I only ended up turning their

171

techniques on them: saying no to trips home, not answering their phone calls, knowing that little by little I was wearing away our feeble bond; rather like tying off the umbilical cord to halt the exchange of blood between parent and infant until the connection ceases and eventually even the remaining stump withers and dies.

'It's easy for you,' Essie said, and a part of me wanted to shout: *It's been the opposite of easy! It's been painful, and miserable and demoralising*! But I was so happy to be Essie's confidante that I remained silent. 'You're so clever and serious, I bet you've got your whole career planned out. Me? I don't know what I'm good at; I mean, things are going pretty well at *The Dawn Chorus*, but I still don't really know what I'm good *for;* I don't know what I'm doing with my life, all of it feels like it's completely tied up with my family and before you know it, I can see it: I'm going to be thirty and still spending my summers in Kent, being told what to do by them because I've no imagination, no ambition, not enough of a brain to get myself out and away and doing something I actually *really* want to do. I'm pathetic.' Essie flashed another toothy smile, but her voice was a tight scratch.

'No. You are not pathetic. You are beautiful.'

'That's sweet of you to say.' She looked at her cocktail glass morosely, unconvinced.

'You don't understand. You're so charismatic. Everyone loves you. Your family clearly adore you.' Or why else would they be so invested in everything about Essie? Would that I had even a tenth of the attention and engagement Essie's whole family had with her life.

'Mate!' She started to laugh, but still focused on her drink and her own lack of self-esteem. Her features were flushed, washes of emotion entering her kaleidoscope eyes. Essie had no idea how beguiling she was; how bleak her life could be if she didn't look like her, lacked the *It* factor that Essie was imbued with.

'You're utterly magnetic. You belong on camera,' I blurted.

Essie's smile lost some wattage, a flash of weirdness robbing it of some power. 'Steady on, April.'

At this, I feared the redness would arrive. I had said too much, or, as usual, not enough of the right thing. I made my excuses and took myself to the bathroom. When I returned, ready not to be weird and try to seem averagely acceptable, Essie's father had just arrived.

'Well, aren't you both a sight for sore eyes. Esther's friend, I assume?' Con didn't wait for an answer and immediately gave me a double kiss while holding onto both of my hands. Essie stood up and Con grabbed her into a bear hug. 'Come here, fruit of my loins,' he said and gave her a string of kisses on her cheeks. Essie screwed up her eyes, her smile as wide as I'd ever seen it.

'Dad-*dy*,' she said, finally breaking their embrace to encourage her father to take the seat next to her, leaving me to sit opposite Con. 'Daddy, April. April, Daddy.'

'Lovely to meet you, Mr Laycock,' I said, suddenly incredibly nervous. I knew how much her father's approval meant to Essie and I didn't want to let her down. I wanted Con to think me pleasant, charming, good enough to be Essie's friend.

'Mr Laycock? You make me sound like my father. There might be snow on top.' Con ran his fingers through his hair, which was chestnut brown with an extravagant sweep of pure white fanning from the centre of his temple to his crown. 'But there's fire in the furnace.'

Essie laughed and nudged her father.

'Call me Con.' He smiled so wide I could see the gold of one of his crowns. 'Or call me whatever the hell you please. Now, who've I gotta screw to get a drink round here? Go on, Esther, go and flash that waiter there. Let's have a bottle of Bolli, eh?'

I knew ordering a bottle of expensive champagne was an ostentatious gesture and yet I was impressed anyway. Con saw my delighted surprise and winked at me. I beamed back.

'I need the loo,' Essie said, rising from her seat. 'I'll give them our order on the way past.'

Con watched his daughter move across the room. He and I were then alone, sat opposite sides of the table. 'Is it me, or has she put on weight?'

I was aghast. My father was unexceptional in every way, but I knew he'd never say anything like that. Though perhaps that was because he chose not to notice anything about me at all.

'Esther? No. She's as slim as ever,' I said.

A moment or two of uncomfortable silence.

'So, you and her work together?'

'That's right. She's great to work with.'

'Is she? She doesn't go around the place breaking things all day; forgetting her own name?'

'No!' I laughed. And then I stopped because I could see Con was serious. 'She's really good at what she does. She's got a brilliant attitude, so hard-working, great ideas. She'll be promoted before me, and I've been there longer.' I had never voiced this thought, this fear before, but it was true.

Con looked out onto the restaurant floor. I worried that my defending Essie may have offended him.

'I like your hair,' I blurted out. It was the only feature he had that came to mind in that moment, but it sounded so personal when I said it.

Con brightened immediately. 'You go for the distinguished look, do you?'

I didn't want to say that I did not 'go for the distinguished look' for fear of offending him again, so thought of something at least neutral.

'It suits you very well.'

Con viewed me side on.

'Take that plait out,' he said.

I looked at him confused.

'Go on, take it out, give your hair a bit of a . . .' He opened his palms and pushed them up into the air by his ears and then waited for me to do as I was told.

I was not at all comfortable, but I was desperate for him to think well of me. I obeyed, pulling the bobble off the end of my hair and using my fingers to untangle the strands and give them volume as he had directed.

'There,' he said. 'Much better.'

I could see Essie was returning from the loo and smiled at her with what I can now place as relief.

'Very nice,' Con said, still staring at me, assessing me, just as Essie retook her seat.

'What's very nice?' Essie asked him distractedly as she began to peruse the menu.

'This place,' Con told her without even a beat of hesitation.

ACT III

'Be aware that certain choices you make can distort your players' faces. For example, unless you ensure the correct tilt, the position of the camera using short lens close can make an actor's teeth and mouth appear much larger than they are. In other words, without any kind of special effect, it's perfectly possible you could shoot someone ugly even if they are, in reality, beautiful.'

FILM SCHOOL LECTURE NOTES TRANSCRIPTION

17

April, the day before the gala screening

My boyfriend thinks I am Essie.

Jags is still staring at the back of me in Esther's dress and if I thought I was scared when I first saw the dress, now I am petrified: I don't know who the man I love is anymore.

Jags cannot see my face in the mirror from this angle, but I watch him flick his gaze down and back again, as though he needs to be sure I am flesh and blood, not an apparition. Then, something in his demeanour seems to shift; he looks more like Jags again.

'You owe us an explanation,' he says. 'You have no idea what you've put April through; you're supposed to be her friend. Do you even care? . . . *Essie?*'

He steps into the room. I have no choice but to turn around and show myself.

'April? . . . *April*. Why are you wearing Essie's dress? Where did you find it? What's with the hair?'

'You called me Esther.' A fracture across the syllables as I say her true name.

'What?'

'I've never heard you call Essie, *Esther*.'

179

Jags appears bemused rather than caught out, but then he's had a lot of practice in portraying emotions that are not real, I remind myself.

'Haven't you? I don't know . . .' He searches the air either side of him for whatever point he's seeking to make. 'I'm pissed off; shocked. I thought she was dead and now she'd dared to show up on your doorstep, for god's sake. It's like when you call me *Jagdeep* when things are heavy.' He checks my expression. Is he trying to see if I'm buying it, or if I'm holding something back? 'Anyway, you haven't told me why you're wearing the dress Essie died in . . . And your hair; what's happened to it?'

'I just had it done. The dress, someone delivered to me.' I guiltily view my body in Essie's dress. I never should have put it on, no matter how strong the pull to feel closer to her.

'How? When?'

'In a black box, about two minutes ago.'

Jags's hands are on his hips now, the stance of someone trying to get to the bottom of something, but it seems to me this could well be a trick of transference.

'Why are you here?' I ask him. 'You said you couldn't be with me today.'

'Did you see whoever delivered the dress?'

'No. And there was no postmark, not even an address for me on it. Did you notice anyone on your way here, Jagdeep? Come across something or someone suspicious?'

He goes to sit on the end of my bed. 'April. Honestly, you're really freaking me out, looking like that, speaking like you are. Is there . . . I hope you know if there's something you're not telling me, you can. I need to know.'

'Such as?'

180

'You tell me! You're the one stood there, in *that*.'

'Have *you* something you want to tell *me*, Jags? You haven't told me what you're doing here yet.'

He sighs. He seems tired, exhausted with the fighting, the suspicions, the acidity between us. 'I decided whatever Mum thought she needed from me today, it was more important to be with you.'

How I want to believe him. How I need to. Why else would Jags come here and besides, who or what else have I got in my life now with Essie gone? One more question before I can abandon my interrogation and be us again.

'Why were you looking over your shoulder, checking I wasn't coming when you thought I was Essie?'

Another sigh. 'If you were to see Essie, standing in your bedroom after what we saw, what would your reaction have been? Remember how you were when you found her in the pool?' He shakes his head. 'If I think I can protect you, I'll put myself in between you and whatever the problem is. Don't you get that yet?'

I think of how decisive Jags was when we first found Essie, how strong he was, how he took control, wanting to shield me from whatever damage he could. I couldn't have got through that on my own. I can't do the screening or any of what happens next solo either.

Jags detects the softening in me. 'Anything else you want to know?'

I think for a second.

'When did you first think you had serious feelings for me? What changed that day for you?'

He sighs once more, but this time, it's wistful. His gaze drifts

181

into the left-hand corner of the room, as though there were a tiny projector, playing his memories up there.

'Just before the wrap party for the film, I know I was an arsehole to you around that time, but I think that was me acting out. I know, it's childish and shows zero self-knowledge, but . . . anyway, the precise moment I knew I was in deep trouble with you was when Essie did what she did on that final scene. She'd made the last couple of days of the shoot a bit of a nightmare for you, hadn't she, but you helped her get to where she needed to be and it was, you *were* . . . powerful, beautiful. I was feeling a bit rattled when I left you in the car park but after I'd driven away, I started to process where my head was at.' Jags shrugs. 'I was at home with my mum, and I realised I didn't want to be there. I wanted to go and find you more than I'd wanted anything else.'

He looks down, a shyness I've rarely, if ever, seen. I turn my gaze to the floor, smiling through the tears of gratitude.

'I think, somewhere, I've always been very impressed by you. April, right from the start. I . . . I've always been ready to love you.'

Jags can almost read my thoughts even in the smaller moments. I wonder, can he tell, does he know, this has never happened to me before? Can he sense I've never heard those words from a man, not even my own father? And in saying this, does he also realise in the space of a single second he's changed something in me forever?

'Take that thing off. Please. I don't want you to look like her,' he says.

I walk to the end of my bed where he sits, stand before him, and undo the clasp at the back of my neck. The gown falls to my waist, and I shuffle the satin past my hips, leaving it to crumple to the floor. I move to stand between his knees and wait for him to see all of me. But Jags's head remains resolutely turned towards the parquet.

'That's not what I . . . How can I say this without being unkind about Essie: you look like her, not like you. She was never my thing.' Even though there's some residual if uncomfortable relief at Jags saying he finds me more attractive than Essie, the undertone of rejection nonetheless makes me take a step back, away from him.

'Don't run away from me; don't be so upset. I'm only here because I didn't want you going back to Lotus on your own. Unless you want to be on your own?'

I almost laugh, but the clag of tears now in my throat stops me.

'Jags. I have had enough of being on my own to last me a lifetime.'

'So, don't push me away. Don't let yourself be alone again.'

I nod, my eyes closed. When I open them, Jags is gently gathering my clothes before handing them to me.

'Come, let's take Essie's phone back to Lotus and get back on track.'

*

The day has turned waxy grey as we ride the bus up to Lotus, Essie's phone in Jags's pocket because I can't bear to have it on me. I cannot wait to be rid of it.

We enter Lotus's atrium, Jags tentatively calling out to check Janine isn't here while I deactivate the alarm. The whole place is beginning to smell now, stale and rotten, the lilies that greet us on the table directly below the skylight brown and broken. Jags and I stand motionless for a moment.

'Let's just drop it down the cushion of her chair and get out of here,' I say. 'Then, we can start thinking about raising the alarm, or maybe we won't have to. When Essie doesn't show up tomorrow, surely Janine or her parents will ask the police to get involved?'

'I wouldn't bet on it,' Jags says and I don't disagree with him. I get the distinct impression that Janine, at least, is rather enjoying her sister's disappearing act. I haven't discounted her as having something to do with what happened to Essie, but given she was, like us, somewhere on the way to the Albert Hall roughly around the time Essie must have died, I can't work out what yet.

Jags and I head into the living space and over to Essie's chair, and I notice again the mess of the place, the stains and dust, the streak of black nail polish on the upholstery of the egg chair. Was that there before? Jags has clearly had exactly the same thought. He bends down and moves to scrape at the stain with his fingernail, and when he brings his fingers back to him, there's a faint trace of nail polish on his fingertip.

'This is recent,' he says. 'Doesn't it look like the black polish Essie had on when . . .'

'Yes. Yes, it does,' I say.

'Could be Janine, I guess, finding it; borrowing it?' Jags says.

'Yes, of course.'

We both stare at the smear a beat longer.

'Right, shall we do this like we planned? Can I have Essie's phone please?' I say.

'Sure,' Jags says, putting on a pair of gloves, while I do the same. He pulls the phone out of his pocket and places it in my hand. I kneel down and carefully go to slip the phone down the side of the seat cushion, bringing to mind how Essie would sit, her legs tucked below her, to help me decide on the most likely place the phone might be lost from her pocket. I settle on a spot almost at the back of the rounded seat. This close up to the upholstery, something catches my eye. I put the phone down, pull off my glove with my teeth, and lick the end of my fingers.

'What are you doing?' Jags asks.

I begin brushing along the upholstery of the chair's seat in quick, systematic strokes. My heart thrashes in my chest.

'April?'

One final stroke of my fingertips.

'I'm gathering evidence.'

'Evidence of what?'

I stand and show Jags what's now in between my fingers: a collection of long, blonde hairs. They're exactly the same texture and tone as my own; exactly the same as Essie's. And I know for a fact they were not on her chair the night we saw Essie in her pool.

'Evidence Essie isn't dead.'

18

Essie, before, The Vanished Woman *rehearsals*

I had hoped the rehearsals for *The Vanished Woman* would help me with my mental state; because if I am being Elena, maybe I don't have to be Essie, trapped in her brain. But the way April has written Elena, it's like I have to be even further away from whoever the real Essie is, become even more vulnerable. I can feel myself getting worse, not better. And now, my heart sometimes races, sometimes stutters to the next beat. And sometimes, it feels like it wants to stop working altogether. At night, I can feel very afraid, too frightened to go to sleep, in case my heart decides to give up after I've dropped off.

'You look like absolute shit,' my sister tells me as I let her in. She's come to Lotus to tell me about some work, *something really decent*, she's set up for me. 'What's April doing to you?'

'It's not her, it's me. Can't sleep.'

'Well, you need to look lively next week. I've got an ad for you.'

'Right. What for?'

'They're pawnbrokers. We're shooting in Catford. All you have to say is a little piece to camera about how if, like you, people are down on their luck, then pawning their stuff is a great idea.'

I think of the shoots I did for Beteille, in Paris and Provence; the enormous squads of people, the stylists, hair and makeup people, the assistants who arranged the couture gowns I wore and made sure I was always in the best light.

'Is this the best I can do now?'

Janine's mouth falls open. 'Are you fucking kidding me? I've been busting my arse to get you *anything* since you fucked up.'

'What if I don't want *anything*? I have enough invested. I have this place. I've cut back on my spending on staff and new stuff like you told me. I don't need to do ads for some dodgy pawnbrokers to make rent or anything.'

Janine's face hardens. 'So, what, are you sacking me? You don't need me to get you earning so you can fund your little acting adventure? Let me tell you, that game will chew you up and spit you out and it sure as shit isn't likely to pay the bills.'

I don't want to hear the echoes of Janine's past acting career now and I don't want to seem ungrateful for all her effort in getting The Most Hated Woman in Britain paid work. 'Of course I'm not sacking you, and thank you for the ad and everything you're doing for me. I'll do it, of course.'

Not because I want to, but to keep my sister happy.

Janine sighs. 'Here. Call this person. I can see you've been going downhill. I think I've found someone who can help.'

She hands me a card which I look at not quite able to take in what I'm seeing. 'You want me to see a psychiatrist?' I view it again. 'A trauma specialist?'

Janine shrugs. 'She's supposed to be good. And if you're not sleeping then . . .'

187

I've never had therapy before. I've always been too scared to have a look inside myself. If I open the can of worms that is being Essie Lay, will Esther Laycock ever be able to cram all that mess back inside again?

'I'll send you the details for the ad shoot.' Janine watches me for another moment. 'And let me see what else I can sort out to help you sleep.'

*

Janine leaves after her swim and I'm alone in my big house. Ever since the rehearsals started, it is getting harder to spend time here alone. There's no one outside my family I trust to get me through it, but being around them has its own set of stresses; my relationship with Jackson seems to have proved to them I'm capable of making only bad decisions. I've been relying on April to plug the gaps, even if it is far from ideal, since Jags is always in tow, leaving me the sad gooseberry. Today is no different from all the other times before it.

'Hey.' I can't believe how nervous, how needy I sound when I call her these days.

'Hi, Essie, what are you up to?' April replies, so breezy, like she hasn't got a care in the world. I can't imagine what that must feel like; to be able to walk down the road without people telling you what they think about you, say something disgusting to your face, tell you they hate you, then ask for a selfie.

'I was just wondering, if you and Jags are going on one of your walks, if you guys found yourself on the Heath, why don't you come to mine for a late Sunday lunch afterwards?'

'Oh, OK. That sounds nice. Let me double-check with Jags.'

Their coming round might kill at least two hours, maybe even three. Then I only have to get through Sunday night on my own before final rehearsals on Monday and then shooting begins. I keep on doing this, breaking my life into little chunks to try to live it a piece at a time. It doesn't feel healthy. It probably isn't sustainable. Also, every time I invite him and April to do something with me, I can see Jags getting more and more resentful. I totally understand why he doesn't want to have me intruding on his and April's quality time together, so the whole thing leaves me feeling like I'm annoying, pointless, and useless. I decide to give the psychiatrist Janine recommended a call tomorrow.

When April and Jags do end up coming round, he acts sweet enough, but I can tell he really does not want to share April with me. He must be so badly in love with her. It reminds me of how I believed that's how it was between me and Jackson, which makes me cry, which then makes April give all her attention to me which, I'm sure, makes Jags resent me even more. All-in-all, being in Jags and April's company means I'm technically not on my own, but today, as with the other times, has left me lonelier than ever. I'm feeling very low when they leave. A few minutes later, my intercom sounds. I assume one of them has forgotten something, but instead it's a delivery: a small, unmarked black box within a box. I open it and find a bottle of pills marked *zolpidem* inside.

These should help you sleep. Jxxx

'Thanks, sis,' I say to the air, immediately popping two pills free and swallowing them without water.

189

*

I don't so much sleep as am completely zonked out by the pills. When I wake, my head is heavy in a way I can't shake, even when it's time for my final costume-fitting. Elena only wears one outfit the entire film. My take on this is that even changing her clothes means giving Antonia, and therefore her father, some kind of insight on her inner emotions, which she does not want to do.

The white dress looks kind of vintage and is supposed to fit tightly around my frame. The costume designer is having to adjust the side seams again this morning, because of the weight I've lost recently, what with the stress, the not sleeping, barely eating. I look at myself in the full-length mirror, in Elena's plain dress, my hair pulled into a low plait at the base of my neck. I look like me, and I don't. I look like someone I know. I look, I realise even through my medicated fuzz, like April.

19

April, the day before the screening

'Jags. I'm not sure Essie is dead. I think she's been here,' I gesture to the egg chair, 'painted her nails and brushed her hair at some point between when we left the morning after the awards and now.'

'That's . . . mad,' Jags says.

'You know how she was about keeping her chair how she liked it.'

'Yeah, she was obsessed, like OCD with her tissues every five minutes. But you can't really think she's alive?'

'I know it's crazy, but it really looks to me like she's deliberately not cleaned up after herself this time; set it up for me to notice. I feel it; I know it,' I say, but even I can hear the hysteria in my voice. Could it be I want her to be alive so badly, I'm looking to conjure her back by sheer force of will? No. I have Essie's hair caught between my fingertips and she wouldn't leave it for me to find unless she wanted me to find it.

'Can I see?' Jags holds out his hand and I rub my fingertips together until the thin clump of hairs flurries through the air and into his.

'Shit. I think . . . Maybe you're right.' Jags squishes his eyes

191

together as though trying to rid them of sand, or scales. 'If you're right, this changes everything.'

*

Jags and I have headed into the kitchen to sit around my normal writing spot and consider whether Essie being alive could really be true and what we may need to do about it. This distinctly feels like the third act, the point in a five-act story at which the action accelerates.

'The thing is, we both saw her that night,' I say.

'You could have only been at the poolside for less than a minute. She could have held her breath that long, right?'

'But what about when you touched her, when you used face ID? You said she was—'

'*I said* she was the same temperature as the water.'

'Was she breathing?'

'She could have been. I just assumed, like you did, she was dead. I was breathing pretty heavily when I turned her in the water. Would I have noticed if she snuck the odd breath? No. I don't think I would.'

'This is crazy. Essie wouldn't do that to me.'

'No, I think, you are right: Essie is alive. Essie is alive and she is fucking with you. Think about it. Who else but Janine had access to Lotus Lodge? And Janine has the awards ceremony as her alibi, then she went off with Jonathan. Who else could come into Lotus, take the dress off, and send it to you?'

But Janine was late to the ceremony, even later than we were. She said she'd been talking to journalists on the red carpet, but how can I know that was true?

192

'I don't know who else might have accessed Lotus, who else might have keys besides us and Janine. The champagne bottle, the pills, the way Essie was – could none of that have been real?' I ask.

'Nah.' Jags shakes his head. 'Think about it: it's so obviously a setup, isn't it? I mean the film star facedown in the pool, after a drink and pills binge, bit of a cliché, wouldn't you say?'

'Yes. Yes, I suppose it is,' I say, but the whole thing is so perplexing. The idea of Essie being alive, however, is deeply tempting.

'April, the more I think about it, I *know* she's alive. Honestly, I've been watching Essie, watching what she's like with you, and I saw how her mind was ticking over when you changed things up around the shoot for the film. You stuck to your plan until you got the result you needed from her, didn't you? And that's exactly what she's doing now. The only mistake I think you can make now? It's blinking first.'

Essie alive, trying to send me mad, to punish me for putting her through what I did during the shoot; but still living? The possibility of her still existing is so magnetic, my mind seems to snatch it from the realm of theory and convert it into belief because I so deeply want it to be true. I don't want her dead.

'What if we're wrong, Jags?'

'We're not.'

'But if we are, how much more trouble would I get into? Impersonating her when I accepted Janine's call on Essie's phone? Delaying the proper investigation into her disappearance?'

'If I am wrong, which I'm not, then it's simple: you say you thought Essie was messing around with you, playing a game, trying to manipulate you with an elaborate prank, like, I don't know, a PR stunt, maybe one that's all Janine's idea. There's nothing to lose, well, there's plenty to lose if you let her win. Let her take control, god knows what that means for your first-look deal.'

I take a long breath. I want Essie to be alive and I want to be in control of my career.

'OK, so what, exactly, do we do now?'

Jags gets Essie's phone out. 'The first thing we do is switch this on, clear the voicemails or whatever and post something short and sweet on Instagram as Essie, something that takes the heat out of the #RIPEssie rumour mill and shows her we know exactly what she's up to.'

'And then?'

'Wait for Essie's next move.'

I can't help my impulses when it comes to her: I immediately start to compose something in Essie's voice in my mind, just as I had when I was drafting *The Vanished Woman*. I can hear her unmistakable cadence in my very soul, the voice I've had in my head since I was twenty-one years old, the one I hope so desperately to hear again, even if she never wants to hear from me.

'Oh god, Jags, I really don't think I can do this.'

If I crossed a line the night of the awards, then this is an even thicker, indelible mark. I will not be able to go back to the other side. My skin begins to prickle, a gathering of heat around my neck, Jags picks up on it.

'Need a minute?' he asks. 'Why don't you get some fresh air?'

'Yes. I think I will.'

I head to the other side of the kitchen, grab the set of keys

194

for the back door, and let myself out onto Essie's wide veranda with its prized view over her substantial garden. I grip onto the stone balustrade as I take in its defining feature, the dominating lotus pond, the withered heads of the summer's past blooms; mud-coloured, bent sticks against the grey of day. I think of Essie as the shoot for *The Vanished Woman* progressed, how, as I altered the script and my direction, her vulnerability, her response to the messages I was sending via Elena and Antonia's story, seemed to shine through her. She was never more compelling on screen than she was when she gave herself over to my story. Like the spent flowers I'm looking at now, can I make Essie open and bloom again? Can I coax her out if I take on her identity?

I realise I am shaking. What did I do to myself when I made sure Esther Laycock would be part of my life again? What was I thinking, given everything that went before? It was always going to end in trouble. It was trouble from the very beginning.

I decide to walk the perimeter of the grounds while I go through how Jags's plan might work and the millions of ways it could go horrifically awry.

There's nearly half an acre around the main house at Lotus. As I progress down the path to the furthest reaches of the garden, I turn to view its great windows, which stretch over three floors, and the balcony from Essie's huge master suite overlooking the grounds and woodland beyond. From the path skirting the wooded area, I peer through the trees to the annexe on the boundary of Lotus's grounds. Essie told me guests at her legendary celebrity parties – the ones I didn't get to attend – would stay there. Janine, I believe, made the place her home for a time until all those ten per cents added up enough to pay for her own place in Chelsea, across town from Essie and close to Con and Una's London residence.

I head towards edge of the woodland, eschew the path to the annexe, and turn for the gravel down the side of the main house. I pass another outbuilding, a double garage where Con, I was told, had housed yet another classic car purchase, one he couldn't fit at his own home. Essie told me when he bought the thing, he tried to justify keeping it at her place because it was really a gift for her. How easily I can imagine Con saying this, in his insistent, unctuous, all-women-are-goddesses tone, as though he were next to me. My body gives an involuntary shudder, even before I notice something odd in the stretch of gravel running up to the garages.

A dark spot.

I walk to the stain, noting something familiar about the blackish grey tone. I find myself dropping onto my haunches to touch the ground. My fingers find a soiled patch of small rocks. They're wet. Though the clouds have been pregnant with rain for days, the downpour is yet to fall. I dare to smell my fingers.

Engine oil.

20

April, the day before the screening

Jags's car, parked at Essie's house, leaking oil onto the gravel. Jags planting the nail polish stain and strands of Essie's hair to throw me off the scent of the truth: an affair gone sour, turned violent? It's crazy, I know, but the coincidence of the engine oil means I must scratch the itch, if only so I can completely eliminate Jags from my suspicions and crack on with our next move.

I eye the two garages located behind me, then look back through the large side window into the kitchen to check Jags is not in there. I find myself peering up at the CCTV camera trained on the garages, even though I know they're not functioning. For whatever reason, I feel watched once more, and so vulnerable. Ever since Jags called me Esther, there's an anxiety I've not been able to fully shake.

I can't stop myself from wanting to investigate, starting with the garage nearest me. It's the least modernised of the two, with older-style wooden doors and two windows so grimy that when I look through them, all I can see inside is a greasy blur. There's a padlock holding the doors together, heavy in my hand, rusty.

I give the padlock a shake, more in hope than expectation, but its mechanism springs free in my hand with a dull, scratchy clunk. I drop it to the gravel, pull one of the reluctant doors open wide enough for me to squeeze in, and look inside. There is a leaf blower, various spades, a scythe, shears of different sizes and lengths hanging on nails on one of the walls, and a well-used sit-on lawnmower, which could have made the stain outside though I don't see any trace of a leak. No Grey Lady. I slide out, push the door, click the padlock to a close, and move on to the next garage.

This one is more modern, with a manual retractable white metal door and no windows. I try the handle, giving it a further forceful tug that makes the door clatter in its runners but does not release the lock.

'Looking for more clues?'

I jump at the sound of Jags's voice behind me.

'Um, I was just—'

'Found anything interesting?'

'No.' I breathe over the nerves in my chest. 'I was thinking about trying to get this garage open.'

'Why?' Jags asks, and I can hear exhaustion and perhaps even a trace of hurt in his voice. It leaves me feeling like the one who may be hiding something.

'I don't know. Just a hunch.' I attempt to introduce quiet mirth into my voice, but it doesn't quite work.

'Essie keeps a load of keys and stuff in that drawer in the kitchen, doesn't she?' Jags says, and I detect a tightening in the air. He knows I don't fully trust him. Part of me wants to tell him it's not him, it's me that's the problem, but I don't want to out my mistrust so emphatically.

'They could be in there,' I agree.

'Do you want to go and get them?' Jags asks.

'You're closer, why don't you have a look?'

Jags sighs. 'If they're not in there, I think you'll want to see it with your own eyes.'

'If you say so,' I reply with a forced lightness, barely masking the fact that, unfortunately, what he's said is true. I return to the back door, moving to pass Jags with an unease I'm sure he senses. I re-enter Essie's vast kitchen and start to search the drawer next to the wine fridge. Layers of life's detritus: Supper receipts, spent corks, old utility bills, the warrantees for appliances; a business card which I assume is for the psychiatrist Essie was seeing. I take it in my fingers:

Dr Jaiyesimi Abiola, Psychiatrist
Anxiety disorders, PTSD specialist

Jags is staring out of the back door, like a waiter looking away as you enter your PIN number into a card machine, feeling like he needs to give me some privacy as I indulge my paranoia. He doesn't see me as I slip the psychiatrist's card into my pocket. Below it, I see what looks very possibly to be the garage key. I hold it in my hand, unsure whether I should pretend I couldn't find it and come back later and alone to see what vehicle may, or may not, be inside.

'Got it?' Jags walks to me now.

'I think so,' I say, holding up the small chrome key between us.

'Do you want me to try it?' Jags says, his fingers about to pluck the key from mine.

'It's OK. I can do it,' I say, hoping he has not picked up on my growing dread.

We both leave the kitchen, moving back across the gravel towards the garage. We tread over the engine oil stain, Jags either not noticing or choosing not to mention how unmistakably similar it is to the one his car left on the Kensington driveway the night of the awards. I think back again to him in his jogging pants and sliders, the morning after. Tremors are asking to rock my torso. I don't want the lock to open. I don't want to know what's inside the modern garage after all.

I put the key in the lock and effect a determined attempt at turning it.

'Oh damn. It's stuck.' I look to Jags as I yank the key out. 'Won't budge.' I shrug, go to take a step away from the door. 'Not to worry.'

Jags comes to me and takes the keys before I can stop him. 'Here. Let me try,' he says.

The lock gives with ease and Jags yanks the door open with a force that makes me shudder once more. Inside is a car hidden from full view by a silvery sheath but is undeniably not dissimilar in size from a Ford Mondeo. I swallow.

'Go ahead, take a look,' Jags tells me. I know he's picked up on my nerves.

'OK.' I make myself approach the vehicle, hoping he can't see me quaking.

The rumble-bang of the garage door being snapped to a shut behind me makes my breath leave me. And now I want to be on the other side of that door. I don't want to be here, thinking the things I'm thinking, about Jags, about Essie. I wish I could un-take every step that put me behind that garage door, now shut tight.

All the while, Jags watches me calmly. 'Can't be too careful, can we?' he says. 'We don't want Janine finding us snooping

200

around her sister's things, do we?' I find I am frozen. 'Aren't you going to see what's under the cover, April?' Jags looks at me, swipes his head through the air in the direction of the concealed car.

I still cannot move; cannot even inhale the air around me.

Jags steps towards me. I cringe.

'What are you afraid of, April?' Jags says, nearly at my side. I notice a huge pipe wrench hanging on the wall – at least thirty pounds' worth, at a guess – right next to him. If he isn't who I think he is, if he was having an affair with Essie, if he was the one who hurt her, he could now hurt me, use the pipe wrench to crack my brain free from my skull.

'I'm not afr—' I begin.

It happens in a smear of motion, his fist coming towards me, reaching for my head, a blur of skin near my eye as I brace for the impact of his blow.

A sudden puff of air on one side of my face, all of it happening lightning fast but in the slowest of motions.

My eyes squeeze themselves shut.

An inhalation. My last?

Stillness now.

I open my eyes.

Jags holds an awkward armful of silvery covering and appraises the car he has just uncovered, and then me. A white, sleek, if dated, vehicle sits before us.

'A 1989 Lotus Esprit, if I'm not mistaken. I think we can assume, from the leak it left on the way in, this old girl requires some work,' says Jags.

I nod, my eyes closed. Relief and shame flowing over the panic and fear in my veins.

'April,' Jags says it firmly, kindly, but he's clearly exasperated. 'You have to stop doing this to me. You need to stop doing it to us, or how can we keep being an *us*?'

I drop my head into my hands, close my eyes.

'I'm so sorry, darling, can you forgive me?' I ask him. 'My imagination's playing tricks on me. This whole situation is . . .' I let the sentence peter out to nothing.

Jags drops the car cover to the floor and takes me in his arms.

'I can't keep fighting fires with you the whole time,' he murmurs, his mouth next to my ear. 'I don't want to spend the energy I should be using to protect you to defend myself against your suspicions.'

He cradles the back of my head, and the idea he would have considered smashing it appals me. I kiss the side of his face. I kiss him again; my lips now inching across his cheek, towards his mouth. 'It won't happen again, I promise,' I say.

He holds me back from him, two hands on my arms.

'Would you like to know where The Grey Lady is, now you know it's not tucked inside Essie's garage?'

I almost laugh at myself and move to kiss him again. 'Please. You don't have to tell me anything,' I say.

'I had to scrap her yesterday.' He moves away from me, puts his hands in his pocket, and looks upon Con's showy classic car with unhidden envy. He retrieves the covering from the floor and throws it back over the vehicle. 'Sadly, she is no more. There was much more wrong with her than it seemed.'

'Oh Jags, I'm so sorry.' I help him tug the silvery sheath down over the Esprit. 'Let me help you get a new car.'

He smiles a smile so tender I could dissolve. 'I don't think so, but thank you very much anyway.' He comes over and kisses

202

the side of my face, then my forehead before finally moving to my lips, once, twice, three times. And I could devour him, or be devoured, or both, my mind overloaded by desire and longing for him. I kiss him more deeply and he me, before pulling away. 'We need to get back to the plan.' He takes Essie's phone from his pocket and he hands it to me. 'Here, take a look. Have a *snoop*. Tell me, what do you notice?'

'You switched it on already?' My stomach falls away.

'Yes. While you were getting some air. I wanted to check there was nothing nasty waiting for you,' he says, and then, on reading my anguish adds, 'There wasn't. In fact, there was hardly anything at all. Look for yourself.' I begin to tap and scroll, eyes greedily searching for the quickest way into Essie's mind, her life, her secrets. But my desperation is not rewarded.

'Besides the messages that came in after approximately five o'clock on the night of the awards, she's deleted everything: texts, WhatsApp messages, even her call history. All of it—'

'Vanished . . .' I say and we both let the word sit in the air for a moment. 'It's as though she knew someone would be looking through her phone and she wanted to cover her tracks. Why?'

'You know why. Essie's up to something. The wiping of her messages practically confirms it. But that's not all. I had a quick look for J.'

'You know who J is?' I ask.

'Not yet. Essie's got loads of contacts starting with J. I was hoping to find a thread that sounded a bit like whoever wrote that note you took. But there's nothing. No messages, just a bunch of Js in her contacts, but there's something else too. Take a look,' Jags says.

Unlike all the other contacts, which are all organised by

surname, Essie's 'Js' are Christian name first: Jonathan, Janine, Jackson, even the psychologist whose card I found earlier.

'Now. Check out the contact under Jude Lancaster.'

I scroll.

Below Jude's contact. Three words.

Just you wait.

'Look at the number,' Jags says.

I tap on the contact, heart thumping.

'It's the date she disappeared,' Jags says. 'Still think there's a chance she's not fucking with you?'

I say nothing, mouth dry, head fizzing.

'Now, do you know what you'd write on Insta as Essie?' Jags asks me.

I can't help it: I start to hear Essie's voice in my head, something between breezy and reassuring. The headline I'm shooting for is: *Shamed Essie breaks social media silence.* Or, better still, no headline at all.

'Yes,' I whisper.

'Don't you think it's time you went ahead and posted it?'

*

Jags has to get back to his mum, so I spend the next hours alone and nervous at the back of the utility room of the kitchen at Lotus, hiding myself away in case Janine, or even Essie, arrives for some reason. I'm reading and liking comments on the post we put up on Essie's account: a lick of my blonde extensions on one side of a view out onto the pond with some breezy text to go with it. So far, the comments are reassuringly anodyne. My task now complete, I move to leave as quickly as I can.

When I reach the atrium with Essie's phone still in my palm, it trills to life and I immediately panic. Janine. It's all I can do to watch the call ring out and wait for the voicemail. But it doesn't arrive. Instead, Janine sends a lengthy text message straight after her call; the words appear with such speed they give every impression of having been ready drafted:

Esther, good to see you're back at Lotus after getting us all so worried after the awards. However, this does not change what happens next. I wanted to tell you in person, or at least over the phone, I am very worried about you and have been for some time. I do not believe you are in your right mind. I believe, and Dad agrees, you currently lack the mental capacity to make safe decisions about your property and finances. Therefore, I am applying to the Court of Protection for deputyship. Our aim is to ensure you have the flexibility and freedom to live your life how you choose it day by day, including a generous allowance, but to also guarantee people with consistent mental capacity to have the reins when it comes to Lotus Lodge and your investments. We want to ensure everything you have worked for is safeguarded from those people whom we know seek only to exploit you.

With love, as ever, Janine xxx

PS Feel free to call me back to discuss, but I'm afraid my position is currently non-negotiable.

205

The message provokes a surge of feelings, including the distinct clink of the penny dropping. I know story breadcrumbs when I see them, and Janine has been doing this in plain sight. Even if Janine believed Essie had come to harm, why would she pursue the person responsible when there's the small matter of her fortune at stake? With Essie out of the way, the estate Janine has been working to take charge of would be hers; not only that, but the sweet vengeance of finally proving to her parents she was better than the golden child all along. This realisation brings relief, but also outrage on Essie's behalf, and mine. Janine is surely casting me as the villain who almost broke Essie with my film, when she was the person with the darkest of intentions.

I google Dr J. Abiola. She's not only a specialist in PTSD, but has also appeared as an expert witness before the Court of Protection in a number of deputyship cases, which I learn is known as a conservatorship in the US. I would wager everything I own on Janine having sent the doctor Essie's way to help build her case about her sister's inability to control her own affairs.

It's getting late. I don't want to be here at Lotus another moment, and I have to try to get some rest ahead of the screening tomorrow. As I leave, I look around the atrium one last time, imagining this large, still house is not a mausoleum, but only waiting dormant for its mistress to return. I deeply hope the possibility of Essie still being in the world, even if it is only to toy with my sanity, is real. If I can believe this, I can make the most of the screening tomorrow and secure my first-look deal the following day. If I can't, and if Essie is not still alive, there is a chance that very soon what is left of my life will barely be worth living.

I get back to my flat and enter my room for the first time

since leaving with Jags this afternoon. The lunar white dress is lying in a heap on the floor where I left it. And I feel it: the powerful sense that somewhere, Essie is laughing at me, enjoying the slow torture she's inflicting on me: finding 'her body', the oh-so-convenient arrival of her acceptance speech, the inexplicable return of her dress, and, of course, the undeniable message, surely, from this side of the grave: *Just you wait*. I resolve not to blink first.

I gather the gown in my arms and go to throw it in the bottom of my wardrobe. I may have made mistakes, put Essie in a place that left her vulnerable, but if Essie really is alive, then she is putting me through just as much.

A metal scrape on the underside of my forearm.

'Ow!'

I look at my arm: two tracks of raked skin, drops of blood forming. I squat, pinching pieces of fabric carefully between my fingertips, hunting for whatever punctured me. I find two sharp pins, pearls at one end, pushed through a fold of material near the clasp at the back.

The pins hold a soft rectangle of pale blue paper to the dress lining:

Dry Cleaners of Distinction, Theydon Bois

207

21

Essie, before, the first day of shooting

We're back at the old church rehearsal space, the big table cleared to one side for April to direct us moving through the script. She's still acting like April, that low-level awkwardness with herself, but she's also sort of like a put-upon god here, making us do and say things in a certain way, then trying again, encouraging us to reach the point where our actions finally match her vision.

I don't have much to say in this scene, but the camera will be on me as I follow John, Elena's father, and Antonia, the therapist, as we walk circuits of the courtyard, then out into the gardens. My character does this walk daily, and in this scene, John decides to accompany Elena. Antonia tells him she's unsure it's a good idea to mess with Elena's routine. As usual, Elena has no say in the matter, in every sense.

'What I need for you to convey is that you're listening to absolutely everything they're saying, but that you're one hundred per cent not listening,' April tells me.

From across the room, Juniper Jones is watching my reaction with intrigue. So far, she's only speaking to me when we're in character, clearly still upset I was given her role and she was shunted off to play the therapist. I can tell she doesn't think I can take directions like the one April is giving me now, which is making me almost doubt myself. I try to access the little voice inside I've been listening to whenever I have to be on screen, the one that tells me to get on with the job and do exactly what I'm told and then no one can be mad at me.

'Right,' is all I can manage to say to April. She walks back to her spot, perched against the back of a chair, the script pages in her hand and her eyes still fixed on me. I have nothing to say and yet I know the success of the whole scene, the whole movie depends on me. I take a breath, centre myself, prepare to listen to every single syllable and beat of Antonia and John's conversation, and allow the tiniest of micro gestures to show the camera how hard I am trying not to be seen to be listening while revealing nothing of what I'm feeling to my father.

                    ANTONIA
    We could go into the garden if you like,
    but we shouldn't go too far.
                    JOHN
    (blusters, almost jokingly) And how far is
    far enough?
                    ANTONIA
    What do you mean?
                    JOHN
    How far would you go to get what you want?
    (walking, proprietorially)
                    ANTONIA
    Here is fine. It's enough for now.

JOHN
For now.
(He nods and begins to walk past Antonia
and Elena back to the house.)

'OK, thank you.' April calls an end to the scene, and we move on to the next, which I take to mean I've done OK. I catch Juniper's reaction too. She looks quietly but seriously pissed off. I seem to have managed to give April whatever it is she wanted. All I have to do now is to keep being absolutely perfect for the rest of the day.

*

It's dark when I finally leave the rehearsal after what has been one of the most intense and demanding days of my life. I had to bring my all to every single moment. Now, I feel as though I've just come off a rollercoaster. I'm disorientated, in a blur of Essie/Elena. I may have escaped Janine, Jude, or some floor manager or producer telling me what to do and when to laugh, but I have two much more powerful mistresses now: Elena and April, with Juniper assessing every little thing I do, or don't, for good measure.

As I slump in the back of my car on the way home, I feel my heart struggling to beat normally. I'm in practically every scene and each of them asks me to give myself over to it while saying almost nothing; I have to lose myself so Elena can take over. The car feels small, the air close and heavy on me, the pressure, the madness of what I've taken on weighing heavy on my chest. I know why I need to be stronger; what I don't know is how.

Perhaps my session with Dr Abiola tonight will give me a way forward. Our first few meetings have been tough, going over the hurt Jackson caused and the hopes he killed: the babies I will never see, the woman I thought I would be next. I feel as though I could be getting towards some answers, or at the very least the shape of the problem that is me. At the end of today's session, Dr Abiola suggests I may have a form of post-traumatic stress disorder that's led to some kind of disassociation issue. It sounds quite dramatic, and it takes all my strength not to make a silly face and ask her, *Does this mean I'm officially mad?* but I can't find any reason to argue with her. I'm not sure if I've felt totally like one person for years, or if it's the process of being Elena for April that's breaking me further into pieces. The psychiatrist suggests I need intensive sessions for at least six months and, again, who am I to argue with her because, really, who am I at all?

When I finish today's session, it's only nine. I don't want to be alone in my messy, massive house tonight. It's Friday. There's a chance I won't see another soul until Monday morning. I call Janine.

'What you up to?' I ask her.

'Seeing a man about a boat,' she says.

'Right.'

'I'll update you about it tomorrow actually. Huge tax advantages through investing you'd be mad to ignore. If you put just ten per cent of your portfolio in—'

'Do whatever you think is best.' I don't care about *investing* or *tax advantages*. The only thing I care about is not being alone all weekend. 'Are you—'

'Sorry, gotta go. I've told your driver to get you there by eight, sharp, tomorrow.'

211

My mind is still half in the conversation with the therapist, half in Elena's head, and I can't remember what I'm supposed to be doing tomorrow. Janine's voice pokes into my silence.

'The pawnbroker's ad? It might not be luxury skincare or German cars, but it's the best you can do right now. Your little film project isn't likely to pay the bills on Lotus to the end of the year.'

'But you were talking about taking out money to invest in—'

'That's not liquidising assets to pay for day-to-day life, it's a sophisticated means of delivering long-term income while enjoying a lifestyle benefit. You can't afford not to do the ad. Your stock's still bouncing along the bottom. The only thing you've got is not being a diva, so, do yourself a favour, don't trash the last thing you have.'

I wait for my sister to finish. Her words seem to be snipping at my mind, breaking it down into even smaller, colder little pieces. And now, I have the prospect of a whole evening on my own, with only a cut-price shoot with people I don't know on the other side of town ahead of me.

'Janine, I don't suppose you could get any more of those pills for me, could you?'

A pause.

'They can be with you by bedtime.'

'Could it be any sooner?'

'Jesus, you sound like an addict,' Janine says.

'I'm not!' I cry, sounding super-defensive and one hundred per cent like someone who is not using their meds as directed.

With no other option, I call up my driver. 'Can you take me to Crouch End, please?' I tell him, my voice fluid with the shame of knowing I'm about to show up uninvited at April's

212

place. 'Essie? Hi, come up! We were just having dinner,' April tells me down the intercom when I arrive.

'Oh god. I'm so sorry.' I completely hate myself in this moment. 'I'll leave you to it.'

'No! Don't go,' April says, and a second later, the buzzer sounds and the front door into her building releases.

Jags is waiting to greet me at April's door. 'Essie. What an unexpected pleasure.' He says it not sarcastically, but I still hear an edge in his words. I know I'm not welcome, but I go inside anyway, the idea of turning around and finding my driver again even more unbearable than being here. On a small table in between the kitchen and April's living space, a tablecloth, a large bowl of steaming pasta, two bowls, two glasses, two chairs.

'Jags, could you be a love and bring that seat over?' April asks.

'You got it.' Jags drags over an accent chair that's far too low for the table.

'Thank you,' I say, pulling it towards me.

'No, you don't,' Jags says, smiling, as he offers me the better chair instead. His knees come almost to his chest when he sinks into the other seat, stretching to the level of the table to pour the wine. April looks at him lovingly.

I end up staying only long enough to eat a few mouthfuls of pasta and then cry in the back of the car all the way home. My driver doesn't notice or care, or both. I call my dad.

'We're not crying again, are we, girl?'

'No. OK, yes.'

'I told you working with that April was a bad idea. She's no good that one, I'm telling you.'

213

'Dad, can we please not talk about her now. I just needed to hear a friendly voice.'

'I'm not your friend, I'm your dad, and if I don't tell you the truth about things, who will? Speaking of which, your mother saw the story today, the paps caught you on set or some such? Anyway, apparently, that white dress that April's put you in does you no favours and you should get it sorted. Want me to put her on?'

'No thanks, Dad.'

A pause on the end of the line.

'It wasn't me and your mum who fucked it all up for you, you know. You can't blame us for the fact you've been reduced to am-dram in rags for that April.'

'I have to go, Dad,' I say, a cry fighting its way out of my throat again.

'Suit yourself. Oh, don't go crying again. You know you'll always be my number one girl.'

Another gush of tears and I get off the phone before he or I can say much more. I know my dad loves me, so why does he rip me in two?

By the time I get home, the pills are already waiting for me in their little black packet on my doormat. I dive on them, pop two, and wait to feel not like Essie, Esther, or Elena, but the absolute relief of feeling like no one at all.

22

April, the day of the London gala screening

I can't help it: my first thought is that Jags lives with his mother in the same area as the dry cleaners whose tag was pinned inside Essie's dress. But then, I remind myself, so do a lot of other people, including, as a google search tells me, a good number of faces from the TV industry. I'm determined not to jump to any wrongful conclusions again. This is how I operate in my normal writing process; I don't rush to make up my mind, or follow the most obvious arc for my characters. Instead, I truly get to know their lives, their emotional landscapes, the choices they have faced up to the point where I allow the viewer to meet them. Then I permit what feels like an intuitive beginning, middle, and end of the story to reveal itself to me, and then to my audience. And when I was directing *The Vanished Woman*, I didn't design a shot or the lighting to hammer home when a viewer should feel anger, pity, or arousal over Elena, but used my framing to nudge them towards reactions that would feel entirely self-generated.

The journey to the penultimate stop on the eastern end of the Central Line takes half an hour longer than I expected. This means, instead of getting to the dry cleaners before its shutters rise, I have to lurk outside and wait for the steady stream of commuters dropping off and collecting their items to clear.

I feel as guilty and shifty as I ever have since the night I saw Essie in her pool. I've pulled my new blonde hair into a tight bun and have used the brightness of the spring sun as an excuse to wear my sunglasses. I catch my reflection in the dry cleaners's window and am embarrassed to admit I look exactly like a background actor I've told to look mildly suspicious. Then, a thought pokes its way through to the front of my mind: *Will I ever get to cast anyone again? Will I ever get to direct again if I don't get ahead of whatever's going on with Essie?* It's the thought of not ever having that level of control, that kind of power over people and their response to me, those temporary nuclear families I assemble for myself, that drives me inside the dry cleaners.

I've practised what I would say, but now I'm here, looking faintly ridiculous, I feel my words leaving me. I approach the counter slowly, scanning the rack of items awaiting pick-up, looking for some kind of clue. Next to it, a wall of fame. I spy a TV chef, two soap actors, several reality stars, all of them I recognise, but none of whom have names beginning with J.

'Can I help you?' A man in his sixties pulls off his glasses and rests his hands on the counter.

'I wonder if you can. I believe you may have cleaned this dress?' I show him an image on my phone.

He immediately stiffens. 'Yes. We were so very sorry. It's never happened before. We've offered compensation, of course. You work for . . . ?'

I allow myself to think for a moment. 'No.' I look behind me. 'Can I count on your discretion?' I lean towards the man over the counter, he does the same, eyebrows raised, ready for a morsel of something juicy. 'The dress was a gift,' I tell him, 'from an admirer. But I don't know who.'

He nods. 'May I say something?'

'Of course.'

'I can understand that perhaps you may not have wanted it, that perhaps you were somewhat overwhelmed to have received such a gift from someone not declaring their identity, but that was a very fine gown and it smelt as though it had been dipped in chlorine. That's not something you want to do with any garment made of white satin.'

I roll my eyes, making it clear the gesture is at myself. '*I know.* It's a long story, but I was trying to make a point, to get the attention of my *admirer* before I returned it to the sender's address, but it wasn't residential, it was a business. I was wondering if—'

The man behind the counter clears his throat. 'We take the confidentiality of our customers *very* seriously.' He stands back from me and takes a pole with a hook on the end of it and uses it to push along the items awaiting collection on the rail along the wall. 'There is no way I could comment on who may or may not have brought a garment in for dry cleaning.' The man gives me the most peculiar look, as if he's waiting for me to protest. Then, he tilts his head and eyes the patch of wall he's just revealed in an exaggerated fashion.

A signed black-and-white publicity shot I hadn't noticed before grins out at me. The shock must be showing on my face.

'Not who you were expecting?' the man behind the counter asks.

I shake my head as he lets the clothes on their hangers return to cover the photo again.

217

'It was such a beautiful gown. We were, of course, morti-fied when it was stolen.' *Stolen?* 'We've installed more CCTV cameras, as you can see.' He points to three cameras in turn, their red-lit eyes seemingly all on me.

'Stolen, yes. And you didn't see who took it?' I ask.

'Our old camera caught the thief's hand, a bit of arm: dark clothes, a glove. We did report it to the police. Wait, is that how you found us?'

I think on my feet, wanting to stay as far away as I can from anything that might bring me into contact with the police. I shake my head.

'Another slightly complicated story. And a gut feeling.' A customer walks through the door. 'Thank you so much for your help,' I tell the man. 'And for your continued discretion.' I nod and give a little smile, before turning to leave.

'Of course,' I hear the man say demurely, watching me as I leave the dry cleaners as quickly as I can.

I walk back to the Tube, typing feverishly on my phone, sending the message I now know I must.

My phone pings. A WhatsApp notification.

Not from the person I've just messaged, but from a number I don't recognise.

I've been sent a video.

I stop walking, look around me, see who may be watching. A thrust of dread in my chest. I know that I do not want to watch the video and that I have to. I steel myself and tap the play arrow.

Silence. No audio at all.

On my phone's screen, Essie's room. It's in perfect order, nothing like the chaos I saw in Janine's wake the morning after

218

the awards. No noise as the camera slowly takes in the order of Essie's designer bags and shoes, as though viewing the exhibits in a living museum, before moving through her bedroom to enter Essie's dressing room. Now the footage speeds up; it's shaky, more like the 'found footage' you might see in a horror movie. My breathing speeds up, my stomach falls over itself.

The person filming goes into Essie's dressing room. Now, the intruder films their own hand, large, in a substantial black ski glove at the end of a thick arm, also clothed in black, go through Essie's drawers. Some items they appear to be tucking into a bag under their arm, others – bags, shoes, underwear – are left strewn around. They return to Essie's room, pull out more drawers, opens cupboards as though searching for something. Next, they move to Essie's bedside table, one-handedly ransacking each compartment in turn until they find what they are looking for: her jewellery and passport, which they appear to shove in their pockets off-screen. This has to be the same person who stole the white dress. The scene fades slowly to black. Just when I think the video is over and cannot possibly be more sickening, more shocking than it has already proved: a bright flash.

A familiar image.

Essie, facedown in her pool in her white dress.

The camera pans across her still shoulders, the back of her neck visible as her extensions part and float away from her scalp, before the shot switches to trace the line of her arm to her fingers, the black-varnished nails below the water's surface.

The pavement seems to be shifting below my feet. If I don't sit, the ground will rise to meet me.

The final shot.

The camera moves in a way that suggests relish, or, an assured understanding of the art of generating maximum horror on film. Whoever made this has a natural gift for direction.

A shape coming into focus now.

Essie's dress, soaking wet, in a heap on her poolside.

The video ends.

My own scalp feels cold and light. I may faint, right here. I barely manage to stagger to the nearest bench when a message flashes up from the video's sender:

I KNOW WHAT YOU DID. I KNOW YOU HAVE HER PHONE. STOP BEING ESSIE. STOP INVESTIGATING WHAT HAPPENED TO HER. IF YOU DON'T, I WILL EXPOSE YOU. YOUR LIFE WILL BE OVER. JUST YOU WAIT.

I hear someone shriek. A woman swerves to avoid me, and I realise it is me making the noise. I cannot stay here, but I don't know if I can move either. I push myself off the bench and try to make my legs run. I am the star of my own horror movie. I manage a stumbling jog to the Tube, my limbs liquid. Essie cannot be alive now. Everything about that message suggests she has come to terrible harm.

When my phone pings with another notification, I am more afraid than ever to look at it, but the compulsion to see what's going to happen next is even stronger. I must get the truth from whoever knows what happened to Essie before they have a chance of exposing mine. And now, I may be getting closer.

The person I believe is J has agreed to meet me this afternoon.

23

April, the day of the London gala screening

I've used the oldest trick in the book to get J to agree to meet me: the possibility of starring in a movie. I call Jags before heading into the Tube station to tell him about the video, then about J.

'OK, calm down. This doesn't change anything, not really. This is Essie blinking first. In fact, this is our strategy playing out exactly how we want.'

'But Essie couldn't have filmed herself like that.'

'It will be someone on her payroll. Trust me.'

I desperately want to believe him. I take a deep breath, try to refocus.

'Where do you think we should meet him?' I ask Jags.

He doesn't have to think about it. 'It's got to be Lotus. If they've got something to hide, I'd say being back at the scene of the crime, whether that's murder – which it isn't – or setting up the place so it looks like Essie ended herself, it gives you the best bet of catching them off guard.'

'You'll be there, won't you?'

'Of course.'

I take another deep breath before speaking again.

'The dry cleaners, it's actually in your neck of the woods, shall I come and find you? We could get to Lotus together?'

A short pause on the end of the line. 'That would have been nice, but I'm about to get the bus with Mum to a doctor's appointment. I shouldn't be too long, I'll see you there, OK?'

'OK. Please hurry. That video, it's petrifying.'

'I won't be afraid when I see it, I promise you.'

*

When Jags arrives at Lotus just ahead of J's arrival, I show him the video immediately. His composure doesn't alter at all as he watches.

'Well?' I ask.

'There's nothing on here that makes me think the intruder isn't the woman herself.'

'But how did she film her own body in the water? That doesn't make any sense.' And yet the theatrical nature, the staginess, the care of the direction make something about it not quite add up to a robbery gone wrong, or a crime of passion by Jackson, or an act of revenge by Jude. Looking at it again, the whole thing seems crafted. The realisation makes my head feel effervescent again. I jump when I hear a key in the lock.

Jags and I look at each other, the seconds expanding as we wait for the door to open.

'Making yourself at home again, are we?'

I smile over my nerves. 'Hi Janine, here for a swim?' I ask, knowing now she definitely won't be here to swim, or to spend any time with her sister. She's most likely come to retrieve some paperwork, or raid what's left of Essie's jewellery, all in Essie's *best interests.* Whatever she's here for, Janine needs to get it quickly and before she sees J arrive.

'We were about to about have a dip. I think we've just missed Essie.'

Janine comes to where we are in the living space, our bags packed with towels and costumes in preparation for this eventuality.

She looks at Jags and me, clearly appalled to see us there. 'This . . .' she moves her pointed finger between Jags and me, '. . . is weird.' Janine angles her head in the direction of the stairs, then to the entrance to the kitchen. 'She definitely still out?' Janine clearly saw my new post on Essie's Insta, a vista of the heath with a short caption suggesting she was about to 'walk all day alone'.

'Weird?' I feel the threat of colouring-up sweep through me as I refer back to Janine's previous comment.

'Did Esther *really* give you keys?'

'Yes.' I breathe through my relief, happy to be able to say something truthful, but still desperate for her to leave before J arrives. There are too many questions, too many things we know and Janine does not. 'Just after Cannes. She gave me a set and said Jags and I could come to Lotus whenever we liked.'

Janine scowls to herself before getting out her phone and taking pictures of the mess of Essie's living room, walking around me as she snaps the table where I found the note that came with the white dress. The rise of panic now across my breastbone. She needs to be gone. What could Janine be looking for?

'I think it's time Essie got herself a housekeeper again!' I try to joke, as Janine moves to another surface covered with detritus.

223

'Where does she keep her stash of pills?' Janine asks me.

'Pills? What sort of pills?' I say, feigning total ignorance.

Janine spins around and stomps out of the living room up the stairs towards Essie's quarters. Jags and I watch as she disappears, and we listen as she moves about on the floor above. I look at my watch, then at Jags in panic. J is due any minute now. Jags mouths: *It's OK*. I thank god when Janine emerges, running down the stairs at speed, with a small squarish black box that rattles as she moves. As she reaches the bottom of the stairs, she pops it in her bag, satisfied with securing, I'm sure, evidence of addiction to prescription meds to fortify her deputyship case, another piece of evidence to prove Essie should be relieved of everything she's ever worked for. I watch from the doorway to the living room as the front door swings shut. It is nearly at a close when Janine stops and sticks her head in again.

'April!' she shouts.

I walk out into the atrium. 'Yes, Janine?'

'You should stop coming here when she's not around.'

'With respect, Janine, I don't think that's up to you,' I say, trying not to sound as combative as my words doubtless are. A faint narrowing of her eyes and behind them, something being articulated, though not spoken: *Let's see for how long.* Finally, Janine slams the door to a close just as a message arrives in my inbox which only adds another layer to my turmoil. I return to the living room to show Jags, who reads it out loud:

'Hi April, been a while. Great news about Essie's win and, clearly, you should have taken Best Director. The reason why I'm getting in touch is that the truth is, ever since I heard Essie's speech, I've been feeling guilty. I was very hurt when you recast me as Antonia, but I should never have made Essie

224

suffer because of it, as I realise I did. Do you know if she'll make it to the screening tonight? Best, JJ.'

'What should I say to her?'

'Say, you're not sure what her plans are but you hope she comes.'

Jags appraises the message for a moment longer before stroking his chin. 'Maybe Juniper's on Essie's payroll now. She could be the one who filmed Essie's "body".'

I shake my head. 'I'm pretty sure the reason she didn't make the awards was because she was filming in LA.'

'Let's see. Some of that footage in the video looked a bit *professional* . . . Didn't you say Juniper always wanted to direct?'

'Everyone has *always wanted to direct.*' I say wearily and largely to myself, just as Jags's phone goes.

I hear the same rat-a-tat Punjabi, a phrase I've heard him use each time his mother calls: 'Sat sri akaal, pahn-chod.' I mouth it to myself. While Jags is still on the phone doing his usual *Yes, Mum/OK, Mum* routine, I text Juniper back:

Just seen your email. Lovely to hear from you. Trust all is well. I don't know what, if anything, Essie is planning for tonight, but looking forward to catching up shortly. April

I hit send feeling satisfied – there's not an untrue word in the message – when the intercom sounds.

Jags tells his mum he has to go. He and I share a look.

'Could you get that please?' I say.

Jags smiles gravely. 'You've got this, April.' The tips of his fingers find my face, move below my jaw, the sweet point,

225

which lifts me, makes me tingle, makes me believe in our future. 'I believe in you.' He takes a step away from me.

'But you're going to help me, aren't you?' I ask, having sensed him pulling away from me just when I need him most.

'I'll be in the next room, but it'll make no sense if I'm hanging around. I'm no one,' Jags says, somewhat regretfully.

The gate intercom buzzes again. Jags goes to press the button that opens it.

'But you're everything to me,' I call to him.

Jags walks back to me and takes both my hands in his. 'And I can't believe how lucky I am for it.' He kisses my head. Now the doorbell sounds. 'You'd better get that.'

I watch as Jags walks to the kitchen; I know what he says makes sense, but still, even though he isn't far away if I need him, the thought of being in the room with J, the person most likely to have some involvement in Essie's disappearance, sends my heart rate soaring. But what choice do I have than to go to the door? As I notice the dirt and the grime on the floor again, I feel as though I should apologise for the place, for Essie. But then I remember what the person on the other side of this door did to her. I take one final breath before opening it.

There is J.

Brazen.

Blue-white teeth exposed by a sharkish smile.

Perfect hair: grey locks texturised and slightly crispy with a product best used by those twenty years his junior. A pink shirt tucked into thin-legged trousers, the faintest suggestion of makeup on the line of his collar. An architect of Essie's downfall.

'Hello, Jude, lovely to meet you. Thanks so much for coming.'

'My absolute pleasure, though I must say, I was somewhat taken aback by the venue.'

I step away, allowing Jude Lancaster to walk into the atrium, no trace of visible hesitation or guilt. 'Bloody hell. I realise the old tart's struggling, but really, she could get someone to take a duster out every now and then.' Jude casts his eyes about the grimy atrium. 'I had hoped she and I might talk, but assume she's made herself scarce?'

I nod. 'She's been under a lot of pressure. She has had other things on her mind besides housekeeping.'

Jude spins around to face me.

'So, you've obviously seen her since the *Unpleasantness* at the Albert Hall?'

I don't indulge Jude's fishing for gossip and stick to the facts. 'I sometimes work out of here, it's very discreet for important meetings with leading talent.'

Jude smiles demurely while his dark eyes shine with the sense of his own brilliance. 'Quite.'

'Would you like to come through to the pool room?' I say, watching for any signs of guilt, or at least wariness, but find none. I wonder, though, does a man like Jude experience guilt at all? All things being equal, he should have suffered the same fate as Essie, worse in fact. But all things aren't equal, so after a brief spell in rehab for 'sex addiction' and an excruciatingly insincere 'I apologise unreservedly if my actions were unexpected and caused offence', he went almost immediately back to each one of his TV and brand deals. 'Have you been here before?'

'Been here? I found the place.'

227

'Oh, I thought it was her father's idea.' All these men happy to take credit for Essie acquiring Lotus, no sense of her agency, or her money, making the purchase possible.

'Nope.'

We take seats opposite each other on the sofas either side of the vast glass coffee table.

'Can I get you a—'

'It was consensual, you know. She cared about me, I cared about her, still do, despite all those appalling things she said in that dreadful video.'

I take a moment to ready myself. Jude picks up on my intensity and sits forward on his seat, ready to hear what I want to say to him.

'Jude. The part I'm considering you for . . .'

'Yeeess.' His eyes flash with excitement. My god, the vanity of this man: Jude actually believes I would cast him in my next movie.

'I'm requiring whomever I choose to leave their comfort zone well behind.'

'Mmmm. I've heard on the grapevine what you put Miss Esther through. Sounds like you made her beat herself up good and proper.'

I ignore this. To accept anything even faintly critical from him regarding poor treatment of Essie is so ridiculous to be almost comical. 'I need to know from the off you're serious about exploring sides to your character to which you and others are unaccustomed.'

'I have hidden depths, Ms Eden.'

'I'm sure you do. What today is about—'

'You'll tell me more about the part?'

'I will, but first I need to be sure my players are willing to go there; to harness the discomfort.'

'I can assure you I—'

I press the remote control to activate Essie's enormous cinema screen. And there she is, as high as the wall, between Jude and me. Essie in bed, her nakedness barely covered by a white sheet. Post-coital relaxation, unguarded. She does not know Jackson, a self-styled health and fitness influencer and 'man of her dreams', is filming her.

'What really went on between you and Jude Lancaster?' Jackson asks Essie off-camera.

She turns back on her front, rubs her eyes, but keeps them closed. Jackson pans back to himself while off-screen, Essie seems to giggle at the memory. Now Jackson's shot closes in on Essie's face. I watch Jude, defiantly keeping his eyes on the screen, every few seconds looking to gauge my reaction to his apparent absence of discomfort.

'Every Friday after we finished filming for the week,' Essie says, 'Jude would come to my dressing room and help me choose what I would wear for next week's shows from the racks of clothes we got sent. It was normal for me to be in my underwear, sometimes not really in that, if Jude thought my bra straps were showing.'

'Did he touch himself?' Jackson asks off-camera.

Essie gives a girlish laugh. 'He did.'

I look to Jude who's attempting to appear unmoved, almost bored.

'When did it stop?' Jackson asks.

'When the eighteen-year-old TikToker landed a gig as the new soap correspondent,' Essie says, and then there's her laugh again. 'She's his target now. The cheeky uncle who makes all the ladies giggle . . . He's still doing it, you know?'

The video ends. I've watched it a hundred, perhaps a thousand times, but seeing the video that ended her happiness, got Essie cancelled, aligned her to predators like Jude Lancaster, made her so lonely and desperate she would agree to work for me, still has a certain shock factor. I take a deep breath, turn off the projector, and focus on Jude, who now seems to be affecting tears. I've always thought there was a certain cheesiness about his screen presence, a campness in the flesh, but these fake tears, which he is now attempting to dab from his dry eyes, have taken this to a whole other plane.

'I can see you're very moved,' I say.

He looks to his lap then sweeps his grey head up to meet me in the eye. 'I'm not the man I was. I have received treatment. I did wrong by these women, but a man can change and grow and deserve to explore new things, even, in fact *because* of past wrongs. I appreciate every opportunity God gives me now, after my humbling.'

'You said it was consensual.'

Jude's glance skims mine momentarily. 'Perhaps I was kidding myself. Maybe I've been an old fool longer than I've known.' He smiles ruefully before brightening. 'Perhaps this is something I can call on for the part?'

I nod. 'The role is a man who's wounded women, who's repulsed women.' I pause to assess his response. His features stiffen almost imperceptibly, but I see it clearly. Jude Lancaster is a man who hates women, particularly when they are in control, as I am now. 'You realise if we agree the part is right for you, you will have to submit to what I need from you every

230

day?' I say, and if there has ever been a moment I have extracted a sliver of enjoyment from any of this, it is now.

'It would be my life's honour.' Jude bows his head, his hair barely moved by the gravity that wants to bring it down.

'I don't respond to flattery or any gifts you might send me, like Essie did.'

Jude looks up at me quizzically.

'The white dress,' I say. 'Essie showed it to me.'

'That was Essie's?' Jude's face collapses into each one of its wrinkles, the foundation, I imagine, concertinas like grease around his eyes. '*That* white dress?'

'Yes. I thought you'd bought it for her, by way of an apology, perhaps?'

He shakes his head. 'Apology? Noooo. It was the most peculiar thing. That dress showed up at my house before I left for the studio, the night after Essie's little speech via her charming sister. There was no postmark, not even an address, it arrived in an unmarked black plastic postbag. I honestly don't know how it reached me. And the state of it.'

'What kind of state?' I ask.

'It was soaking wet.'

I don't say anything, merely make a face suggesting I find what he's telling me as strange as he does.

'I didn't know what to do with it,' Jude continues, 'so I called my dry cleaner to collect it, and a day later, they call to tell me the thing'd been nicked! The whole thing was completely bizarre. Do you think Essie thought it was from me, then returned it soaked through as some kind of protest?'

I shrug. 'I don't always know what goes on inside her mind.' It's true; try as I might to make it otherwise.

Jude resets himself in his seat, clearly eager to change the subject, swap the topic of conversation from Essie to him. 'I have to say, I was surprised but thrilled when my agent said you wanted to sound me out about the part. I'd heard from a Hollywood pal of mine you had your heart set on Martin Russo as your silver fox for the next project.'

I only sent Martin's agent the script yesterday. How quickly news travels when celebrities of his magnitude are involved. The scrutiny and speed of this finding its way into the outside world at once excite and appal me. If I don't get ahead of this situation soon, it will surely get well ahead of me. I take a breath and recompose myself.

'Jude, in our industries, I think you and I both know we shouldn't believe everything we hear.' I glance back to the screen where Essie's video has just played. 'Or see.'

*

I spend another half an hour with Jude, asking much of him, but promising nothing in return. He feels no remorse about what happened to Essie after the video, compared with what happened to him. He cannot see the injustice of it. But while our time together confirms he is indeed a dreadful human being, it's not done anything to convince me he is implicated in whatever Essie may be up to. He has no motivation; he's lost nothing in the whole Essie cancellation debacle, and besides, his story checks out against what the man at the dry cleaners said.

I send Jude away and wash my hands many times after he leaves. And when Jude Lancaster's agent calls mine for feedback, it will be with some relish that I ask him to communicate that having met him face to face, I find Jude wholly unsuitable for any role in my work now or at any point in the future.

Jags returns once Jude has left.

'What did you make of that?' I ask him.

'Essie's messing around with Jude's head like she's messing around with yours.'

'You think so?'

'I know so.'

My phone rings. It's my agent, telling me that Martin Russo's agent is keen to speak as soon as possible about *The Longest Road*. I'm thrilled, but now I need to get back to my place to prepare, rehearse how I'll pitch to his LA-based people that April Eden is the director who has the King of Hollywood's next project. And then somehow I'll have to get myself in the zone for the gala screening of *The Vanished Woman*.

'Will you come back with me to my flat, so we can get ready for tonight together? I could even introduce you to Martin's agent if there's an appropriate moment,' I ask Jags as breezily as I can, aware I'm dangling the opportunity of making a connection that could lead to future work to help entice him to my place.

'I'd love to, but Mum needs me to do something for her.'

'Of course.' I swallow the disappointment in my voice, but I'm becoming so very tired of only getting what sometimes feels like the dregs when I need the best of him. 'One day soon, I'd like it if you put what I need to the top of your list. Not every time, not right now, but soon.'

Jags comes to me, kisses me on the forehead by way of an apology. 'I'm going to call a cab. Call you one?'

'No. I'll walk.' I plan to start getting my red-carpet patter ready as I do. I leave Jags at Lotus waiting for his ride and I make my way back down Highgate Hill alone.

*

As I walk, instead of focusing on the potentially life-changing task in hand of preparing to wow Martin Russo's agent, I find myself processing all that's happened today. After so many developments, my trail of clues seems to have come to a maddeningly dead end. By the time I reach my flat, I know I'll have to improvise my pitch to the LA agent. I sense another opportunity, another night ahead of my life that should have felt sweetly triumphant, turning sour and soiled because of Essie. I'm beginning to feel no longer aggrieved, but angry and frustrated.

If only I could see Essie's call history, who was she contacting, colluding with, if she really did fake her own death for my benefit. And even if it wasn't fake, who was the last person to speak to her? Was there someone who ensured she was home alone at Lotus so they could do what they did, if they did anything at all?

It's more in hope than expectation that I google 'Is there any way you can recover a phone's deleted call history' as I wait for the agent to join our Zoom. With something called a phone rescue app I discover it is indeed possible.

And I manage to do it.

The agent is running ten minutes late, according to his

assistant, when I restore Essie's texts, her messages, and her call log, the thing my gut is telling me to focus on. At first there are no particular surprises; multiple calls and texts to Jonathan, Janine, me. But there's someone else. An unnamed contact. She calls the number many times a day. On the day we found her facedown in her pool, I count no fewer than six calls. This was the very last person she must have spoken to before Jags and I arrived at Lotus, approximately forty minutes before we left for the awards and then told Janine to check on Essie.

I decide to dial the number with my phone, not Essie's.

Whoever answers this call, they surely will know exactly what happened to Essie and where she is now. I draw a deep, adrenalised breath, my finger poised above the dial button.

'April! Can you ever forgive me?' Martin Russo's agent fills my screen. 'Damned actors! Always some crisis, right?'

'Yes. Always,' I say, laying the phone down, the tantalising number waiting to be dialled. Essie's mystery contact will have to wait.

*

I manage to acquit myself surprisingly well throughout the hour-long call, even when I have to interrupt it halfway through to let in my hair stylist and makeup artist (I've decided to wear my Essie-like hair in an updo so as to not risk being accused of trying to ape my much better-looking muse). Perhaps I do so well on the call because I realise getting Martin Russo on board and securing my deal feels very much like they are life-or-death matters. I'm facing a scenario that will either make my life, if I still have one to live freely, or kill all my hopes.

235

There's barely any time to get ready before I'll have to leave for the screening, further postponing my call to the person who must know what happened to Essie. I don't have either the time or the privacy to call now, but when I come back from the screening, I will finally have the chance to discover at least some of Essie's secrets.

24

April, the night of the gala screening

The makeup artist has only just left when Jags arrives so we can take a car together to the screening. To help steady our nerves, I'm ready with two glasses of that fine whiskey we drank two days ago, the last time we had sex. When I let him into my flat, I notice Jags is carrying a black leather holdall, which makes me feel hopeful he might stay over tonight, but I don't say anything for fear of scaring him off. Still, I wonder if my bit of Punjabi might impress him as he leans in to kiss me on the cheek.

'Sat sri akaal, pahn-chod,' I say, handing him his glass.

Jags features twist with unvarnished disgust. 'What did you just say?'

'Sat sri—'

'Don't!' He walks away from me and swigs his whiskey down in one. 'Just don't.'

'I'm sorry,' I say meekly, reeling from his repulsed reaction. 'I assumed it was some kind of pleasantry. I thought I've heard you say it to your mum when she phones.'

'You heard wrong.' Jags sighs and appears to regroup. 'I'm sorry . . . You look great, by the way,' he says somewhat functionally. I had so hoped he might look at me and do that thing I've seen some men do to women like Essie: hold my arms up so they're either side of him, lean back to take all of me in. Now, I've ruined it. I turn away from him, throw my whiskey down in one glug, and pray the night will improve from here.

Jags gets the notification to say the car is waiting for us outside and we leave without saying much more to each other. We're almost out of the entrance to my building when he realises he's left his holdall upstairs. I give him my keys and watch him run back up, my chest heavy with hurt over him clearly not planning to stay with me tonight after all.

I'm still wondering about the words I swear I've heard him use whenever he answers a call from his mother, so I pull up Google Translate on my phone. It takes me a couple of attempts but soon enough, I understand why he was so taken aback. As Jags jogs back to the car, bag in hand, I kill the screen that tells me I apparently greeted my boyfriend with the words: 'Hello, sister-fucker.'

Why would he say what is apparently one of the most offensive things you can say in Punjabi, to his beloved mother? Perhaps she's not as beloved as Jags has had me believe. Or perhaps the person on the end of the line isn't his mother at all.

Jags reaches for my hand in the backseat. This time, it is me who is reticent to return his affection.

*

Hundreds of people from my industry, many household names, dozens of esteemed stars (and a good number of would-be stars and reality-show regulars, if Jonathan has anything to do with it) are waiting to watch *The Vanished Woman* in Leicester Square tonight. Some are film lovers, but others, many others in fact, are mostly here to see and be seen on the red carpet and at the post-screening VIP reception in the rooms above the cinema.

I step out of the car and the camera flashes begin. I want to walk on by. I don't want to smile over my churning emotions alone, as Jags lurks out of frame, out of step with who I want him to be. But they bray and shout at me to move, to turn, and then to walk on and make room for the next woman. It's only after I walk away that my compliance to the demands of those yelling men, mostly white and the same age as my father, strikes me as absolutely extraordinary. When did women sign this off? When did we accept as normal that men like those photographers are entitled to scream at women who have the kind of fame and impact they can only ever imagine and never achieve? They command us to twist our bodies this way and that, strike coquettish poses, and we signal to them it's completely OK by complying. Essie never told anyone it was acceptable to pursue her like they did, writing all those terrible things about her without a thought, and yet she never really appeared to rebel. Until now. Perhaps. How did a whole system, including its victims, tacitly endorse the horrific things happening every day to famous women?

I stagger through the subsequent excruciating red-carpet interviews where I manage to dodge questions on whether Essie will show up. I'm so thankful when Jags and I are finally shown to our seats. The house lights will go down and I'll have some respite for the duration of the screening.

But any relief is extinguished. Before the lights dim, there's a tap on my shoulder.

'Hey, April.'

It's Ed. The commissioner who dangled a first-look deal before me at the Albert Hall and with whom I have a make-or-break meeting tomorrow.

'We're still on for tomorrow, but wanted to give you the heads-up about something in case you hadn't seen or heard.'

'OK,' I say, catching Jags's eye. I know I'm not going to like whatever Ed says next.

'There's some crazy shit starting to swill about Essie. I don't know if this is some genius PR stunt, but I just got a tip-off that a very reliable source is about to break the story that – and this is ridiculous – that Essie really is dead or something, that she killed herself the night she won Best Actress and has been timing her social posts, or some batshit. I know, sick, right?'

'That's crazy,' I croak, blood sweeping across my arms and décolletage.

'Totally, *totally*,' Ed says. 'I mean, she's showing up tonight, isn't she? My assistant said her social posts seem pretty upbeat. Be great if she'd put in appearance, put all the other nonsense to bed.' He looks over his shoulder, as though Essie might be about to surprise him, or me.

'It would, but I wouldn't bet on it,' I say. 'I mean, she's fine, but I think the whole process has taken quite a bit from her, if I'm honest.'

'Mmm, mmm. Anyway, if you were able to get word to your leading lady to, you know, show her face at some point, call off the dogs, it would very strongly be in your interests ahead of tomorrow. Oh and . . .' he looks over his shoulder while raw panic surges through me at the thought of the

240

whole sorry story unspooling, my life with it, '. . . if you wanted to close on Russo, now would be a very good time.'

'Martin Russo is here?'

Of all the things he could do tonight in London, Martin Russo has chosen to come to a screening of my film. He must be getting serious about attaching himself to *The Longest Road*, which in any other circumstances would have me punching the air. But now, thanks to my dreadful choices, I must live even the most brilliant moments of my life in a kind of purgatory, constantly crushing me somewhere between hell and an almost reachable heaven.

'He is indeed,' says Ed. 'And he looks *ready to party*, if you know what I mean. I'll see you tomorrow. Hopefully we'll both have good news for each other?'

'Hopefully,' I say.

Ed disappears into the gloom of the movie theatre behind me. I look to Jags who's been listening to my conversation with Ed.

'I thought she might pull something like this,' Jags says, before moving to lift his bag onto his knee. He unzips it enough so that I, but no one else, can see what's inside.

I gasp.

Essie's white dress.

'Why did you bring that here?!' I whisper.

'People need her here. After it's over, at the end, you let your hair down, get the dress on, and let's get Essie papped from behind. I mean . . .' Jags leans in closer to me, whispering into my ear, '. . . you fooled me.'

'Oh god.' I look around me, end up giving a couple of members of *The Vanished Woman* crew two rows behind a weak

241

wave. 'I can't. Not here. Not ever.' I may as well turn myself in, I consider, but then when I imagine it, the things I'd have to admit, I harden against the possibility.

'Listen,' Jags says, 'get the right picture out there and the internet will just about break with images of Essie's secret re-emergence into public life. Then you can walk off into the sunset with your next feature, we finally get to work together, and Essie crawls out from wherever she's been hiding and asks you nicely for her part back. Sounds like the story only needs to hold long enough for you to seal the deal.'

It's true. He's right. If we can only persuade the world Essie has not gone forever, long enough for my contract on my first-look deal to be announced, with Martin Russo signed on to *The Longest Road*, then all of this madness would have been worth it. Can I do it? Is the risk worth taking? Or would doing what Jags is proposing only confirm my monstrousness, my dark dedication to my career in the context of a life that's not delivered any other joy? But god knows, if I do go through with it, I won't be the first woman who sacrificed so much in the name of surviving long enough to make a Hollywood movie.

Applause breaks out around me. But instead of warm and flattering, it sounds tinny and mocking, with the commissioner's sickening warning in my ear, my life-changing deal hanging by the thread of a fraying lie. And if I'm shown to have concealed a murder or tampered with evidence, impaired a proper investigation, then forget my career; my freedom, surely, is on the line too.

The film is about to begin, but rather than burst with nerves over the audience's reaction to my first feature film, the project my whole life has been building up to, my stomach instead brims with dread over one notion: how do I become Essie Lay tonight and get away with it?

*

I look at the screen, at wonderful Essie in all her brilliance again, but while the audience is rapt, Jags walks me through his plan. Once the screening is over and the party gets going, I'll slip on Essie's dress and get Jags to tip off the paparazzi as I disappear into the VIP area, which they cannot enter. I know there's a storage room where the sponsors are keeping goody bags and bottles of gold-flecked rum for the party. Locking myself in there to transform into Essie and then back into April once the job is done is my best bet. Once the press get their stolen image of 'Essie', we'll head up to the roof terrace and post an image on Essie's Instagram of me from behind, overlooking Leicester Square.

As the final credits are finishing, I make myself mentally sidestep the many risks, the ludicrousness of the whole escapade, to focus on how I might direct myself best to be Essie. I think of her dancing, her back curved, her arms pointed out before her. Shot from behind, with the white dress, my extensions down my back, I could create the illusion of the silhouette of Essie in all her glory. If my visual impression fooled my boyfriend, surely it will be persuasive enough to convince the paparazzi?

'Get up.' Jags voice cleaves into my thoughts.

'What?'

'Get up,' he repeats.

The house lights are on. People are standing, clapping. I was

243

so lost in my scheming, I'm missing my own standing ovation. This moment, this sound, this place, this entire scenario is something I've dreamt about, fantasised about for decades; the disinfectant for all my life's disappointments, my loneliness, but now that it's happening, I'm not really here. I stagger uneasily to my feet and stand for the most fleeting of seconds to take my applause before it dies. I fall back in my seat again. The moment to savour, the window to feel if not loved, then at least admired and appreciated in the home town of my choosing, now lost.

I move up to the VIP areas through handshakes and hugs, against a soundtrack of compliments; endless, overwhelming compliments like I've never known. Ed tells me my work is one of the greatest British films of all time while embracing me like I've already saved his job. I should be loving every second, but instead every kind word, each gesture of reverence leaves me feeling sick and unworthy.

The party gets underway, and I lose the worst of my nauseous panic to a large gold-flecked rum. I lose Jags too, who seems to be in a more sociable form than I've ever known him to be, hobnobbing with some of the crew, chatting to the cast. I only ever saw him like that at the wrap party, the night I thought I may have found a genuine partner in Jags, those hopes now as frayed as my nerves. Normally, I would want to summon him, ask him to be by my side tonight, prop me up, but I'm beginning to feel as though I no longer want to ask any more from him. If my relationship with Jags had three acts – act one being when he first came into my life, act two being when he appeared to have deep feelings for me – then I get the distinct feeling we are deep into act three, possibly our final act, our story having run its course.

As I drink my third gold-flecked rum of the night, I realise the thing I want most is for someone to give themselves to me willingly, to abandon their needs to satisfy mine, to tell me all the reasons I should be loved, to make me know this, regardless of whether my career is a startling success or a disaster, whether I'm thrown to the dogs for what I've done to Essie, regardless of whatever I am, that they love the essence of me. I know, I have always known inside me, Jags is not that person. I should have known how easy it is for someone to lie to themselves and yet it's a trap I have thrown myself into with Jags.

But I cannot tell Jags this now, nor can I put off the immediate task in hand any longer. I retrieve Jags from an animated conversation with my casting director, bristling that I need him to halt his schmoozing to help enact the plan which, after all, was his idea. I feel very alone, even as the two of us head as discreetly as we can away from the crowds and up to the storage room. Jags hands me his bag. He doesn't kiss me, or wish me luck, only disappears back down to where the paparazzi are waiting. I am alone in the storeroom, and alone in my life. Jags is no partner. He isn't a man I know well enough to love or be loved by; like me, he's a self-interested person on the make who feels life owes him more than the hand he's been dealt.

It is not because I trust Jags that I take off my own gown, free my hair from its updo, and pull the white dress from his bag, ready to go through with tonight's strategy. It's because I have no idea what else I might do to play the hand I have any better.

Essie's dress is creased and does not look as glowing as it once did. But nonetheless, as I slip it over my head, let it hold my breasts and waist and smooth the shape of my thighs, I feel the transformative power of the garment once more. The way

245

it's designed to push the female body into a perfect shape, even mine, gives me an injection of momentary satisfaction.

I'm inside the room for a couple of minutes, hiding behind the door, waiting anxiously for Jags's text telling me to get to the agreed-upon spot in time to be papped from behind. After a few minutes more, the dress is beginning to dig into the flesh above my hips, the central band bites into my natural waist; the rigidity of the built-in corset feels like it is chaffing the sides of me. In fact, the dress feels as though it's trapping me, as if it hates the body it has captured. And it hits me. *This* is what being Essie Lay was really like, pushed and pulled to make something desirable for all who may view her, regardless of the pain this may cause to the object beholden. Far from propping up her self-esteem and making her feel loved and wanted, it must be truly miserable to be as watched, as invested in by others, as Essie Lay.

Jags's one-word text cuts into my epiphany about Essie.

Now.

Feeling startlingly sober, my heart banging within my constricted chest, I open the door. I head to the side entrance to the VIP area and stand there, my back to the landing outside it, my head down, as though simply messaging someone privately on my phone away from the A-list throng.

After an agonising wait of only a few moments, I hear sounds behind me. Men snapping their cameras, panting up the stairs. They don't say her name, yet, trying to capture her unawares, to take a picture of her arse before she knows what is happening. Then, the noise begins.

'Essie! *ESSIE!* Made any more video nasties recently?'

'Turn around, love, let's see 'em.'

'To me, Essie. Come on, give it up!'

'Where've you been, Essie?'

'You're supposed to be dead, aren't you, love?'

At these words, at the sense of the pack of them closing in on me, I flash my access-all-areas wristband, push through the security guards, my head still down. The security guard holds the snappers at bay as I head past the VIP area, back to the storage room, their enraged shouts as I disappear telling me I've achieved what I needed to: the media have their sighting of Essie; I have my breathing space. But for how long? My actual breathing is seriously restricted in the dress, it emerges from me quick and hot, as on the other side of the door, I can still hear the paparazzi calling for Essie. What if one of them manages to get in and sees I'm not her? I've committed no crime, I tell myself. They merely assumed I was Essie. The press mistook me for their target. They only have themselves to blame, not me. I close my eyes and attempt to level my breathing within the tight tube of white satin I cannot wait to remove. I'm about to release the clasp at the back of the neck when the door handle turns.

My breath stops entirely as the door begins to open.

I'm trapped.

'Can I get out this way? . . . Well hello there.'

I gasp.

'Didn't mean to scare you,' he says.

'You didn't,' I say, so relieved, then stunned.

Martin Russo takes a step towards me, a powerful vapour of rum radiating from him.

'Maybe you were a little . . . surprised?' he drawls, and I nod dumbstruck. He takes another step. 'Is it a good surprise?' Now, his hand is on my waist, as the other moves to brush the skin down my neck. I could die right here.

'The best,' I hear myself say before I can think of anything else.

He kisses me.

Martin Russo, his lips smooth and muscular, his cheekbones now under my fingertips, kisses me, April Eisdale. Martin Russo is kissing *me,* the backs of his soft knuckles skimming the skin below my jaw, my whole body pulsing with love for myself in this moment because *he* wants *me.* I am imperial, immortal. I am desire. I have no thoughts of Jags, only Martin Russo's body, which I pull to me, before slipping my fingers into his famous hair.

Our kissing is becoming more heated, more needy. Where could this go? Where might I take it?

'You're so beautiful, Essie.'

My heart falls.

Martin Russo wasn't kissing April, but another woman, a better one, one people love so very easily: Essie.

'Martin. I'm April Eden, the director.'

He blinks through his drunkenness, an inebriation that serves to reassure me he won't be rushing to tell anyone he was so out of it that he confused the director for the leading lady in a store cupboard tryst. After a beat, Martin's Hollywood gentleman persona seems to take over, and for one horrible moment, I feel like a member of the public. I'm truly April Eisdale again: unexceptional besides her determined inability to form meaningful relationships; outside of love.

248

'April . . . Ap-ril. *Sure*. That's what I said, what I meant.'

He almost goes to kiss me again but stops himself. I stand myself straight while he clears his throat.

'I'm glad we bumped into each other, actually,' I tell him.

'Oh yeah?' He smiles, the utter gorgeousness of his fêted dimples still punching through my disappointment.

'If you don't get your Oscar this year . . .' I begin, calling to mind how the buzz seems to be turning against him amid his custody battle, not to mention his war with alcohol, which he is clearly losing, '. . . you know my project is the one that's going to give you another shot. I'll forgive you for calling me by another woman's name if you commit to attaching yourself to it.'

'Ha!' He looks at the ceiling, then me, as though viewing me for the first time. 'You're tough. I like that. And my agent loves the script and your pitch today.' His half-closed eyes regard all of me again. 'I gotta feeling you could be pretty good for me, Ms Eden.'

He moves into my space once more. And I let him, because this time he's coming for me, not Essie. We kiss again. My phone goes. I break away from Martin to look at it: Jags.

'That your boyfriend?' Martin asks.

I don't answer him, only let his lips find the skin of my collarbone. The deliciousness of the sensation gives way to the realisation Jags has never kissed me there. My so-called boyfriend has barely kissed me anywhere.

My phone sounds a text notification. Jags again. Martin sees my troubled reaction and steps away from me, holding his hands in the air in surrender. 'Looks like you've got somewhere you gotta be.'

249

'I do. Tonight, I do,' I say, my body crying out for more of Martin, my mind grasping that it can't have that now.

'So, what about tomorrow?' Martin drops his blue eyes to the floor before sweeping them up to meet mine and examining my face as though he wants to find a way into my soul. It's as arousing as any touch.

I kiss Martin Russo's iconic mouth a final time.

'Tomorrow, everything can change.'

I make myself leave Martin, escaping the storeroom via the service staircase to head up to where Jags is waiting on the roof terrace. There's an air of strange triumph about him as the wind blows around him against the gaudily illuminated night down in Leicester Square. I don't really know who this man is; I don't feel guilty in the slightest about what I've just done with Martin Russo.

'I can't believe I pulled that off!' Jags says, apparently blown away by his own brilliance, too wrapped up in himself to note the telltale smear of my lipstick, the change in me. 'If it isn't already,' he says, voice soaked in self-congratulation, 'what I set up is about to light up newsrooms across the world, but let's give them that one last shot.' He takes out Essie's glinting phone. 'Go on, stand there so I can shoot you from the back and we'll post it on Insta like we agreed.'

The lingering taste of Martin Russo in my mouth, the sense I'm moving into thrillingly dangerous territory, fills me. I go to the edge of the terrace and look below, onto Leicester Square, a place that everyone new to London believes is the absolute epicentre of town. I know now this isn't true, but tonight, I do not care. Standing with my back curved, I point my two fingers out across the square, tilting on my hips, aping Essie's dance moves, as though the whole of London's film industry, as if the King of Hollywood, all belong to me.

Then, I drop my arms, turn, and walk back to Jags. I put my palms firmly on each side of his face, and I kiss him, thinking all the while of the hot muscularity of Martin's mouth as I sense the flaccid reluctance of Jags to my apparent passion. I pull back from him.

'I don't want to post that picture, Jags. I don't need to. It's not going to happen.' I drop my hands away from his face, catching a glimpse at his confusion, then anger that I'm deviating from his will. I turn my back to him.

A phone rings. Mine.

Janine's name on the vibrating screen.

I don't answer it.

'I'm getting out of here,' I say, moving towards the exit.

'Well, I'm coming too!' Jags says following me, sounding uncharacteristically desperate to be by my side.

I run back inside and sneak into the stairwell where I can change out of Essie's white gown and back into my own dress, Jags acting as lookout. I pull my hair into a non-descript pony-tail, and then we leave, managing to jump into a black cab on Charing Cross Road without speaking to anyone, or each other.

My phone rings again. Janine. Jags watches the screen warily as the ringing dies unanswered. He shakes his head, just as his phone goes too. His less than cherished 'mother', her timing impeccable, as usual. Something in Punjabi I don't recognise, and then: 'I'll be coming home soon, OK? Not long to wait.'

Jags finishes up on his call and my phone rings once more. Janine again.

'You'd better answer that, April.'

'I don't want to.'

'Answer it.'

Jags's finger manages to reach my screen, swiping over it to accept the call. I glare at him while the sound of faint weeping fills the taxi. I tentatively put my ear to the phone.

'April?'

Janine's voice sounds like a wounded child's. I know what she's going to say before she speaks the words.

'It's Essie! They've found a body! Come over! We're all at Lotus.'

ACT IV

'Your hand determines the power of your characters and to what extent they appear in control of what is happening to them. It might be you show your main player leading the way through a scene, pushing the action forward almost at the power of their will. Or you could choose to move the camera in a way that seems to drag the main character through whatever your story decides to put them through, and to which they might naturally seek to resist.'

FILM SCHOOL LECTURE NOTES TRANSCRIPTION

25

April, back then

'Esther's friends stopped coming to Signal House last summer. I rather liked it that way,' said Janine to her window, me sandwiched between her and Essie in the backseat of Una's SUV. I watched Una glance into her mirror to gauge my reaction to her eldest's sniping, a look that appeared to tell me she was in quiet agreement with her Janine.

'Janine,' Essie cautioned without too much conviction.

'Do *your* friends stay often?' I asked Janine, even though I could tell this was not the case. I could recognise that she, rather like me, carried the tang of immediate unlikability, or perhaps for her it was simply a case of paling into insignificance against her infinitely more compelling younger sister.

Janine ignored my question; Una changed the subject.

'You're not crying again are you, Esther? It was only a few weeks of your life. You didn't really imagine you were serious?' Two days earlier, the footballer had been photographed leaving the hotel room of not one but two 'mystery blondes'.

'You and Daddy got serious pretty quickly,' Essie responded glumly. Inside, I winced not only at this idea but also at the girlishness of Essie's *Daddy*, while Con himself, who was driving, flashed a huge grin, but not at Una. Instead, he seemed pleased with himself for bagging her so comprehensively, perhaps satisfied at the memory of keeping his starlet dancer earthbound with a pregnancy.

Ignoring Essie's comment, Una said, 'All this drama seems a bit much for someone you hardly knew.' She gave a self-regarding shrug to the windscreen.

'I knew him. I knew him just like Daddy knew you were the one for him,' Essie told the motorway verges skimming past her window.

'You thought you did, anyway,' I said sympathetically. Janine rolled her eyes and puffed out a breath through her teeth. Con, meanwhile, seemed as though he appreciated my kindness to Essie. He smiled at me, and I politely smiled back.

We pulled into the driveway of Signal House. There was no point in me trying to 'play it cool', even if I knew how. The house, a great palace of white render and glass, was stunning; it looked like a superyacht stranded on dry land. A housekeeper emerged to greet us and took all our luggage in, including mine, which made me feel embarrassed somehow. But how lightly the Laycocks wore their wealth: no guilt, no shyness, just a wholly assured ability to hand over the heavy lifting to lesser people, and focus on living the best of lives.

We went inside. Con seemed to monitor me as I headed towards the wall of glass at the back of the vast, open ground floor. The scale of the place alone was overwhelming, and the view past the manicured lawn to the hidden foreshore and then out to the water created the sense we were only a short stroll from a sea of diamonds. It took my breath away. I hardly noticed the faint smell of sewage emanating from somewhere,

256

or that Con had arrived to stand next to me. I could tell he was not admiring the view, rather my reaction to it.

'It's nice to see someone really appreciating this place,' Con said, hands in his trouser pockets. I turned to him and as close up as he was in the moment, I could see his eyes were an amalgam of colours, like Essie's; an odd familiarity that disarmed me.

'I could wake up to this view every day and never take it for granted!' I blustered.

'I'll bet,' Con said. And there was something in his tone, the way his voice slid up and down the syllables, that made me not want to look at him, even though, in fact especially because, I could feel his eyes on the side of my face. I wanted to say something like, *I didn't mean it like that*, but to call out his tone as laced with innuendo would be to somehow create the very lasciviousness I sought to neutralise. This particular type of silence, I have come to realise, was one of the defining features of young womanhood.

'April,' Una called from the foot of the spiral staircase that dropped into the centre of the great room from the floor above. I don't know how long she had been stood there. 'Let me show you to your room.'

'Thank you, that would be great,' I said, meekly smiling at Con, then at Una, who was resolutely unsmiling as I left her husband to follow her up the winding column of stairs onto the wide corridor above. I noticed, as I ascended, there were cracks here and there in the plaster and that the treads were a little lopsided, but in that moment, they only seemed to lend an additional charm to the place. As I followed Una down the first-floor corridor, I passed the sound of muffled crying from a bathroom: Essie. Una ignored the sound of Essie's pain. She also pretended not to see Janine slam her bedroom door as I went by.

'Here we are,' said Una when we had reached the very end of the walkway. She opened the door to a small room that looked like a study. I walked inside and with a flick of her chin, she gestured to two white towels, one large, one smaller, folded on the small single day bed inside. 'Don't walk around in them.'

'That's not the sort of thing I generally—' I started to say but was cut off.

'Gin on the lawn at seven,' Una said as she closed the door while still speaking, perhaps indicating she'd prefer it if I stayed on the other side of it for the hour and a half until then.

I dropped my bag on the floor and flopped onto the slim bed. Despite Una's chill, I was delighted to have a couple of nights at Signal House, away from the bank, in luxurious surroundings, and with Essie. I closed my eyes and tried to savour the moment when, despite myself, I thought of my own parents' home. I wondered for a moment if my father and mother ever talked about me and if they did, was it with hope that I might one day 'come to my senses' and apologise for leaving them behind? Or was it, as I suspected, with resentment: the only child they conceived had proved so unlike them? I opened my eyes to derail this train of thought and gasped when I found Janine's face peering at me from across the room.

A hideous wall of photos; Janine, frozen in time, aged about eight, I guessed, pictured in a black leotard, black tights, tap shoes, and an ill-fitting top hat and tails, with a cane held between her skinny arms at the level of her bony knees. Next, Janine the aspiring actress a year or so older, in a simple white

258

T-shirt, her hair much fairer, her face in conventionally attractive proportion, her nose almost button-like. Another image from around this time, Janine sitting on the lap of a dame of the theatre, in Victorian vagabond costume. Next to it, aged twelve or thirteen, Janine is standing below a boom microphone, clearly on the set of some children's TV programme. Finally, Janine aged no more than fifteen. Here I could see how puberty had taken full control of her face, accelerating the growth of her nose and chin. That image, a soft-focused publicity shot in black-and-white, was the last of the series. It seemed this was where Janine's acting career ended and her transition into the woman she would become truly began. I could almost feel sorry for her if she wasn't so awful to Essie. After viewing the tribute wall to Janine's thwarted acting career, I no longer felt Signal House was quite so relaxing.

I dared to leave my confines, checking the gangway for signs of Una before going to Essie, who was still in the bathroom, weeping.

'Esther? Are you OK? Would you let me in?' I said from the other side of the door.

'Just fucking leave her alone!' Janine shouted from her room.

'It's OK, April,' Essie said. 'Go and wait in my room. It's at the far end. I'll be with you in a minute.' I could hear Essie blowing her nose as I headed to her room, quietly thrilled to have a moment alone in her private world. Her quarters were large, with a huge window facing out onto the lawn. I could see a layer of ocean beyond the pebble beach and the low wooden fence near the sunken public footpath that bordered it. In this part of the house, the smell I'd detected downstairs was even more insistently organic than it was on the floor below.

259

The room was just as I had imagined it: very feminine, with peaches and pink and mint greens. There were photo collages of Essie with her father over the years; as a sweet toddler at the zoo, sitting on Con's hip while she offered a giraffe some leaves to eat; by his side with a helmet on in a Jeep; perched on top of a sand dune; dancing with him at some kind of corporate-looking ball in a dress that looked too sexy for a teenager to be wearing. I found I was as repulsed by this as I was jealous. I could recall no moments of intimacy and pride with my own father, but could not bear being as physically close to him as Essie was to Con.

Also on the wall next to her dressing table were photos of Essie with a few pretty, flip-haired teenaged girls, the types who went to private schools like Essie did, girls who knew how to dress, girls who knew how to smoke and ski. They made me feel suddenly territorial over Essie, and so glad I'd bought my Canon camera with me, as well as the video camera I'd 'borrowed' from *The Dawn Chorus* so I could document our weekend together, perhaps generate something that would allow me to show Essie how others might see her, all her beguiling beauty and charm she could not see.

My ambitions had recently been crystallising, as I realised how I could marry my observations of other people with the emotional connections my writing allowed me to forge between my own life and those around me. I was finally happy with my draft of *Singular* as a short film. In Essie's room that afternoon, I decided I would take pictures of her that would make it into her collage of friends. Even if I wasn't in them, she would know they were taken by me. I also wanted the chance to experiment capturing landscapes, perhaps shooting some footage of the beach after dark, as well as some video of Essie, something that might help her realise how much more she was than she thought; how absolutely perfect to star in *Singular*.

'Oh god. I look such a geek on that one.' Essie was at the door, her nose red, her face puffy. 'And look at that hair!' She peered in close to look at the image of her and two other girls squeezed tightly together on a fairground waltzer in a strappy pink vest. She would have been about sixteen.

'Are these girls your best friends?' I asked and when I did, the words *best friends* seemed to catch in my mouth.

Essie sighed. 'One of them was. We had a bit of a falling-out after the summer holiday last year, I suppose.' She bit her bottom lip for a second before snapping herself out of evidently still painful memories. 'You settled in OK? Sorry about the smell, by the way. The house is only two years old and already the whole drains need tearing out or something.'

'That's a shame,' I said. 'It's such a beautiful house.'

'Daddy's suing the builder.' Essie said, moving to open one of her windows and sneaked a glance over her shoulder and dropped her voice. 'Your room's probably creepier than your bank place – all those photos of Janine.' Essie did a funny little jazz hands type pose and we both laughed. I loved being there, with her, like that. I dared to use Essie referencing Janine's theatrical forays to turn the conversation towards the idea of getting her on film.

'Did you never think about acting, Essie?' I asked, watching her cross the room once more to reach her dressing table where she bent to view herself in the mirror.

'Me? No way. Actively encouraging a load of strangers to look at me and judge me?' Evidently unhappy at what she saw

261

in her reflection, Essie visibly shuddered at the idea of putting herself in the spotlight. 'No thanks.' She ran her fingers over the patches of skin under her eyes, pursed her lips in dissatisfaction before spinning around to face me. 'Fancy fixing my face before gin o' clock?'

'It would be my pleasure,' I said, happy to have a chance at making Essie feel better about her appearance, but deeply disappointed at her shutting down the idea of getting in front of mine or any other video camera.

*

I changed into a new dress for the evening, a white, knee-length, polyester thing with spaghetti straps that made me feel like a new and different April, someone, perhaps, who looked like they were cool enough to be close to Essie. When it was time to head to the lawn, I picked up my Canon camera before leaving my study-room quarters. I wanted to get some shots of the vistas, but mostly of Essie in the sunshine. I was also considering asking her if she'd come with me when I planned to shoot on the beach after dark, under the guise of me needing a focal point against the night sky and darkened sea.

The forecast predicted a very hot spell coming. By the time Essie and I made it to the lawn, four white loungers had been set up, as well as a small wrought iron table laid out with the bottles, crystal glasses, and bowls holding ice and lemon slices required for 'gin o' clock'. Janine, Una, and Con were already there. Mother and daughter had their feet up on adjacent loungers, Una reading a copy of *Red* magazine, Janine scowling, clicking on her iPod, earbuds in, while Con stood by the table,

262

facing the sea. The building heat had already burnt any clouds clean away from the faultless sky. Essie surprised me when she linked my arm for a moment as we approached her family, as if to say, *I'm so glad you're here*. I could not have been happier in that second. I already knew I was in for a night to remember.

Una wore a backless green halter-neck dress, revealing pale, freckled stretches of skin. Her hair was expensively highlighted shades of bronze and blonde, rather like Essie's, though worn shorter, in layers to her shoulder that moved with the sea breeze. She greeted us with a cool, 'Hello, girls.'

Janine, in shorts and a vest, meanwhile, did not look up when Essie and I approached, but I heard her mutter a sarcastic, 'Here comes the dream team.'

'You young ladies look lovely.' Con, in pale linen shirt and trousers, gave Essie, then me, a double kiss before handing us each a cut crystal glass of gin and tonic.

'Thank you, Daddy, so do you.'

'Cheers.' Con clinked Essie's glass, then mine, the top of his fingers catching mine around our respective glasses in a way that almost made me apologise, though the contact was not my fault. 'So, April, Esther tells me you're an Oxford woman,' said Con. 'Very impressive.'

Janine snorted behind me. 'Ha! I've heard it's full of toffs and virgins.'

'That true?' Con asked me, and I felt it again, an ambiguity in his meaning, one that if I acknowledged would render me somehow complicit.

'Well, there's a lot of people you would say are from old money there, but they tend to mix amongst themselves,' I said, looking for some kind of backup from Essie, who was by now

263

engrossed in texting. It was obvious she'd tried to contact the footballer with disappointing results.

'And what about the virgins?' Con asked. On her lounger, Una turned a page on her magazine so emphatically I heard it tear.

'Oh, I don't know anything about that,' I said to the grass, acutely aware of Una and Con monitoring every nuance of my reaction, though for entirely opposite reasons.

'I'm sure you don't,' Con said before taking a sip from his glass, and though my gaze was now on the water, I was confident he had winked behind his crystal tumbler.

'What a view,' I said, turning so I was addressing Una and Essie, desperate to change the atmosphere, bring the other women into the one-to-one Con seemed intent on pursuing.

Essie looked up from her phone and smiled through wet eyes. 'Daddy chose this place, didn't you, Daddy? For all of us to escape to.' She reached for Con's hand. He took it as she gave him a gooey type of smile. I stood between them awkwardly. 'Clever Daddy. Why can't they all be as good as you,' Essie said, giving his palm a final squeeze before returning to her phone.

'Mummy did the interiors, you know,' Janine called out. 'It's her house really.' Janine, it was clear, wasn't actually listening to music. Una gave her eldest a terse little blink at acknowledging her contribution to the Laycocks' sumptuous lifestyle.

'It certainly is lovely,' I said over the fresh thrust of jealousy in my chest. Their lives seemed like a collective effort, making me think once more of the disparate collection of poorly connected individuals that was my family. I felt so out of place in this moment. I was so overawed by the view, the house, the febrile dynamics of the Laycocks – which, while far more

264

complicated than I'd imagined when seen from a distance, were still more cohesive than those of my family – that I'd even forgotten to try to deploy my vocabulary. 'Lovely?' I corrected myself, shaking my head. 'Lovely doesn't do it justice at all, actually.'

Essie's phone rang. The footballer. She answered it and began walking back in the direction of the house, leaving me standing with Con. I snapped her with my camera as she went.

'The view's even better from the end of the garden,' Con told me.

'Is it?' I spied an opportunity to leave the awkwardness on the lawn. 'I might take a quick stroll; get some seascapes.' I touched the sides of my camera, hanging off my neck, so happy to have it there, like a trusted friend who could not leave my side.

'Why don't we go and see,' Con said to me.

'Oh, I can go on my own.' I heard the tiniest trace of panic in my voice.

'I'd be happy to show you the way.' Con ostensibly eyed my camera, though I felt very much as though his gaze was lingering on my breasts.

'Janine, why don't you go with them?' said Una tightly.

Janine, in response, gave a quick, petulant shake of her head. 'I can see things clearly from here.'

Things. The view, or whatever Con was doing to justify his wife's and eldest daughter's unspoken suspicions? At this point, Essie remained the only member of the Laycocks blissfully blind to their patriarch's flaws.

Una breathed audibly. 'Don't be long, please.' And in Una's voice I heard the strain of desperation.

265

I had no choice but to allow Con to come with me to the far end of the lawn.

'This way.' He opened the gate in the low wooden fence that separated Signal's grounds from the public footpath and the shore below. If I followed Con, Janine and Una would not be able to see us.

'It's OK,' I said. 'We don't need to go too far.'

'And how far is far enough?' Con's hand had found my arm, which he was pulling towards him, in the direction of the beach. I glanced back to Una and Janine who, behind their sunglasses, were surely watching as much as they were able.

'What do you mean?' I tried to make my voice sound light, but I failed, my nerves cracking through. The truth was, I had not been quite myself since the incident with the footballer's friend in The Boys and Girls. In fact, looking back at my earliest encounters with men, when I thought the only thing I had to offer them was my supposed innocence, I had begun to wonder if I had ever really been in my right mind. A quiet part of me was beginning to wonder why I allowed men to treat me poorly, to fuck me so roughly. Was there something in me that encouraged men to leave me feeling sore and used because that way, I could get there first, I could own the fact I was worthless before they could? Maybe this was my maladjusted way of retaining control, some mastery over my unlovability, while extracting some of the human, physical heat I craved. But I was getting to the point where I did not want to resort to this anymore.

'How far would you go to get what you want?' Con said, his slow, unctuous words slithering into my ear, then creeping across my reddening face and chest.

'Here is fine,' I said, lifting my camera to my face. I began to take some shots of the seascape ahead, making the world around me into something I could construct, something I could control. Con forced his way into my frame. I did not want him there. I shifted my view to free my perspective of him, but again he entered my field of vision and I was made to watch his gaze sweep all over me, as though appraising a car he intended to test drive.

'I think that's enough for now,' I said with a confidence I only felt when I had a camera between me and the world. But when I lowered the lens and saw the seriousness of Con's expression, I heard myself giving him a fake laugh before I even realised I was doing it.

'For now,' Con said slowly, injecting innuendo into a space I had not intended to create.

I felt unsteady as I walked back over Signal House's cushion-like lawn, Con a step or so behind me, enough so I could feel him looking at every bit of me. When we got back to the rest of the family, Essie was slumped on a lounger, Una with a stiff palm on her back.

'Time to pull yourself together,' Una said to Essie, though she was viewing me with an undisguisable tension in her mouth. 'Few men are worth your energy.'

*

In her distress over the footballer, and the complete lack of sympathy from Janine and Una, Essie ended up getting drunk even before the main meal was served.

'Sorry, everyone,' she slurred slightly. 'I think I should

probably leave you to it. I'm no use to anyone. I'm going to bed. Good night.'

I was sad to see Essie in such a state, and disappointed there was no chance I'd have her company, or the chance to shoot her, on the beach later. I wanted to leave the table too, thinking now was the moment to be honest about my filmmaking ambitions and Essie's role in achieving them. Perhaps that would make her feel better about herself tonight and give her something else to focus on in the longer term instead of bad men like the footballer. But when Essie stumbled out of her seat, and I moved to follow her, I was stopped.

'Don't go before you've eaten, girl. Let Esther get her beauty sleep,' Con said in a jovial way, but in a tone that left me in no doubt I had to remain for the duration of the meal. I retook my seat and watched Essie disappear up the cracked spiral staircase.

It continued to prove an excruciating dinner. Janine ribbed me further about Oxford, grilled me about my family, and successfully revealed my lack of friends. All the while, Una ate and spoke very little. Con, meanwhile, seemed to relish the spectacle of Janine depleting me, then took the opportunity to play the good father figure to Janine's bad sister, variously countering Janine's questions and commentary with things like, 'I'm sure April's had lots of friends. Plenty of boyfriends too,' and, on learning I had little contact with my family with a wholly unrelated, 'Dads, we can't help it. You may be all grown-up into beautiful young women, but to us, you'll always be little girls.' Una blinked away his lasciviousness, while Janine tutted. Occasionally I could see her cringe over her father's behaviour, though she never asked him to stop.

268

The night drew on. Una took herself off to bed soon after the housekeeper served coffee and cleaned up the table and dishes. Con asked Janine to keep him company while he watched an old movie in the expansive den. I decided that leaving them at that point would no longer attract Con's ire, so I made my move to be alone.

'If you don't mind, I'll leave you to it. I'm going to practise shooting some night skies down on the beach,' I said. Janine half snarled, while Con tilted his head and smiled in a way that made me want to get out of the room as quickly as possible.

I went to my study-room, grabbed my video camera, along with the pashmina I'd packed, and left the house, walking beyond the boundary of Signal's grounds and to the clean, calm solitude of the beach.

So bright was the moon, so warm the night on my skin. It was a shame Essie wasn't with me, but I knew the sequences of fast-moving clouds I captured racing across the lunar face, the splintered reflection of the moon on the sea's surface would look spectacular. I hoped I could use them, perhaps in a dream sequence I might add to *Singular*. I took my video camera off my shoulder, lay my pashmina over the pebbles, and gazed into the stars, listening to the waves. I was so happy to have a moment of aloneness that for once felt exquisite. I was reassured in the knowledge I would be there for Essie when she woke, and that the weekend would have surely cemented our friendship. When she sobered up tomorrow, *that* would be the right time to bring her into my plans for the short.

I was about to head back to the house, anticipating an undisturbed sleep away from the bank when, in a break in the waves, I heard the grind and clink of feet on the pebbles. I was not alone after all.

*

When I returned to the house, I did not sleep. I bathed for a very long time, and then I took some shots of myself in the mirror with my Canon camera; images of the lower half of my body on the end of the bed, as though cataloguing the various parts of my body and therefore processing what had just happened to them. Nothing felt quite real.

Once I dried myself and dressed, I lay on top of the duvet fully clothed from head-to-toe in the jeans and long-sleeved jumper I had removed from my backpack. A summer storm the forecast had not predicted began, and rain hammered against my window. When I heard a dripping sound, I realised it was coming from the carpet below the windowsill. Water was pouring in around the windowpane, which did not sit true in its frame. I rolled up the larger of the towels I'd been given as best I could to plug the length of the leak. By this time, the stench of sewage was all-pervasive, the excess water must have overwhelmed Signal's already fragile drainage system.

When it finally happened, my sleep was terrifying and gluey, I dreamt I needed to scream but could not force the sound from my lungs no matter how hard I tried. I was ripped free of my nightmares by an equally disturbing noise. Una, half-moaning, half-shrieking. 'Con! Conrad! Ambulance, now! It's Esther!'

I yanked open my door to poke my head out in time to see Janine thundering past to Essie's room, Con shouted something like, 'Christ! Hurry!'

Overheated in my dreams, I must have pulled off my clothes in my sleep and had ended up only in my underwear. I had grabbed the first thing I could reach – the smaller of the white towels – to cover myself up and ran to Essie.

Her bedroom door open, Essie was slumped over her mother's shoulder. There was greenish sick on her chin and on the floor. Janine, knelt behind her mother, slapped Essie's face. 'Esther. Esther! Wake up! You've done something stupid,' she said.

Con was stood to one side of the bed, a hand on his forehead; Essie's hero, wordless, powerless, and without use in her crisis. He did not, or could not, look at me as I stood in the doorframe.

'Oh god,' left my mouth.

Una, who was alternately patting Essie on the back and stroking her hair, stopped and turned her head to say something to Janine I couldn't hear. Janine got up and approached me as I stood in the doorway.

'My mum asked you not to walk around like that.'

The door slammed closed on me.

*

It was clear the Laycocks did not want me to come with them to the hospital, but neither did they want to leave me alone in Signal. And with the sickening smell of the home's effluent stinging our throats and nostrils, I wonder too if they did not want to risk someone acknowledging all the shit in the air. In the end, I simply got in the car with them, and no one had the words or energy to stop me. I squashed myself in as far away from Janine as possible, and so there was no chance of meeting Una's or Con's eyes in the rear-view mirror.

Essie had, the doctors decided, made 'a cry for help'. Her stomach was pumped, and she would be sent home after a period of functional observation and without, it seemed to me, much curiosity over her mental state. It was only Janine who appeared to have a more proactive approach.

'She's just tried to kill herself. How are we planning on stopping her if she tries again? Shouldn't she be sectioned or something?' I overheard her say through the curtains drawn round Essie's bed. Una and Janine did not allow me to be by Essie's bedside, while Con remained peripheral and silent. I did sense some shame about him, though whether this was the disgrace over his behaviour, or whether it was over the indignity of what had happened to Essie, showing him to be the purveyor of faulty goods, I could not tell.

By the time Essie was out of the woods, but still needed to be kept in the hospital for observation, the family decided to stay on at Signal House for a further few days. Con, Una, and Janine were standing in a cluster by the nurses' station, while I was listening in, a plastic cup of vending machine black coffee in my fist. I did not want to stay, I very much wanted to be clear of the Laycocks and of Signal House by this stage, but neither did I want to leave Essie.

'I could stay here and watch over Essie if you all want to go back to Signal and get some rest,' I said to Una's back.

She turned and I could see both she and Janine were horrified at the notion, while Con shifted on the spot with his hands in his pockets and looked in the other direction. Una widened her eyes, gesturing to encourage him to say something to me.

'You should get yourself back to London,' Con said eventually. 'I'll drop you at the station.'

'I'll do it.' Una pulled her handbag onto her shoulder. It seemed there was to be no further discussion and not a second to waste. I was profoundly grateful not to face a car journey alone with Con, but the idea of being with Una made my head spin.

The drive back to Signal House to collect my things before heading to the nearest station proved unbearable. My mind churned over everything that had happened in just a few short hours; my body wished it could shrink to nothing, and get as far away from Essie's mother, from all of her family, as possible.

Because only hours ago, Una's husband had demonstrated he was willing to go as far as possible to get the thing he wanted from me, even if I had not given it freely. In the minutes and hours since, it had left me at turns dazed, disgusted, and feeling filthy. Bruises were already blooming on my thighs and wrists. I wonder if Una saw them too; something made her drive so fast that I gripped the seat either side of me as we sped towards the nearest place she could get rid of me.

'I take it from what you said at dinner yesterday you have some difficulties with your father,' Una said finally, eyes fixed on the road ahead.

'Yes,' I said very quietly.

'I had a poor relationship with my father,' Una said. 'The biggest mistake you can make in that situation . . .' She turned to look me for a moment, her tired, tearful eyes catching mine for a second, before she directed her attention back to the road, '. . . is trying to fix it by finding someone you hope might replace him. I would not recommend it.'

273

I felt the fear of exposure, of having allowed – as it had seemed to me back then – her husband to do what he had done to me on the beach. I felt myself to be an open wound, raw and terrible, not capable of being bandaged or masked, only of festering in full view.

'Would you mind stopping the car? I feel a little sick,' I said.

Una jerked to an emergency stop, lest I sully not only her family, but her precious SUV too. My head was flung forward and snapped back, my neck screaming in pain to add to all the other agonies about me. I managed to open the door and went to stand, bent double, my hands on my knees, on a grassy verge near an overflowing litter bin.

'I need to get back to the hospital,' Una called through the open window. 'Keep following the road for another mile or so and you'll reach the station.' She performed a screeching U-turn and sped off away from me.

It was far longer than 'a mile or so' to the station. I walked for more than an hour, dazed, tearful, in pain, and cold in my bones, even though the sun was already blazing in the early hour. I waited a further two hours for a train back to London, so profoundly alone on the platform, desperate to know how Essie was doing, dying to hear her voice and be reassured she was OK. I did not want to be alone in the hell of my own body that day, and I did not want to leave Essie with her horrid mother and sister, and with the father she should know better than to idolise. I had already decided, though, I would not tell her about what had happened when we spoke next. Essie seemed, despite her dazzling confidence, so vulnerable that I did not know if I would ever tell her what had happened. I had no idea I had already spoken to her for the last time until the day

274

she accepted my invitation to the table read of *The Vanished Woman*.

And after what had happened to me at Signal, I put the camera away in a box in a far corner of the old bank. I wrapped it in the brand-new white dress I would never wear again but could not throw away. I moved the box without opening it when I finally bought my own place and left the bank. I was not able to develop the film until my life changed and I could not avoid facing that part of my story any longer.

*

After our weekend at Signal House, Essie didn't come to work. She had, apparently, told the series director it was glandular fever, and she could not be sure of her return. I was so worried about her, whether she may have tried to hurt herself again and this time succeeded, particularly as the tabloids had revealed the footballer had impregnated one of his 'hotel blondes'. When I tried to call Essie, her phone rang out and went to voicemail. I imagined Janine had confiscated it and was screening her calls.

Essie didn't come to work that week, or the week after, or ever again. My only friend, the person I had hoped would facilitate my first foray into film and the creative life I thought might save me, was gone.

The next time I saw Essie, it was months later on the children's TV show *All Aboard*. I froze when I caught sight of her face coming out of twenty TV screens stacked on top of each other in rows in a shop window on Tottenham Court Road. I was shocked, but not wholly surprised. She was an absolute natural, destined to be where she was, right in front of the camera. Though it seemed a travesty that her beguiling, open personality and charismatic beauty were not being deployed to create art, but instead being squandered on creating craft curiosities from kitchen foil and sticky-back plastic. But what was my destiny? What would become of me now that my short time travelling in her slipstream was over and Essie's career only beginning?

I remember that time very well, including how I had to reimagine my immediate future. I never did make *Singular* as a short. Like the camera, I packed that script away. Eventually, I began to write other projects, paid my way through film school and hustled to get an agent and my first paid gig in a writers' room for a popular soap, before getting commissioned to write shows, ultimately penning *Encounters*. As I ascended my chosen career, Essie did hers. Our successes were not side by side as I'd dreamt, but adjacent, and for a long time, I struggled with why that had happened, why she had frozen me out. Maybe, I sometimes reasoned, Essie had come round to how unlikeable I was; or perhaps, I thought, she did not want to see me because she was embarrassed by her cry for help. Maybe, I thought, she was embarrassed by me, the dull, civilian acquaintance, as her star rose. I considered every rationale for my severance, except for the real reason she could no longer be my friend.

*

After some time, when the worst of the pain in the aftermath of that weekend in Signal House receded, I was able to remember my strengths: my intelligence, my work ethic, the life I lived inside myself, which enabled me to see into the lives of others, and eventually delivered my creative success.

I'd always hoped there would be a point in my life when I felt ready to finally free my old Canon camera from my white dress and develop the film from the Signal House weekend. It was always going to be a moment when I felt there was enough distance between who I was then, and who April Eden is now. That moment arrived the day my first feature was officially greenlit, after I'd managed to attach Juniper Jones as my lead and persuade my financiers to back me. The working title: *The Vanished Woman*.

It was time.

I unwrapped my Canon camera from its dusty white shroud, imagining I could still detect the stench of Signal on it. I took the film to be developed, later bringing the packet of images back to the flat. I knew I was alone and safe, but still my pulse pounded in my head because I knew what was coming.

After the shots of Essie on the lawn, the beach in the early evening, soon I would see the images I took of myself in the mirror after midnight on that thunderous day. I knew I was going to see my twenty-two-year-old face tear-stained in the mirror, the skin on my shoulder darkening, the strap on my dress snapped. I knew I was going to see my thighs, close-ups of the marks where Con's fingers grabbed at me, held me in place. *I should have stopped him. I should have said something*, I heard myself say, before a kinder, wiser voice told me, *He never should have done that to you.*

After flipping through the series of beach shots I took in the afternoon, I braced myself to see that last set of pictures. But no.

Following the beach series, there were two images I did not

take, both shots of Signal's lawn at night, the moon high in the sky, and both captured from a vantage point on the upper floor of the house. The first, me returning from the beach. My face is swollen with tears that still look to be pouring down my cheeks, although my expression is blank, numb. One hand rubs the wrist of the other carrying my video camera as I walk, the torn strap of my dress blowing free in the breeze. And in the next frame, Con, walking back to his family's beach home, his hands in his pockets, a faint, self-satisfied smile on his glistening face.

I wonder what stories Essie's family must have told themselves and each other about me to make her cut me out of her life. Did they go so far as to say I'd successfully seduced Con, or merely that I had tried, and Con had nobly resisted? After I saw the images Essie took, I realised that Essie hadn't been convinced that I wasn't likeable, or that I would never be powerful, but that I was dangerous.

I may have needed to create *The Vanished Woman* to tell the world my story, but my real target audience didn't need me to make her the star of a motion picture to know my truth.

Essie knew it all along.

26

Essie, before, The Vanished Woman *shoot*

April has become even more intense these past couple of days. Maybe running the shoot is getting to her, being first to arrive, last to leave, the person in this operation with whom every last buck stops. I watch her as she's deep into what looks like a pretty serious conversation with Juniper and the actor who plays Elena's father John. We're preparing to go again on the scene where I follow in their footsteps, transitioning from the courtyard to the garden. April finishes up with Juniper and now she's coming over to me.

'They're playing this a little differently than how we rehearsed, but you're going to do exactly what you did before, OK?'

'Listening but not listening. Got it.'

April nods and walks away. 'Places please!' she calls. 'Quiet. Let's go.'

The scene gets underway.

'We could go into the garden if you like, but we shouldn't go too far.' Antonia/Juniper says this much more warily than she did the last time we rehearsed.

'And how far is far enough?' Elena's father says to Antonia,

279

but not in the rambunctious kind of way he did in rehearsals; the way he says it now is almost flirtatious, kind of creepy.

'What do you mean?' asks Antonia, trying to laugh it off, but it's clear John has freaked her out. All the while, as Elena/I listen, and I don't hear.

John stops, blocks Antonia's path, and says, slowly, slimily, 'How far would you go to get what you want?'

'Here is fine. I think that's enough for now.' Antonia is still trying to minimise John's tone, but it's impossible not to acknowledge. I absolutely hear this but say nothing, apparently hear nothing.

'For now,' John says, and when he does, from the corner of my vision, I see him slide a finger down Antonia's cheek.

'And cut!' April shouts, and my heart stutters in my chest. I run straight to my trailer and pop another pill.

Today feels strange, dangerous. Later on, we film more scenes that April directs so the interaction between Antonia and my screen father are completely different to how they read on page, and how they seemed at the first table read. Under April's direction now, Elena's father is slowly but surely becoming more predatory towards Antonia and cruel to Elena. Everything John has said in the most recent scenes play as an innuendo. Antonia seems more and more unsure, even afraid of John. As for Elena, she has chosen to either not see or care what he's doing, that is, until the next scene.

'Essie, are you hearing me?' April says as we prepare to go. 'I need you to tell Antonia not to listen to John, not to do as he says, as though this the most important message she could deliver. This is the moment Antonia realises she needs to protect Elena from John. Does that make sense to you?'

'I think so,' I say, but I don't know why she's decided to make John such a horrid character; that bit really doesn't make sense to me, especially not through the medicated fug I'm doing my best to mask. Picking up on my confusion, my likeliness to hold back, April asks me, 'So, can you go there for me?' She looks so desperate to get this scene in the can, a feeling I share in this moment. It's the last scene scheduled for today and we both know the light is fading.

I nod.

'OK, let's go again!' April shouts. The set goes silent.

I take a moment to recentre, make myself listen to the back and forth between John and Antonia as though I'm hearing it for the first time, try to call on something that might help me now. And I find myself thinking of what I saw that awful weekend April came to Signal. By the time it gets to my line, I'm there: twenty-one again, looking out of my window, down onto the moonlit lawn after midnight, April walking back to the house, something about her puffy, damp face and the way her white dress hangs off her shoulder that I don't like; I don't want to see. And then, I look at my own shoulders, the three white strings for straps. It's just like April's dress that weekend. Jesus, is it *that* dress?

'Don't!' I cry.

John and Antonia are barely through their lines. John is startled by my outburst, Antonia momentarily stunned before seeming boosted to hear me back up her resistance to John.

'Don't listen to him,' I say firmly, darkly. I know I've said it exactly right, exactly how April wants me to. I feel as though Elena is shining through every pore of me, and I know this is just what April wants too. She lets the scene run for a beat or two

281

longer than expected, capturing my response to my own outcry, as well as John and Antonia's silent reaction. I allow myself to look at John, a defiant look that dares him to say something to me. *Tell me why Antonia or I should listen to you? Why should we do what you tell us?* And after I do, I look to Juniper/Antonia's face and it seems to me that both character and actor are digesting something, something they both begrudgingly appreciate. April lets the scene run for another few seconds.

'And cut!' she finally shouts. She doesn't move for a moment, her head bowed low. She looks to be breathing heavily, her hands on her hips as she falls back into her director's chair, as though she's just finished climbing a mountain. Getting that performance out of me has left me feeling overloaded with emotion and empty all at the same time. It looks like extracting it onto film from me has done the same to April.

The scene done, Juniper moves through the set, brushing past me on the way to her trailer. I've got used to her acting as though I'm a ghost unless we're in the middle of a scene. But when she rushes away from set this time, she stops and says one word to me.

'Outstanding.'

If my latest pill wasn't already kicking in, I would probably cry with joy and start gushing in Juniper's general direction, but I don't know who or what I feel anymore. I'm not Elena now the scene has ended, but I don't yet feel like me. And a part of me thinks I'm being made to feel, somehow, like April. And if me, Elena, and April are becoming mixed up, then the same is true of John and my father. The two characters are starting to merge into one terrible man. As I leave the set, loads of people from the crew are calling out *Bravo!* and *Superb!* and it's all I can do

282

to half-smile at the floor and get to my trailer as quick as I can before I start crying in front of anyone. Because while the more Elena and Essie fuse in my performance, with elements of April now blurring in, the more I feel the people around me genuinely respect me. But it's becoming even harder to respect myself.

*

Two days left until we're due to finish. There's a rumour swirling around set that April has arrived with an updated shooting script and no one is happy; her financiers, the director of photography, lighting. April is on her mobile. She appears calm, except for the flush from her forehead to her neck. She looks like she's trying to justify herself to one of the people she's pissed off with her last-minute changes. Something tells me I'm not going to like these changes either.

I head over to her once my hair is fixed into its April-like plait and I've got my Elena/April white dress on. I've not said anything to April yet about the dress, the story, what any of it means. I can't find the words, or perhaps it's that I don't want to.

'Essie. I've made some changes to the script,' she says, not looking up from the monitor.

'I did hear something,' I say.

April nods but doesn't look up as her assistant passes me the pages in question. I scan them. Once it's becoming clear how the story has changed, I'm reeling. I feel as if those hiding places from the words I need to say, the truth, are running out.

'This is . . .' I say, 'this isn't . . . this isn't what I expected.'

'I thought it was kind of obvious,' April says, quietly, but

283

confidently, her eyes still fixed on the monitor. 'But as we've been shooting, it struck me I might need to give my audience a helping hand to know what's really gone on.' April finally breaks away from her monitor. She's different today. 'Are you ready for that?'

I stare at April; it must be the light or the fact that I've already taken a pill today, but when she speaks, her face seems fuller. She looks younger, like she did back then.

'Essie? Are you good to learn this now?' She gestures to the pages in my hand.

'Yes,' I say, but I'm not. I don't want to *learn this*, not today, not ever.

*

The shoot is a disaster. I did not shimmer with Elena's spirit like yesterday. I slurred and I stammered. I forgot my lines, barely heard anyone else's. April has had to call off filming for the rest of the day. I've staggered back to my trailer where I want to fall asleep straight away, but April has followed me.

'Knock-knock,' she says, already opening my door. I can tell from her voice she's still in full April the Director mode.

'April, listen, I'll stump up whatever I've cost you today, obviously,' I tell her, desperate, for once, to be alone.

'Essie, it's not about the financial cost. I've already messed that up today, but I did that because I want us to make the right film,' April says, stood in the doorway, not even bothering to come in, afraid, maybe, that if she did, she and I would both need to face up to what has been going on between us, the story she's trying to tell. 'I'm a novice female director. I need to do the

284

film the right way and we need to control the narrative about you being good enough to open this film, to show everyone Essie Lay can go toe-to-toe with Miss Juniper, and that I'm competent enough to control a functional set.'

'Control me?' I say.

April doesn't say anything for a beat.

'You know what I mean.'

I feel as if I'm beginning to think I do. And I don't like it much. It's me who needs to be in control of me.

'Tomorrow, I promise I'll be better.'

*

Finally, the last day of the shoot. Today, I don't take a pill. I have to prove I can get some kind of control back, even though I know I am craving my tablets. My insides are cramping and cringing, and my mind is begging me to let it float away and not deal with any of this. But I'm not giving in. Stories have started to leak about life on set: leading ladies at each other's throats, creative differences between the female director and her 'troubled' lead, standard women-baiting shit. Only some of it is true, with the actual truth too great for April and me to acknowledge directly yet.

In this final set of scenes, I have to narrowly avoid stepping onto a shard of glass Antonia has left outside for me, knowing how Elena does slow, repeated circuits of the courtyard of her father's house in the afternoon. Antonia wants Elena to be made to feel something, anything, to finally make her open up, and she's desperately hoping that putting Elena through physical pain will mean she'll need to call Antonia for help. She wants

285

to see Elena when she's not in control of what she shows and doesn't show to Antonia. When Elena nearly steps on the glass and sees the lengths Antonia is willing to go to get to the truth, she gives Antonia the information she wants, before giving her an alternative version of what happened, then another.

We're about to do the first take of the scene when April approaches me with a page in her hand. 'The choreography is the same. You just have fewer lines now.' She hands me the page.

I read it quickly. In fact, I only have three lines now, so powerful, April knows I'll be able to recall them easily. April has walked back to her spot. I have no time to think, I only have to act now.

'And action!' April calls.

Three cameras follow me as I take slow, measured steps. Juniper/Antonia walks into the scene to sweep the leaves from the yard, only she's really there in the hope of seeing me bleed. At this point I'm supposed to stop before my foot touches the razor-sharp end of the shard of glass Antonia has left waiting for me. Instead, I drop the arch of my foot onto the spike of glass.

It's like an out-of-body experience. I feel the pain, sense the blood, warm and sticky already under my foot, but somehow, I can fly through it, right over the agony. I say my line.

'You know why I vanished. You've known all along,' I tell Antonia/April.

'I didn't. I don't,' she tells me.

'My father hurt you.' I feel something moving through me into the camera and back to April: the truth. 'And when he did, he hurt me too.'

This too is true. After I accused my father of what he did to April and he denied it so strongly, so much so that I began to

286

doubt what I saw, I had a world of making up to do. It led me to say yes to a career and a life I didn't want but suited him. And all along, in my heart, I knew what he'd done to April and also why my old friends didn't want to come to Signal House anymore.

Juniper/April notices the blood on the ground.

The next line is mine too, but I decide to wait before saying it, allow more of my blood to trickle out onto the stone. I stand in my pain, my mistakes, and own them. Antonia has no choice now but to see she has been looking at everything the wrong way round this whole time. She falls to the ground in horror; this is not in the script. Next, she takes off her top, leaving her only in her vest and slacks, and holds my wounded foot in her hand before dabbing it with her shirt. She does not actually say the words *I'm sorry*, but it's writ large in the way she's tending to me. It's urgent, but also careful. And now, it's time for my final line. I decide to offer Antonia my palm to help her back to her feet. She hesitates, feeling unworthy of my helping hand.

I wait a moment, allow her guilt to linger for a second or so longer, before signalling she doesn't need to stay down, floored with regret for putting me through pain anymore. The pain has been ours to share, though a man was the cause of it.

'Walk with me,' I say to her, and I hope April hears it too. Let's walk side by side now we've made this brilliant thing together; let's heal, let's fucking well take on the world with *The Vanished Woman*. That's what I'm going to say to her, after I've said I'm sorry, as if that will ever be enough.

Antonia peers up at me uncertainly.

The viewer won't know if she ever accepts my hand, or if we ever really end up in partnership, not in opposition, because before we can shoot another second, I hear April's voice.

287

'And cut! That's a wrap.'

Juniper retreats, bloodied shirt in her hand, seemingly overwhelmed. Meanwhile April rushes over to me, then stops. It's like she's asking for permission to give me a hug. I go to hug her first. And now I am crying. I owe April so many apologies: for what my dad did, for what I did by cutting her off and trying to make the truth vanish all those years ago.

'Can we get a chair and some first aid please? Water and a towel too!' April calls out and one of the crew runs straight over with April's own director's chair for me to sit on, a small towel and a green box which he fishes about in for wound dressings. 'It's OK, I've got this,' she tells the crew member, relieving him of the first-aid box, while I lower myself down into her chair. I watch while she first pours water carefully over my wound, then dabs it gently with the towel.

'You might need stitches,' she says.

'I don't think so,' I say, watching her still. 'Thank you, April.'

She keeps her head down, still focused on my wound, not able to meet my eye. The film, everything that led to it, must have taken so much from her, demanded so much bravery. 'Please. Don't thank me,' April says quietly. 'Everything I've done with this project; I've done for me and me alone.'

'April,' I insist, 'you've given me so much; a chance I know I didn't deserve. I know I've let you down, in so many ways.' April continues to fuss with a roll of gauze. 'April. Stop. Please, listen to me. I understand what my dad did to you, OK? I should have been so much better to you. I should have stood up for you, I should have stood up for myself, for what I'd seen with my own eyes. I'm so, so sorry.'

'I should be saying sorry to you,' April says, finally pausing in her wrapping of my foot in dressing. 'I never meant for you to get so hurt.'

I let out a dry laugh. 'Oh April, I've been hurting a very long time. But things will get better from here, for both of us. Come over tomorrow, just you. Let's talk properly, put our world to rights.'

Tomorrow I'll say sorry for everything. I'll say sorry over and over for what my father did to her that weekend at Signal, say sorry because even though I saw her and I knew, I *knew* what he'd done and that's what took me over the edge that night, not the stupid footballer. And in the morning, in all the years that followed, I didn't let myself believe the truth not only because of the pressure my father put me under, the emotional and financial blackmail, but also because I chose not to. I was too weak to face up to reality. I've been too weak all this time, until now, until April came back into my life and rebooted the whole damned thing.

April's eyes fill with tears, as she goes to pass the roll of gauze around my foot once more, the blood continuing to blush through the layers. 'I don't deserve your friendship now,' she says.

'You do, April. You're a brilliant, beautiful woman and a brilliant, beautiful friend; the best. You deserved more from me,' I tell her, because I know she's always had low self-esteem and I know what my father did to her would have made her feel worthless. I know because that's how I was left feeling after I let Jude do what he did, and how I felt when I realised Jackson had betrayed me.

'I don't deserve anything,' April gulps.

'You do,' I insist as she applies a piece of sticky medical tape to my foot. 'I think it's fine now, April. I don't think it's going to

289

bleed much more. You go and do what you need to do.' I look around the set, the crew embracing and slapping each other's backs. She deserves to go and be part of it.

'Go on,' I say. 'I'll be fine now.'

April nods, reluctantly rising to her feet and disappearing into a cluster of hugs and high-fives. I watch her for a moment, looking as uncomfortable, as unhappy as she ever did, and I wish it wasn't so. I hop back to my trailer and a wash of euphoria breaks over me, the immediate pain and shame of being made to face up to what happened now giving way to something else, a high better than any pill. Reckoning with my family and reconciling with April will be painful, but it will be the start of a new and better life for me.

I take off Elena's white dress for the last time and start to get ready for the wrap party. I'm looking forward to being in April's company, to start properly repairing the damage done to her by my father and by me. The first thing I can do is cheerlead her victory lap today, start doing what I can to build her up to where she deserves to be.

I'm ready to leave my trailer. Just as I'm about to open the doors, I hear raised voices outside. I step back and peer out through a gap in the blinds.

'I can make it worth your while.' April stands a metre or so from Jags, her arms folded across her, not wrapped around him like they always are when I've seen them together.

'I think I've shown my face enough,' Jags tells her.

'But it's the wrap party. Everyone will expect my boyfriend to be there.'

'Well, that's not exactly my fault, is it?'

'Please.'

Jags gets his car keys from his pocket. 'Call me over the weekend about what you want to do next week.' Jags notices April's skin starting to colour. 'Oh god, not that again. Sorry, I don't know what it is, but I can't be around that. Call me, OK?'

He turns and walks in the direction of the car park. I can't believe the way Jags has spoken to April. I rage on her behalf, but don't want to hand her the extra humiliation of knowing I've seen her normally adoring boyfriend treat her like shit. I leave it a few seconds before emerging from my trailer. April's smile tells me she doesn't think I've seen or heard a thing.

'Hey. How's the foot?' she asks, not acknowledging the wateriness of her eyes. My heart breaks for her. How can I do nothing now, after all she's done for me?

'It's fine. The cut wasn't as deep as it seemed, but I am going to pop back home, get some looser shoes, then I'll be back to celebrate everything with you.'

'Everything? Are you sure about that?' April asks, hands in her pockets, gaze on the ground. 'Will you say anything to your father?'

'I . . .' I haven't thought that through yet. 'I need some time to process it all. Right now, I can't imagine wanting to look at him.' I think about how he lied to me, to Mum and Janine after that weekend, and how none of us really believed it but went along with his story that April had come on to him. It doesn't matter what I say to him now. He and I, Mum and Janine aren't the most important people in this. 'What would you like me to say to him, April?'

'Nothing. Say nothing. I've heard what I need to hear, from you.'

291

I nod, her words painful but necessary for me to hear. 'You don't have to make any decisions now; you don't need to think about anything but enjoy the fact you've got your first feature in the can. Congratulations, April. You did it.'

April closes her eyes, lets a breath out through her nose. 'Yes. I did.'

The air fills with music. Someone on set has just started pumping out Rainbow's 'Since You Been Gone' full blast, which feels about right at the end of a shoot about a woman who sends other people mad by disappearing.

'You'd better get back to everyone,' I tell her. 'I'll see you at the party.'

April nods and I move to her for a final hug. It's a short but firm embrace before April turns to return to her crew, her head bowed down. Poor April, wounded by the past, heartbroken by a shit guy in the present. I wish I could do more to make this day better for her.

I head back to my car. On the other side of the car park, I see Jags.

'Where to?' my driver asks.

I think about it a second. 'See that piece of shit there?' I point to Jags getting into his ancient Ford Mondeo.

'The grey old banger or the bloke driving it?'

'Both. Follow them.'

27

Essie, before, the evening of The Vanished Woman,
wrap party

I follow Jags across town. He heads to a multistorey car park
in Soho, where my driver and I wait while the man himself
stays sitting in his car for a few minutes. When he gets out
it's obvious what he's been doing. Jags's hair is teased up into
very un-Jags-like little tufts and he's not in his usual preppy
trousers, sensible, if pec-hugging T-shirt, and tailored pea coat,
but ripped jeans and a leather jacket. Jags has gone through
some radical image change in the space of just a few minutes.
So have I.

For years, I've kept a standby disguise in the car for emergen-
cies, or for when I want to go for a walk or a coffee like a normal
person. It consists of a brown duffle coat, bobbed brunette wig,
and my fake glasses. I try not to think about the many times I've
been in a tight spot and had to dig out this gear: doing the walk
of shame from some guy's house; buying the morning-after pill;
waiting it out at the walk-in sexual health clinic, having to avoid
going private so Janine wouldn't see the expense and know I'd
screwed up. All normal, uncomfortable things many women
find themselves going through, but not every woman doing

them is worth up to ten grand for anyone with a camera phone in the right place at the right time. And people wonder why I'm not completely 'normal' after twenty years of living this way.

I ask my driver to wait and leave my car to track Jags down the gloomy car park staircase and into Soho. Thankfully, he doesn't go far. I follow him into a cocktail bar in Kingly Court. He slips himself into a leather booth, me into the one behind it. From here, I watch him rubbing the ends of his hair into fresh little peaks with his fingertips, checking out of the window. Someone is nervous.

A waiter comes to take my order.

'A sidec—' I just about stop the potentially incriminating words before they come out. 'Negroni, please.'

The waiter moves on to takes Jags's order. He's facing me, his head peeking out just above the booth, but he's so involved in himself, he doesn't see the strange-looking brunette in the next seat.

'I'll take a bottle of rosé please, two glasses,' Jags tells the waiter.

'Still, sparkling, dry, sweet?' the waiter says.

'Still, sweet,' Jags says. He messes around with his phone while he awaits his guest and gets started on the wine when it arrives. Soon after, she shows up: tall, confident, and no more than twenty-three. Jags stands up and gives her what feels to me like a seriously overfamiliar, lingering hug and a kiss near the mouth.

'Jessica. Wow. I thought you looked stunning in your profile, but you're even more beautiful in real life,' Jags tells the girl. What an arsehole. He left his girlfriend's wrap party for a Tinder match.

'Cheers,' the girl says, sitting herself down on the opposite side of the booth with her back to me, even though Jags has made space and lined up two glasses on his side. Smart girl.

'May I pour you a drink, Jessica?'

'Sure.'

Jags hands her a large measure of syrupy-looking pink wine. 'So, Jessica, you're a student nurse.'

'Junior doctor.' She takes a small sip.

'Doctor. Wow!' Jags says.

'Your profile said you were twenty-nine?' says Jessica flatly.

'That's right.' Jags puts up his hands in surrender. 'I suppose you could say I've not had the easiest time of it lately; maybe that's aged me a fair bit. But enough about me!' He grins at the poor girl, and although nothing's changed about him physically – he's still technically a good-looking guy – the desperation and the sliminess make him repulsive. I think, suddenly, of my father and my stomach tightens.

'And you're not in a relationship?' she asks him, though she's clearly not interested in the answer and looking only to play this lying loser for sport. I wish I'd have been more like her, I find myself thinking. Why didn't I kick Jackson's tyres harder when he burst into my life like the cut-out-and-keep perfect man for me? Like Jags's boosted profile, he was so obviously too good to be true. Why did I let Jude do what he did to me, then let him do it to someone else? Why did I accept my dad's lies when I knew the truth of what he was? I have to get tougher, be stronger, from this moment on.

'Ooh, cut to the chase. Why not?' Jags switches from jovial to hammy, oh-so-serious and sincere mode in a split second. 'That's right, Jessica. I was engaged, but my girl died before we were able to get married.' Jags lets the fake tragedy seep into the air. 'Anyway, so this is me, doing my best to get out there, like my mates keep saying it's time to.'

Mates? I've never seen or heard of any mates.

'What was her name, *your girl*?' Jessica says.

'April.'

I almost spit out my drink.

'Do you mind me asking what she died of?' Jessica asks. 'She must have been very young.'

'Cancer. Thyroid.'

Interesting how Jags has chosen a relatively obscure type of cancer; one he might not need to know too much about.

'I'm sorry to hear that,' Jessica says. 'Was she in hospital long?'

'In and out for nearly two years,' Jags says grimly, faintly shaking his head at the supposed memory.

'Which one?' Jessica asks.

'*Which one*?'

'Which hospital?'

'Oh, there were lots,' says Jags. 'So many appointments, incredible consultants, nurses. I think what the NHS did to try to save her was just amazing.' Jags gives his date his best smile. It's incredibly creepy.

'Yeah, there are some great NFT specialists in London,' Jessica says.

'Yep. Brilliant people.' Jags nods.

'One day I hope to specialise in nose, face, and thyroid, actually.' Jessica sits right back in her seat, appearing to be assessing Jags, who appears to be suddenly more guarded now his date might know more about his dead would-be wife's

296

cancer than he might. He gazes out of the window for a second before redoubling his efforts.

'Wow, it's amazing to think you could one day be an NFT specialist, the sort April and I spent hours with. Maybe you'll go on to save lots of Aprils.' He looks out the window once more, as if he's imagining his beloved fiancée on the other side of the glass.

'It's HNT.' Jessica tilts her head.

Jags blinks. 'Yeah, that's what you said.'

'No, I didn't. I said nose, face, thyroid, NFT. It's head, neck, thyroid, *HNT*.'

A bit of a pause, before Jags mumbles, 'Difficult times. I think maybe I've tried to forget—'

'You said you were an actor?' Jessica cuts him off.

'Guilty as charged,' Jags says.

An actor? When he gave April his card it said he was a business affairs specialist. Why would he lie? Does April know he's a complete liar? I stare into my negroni, trying to make sense of it all. When I look up, I see Jessica grabbing her bag.

'Well, if I were you, I'd be looking for a refund on my tuition fees.'

And she's off, leaving Jags reeling, me still processing what I've heard.

'Jessica, wait. I'm sorry!' Jags stands in his booth, turns to watch her go. 'I only wanted to . . .' He finally notices someone is watching him. 'Can I help you?' he asks me.

I leave my booth, slide into the seat opposite his.

I think I may have worked out what's really going on with Jags.

'Let's see,' I say.

'Sorry, do I—'

I take my glasses off and wait for *him* to work it out.

'You!?' He falls back down into his seat, then makes himself sit up again. 'Essie, I don't what you think you've seen, but it's been a really long day, and my mum's probably expecting me ages ago, and she's not very well, so I'll be going now.'

'I need answers,' I tell him. This is one bad man I'm not going to allow to escape the consequences of his actions.

'Essie, I can't imagine the pressure you've been under, so, how about we call it a night now, and if there's still something on your mind the next time I see you, then, go ahead: shoot. Grill me all you want over a sidecar or two, OK?'

'That's not what I want.' He tries to stand, but I think he realises by now he's not going anywhere. 'Sit down, Jags. Love the hair, by the way.'

Jags goes to mess about with his tufts again before stopping himself, getting out his wallet and flapping about with it before chucking three dirty tenners onto the table.

'I know because you're famous you might think you can boss little people like me around, but I'm not one of them.' He can't seem to get his wallet to shut properly, the faster he goes to snap it together, the more it seems to want to pop open again.

'Sit down, Jags.'

He holds my glare for a second. Then, it's like a switch has been flipped behind his eyes again.

'Oh my god!' He shouts it, a mad grin on his face. 'Oh my god! Essie Lay! I don't care what they say, I absolutely *love* you!'

Jags bends down, his face next to mine. 'Not now. Not here.' He gets out his phone and pushes his face close next to mine again. 'Oh my god, new profile pic alert!' he yells, and one, two, three sets of tables, look our way. Then, even more pick up on something happening. Within five seconds, forty people I've never met now want a piece of me. My trusty disguise blown, my willingness to pose for selfies clear. As a tide of people run towards me, Jags tries to disappear into the night.

The people in the cocktail bar paw at me, shriek, and snap away, but I'm too focused on my mission to let them win. I manage to pull myself free of the crowds and run out of the cocktail bar, a backdrop of boos and people saying what a bitch I am trailing behind. It's water off a duck's back. Almost.

I run as fast as I can back to the car park, taking the short-cuts and side alleys I've used many times to give fans or paps the slip. When I make my way up the storeys, Jags's car is still there. I wait. Seconds later, he turns up panting and obviously furious. Something inside me relishes seeing him like this, the real him I've detected round the edges of Mr Nice Guy all this time. He grabs his car door open, starts the engine, and gets ready to escape. But when he looks out of the windscreen to go, he sees me, blocking his exit.

*

Jags and I have been talking in his car for a while. He was pretty angry at first, but I found a way to calm him down.

'What was it that first attracted you to April?' I ask him.

He looks to his hands, clasped between his knees. 'She looked . . . she seemed different. Something about her just drew me in. Despite myself, I felt this connection I couldn't ignore.'

'And when would you say you thought you were really falling for her?'

299

'*Really*?' Jags turns to me.

'I'd like to hear you say it.'

He looks to the ceiling of his car, slouching where he sits. 'I can't remember when, exactly.'

'I need details.'

Jags is quiet for a second, then pulls himself up, cups the back of his head in his hands, and smiles at the ceiling of his grotty old car.

'The day I knew how truly in love I was, why I think it was probably today. You'd been acting like Joan Crawford on a bad day, losing-your-grip-on-reality-and-the-limits-of-your-own-ability meltdown territory. Anyway, for some reason, April didn't lose her mind with you. If anything, the more mental you were, the more unhinged, the more patient and in control April seemed, which is how she made the last take today so brilliant. I love powerful women, you see. I couldn't resist her in the end. So while I did indeed head home to see my mother, it got to about . . .' Jags checks his watch, 'eight and it dawned on me I needed to get back to April, be with her at the wrap party, stand by her side, see if she'd give me a chance.'

Jags looks to me, satisfied he's said enough, happy he's managed to dig the knife into me along the way. All this time, he's thought I'm a pushover, a fragile little mess. He has no clue how much abuse I've taken from much bigger fish than him, whole schools of them, in fact. But I'm not going to take it anymore.

'All right. Almost plausible,' I say.

'So we're done and I should go to the wrap party now?' Jags asks.

'Just one more question,' I say.

He turns his palms out and spreads his arms, like he's showing me what an open book he is. 'Shoot.'

'When, exactly, did April first hire you to play the role of her boyfriend?'

28

April, the night of the gala screening

Jags and I are on our way to Lotus in the back of a taxi. I've dropped off Essie's white gown at my place, where I hastily changed into jeans and trainers. I've told Jags he should get out of the car and head back to his mother's, but this is one occasion when he seems to want to prolong the night with me. When I come back, he's still there, likely more out of ghoulish curiosity over what's happened to Essie, than any genuine care for me.

'You don't need to be here.'

'I don't think you've ever needed me more. You don't need to push me away now. I want to be there for you.'

I haven't got time to argue with him. I tell the driver to take us to Lotus.

My mind feels lost in a universe of wrenching and bizarre possibilities and questions as we get closer. Firstly, what the hell has motivated Janine to bring me into the inner circle at Lotus now? My brain then gallops through the many, varied, and disturbing scenarios I could be participating in: Essie is dead and Janine knows what I have done and is playing out how best to traumatise, humiliate, and punish me; Essie is dead and Janine killed her and is seeking to neutralise whatever threat I may be to her seeming innocence; Essie is alive and Janine is in on the whole thing and I'm being summoned for torture and reprisals at best, at worst to make it easy for the police to arrest me. But Janine sounded genuinely distressed on the phone, displaying the kind of anguish I'd expected to hear that morning when Essie had first vanished from her pool, though Janine had not realised. Or did she know much more than even I did?

The taxi finally swings into the dropped kerb outside Lotus's main gates.

Jags checks the driver isn't listening, then whispers, 'Don't say anything you don't need to. Oh, and don't use your keys, we should get Janine to let us in. Let her feel she's the one in control.'

'OK,' I say, throat thick, stomach heavy.

Jags leans out of the window and speaks through the inter-com at the electric gates. I hear Janine on the other end of the line, her voice slow and solemn. I get out of the car and move across the gravel to Essie's front door, a wave of nausea rippling through me.

'Here,' Jags says as we're nearly at the door.

'What?' I see a blur of diamante in the gloom. Jags is hand-ing me Essie's phone.

I don't have time to ask why now, or protest; I barely have time to shove it in my pocket before Janine opens the door. Her face is swollen and blotched. She's clearly been crying for some time. Oh god, Essie really could be dead, and I have her phone in my pocket. The truth of her loss and the danger I am in pushes into my heart like the point of a freshly sharpened knife.

303

'Is she really . . .' My throat closes before I can finish the dreadful question.

'Come inside,' Janine says.

Something's changed about the place. The marble floor shines. The whole place looks to have been steam-cleaned. A clean-up orchestrated by Essie's killer? There would be no motivation for Janine to portray Essie's life as anything but chaotic, so who else could have done this? We pass the atrium table, polished to a high shine, the vase of rotting flowers now replaced by a funereal display of white lilies which makes me shudder; another move by Essie's killer, another means of tormenting me?

'Are the police here?' Jags asks Janine.

'They just left,' she says and at least there is some cold comfort in that. They may come for me eventually, but not right now.

The three of us walk through to the living space. The carpet is immaculate, the cream sofas gleam, Essie's egg chair looks like no one has ever sat on it. My stomach flips when I think about what Essie's killer must have done to create the impression she had sat there after her death: pluck the hairs from her cold scalp to fool me.

'And your parents?' I ask Janine. 'I can't imagine . . .'

'Mum's lying down. Dad can't speak. I don't know how to help him. I don't know what to say.' Janine paces in front of the glass sliding doors to the pool. 'I thought I should tell you myself. I mean, you were the closest thing she had to a best friend.' Janine cries anew.

My heart fills, then falls. I think I probably was Essie's best friend. But now she's not here, what's the point? What was the purpose of any of it? If she was here, alive, at Lotus, I would dedicate my life to elevating her, I would write stories that would only ever hero her fortitude and tenacity, not her vulnerability. And I would shoot her so beautifully, as epic and poetic as she deserved. I would beg her forgiveness.

'Janine. How . . . where?' I ask her.

'They found her in the river.' Janine sobs out the words, then composes herself to speak again. 'We don't know much yet, but they think she may have drowned. We don't know if there was foul play. . . They're keeping an open mind until the investigation gets into full swing, but, with her history, how's she been lately . . .' Janine lets the sentence trail away, and I struggle to listen for a moment anyway.

They know Essie drowned, but how do they know it wasn't in her pool? They will surely know this soon.

The investigation.

They are coming for me.

If Essie has been dead for days, since the night of the awards, they'll want to know how she has posted on Insta; been spotted at the screening; spoken to her sister from beyond the grave. Perhaps, though, she has not been dead for very long. Maybe this could save me?

'Do they know how long she had . . .' I ask.

'Not yet. We'll find out more soon,' says Janine.

'And they're sure it's her?' Jags asks, still stupidly clinging on to the idea she is alive and we do not face being hauled over the coals and into prison.

'I have to go to identify the, you know, tomorrow.' Janine covers her eyes with her hands, seems to crumble. 'I said I'd go. Mum and Dad shouldn't have to do this. We're not telling the press, we're not telling anyone until we know for sure, but the police . . .' Janine reaches for a large brown envelope on Essie's rattan side table. 'This is what they gave me.'

'You don't have to look, April,' Jags says to me.

'No. God, no, sorry.' Janine moves to take the envelope back.

'It's OK,' I say. 'I don't think I'll believe it until I see it.'

I must force myself to see Essie how she is now: gone, washed up on the banks of the river like junk. I deserve to see the things I can't unsee for the rest of my life. I take the envelope from Janine's fingers, unsure if it's she or I making the paper quiver.

'I know I could be hard on her.' Janine begins to pace again, muttering to herself. 'I know I probably could have done more to help her, but I always did what I thought was best for my sister in the long term.' I ignore Janine and slip my finger under the envelope's tucked flap, bracing myself. My eyes are closed when I eventually free the photographs. I make myself open them.

'Oh god no.'

The first of two images.

Essie.

So white as to be almost blue, Essie on the mud of an exposed shore of the Thames. She lies on her front, naked, her head turned to her right-hand side, her face barely visible; her yellow hair damp and tangled down to the small of her back, where the image cuts off. Her arm is grey green, extended as though she was reaching out for help. It is unmistakably Essie, though my desperate mind wants to suggest it could be another slim white woman with blonde extensions. I force myself to put the top image to the back and view the second. I have a sense, somehow, this will be much worse.

306

Her face.

A close-up.

There are a few strands of her extensions plastered over her cheek and sunken into the mud around her head. Her eyes – somewhere after blue, amber, grey, and green, beyond colour – stare into the infinite space before them.

'When was the last time you spoke to her?' Janine asks me. 'Did she talk to you? Did she mention the deputyship? I wouldn't have been looking into it if I didn't think she was vulnerable. I mean, she is, she was.' Janine continues to talk hysterically, justifying her exploitation of Essie.

The floor feels as liquid as Essie's pool. I put one hand down on the back of her chair and stare through the window into the blue. And I see Essie there, in her dress the colour of the moon, that night, her face turned away from the world forever. And I left her there, I abandoned her so some evil person could steal her things, undress her, before throwing her into the river. Maybe the killer drugged Essie, got her zonked out on too many pills and champagne when she said she wouldn't go to the awards. They let her pass out, rolled her into the pool where she drowned; but then they panicked, and then they took her to the river, where they hoped she'd be washed away forever. An amateur job, but a diabolical effort. They were probably still at Lotus when we arrived, hiding, waiting for Jags and me to leave. But who? Why? What monster did this to my best friend? And what monster did I let myself become to do the things that set this in motion? I will never, as long as I live, forgive myself.

'I need some fresh air,' I say.

'I'll come with you.' Jags moves to follow me, but I don't want him near me right now. I need a partner who brings

307

out the best in me. He has brought out not only my deepest insecurities and my neediness. More than this, he gave new life to the darkest elements of my single-mindedness. I don't think I can be with him now or ever again. I do believe I am truly done with him. I only wish Essie were here to see it, I think she would have been proud of me.

'No. I want to be on my own.'

I take myself out to the veranda but turn on my heels when I see who is already there, propping himself up on the balustrade overlooking the lotus pond.

He hears me and turns.

'Janine said she'd called you.'

Con returns his attention immediately back to the pond and the night beyond it. 'I'm surprised you came, though . . .' He waits for a moment before completing his sentence, ' . . . after what we did.'

'I'm sorry for your loss,' I rush, turning to get away from him.

'Oh, I bet you are.'

How I want to get away from him. But there's a piece of me that has changed since I lost Essie; the night I lost something of myself. Whatever it is, it won't allow me to leave Conrad Laycock's snide innuendos unchallenged.

'What . . .' I swallow. 'What do you mean?'

'You tempt the fathers of all your so-called friends?' Con's words and his oily tone turn my insides. 'You know, Esther was destroyed after what you did. You know that's why she tried to end her life that time? I said to her mother when you wormed your way back into Esther's life, I told her, and Janine: *She's trouble, that one. Esther should stay well away.*'

The unbelievable self-righteousness of men like Con, men like Jude Lancaster. The men who get to walk through life, trampling on the bodies of better women, learning nothing, caring for no one and nothing but their egos, their pathetic yet uncontainable needs. How I wish it was Con's body lying cold and without dignity on the river's sludge, not that of his brave, beautiful daughter.

'You forced yourself on a young girl your daughter had brought for support.' There is a tremble in my voice, but the words are clear.

'Forced? Hardly. And you weren't that young or as innocent as you made out to be. And now, you've finally gone and done it.' Con's lips tremble in a way that makes me want to slap them still. 'You know, she never really recovered after that weekend? I think you're involved in all of this somehow. I think the police'll come after you.'

'The police come after me? You're more responsible than anyone else for Essie being vulnerable. You controlled her. You wrung her dry for money. You used her friends to satisfy your own needs. And she knew, but you lied to her about them, and you lied to her about me, didn't you?'

Con puffs out a gust of air, shrugs. I drive myself into the space next to him.

'I wasn't the first, was I? There was a reason girls who came with Essie to Signal House didn't ever come back. I know what you are, and I think she did too. I helped her realise the truth she always knew.' I force myself to enter the space right by Con's ear. 'You're a fucking rapist.'

Con, his eyes wide in outrage and something else: fear. Is there anything more dangerous than a woman ready to call out the despicable things men do?

309

'Dad?'

Janine is at the door. I don't know how much she heard, but I can't imagine any of this is news to her. If she wants to challenge me now, let her. I will send her my own series of incriminating photographs and she can come to her own conclusions.

'Mum wants to get home now.'

'I'm leaving too,' I say, moving away from Con and back towards the door.

Janine nods, her eyes squeezed tight as though the next words she wants to say are hard for her to utter. 'I know you wanted to be a good friend to Essie.'

I stop in front of Janine. 'I do. I did. I honestly don't know what I'm going to do without her.' My sobs burst free and somehow, Janine and I are hugging each other. In the background, Con makes his move towards the door.

'I know it will be the last thing on your mind,' Janine's mouth is now near my ear, 'it's the last thing on mine, but you know I've had cause to go through some of her documents lately. I don't know why, but she changed her will recently. My sister left a gift for you.'

'I don't care about any of that but thank you for letting me know.' Then, a thought strikes me, as I pull away from her. 'I hope she left you this place, Janine. I'd hate to see it leave your family for any reason.' Janine gives a meek little nod to the floor, a flutter of shame in her eyes. And now I know what's really going on, why she's brought me here: she wants to keep me on-side.

Deputyship was good, it would have given Janine control of Essie's fortune, but it was messy and expensive, and would require legal maintenance as Essie would have doubtlessly tried to prove to the courts that she didn't need her sister to be in control of her money. Death. Death is clean. And cheap. And final. I realise I'm here not to grieve with her, but to initiate the process of Janine neutralising any kind of challenge I might make to the will, or, at the very least, any attempt I might make to muddy the public narrative that Janine Laycock ever had anything but the best of intentions for her talented, rich, beautiful, younger sister. And now, I think I understand something else too.

'Janine, before you go, there's something I want you to know.'

'Oh?'

'Essie loved that white dress you sent her. It was you, wasn't it?'

Janine looks to the door. 'I should probably get back to my parents.'

'I'm sure you thought you were doing the right thing, giving the impression it was from Jackson. I know what you did came from a good place: you probably wanted Essie to feel loved in the run-up to her big night at the awards. You weren't to know it would make her feel a thousand times worse,' I say.

She smiles, eyes closed in faux humbleness, but her mouth twitching with a waiting snarl.

'Well, what's done is done. And that dress is yours now, April.'

I lose a breath. What does Janine know? 'I'm sorry?'

'That's what Essie left you: that white dress.'

Janine mutters something behind her tissue along the lines of how Essie had *no idea she'd be passing it on to me so soon*, but

311

I'm barely listening. The idea of Essie bequeathing me a dress that I know for sure she died in, and was subsequently used to taunt me, makes my head feel like a puff of air.

'You and Jags can see yourself out.' Janine moves to the back door. 'Oh, do you have your keys? While you're here, I may as well take them.' Janine tries to say it casually, like it's of no significance whatsoever that while she's only known of her sister's death for minutes, she is already marking her territory by relieving me of access to Lotus.

I avoid the temptation to touch the bulging front pocket of my jeans, where the keys are tucked together with Essie's phone. I tell Janine as evenly as I can manage. 'No. It's why we had to be let in.'

She nods. 'Next time, then.'

Janine finally follows her father inside. I intend to stay out here for as long as it takes the Laycocks to leave. I view the lotus pond, a ring of spotlights silhouetting the dead heads and shrivelled stalks. They seem to tell me my life without Essie will never be a bed of roses, or even a lake of lotuses, only a landscape of promise spent; death and decay, punctuated only by the soiled white dress that clung to my best friend's body.

What will Janine do when she sees the dress is missing? I will have to act upset and surprised when she tells me the news, all the while knowing the dress is already in my wardrobe. And now I realise my life will forever be defined by lies and fakery; I will never have a true and sincere connection with another human being again, if I've ever had one to begin with. My view of the eerie pond is obscured by a fresh throb of tears. I wipe my eyes and see the pond clearly once more.

And when I do, I notice something.

A stripe of darkness over one the lights on the far side of the pond.

'They've all gone. Shall we get a taxi?'

Jags appears behind me. He lays a hand on my back. I stiffen, rather than lean into it like I normally would. His hand rubs my shoulder now, in apology. 'I was going to take the same one as you, get you home first, but my mum needs to talk to me about something urgently.'

I move away from him and towards the door. 'You should head straight home then. I'll get my own car.'

He nods, then tries to hold my hand. I move my hand away, open the back door to get back into the house via the kitchen, clasping my palms together shut as we walk through to the atrium. I maintain my solitary pose for the duration of the time it takes for us to order Ubers and for his to arrive.

'I was going to wait with you if my ride showed first, but—' Jags says.

'Go. I'm fine on my own.'

Despite the shock of the night, the very fact we know Essie is truly dead, Jags saunters off without ceremony into his taxi. And I think: this is how our final act ends. No drama, no formality, no discussion. I am finishing whatever we may have had together now, only solidifying the truth that has been evident for weeks, maybe even months: the connection between him and me that started the day we wrapped on the shoot has cooled to nothing, if there were anything truly warm between us anyway. As I watch his car turn onto the street and pull away into the night, I block his number, then delete it entirely unceremoniously. Only the endings of things significant and real deserve our pause for rite or ritual, and whatever I had

313

with Jags, I know it is unworthy. A few minutes after, my Uber arrives and drives me away from Lotus. I descend through North London. We pass the street where the old bank I lived in used to be, now a luxury apartment block. I wonder what it's like inside. Then, I wonder whether I will ever get to be inside Lotus Lodge again.

A rush of panic.

I still have Essie's phone in my pocket.

'Excuse me!' I shout to the driver. 'I'm going to change my destination.'

29

Essie, before, The Vanished Woman *Cannes gala screening*

It's 10 a.m. and a scorching sun is already creeping into the shadow of my balcony overlooking the La Croisette and the shining Mediterranean. It's Directors' Fortnight at Cannes and *The Vanished Woman* has a gala screening today at the Grand Théâtre Lumière. Getting selected is a huge deal for the film, for April, and for me. If I've managed to front an independent movie good enough to punch through to Directors' Fortnight, I can't be that bad an actress, or can I? There's a rich history of strong reactions from the audience at this venue; boos and walkouts if they don't approve, and an odd ritual of standing ovations that have been known to last more than twenty minutes, and often come with the expectation that lead members of the cast and crew will cry in response, the audience not letting up until they get their tears, particularly from their leading ladies, or on the off chance the director is female.

A big UK press turnout is expected this afternoon. I suspect the British media is rubbing its hands, ready to trash my performance and how I've dared to think I can un-cancel myself, prepared to ridicule the French selection committee for not adhering to their high artistic, not to mention, moral standards, by including my film. Being cancelled isn't a one-way street, particularly for women. When men are uncovered as wife-beaters and sexual deviants, after a stint in therapy, maybe three months out in the cold, they can come back, or they can simply take the *never complain/never explain* route and act like they've never been cancelled. But this doesn't work where women are concerned.

As well as the grovelling statement Jonathan put out in my name straight after the video dropped, there was also an Insta post telling everyone I was sorry that I couldn't have been better for them, especially the young woman I was accused of using as bait to stop Jude from coming after me. I also apologised to viewers who'd bought into the on-screen friendship that I'd now shown was fake, and to all the brands and their customers who'd dumped me already. Every word was drafted by Janine and Jonathan. Explaining what had really happened or arguing I had been a victim too were not options available to me.

I may not be myself when I'm Elena, but she's the closest thing I've had to having my own voice since I was twenty-one years old and my father emotionally blackmailed me into taking my first on-screen job in TV. He convinced me I needed it not just to help pay to fix everything wrong with Signal, but also to undo the damage of my 'cry for help' and my accusations over what he'd done to April.

'You've cut me to the bone, girl. I don't think you love me at all,' my father had said to me after I told him what I saw. The boyfriend I thought I loved at the time turned out to be a pig, but worse than this, the father I adored was a monster. I was very drunk by the time I got my hands on my mum's meds. I did not really want to die that night, but I didn't want to live with the truth I'd learnt either.

How easy is it to not believe the things staring you in the face because they're too big and awful, because they hurt too much to possibly be true. Here are some of the truths from back then: I left *The Dawn Chorus* to stay away from April. I didn't want to see or speak to her because I didn't want to face the truth about my dad. It's not something I recognised then, and that's not something I'm at all proud of. But it is the truth I'm glad broke through when we shot *The Vanished Woman*.

After I left *The Dawn Chorus*, I managed to get a break as a production co-ordinator on the children's magazine show *All Aboard*. I'd been there a couple of weeks when they'd asked me to stand in for a presenter in rehearsals for a making slot, pasting together some sort of cardboard rip-off of a cartoon franchise. I'd made an absolute pig's ear of the model and ended up joking my way through the mess of glue and paper strips. The next day, I was asked if I wanted to join the presenting team. I was blown away, so flattered, but so scared. I knew I didn't want people to look at me, maybe millions of them, and have an opinion on me, how I looked, what I said, how klutzy I was. So, I talked it over with my dad, even though things had not been the same between us. Maybe I wanted to prove I still trusted him, and deep down, I was so unused to being out of step with him.

'How much they want to pay you?' he said.

'Loads?' For a production co-ordinator like me, what they would pay me as 'talent' was a phenomenal amount of money. But when I thought about what I'd be giving up – the possibility of living a normal life without being stopped in the street or plastered across the tabloids like I'd seen happen to my footballer-ex – I didn't think it could be worth it. Besides, I was pretty good behind the camera, I was doing so well at *The Dawn Chorus*; the senior producers liked my work ethic, my ideas for getting things done. They'd called me 'a production natural'. I'd started to believe there was a path there for me into future success, a road that didn't take me in front of the camera, a place I did not want to be.

'You'd get even more if you had a manager. We'll get Janine to act as one while we get you an agent,' Dad said.

'I don't think I want to do it. I still reeling a bit after—'

'After your loopy little moment in Kent? I think you could do with something to stop that imagination of yours getting you into trouble, Esther. You'd be mad not to bite their hand off. I'll get Janine onto it. She knows how these things work.'

I didn't bother arguing with him, knowing somewhere it would only lead to more gaslighting, more accusations of me not loving him. Dad could see I wasn't convinced yet.

'I've had a few let-downs of late, in more ways than one.' My dad gave me a hangdog look. 'The truth is, unless you want me to sell Signal and destroy your mum in the process, you should get yourself on camera and wring it for all it's worth; pay your share.'

'Are things really that bad?' I asked, stunned at the idea my father could find himself at risk of losing something as major as Signal.

'We all need to work hard and to stay lucky.'

'Right.'

'There's a good girl.'

I hadn't actually said yes, but neither did I say no. That

was the moment when my entire life was set on a path I didn't particularly want it to go on because I didn't speak when I should have. Instead, I let my dad, and then my sister on his orders, do all the talking for me.

Later that day, Janine called the producers on *All Aboard* as my manager. She moaned so much they upped their offer. She would deduct ten per cent from this and everything else I earnt from then on. With a high-profile gig already under my belt, I was a solid prospect to Jonathan's agency, who Janine paired up with soon after. He also took his ten per cent. Together, they created 'Essie Lay'. I was not consulted or asked to consent to killing off my own name.

But today, Esther Laycock, the real me if I can find her, is fighting back.

A knock on my Cannes hotel room door. I open it.

'Hi, April. Hi, Jags.'

Here they are, love's youngish dream, or something like it; April glowing, enjoying the turnabout that happened between her and Jags on the last day of the shoot, when he showed up for the wrap party after all, and stayed by her side all night long.

We're all heading to the screening together in a kitted-out limousine the financiers decided to pay for when they detected the heat around my reappearance into public life, which they want to wring for all it may be worth. I'm in an azure, sequinned floor-length gown. It feels strange being so dressed-up this early in the day but Cannes, I have learnt, is a very strange place. It's like a cattle market for films, as well as for actresses. There are big releases, art house stuff, really bad films; it all gets bought and sold here. It feels like anyone who's trying to make a buck in the industry, or build a reputation, is here. And although

I have a leading part in a production that's already being buzzed about, I'm still not totally sure Essie Lay should be here. Putting her out there again from the photographers and journalists, and TV crews I know will be lying in wait feels like throwing her voluntarily into the lion's den.

We're nearly at the cinema. On this opposite side of the limo, I watch April take Jags's hand in hers, him squeezing hers tightly in return.

I break into their moment. 'Guys, I've been thinking, I should give you a set of keys to my place, let you know how the alarm and locks work.'

April turns to look at me, Jags watching on warily.

'Lotus is too big for me on my own, really. I think it would be nice for you guys to feel it's somewhere for you to be too. Come and work there, have a swim, enjoy the garden. April, you need to finish writing your next project, correct? I think I'll be happier knowing someone else is knocking about the place a bit more too, now that the madness around the film's publicity campaign is starting.'

'Really?' April asks.

'Why not? It's a win-win,' I tell her.

'Essie, that's so nice of you. My flat can feel a little cramped sometimes. It would be lovely to be able to find a spot in Lotus to polish my script,' April says.

'Have a nice dip,' I add and April nods. 'And Jags, you're still living with your mum?'

He gives me a tight smile. 'For my sins.'

'I bet you'd appreciate somewhere to escape to with April?'

'Ab-so-lute-ly,' Jags says, slowing the word for added emphasis.

320

'That's settled, then.' I enjoy a moment of satisfaction. It's short-lived as we're now arriving at the cinema. My stomach flips as we pull in at the foot of the mountain of red-carpeted stairs to the auditorium of the Lumière, a league of photographers at either side. And then, the training kicks in. I stretch my mouth into my 'signature smile' and make myself not hear my voice on that video or think of Jackson, right before he fucked me for good.

Someone outside opens the limo door and the flashes begin It's a dysfunctional homecoming, terrifying but nevertheless familiar. I get ready to step out of the car and turn to check how April's bearing up. She's a rabbit in the headlights, frozen to the spot.

'April,' I say, but she doesn't respond, her eyes wide and fixed on the flashes beginning in earnest outside the limo. Jags too is letting himself look rattled by the barrage of light. 'April? Honey.' I take her hand. 'Come. Try to enjoy yourself.' *While it lasts*, I think about adding, but don't.

I lead her out behind me to a spot in between the two rows of paparazzi and in front of a row of huge publicity posters, my face massive but then fading away to nothing on one side, the white spaghetti straps on my shoulders, behind the place where April's name appears. Now that I'm here, I don't want April ruining the pictures by looking like she's just stolen her body from someone else. Also, it would be good, I think, for her to understand even a little of what it's like to be me, not having any real control even over how I enter a movie theatre, my every movement calibrated to meet the needs of somebody else. How the hell did I get here? Do I really know how I'm going to get out, how I'm going to take back my body, my life?

'Remember what I told you?' I whisper into April's ear. 'Contact, contact, contact. Look into the eyes of each and every one of them. If they ask you to twirl, *twirl*, if they ask you to dip, *dip*. If they want you to walk, *walk*.'

April does exactly as she was told.

Even after my spell in the wilderness, walking for the paps is relatively easy compared to waiting for the moment I have to see myself on the massive screen. All of the cast and crew of the movie are sat on a middle row. This means I'll be able to see it when the viewers in front of me are bored, when they find my performance laughable; when they desert the place in disgust at my attempt at being credible. April keeps on trying to talk to me, but I'm so nervous, I can't concentrate on whatever she's saying. When she's not trying to engage me in conversation, April strokes Jags's thumb, cooing into his ear while I have to use every bit of my strength to stay in my seat. Finally, the title sequence begins.

And there I am. My face enormous, each one of my crow's feet metres long with the first close-up. When the camera pans back to reveal more of my face, I don't even look like me. The way April's chosen to shoot me has distorted everything I thought was OK about my face. I look hideous; my mouth is alien-huge, my head, massively out of proportion. If you didn't know better, you would say that April has deliberately shot me to look as ugly as she possibly could. She has shot me in such a way, with my drab plait and unflattering angles, that I look exactly like her.

I steal a glance at April, and the way she focuses on the screen, determined to not look me in the eye, tells me she has shot me ugly knowingly. Is this another way for her to punish me for what my dad did, just like putting me through the wringer when we shot the film? Or is this simply her artistic choice, because to tell the story she needed to tell, she needed me/Elena to look and feel something like her? Whatever her motivations, April can't bring herself to face me. It makes sudden sense why, every time I've asked if I could see the film before now, she made excuses about 'the print not being ready'.

Up on screen, I look so vulnerable and so unattractive I want to cry, and I feel the same way too: ugly on the inside because of what I let my dad get away with and vulnerable because I'm remembering once more everything the film dug up from the past. I'm without protection at exactly the moment I need it most, when I've put myself on the line for public scrutiny in the most out-there way possible: me leading a movie, my face the one on the poster and filling the screen in every excruciating scene. While no one in the audience has walked out, I badly wish I had. When the house lights finally come up, I also wish I had my disguise kit on me, anything I could possibly do to slip out of here without having to look or talk to anyone.

The whole auditorium is an explosion of noise, so loud, it takes all my will to not press my hands over my ears. And then, I'm glad that I don't.

Cheering.

Clapping.

Everyone is standing. It's happening, a feted, prolonged standing ovation. April looks at me, grabs Jags's hand, then mine. I only sit there, oddly numb. Because I've been here, or somewhere like it, before: lauded and loved by an audience, until they don't love you anymore, until they hate you; because if you're ready to believe these five-star reviews, then you must

323

accept their single stars too. None of it lasts, none of it is real and if I was feeling kinder, I'd make sure I'd advise April to not make the mistake of thinking that it is. I don't know how long the ovation goes on before she takes my hand and pulls me to my feet. The noise goes to another level. It's more vocal, more insistent.

'They're expecting us to cry,' April says gleefully.

'Right.'

More hollers, louder expressions of adoration. I view the audience, braying now, their hands, surely raw. They want their tears. April gives it to them. As her hand finally goes to her face to wipe away a tear, the crowd cheers. She looks to me, she wants me to join her, to give the people want they want from us women.

'It's for you, Essie. I know it was hard to do, harder to see, but look what we've done.' April's dishwater eyes encourage mine to meet the sea of faces, people, almost masochistically slapping their hands together in my direction, to compel me to do their bidding, give them the show of emotion they feel they're owed.

I stare out at all these people, requiring my catharsis for their satisfaction. But I've had my fill of emoting on-demand. Those days are gone. I'm into a new era now. My eyes stay dry.

30

April, the night of the gala screening

I'm back at Lotus. I let myself in through the front gates, ready with a story I left something there should I be discovered by Janine, or Con and Una. But I've come back to lose something, to hide Essie's phone down the back of her rattan chair. But now that I'm opening the door, I have the uncanny compulsion I am actually here to find something, yet I don't know what. What I do know is this is probably my last chance to search Lotus for clues on what really happened to Essie and who was responsible.

As I walk through the atrium, absorbing the over-aweing scale of the place when one is alone here, I feel deeply for Essie, holed up at Lotus with no support in the aftermath of the video that got her cancelled. I sense her killer's hand in the lilies, in every shiny surface, in the obliteration of every trace of what they did to Essie. And yet I sense Essie powerfully too; watching me, waiting. For what? To bring her killer to justice, to work out the identity of the dark figure who stole her things, tormented me to imagine she was alive and halt my investigation while I impersonated her, while they disposed of her body?

'I'm here, Essie. I'm trying my best now, OK?' I attempt to soothe her spirit as I move into the living room. And in the quiet, my mind fills with the awful pictures of Essie. I see her frozen, her cheek in the mud. I slide the doors into the pool area and stare at the water, as though the mysteries might somehow reveal themselves to me, as though Essie herself might somehow magically appear in the water once more.

I walk through to the kitchen, where I head to the drawer where I found her garage key and her psychiatrist's card. I move slowly, the exhaustion of the last year, of everything it took to get Essie back in my life, to try and build something good around her, and all the ways I have failed, seeping into me. I find I'm bent over one of her kitchen counters, my head hanging over my forearms, my breath hot and quick. I must go soon, but I know, I'm not yet finished at Lotus. I consider going up to Essie's room, but I can't face it. I'm afraid. I don't want to climb that dreadful staircase alone, imagining gloved hands touching and stealing Essie's things. I decide instead to take one last look outside and leave Lotus Lodge for the final time. I'll go home, and instead of anxiously waiting for the UK press reviews of *The Vanished Woman*, as I might have done in an alternate existence with Essie still in it, I will drink sidecars alone, rewatching my own print of the film as I finally begin to mourn all I have lost.

I unlock the back door and walk out onto the veranda, the night freezing now, my body shaking with cold and what feels like deferred shock. I look out onto the lotus pond, noticing once more the darkened streak across one of the lights on the farthest bank.

I know I must go to it.

326

I take unsteady steps down from the veranda onto the lawn edging the pond on three of its sides. The ground is chilled and damp under my feet, but I have to see what is blocking the light on the edge where the water appears deepest. My trainers make horrific sucking squelches as I leave the lawn and step down to the bank to get nearer, and I feel I may be risking getting stuck if I don't keep moving.

I reach the light. I cannot decipher what the material draped over the bulb is from here. The second my fingers make contact I wish they had not. A whine of revulsion leaves my mouth.

In my hand, hair, not a few strands, but a thick yellow lock. An extension. Essie's.

I view the ground below me with new horror, the mud-caked piece of her hair still caught in my fingers. Did her killer hide her here first before taking her to the Thames? Nausea rising now. I find I'm staggering backwards. Something hard in the putrid mud beneath my foot, resisting my tread. I shine my phone onto it. A champagne bottle, just like the one that fell into the water near Essie's leg that dreadful night. Something else next to it, glinting through the sludge. I prize the rest of whatever it is free from a suck of mud.

A pill bottle. Zolpidem. Empty.

I can't hold down my sickness anymore, vomiting into the water, the fake hair still caught on my fingers. I squat down to frantically wash it away in the dirty water.

The mud bank, it wasn't The Thames. Those images were taken on the edge of Essie's pond. But the police said she was found in the river. Were those photos not taken by the police, but by Essie's killer, here? Did they hide Essie's body the night of the awards? But why hide the bottles in the mud too? I trudge

327

shakily back to the lawn, and it strikes me there's a sense of mischief about this move. And the strand of hair; why leave it, draped unnaturally across a light at the farthest end of the pond? It's as though I have been led out here.

That cold feeling again, terrifyingly palpable now. I am being taunted. I am being watched. A residue of Essie, in the dark water below the spent lotus stalks, breaking through the slime of the pond's banks. Where next? Where else am I required to be by whoever is directing me tonight? I look about me.

A light.

Flickering on at the end of the garden.

Someone is in the annexe.

I know if I don't go see who is there, I will never understand more. And if I do make myself face who is there, my tormentor, Essie's murderer, then I may never leave Lotus Lodge alive. But the truth is a compelling force, and its draws me away from the pond, across the lawn and to the bottom of the garden.

I walk through the slim strip of mature woodland, avoiding the path. I can now see a shadowy smear of someone moving behind the thin curtains of the living space. A man's silhouette. Another light comes on at the far end of the building. I move around its perimeter without making a sound. I peer through a gap in the side of the curtains to see evidence of life in the living area. A dirty, frosted tumbler on a side table, a phone behind it, but no specific clues on his identity.

The phone.

Can I summon the tormentor by calling the number Essie has been ringing multiple times a day for the past six months, the last person she spoke to? I pull Essie's phone from my pocket, and I finally get to make the call I wanted to before I had to leave for the screening.

My fingers quake as I call the number of the last person who spoke to Essie.

The phone behind the tumbler comes to life.

I clamp my hand over the gasp leaving my mouth.

Whoever owns that phone is implicated in Essie's vanishing and they are clearly squatting on her property, so comfortable they seem to be having a shower, judging by the steam in the air, the ringing phone unheard.

I need a moment to regroup, to observe, to think about what I want to happen next. I walk past the front end of the building, down the side to the back; perhaps I can glean something from a view into the annexe's bedroom. That's my intention as I round the corner, but I stop dead long before I can creep to the back window.

In the darkness, I see her.

The Grey Lady.

ACT V

'By swinging round to the same shot and then showing, not a character of greater significance, but the original character reframed, you, as director, flip the false sense of security you created in the previous shot. You have subverted the viewer's expectations of what they think should happen next and who they are expecting to see doing it.'

FILM SCHOOL LECTURE NOTES TRANSCRIPTION

31

April, after the screening, the final visit to Lotus Lodge

My ex-boyfriend's car. Tucked safely behind the annexe of my dead best friend's mansion.

How could I have been so stupid to have ever trusted him. He lied to everyone else, why did I let myself believe he wouldn't lie to me?

Now there is nothing left to lose.

I walk back to the annexe's front door. I try the handle and find it's not locked. In the least likely place I or anyone else would ever look for him, why would Jags bother? I creep inside, then, hearing the water still flowing in the shower, as calmly as I can, I take a seat near his phone. I view the screen. A notification: *Missed call: Mum.*

'What the fuck!'

Jags stands in the bathroom doorway, a towel taut around his toned stomach; a body I ached to know better, so much so it polluted my judgement. This, after so many years of believing it was only men who were sufficiently basic to do such things.

'April.' He sends a sigh of relief into the air, shaking his head at his own fear. 'Thank god it's you.' He runs back into the bathroom to turn the shower off, and get his story straight.

'OK, you probably want to know what I'm doing here. The truth is my mum—'

'Your mum?' I say.

'Yes. My mother.'

'The woman who calls you three times a day every day since we properly got together?'

'Yes.' He takes a step forward into the room and watches as I make a call with Essie's phone. 'Who are you calling with that?'

I pick up Jags's phone from where it rests, next to the tumbler. I hold it up to him, so he can read the screen when the call from Essie's phone connects. He pales at the sight of the incriminating word I show him: *Mum*.

Then Jags appears to reset. He sighs, then shrugs. 'She's been letting me stay here gratis for months. You paid, she paid more.'

I nod to my feet. 'Enough to pretend you loved me?'

'Just about.'

'Enough to sleep with me, even though you didn't want to.'

'Reckon I got a whole lot more than you paid Jackson to ball your long-lost BFF. Mind you, all told, Jackson got the far better end of the bargain. And Essie seemed to do all right out of your little plan anyway, to a point.'

Jags puts his hands on his hips and views me with a vile mixture of disgust and pity.

'I mean, none of it really worked out how you wanted it, did it?'

I think back to my last moments of innocence, before I put myself and Essie on the path Jags is referring to.

I'd finished polishing *The Vanished Woman*. There was heat on me after the critical reception for *Encounters*, and a buzz about my new feature script. I knew I needed to direct this story and my financiers agreed, greenlighting the project soon after I'd managed to attach Juniper Jones in the role of Elena. I finally felt as though I was about to show everyone that my existence had value, that I was deserving of admiration and, perhaps, affection. But in the sweet, fizzing process of 'making it', still I carried a sourness inside, a part of me I could not be rid of until I faced down what happened to me that weekend at Signal, first at Con's hands, and then at Esther's. After cutting me free of her life, she had taunted me day by day, year by year as she made the whole nation fall in love with her, when not one person ever felt that way about me. And all the while she remained loyal to her father.

I had imagined, before I developed my camera's film, that her father had spun a line about me seducing him, about me being no good, and Essie had listened and accepted his story. But when I saw the pictures Essie took that wretched night, it was far worse than even this. Those photos showed me how deeply I had been betrayed by a person I would have done anything for, the woman I was building my first creative project around. Essie had to have known the truth from that very night, and yet she still treated her father as though he was blameless and I was the guilty party.

I wanted to break Essie's life enough so she would need me and my project, and then use my film to alter how she saw both the past and me, by making her feel something of what it is to be inside my skin, my soul.

First I needed the perfect man to disrupt the status quo of Essie's existence – endlessly available, caring, always listening, loving her unconditionally, dedicated to her happiness, and

335

crucially, appearing as though he would continue to do so, even if he was to see the worst of her. I was having speculative casting meetings for some of the minor roles for *The Vanished Woman*, and when I saw Jackson's publicity shot, while I knew he would not make the cast of my movie, he could have a central role in another project.

'You can think of the role with Essie Lay as immersive; embedded,' I told Jackson when I realised how malleable he might be. I explained I was working on some content around the truth behind celebrity facades in light of persistent rumours about Jude Lancaster and Essie Lay. 'There will be acting involved, some of which could potentially be . . .' I swallowed, '. . . intimate.'

'You asking me to shag a confession out of her?' Jackson smirked, looking both incredulous and aroused.

'I'm not asking you or her to do anything you won't want to do. There will be base pay for three months and a bonus if you secure the truth on film. It goes without saying, you'll be expected to sign a nondisclosure agreement.'

Twelve weeks later, when I watched what Jackson had billed as 'the smoking gun' in the form of a snatched post-coital moment where Essie 'revealed all', I was disappointed; the story lacked moral clarity, the motivations of the character were muddied, leaving the core drama altogether dissatisfying and too nuanced for my needs. Because what Jackson captured told me Essie might have already learnt from past mistakes, even before I'd made her.

JACKSON: What really went on between you and
    Jude Lancaster?

336

ESSIE: I'm trying to go to sleep, you want
  to give me nightmares?

Essie turns back on her front, rubs her
  eyes, but keeps them closed. Jackson pans
  back to himself and off-screen, Essie giggles nervously, uncomfortably.

                (OFF-SCREEN)

JACKSON: If we're going to get married some-
  day soon, we shouldn't have any secrets.

ESSIE: Bloody hell . . . If you really want
  to know . . . Argh! When I first started
  at Daybreak, for the first couple of years,
  I kind of had to . . . Do you really need
  to know?!

JACKSON: No secrets. Let's start the rest of
  our life right.

ESSIE: (pauses) I didn't have sex with him,
  ever. Not once. He pushed me, like, endlessly pestered me. He thought it was
  funny, I guess. I made it into a bit of
  a joke, tried to make it all smaller than
  it was. I felt I really had to keep him
  happy if I wanted to keep my job . . . So,
  every Friday after we finished filming for
  the week, Jude would come to my dressing
  room and help me choose what I was wearing for next week's shows from the racks
  of clothes we got sent.

JACKSON: Go on.

ESSIE: He would sit there with me.

                337

I would . . . They told me it was normal
for me to be in my underwear, sometimes
not really in that, if Jude thought my bra
straps were showing. Sorry, I feel sick
just thinking about it. You have to understand, I needed the job, a house my dad
absolutely loves was about to crumble into
the sea. I was under a lot of pressure on
all sides. So, there we are.

(OFF-SCREEN)

JACKSON: Did he touch himself?

(Essie pauses.)

ESSIE: He did, and I hated it. I hated him.
I still hate him. I hate him for doing
that and I hate him for making me pretend
to be his best friend, all that supposed
'uncontrollable giggling fits'. Sometimes,
that felt worse than getting my kit off
while he got off. Fuck . . . So, now you
know it. I'm a telly prostitute. Anything
else you want to know?

JACKSON: How long did it go on for? When did
it stop?

ESSIE: After about eighteen months. I told
myself it was because I'd just renego-
tiated my contract, doubling my deal,
because he knew I was getting more famous,
more powerful. What actually happened
was he'd moved on to a new target, a mum
blogger who had a regular slot and seemed

338

to think letting Jude use her would help her career. But then he got tired of her after a while and she lost her slot; as did the next one. And then last year, when an eighteen-year-old TikToker landed a gig as the new soap correspondent, she became his target. And I can't imagine she would want to go near him, given the choice, but I don't know if she realises she has one. Everyone knows, it's an open secret, even amongst the press, but it doesn't fit the narrative that's making everyone money: him the *national treasure, the cheeky uncle who makes all the ladies giggle*. I was the last to know what Jude's been doing to that kid. When I found out, I wanted to speak up, but Dad and Janine told me I'd be mad to rock the boat and the girl wasn't underage anyway. Why should I put my career, and the golden-handcuffs contract Janine had 'busted her arse' to get me, on the line for something that was happening between 'two consent-ing adults'? But I know, I know it isn't what she wants, it's not what any of us wants. But I haven't said anything. He's still doing it, you know. I can't stand the thought of it. Do you know what, that's it: I'm going to speak to the channel head. Tomorrow. I can't do this

339

anymore. Even if no one else stands up
for her, I will. It's time . . . You still
want to marry me now?

I wasn't completely without scruples. Essie's on-camera realisation gave me reason to pause as I processed what I'd seen. She'd had clearly grown as a person. Somewhere, I could see that, but soon, this only made my rage burn deeper and harder: she'd offered to protect a young woman from a predator like Jude, but what about me? Why didn't I deserve shielding from my aggressor, her father? Was it because I really was as worthless as I'd been made to feel, both by Con and my parents, in wholly different but equally damaging ways? And not just them, but all the men I've slept with, and so many of the men I've found myself on the opposite side of a boardroom table from? The men who never truly saw my worth, not without me fighting for every morsel of respect, which would only be granted with strings attached anyway?

I regrouped. With a fresh clarity of purpose, I went about my original plan to wake Essie up to the reality of what had happened that summer, becoming more committed as I began to imagine Essie as Elena, finally getting her to say my words, to shine as my avatar. But to make that happen, I would have to dismantle Essie's life as she knew it, making her so desperate she'd let me cast her as my proxy, the character whose story I would push Essie through until she had nowhere else to look but at the truth she'd chosen to ignore. I edited Jackson's tape and returned the cut to him to sell to the media, then made one last money transfer and told him to delete all traces of our contact.

After the story broke, and when I was able to see with my

340

own eyes how profoundly it had broken Essie, when she came to the read through, I wanted to scream and hide – not from Essie, but from the horror, ugliness, and scale of own intentions. Could I really go through with my plan from here, even after I was able to see what a dreadful state it had already left her in? Yes. Once I'd introduced the topic of that weekend and she showed me she didn't care to dwell on what had been done to me, yes, I found I absolutely could. Not only could I continue what I had already put in motion, I wanted to go even further, knowing how much my having not only an enviable career, but also a seemingly perfect boyfriend of my own, would wound Essie in her fragility.

I had hoped by the time Essie was ready to come back into my life, I would have naturally attracted a partner. But the truth is, I had never fully made myself available to anyone since the incident at Signal. Using Jags, I grew addicted to the sense I was making Essie feel as alone and unlovable as I had been made to feel by Con and by her. I also became accustomed to paying him to spend time with me, even when I didn't have Essie as my audience. I would make up some scurrilous excuse; get him to walk with me to rehearse some lines he might say the next time we saw Essie; come to my place for dinner so I could brief him on the next phase of tormenting her. Somewhere along the way, I convinced myself that perhaps he could care for me, even before his apparent emotional epiphany on the final day of the shoot. Over the previous months, Jags showed an interest in my life in that he began to ask me questions, about Essie and our history. And in the spotlight of this attention, I made the mistake of telling him just enough to encourage him to probe more. And when, one day, he appeared fascinated by what

341

I knew about the downfall of Essie Lay, I suppose it was in a bid to impress him, to show him my power, that I told Jags how I was the architect of her downfall, though I did not want to share with him exactly why.

Afterwards, on many of my long and lonely nights, I did, of course, curse myself for telling him how I'd engineered Essie back into my life and my movie. Sometimes I panicked over how deeply vulnerable I'd left myself. And then, a miracle. My decoy boyfriend fell for me for real. I didn't need to feel alone anymore, and I didn't have to worry I'd be exposed to ruin anymore by telling Jags the terrible things I'd made happen to Essie.

'The things us resting actors have to do to put food on the table,' Jags says now, cracking into my memories, rubbing his damp hair with a towel, allowing me to observe the sheen of his skin over the muscles across his pecs and stomach. I think back to when he showed up at the wrap party and knew I would get to spend the night next to the warmth of that body. The way Jags apologised for how he had been earlier that day, the way he had kissed me, properly, for the first time; I wanted to melt into him, realising how deeply I had been aching for us to be something real. And then, I no longer needed to rely on making promises about getting him parts, or offering him morsels of my grand plan with Essie, to keep him interested in me. From that day on, April Eisdale, the misfit with endless dreams above her station, was enough for him, and all her dreams were coming true.

Jags's obvious repulsion for me now cannot compete with the revulsion I feel for myself. I am now alone with the actor I paid to taunt Essie by masquerading as my perfect boyfriend and faced with Essie's ultimate revenge: recruiting Jags as a double agent to make me believe he had genuine feelings for me, making me fall for a practised liar who must have surely gone on to kill my best friend, not only that, but a talent I always knew was capable of bringing my work to life. I always knew Essie would elevate my ability to tell the stories I wanted to tell. In amongst my darker motivations, Essie proved my first instincts about her correct: she was the ideal muse through which to tell my truths.

But what is the truth now?

'The day we wrapped on the shoot, that's when she flipped you, when you told her everything you knew about what I'd done. Then she started paying you. Why did you kill her?' I ask Jags, my voice wavering.

Jags laughs. 'Give me my phone. You're not getting anything else out of me; you've had more than your fair share already. This whole thing has got way too fucked up for my paygrade. I'm getting my last instalment tonight, and after that, I'm gone. I wouldn't stick around much if I were you either, but what do I care, it's your funeral, you know. After hers, of course.'

I gasp at his callousness.

Jags moves to hover right over me. 'Give me my fucking phone back. *Now.*'

Three simultaneous pings: my phone, Jags's, Essie's.

I turn away from Jags and look at each of the phones I'm holding. Three notifications on the screens, but only one message:

WHATEVER HAPPENED TO ESTHER LAYCOCK? COME TO THE POOL AND FIND OUT.

343

32

Essie, after

Jags and April are on opposite sides of the pool room. April is looking terrified, her arms wrapped around her as she stands by my egg chair, while Jags, close to the doorway into the atrium, is doing his best to appear untroubled and unimpressed, like he's waiting the whole thing out until my final payment to him clears.

They both jump when I appear. A huge image of me on my cinema screen to the foot-stomping guitar of Rainbow's 'Since You Been Gone', playing so loud the windows shake. A series of images: me, aged twenty-one, making my screen debut in *All Aboard*. Next, a fast-cut sequence of me on the front cover of a dozen magazines, interspersed with stills of me interviewing film and music stars. And now, photos of me getting older, intercut with headlines about my body, my boyfriends, my emotional state, pregnancy scares, 'fertility worries', fragile mental health.

Then, I transform into the smiling screen wife of Filthy Jude, faking my laughing fits, the deadness inside me invisible to the cameras. Still, the horrid headlines roll across the projection, until finally there's the explosion of hate around my downfall, and the images of me crying accelerate. Meanwhile, the singer whines about losing his mind over a woman who's made herself disappear.

The song slows to a hideous, distorted moan, one final discordant note as a black card appears:

The Vanished Woman
A Film by April Eden

In the room, April breathes heavily, red as the devil. Meanwhile, Jags struggles to maintain his nonchalance, looking around him as though the person running the show is going to jump out from behind. Both of them watch the screen fade, giving way to black-and-white CCTV footage. It's grainy but April recognises what she's watching immediately: the night of the awards, inside Lotus, April being guided away from my body in the pool by Jags. Next, April answering my sister's call as me. Then, over the images of her leaving Lotus that night, the audio recording of Jags ham-fistedly trying to get April to confess the day my body vanished when they were in her flat. Now CCTV of Jags's grey car pulling into Lotus, then slowly making its way to the spot behind my annexe. Janine fills the frame now. Close on her face. We pan out to see two women in sensible coats standing before her, their heads directed to the floor, as Janine looks at photos of my body and starts to cry.

The footage cuts to the video April was sent, the dark, clothed hand, in my room, taking my things, leaving the box containing the white dress on April's doorstep, finally leaving a strand of my extensions on the light at the edge of the pond

345

and pressing the champagne and pill bottles into the sludge with a black biker-booted foot.

And now: me. My blue-grey body on the banks of my lotus pond, wind whipping my hair around my head and into the mud. April watches with her hand clasped over her mouth, shaking.

One final frame, words over black:

> BEHIND YOU

April gasps as simultaneously the living room is plunged into darkness and the lights in the swimming pool come alive. She whips her head around.

'Oh god. Oh god.' April's voice sounds like it did when she first found me in the pool. She moves towards the sliding doors, throws them open. Behind her, Jags crosses the room in grim, fearful curiosity.

'No. No, no, *no*!' April screams when she sees what is waiting for her in the pool.

There I am, in a dress as black as a starless sky, facedown in the water again.

My skin has the look of greenish clay, my arms bobbing lifelessly, my veins, chords of dark purple around my arms and the visible sections of my thighs. My extensions are ragged, rotten on my cold skull.

April makes a high whine as she kicks off her trainers and dives in, watched by Jags. Flailing in the water, she gulps and retches and cries as she goes to grab me. A violent bubbling of white water. Panic.

'Help me!' April cries, but Jags has no intention of assisting her, he only wants to watch the spectacle of April flailing about my body. 'Please!' she manages to squeal as she seems to fight against the water itself.

But April isn't asking for help retrieving my body.

She needs Jags, or someone, anyone, to save her.

Because now April is being pulled down into the water.

33

April, now

Pressure on my shoulders, a vice around my ankle, scrapes of black and blue across my vision as I try to escape the liquid flooding my lungs. I don't want to die, here, swallowing mouthfuls of fetid pool water, watched by a man who despises me next to the body of a friend I failed to protect.

Sudden stillness. I don't need to fight anymore.

My head breaks the surface of the water. Through the blur of water in my eyes, it looks as though Essie's body is pulling itself out of the pool.

'What?' I splutter.

The body walks to one of the sun loungers, picks up a towel, and wipes her face and arms free of as much of the greasy makeup on them as she can. Still coughing up water, I swim to the steps as she strolls back into her living room. I pull myself out and a black towel is thrown in my direction.

'Let's talk.'

Jags watches Essie, open-mouthed as she heads past the sliding doors.

'Don't think you're going anywhere yet either,' Essie calls back to him, as she moves to her egg chair.

I squelch my way into the living space behind Jags, my lungs still trying to rid themselves of the stale, sickeningly warm water and get oxygen to my overwhelmed brain.

'Essie,' I say, following her.

I go to perch on the end of the sofa arm nearest Essie. Jags, meanwhile, leans against the far wall nearest the atrium.

'Don't call me that. You know my name is Esther.'

'OK. Esther.'

'There are two ways this could go.' Esther's voice sounds unusually low, as though she has matured ten years in the last few days. Still, I can't help it: a joy to hear it again. And also this: no body, no murder, no need for the police to investigate and take me away. Though I don't yet know what else Esther has in store for me, I can't help but be overcome with relief.

'I can't believe you're here. I can't believe you're alive. I've been feeling—'

She closes her eyes and raises her two hands by the sides of her dripping hair. '*I* am going to be listened to today. Don't speak over me. Don't speak *for* me. It's my turn now.'

I nod, admonished.

She reaches for the remote control to her cinema screen and presses a button.

CCTV footage from within Lotus.

Her face, her nose and eyes huge, up close to the lens of one of her security cameras. She leans back and it's clear she's standing on top of a ladder. She dips a brush into a small pot of what looks like her black nail varnish and applies a dab to cover the red light that would have told me the cameras were recording.

Now a rough cut of footage of me playing the video for Jude, reminding me it was Jags's idea to keep coming back to Lotus, generating more content for his paymaster, it would seem. Now there's CCTV of Jags running back to the annexe to retrieve his things when he went back inside Lotus while Janine swam, as oblivious as I was. All the while, I thought I was the director out of the two of us, but it was Esther, directing him, and me, changing the narrative of my life when I believed I was doing the same to her. Now, I'm required to watch Esther, teasing hair from her brush, sprinkling them about the seat of her chair. Finally, the two 'detectives', not with Janine in the atrium at Lotus, but in the old church rehearsal space I used for the table read of *The Vanishing Woman*, scripts in their hands as they rehearse their scene. The footage ends.

The real Esther speaks.

'Do you like my film, April? This is just a rough cut, but you get the idea: *She Who Would Not Be Vanished*.'

'I didn't know you could—'

'Do anything but be the woman people wanted me to be? Including you? No. You gave me a brilliant idea after I found out what you'd done to me with Jackson. And I took a course. This is all my filming, my work, my story,' Esther says calmly, but her words are crisp with pride and assurance.

'I'm done with people, with you, directing the story of my life. I know you had your reasons, April. I know it mattered to you that I accepted what my father did to you, but you went way too far. Paying a man to sleep with me? Worse than that, to make like he actually loved me; like he was going to give me a future you correctly guessed I longed for?'

'That was you, ransacking your own things? And you set up the shots of your body on the banks of the pond?' Esther's shots feel assured, accomplished even. She had more to give than Janine, Jonathan, her family, and the public could ever imagine. More than I had even allowed myself to believe.

'He shot them,' she says, gesturing to Jags who gives a half-hearted shrug. 'But, yes, I designed and set up all those scenes and images. And I'll be directing everything about my life from now on. Not you, not Janine, not Jonathan, not whoever or whatever piece of shit wants to make disgusting stories about my body, my shame, my sex, my mind, use all of them as it suits. *Me.*' Esther's voice is tearful, but her back and shoulders are true and straight, as though ready for some noble march. Now, she leans forward. 'My director's cut: I reveal every awful thing you have done to me in your screwed-up quest to avenge me for the sins of my father and maybe bring me down a peg or two because you can't be like me; show the world far from being a woman who elevates others, you're one more person who thought they could use me. I want people to know that Essie Lay isn't going to let herself get pushed into doing things she doesn't want to anymore.'

'Esther, you're right, but I did, I *do* believe you've got so much to give; I do want to elevate you. I—'

Esther cuts me off. 'I understand and I'll say it again: I am sorry. I was young and I was desperate for my dad's approval, I was stupid and I should have been better, but I wasn't.'

The apologies Esther gave me then, and now, they should have been my nirvana moments, the point at which I knew everything I'd done had been worthwhile. I wanted to feel relief and validation, but Esther's apologies have only made me feel even more worthless. I want to make what I've done, and me, better somehow. Because I can't live with how I feel right now.

351

'It wasn't your fault, Esther. None of it was. I'm sorry. I should have been honest, should have come to you, I should have known he would have forced you to believe his side of the story.'

Esther nods. 'I'm never making the same mistake again. He's dead to me now.'

I find my throat has tightened, and I realise, this is the relief; the validation I have needed. I swallow.

'Is there another option; another way you could tell the story?'

Esther's features relax and she takes a deep breath. 'We finish my film, together. We create a work on what fame, what industries like ours, do to women like us. We'll be creating our own genre. And I fund the whole project; I reinvest anything we make from the film, I liquidise my portfolio, the boat stuff, whatever Janine's got me into, I'll get out of, get my money back and go back to the thing I should have probably been all along, a producer. You take what I've started and make it as excellent as I know you know how.' Esther's eyes seem to be flashing from blue through to amber, as her ambitions unfurl. 'I don't want to rely on men to greenlight what I get to do, do you? So, what's it going to be, April? Your choice.'

I go to speak, but someone else is already talking.

'Once again, Esther, what you're saying isn't true.' Jags walks to where Esther and I sit, his hands in his pockets and a smug expression that reminds me so much of my father, and Con, and my male financiers, and every other man who thought they were the first to fuck me.

'The only thing you girls can do, is exactly what I say.'

34

April, now

Both Esther and I turn to Jags.

'I have the dirt on both of you. I could run your careers, your reputations.'

'What about your reputation?' Esther says. 'Think your agent's phone, that's if you have one, is about to ring off the hook when the world knows what you've been paid to do?'

Jags looks momentarily stung by Esther's comments, before giving a theatrical shrug.

'And your family are going to be so proud, or they will be once they know what you've become,' I add, sarcastically.

'April, you know now there is no demanding mum, waiting for her son to come home every day. Like you, I'm already nothing to my family, so there's no further damage to be done.' He smiles with great gratification, as if having a family that hates you is something to be proud of. 'As for my acting career, that's as good as dead currently too, despite the carrots *certain people* dangled before me when they wanted a kiss and a fumble.'

'Don't talk about her that way,' Esther says.

I'm immediately moved by the fact she's standing up for me. A rush of raw emotion bursts free of me before I can stem it. 'I didn't want to hurt you. I'm sorry. I shouldn't have done what I did,' I tell her, and her alone. Esther nods, her eyes closed again.

'This is so touching! Look at you two,' Jags says. 'Now you've come over all sentimental, you can agree on the only course of action that's going to let you leave this situation with your lives as you know them intact.'

Esther and I wait, her moving to be where I am now, next to her chair and side table.

'I want money and a place to live, not Lotus End or whatever you call the hut I've been holed up in. You can look after that, Esther, can't you? As for you, April, darling, I think you owe me that part now, don't you? As long as this little scandal of yours never sees the light of day, you should get the greenlight on the Martin Russo project you've been getting all hot and bothered about. I should think there's a decent role in there for me, after all.'

'And in return, what do we get?' I ask him.

Jags closes in on Esther, relishing the power he has in this moment. He is near enough to view her face closely, in faux tenderness. 'My discretion. For as long as I decide to give it.' Jags takes the end of a strand of Esther's hair in his fingers. She recoils, staggers back, forcing her to grab onto her Best Actress gong to steady herself. 'My silence . . .' Now Jags dares to move a strand of Esther's hair away from her face with his finger, her cringing at his touch, '. . . on whatever terms I dictate. No more *call me Esther, turn the camera this way, stand over there, tell April you love her.*' Esther looks to the floor. '*Make sure you get her over to Lotus, give old April a big old kiss.* Nope. I get to direct you now, Essie; tell you whose bed to lie

354

in.' Jags's fingers now trace the line of her neck down towards Esther's breast.

Esther's breath is audible, her voice raked by repulsion when she speaks. 'No. I don't want that. You won't control me.'

'I don't think you have a choice, Essie, do you?' Jags leans into her space, his hand around the base of her skull now, bringing her head to his so he can kiss her roughly and before I can do anything to stop him. Esther makes a high grunt, trying to shrink away from Jags, but he has a point to prove and will not let her free.

A rush of air makes me flinch, my eyes shutting tight.

A stomach-churning, liquid thud.

I open my eyes, just as Jags's body twists towards me. His eyes find mine, wide, frozen, as he falls to his knees, then crumples to the ground.

His blood blooms into a rapidly expanding pool on the cream carpet.

In Esther's hand, a heavy bronze sculpture of a projector: her Best Actress statuette.

She looks at Jags on the floor, then at me, then at the award quivering in her grip, as though trying to work out what she has just done, as though the whole thing was an out-of-body moment.

Silence.

She is frozen, still trying to summon her spirit back into the body that's meted out such violence.

I crouch to the ground to examine Jags. His eyes are open and unblinking. 'I think . . . Esther, you've killed him.'

She finally moves, dropping the award on the floor, staring numbly at Jags's body.

355

'I didn't know what I was doing. I didn't mean to,' she says. 'I . . . That wasn't me. I snapped. Oh god.'

She blinks, shakes her head, finally taking possession of her senses, of her body again. 'What do we do? Who do we call? Ambulance?'

I see the film of my life, and Esther's, start to play from this moment forward. If we go to the police, Esther does not get the life she deserves. Neither do I. No deal, no Martin Russo, nothing but being the person on the scene when Essie Lay murdered a third-rate actor as part of a bizarre revenge plot. We've both come too far to go to that place now.

'Don't call anyone,' I say, moving in the direction of the kitchen.

'Where are you going?' Esther asks, an ethereal calm in her cadence.

'You want to throw away everything? Now? For him?'

Esther looks down at Jags and does not speak.

'Start deleting your footage. Wipe everything.' I turn away from her, thinking hard, choreographing what happens next.

Esther reaches for her laptop and starts typing, her hands shaking. 'Where are you going? Don't leave me.'

'I'm not leaving you, I'm helping you.' I run into the kitchen to grab a handful of carrier bags from Esther's drawer of domestic detritus. When I return, I ask her, 'Is all the footage clear? Can you switch all the cameras off, inside and outside?'

She nods, types again for a few moments.

'All done? Right, we need to lift his head.'

'I don't want to touch him,' Esther half-speaks, half-cries.

'Lift him, unless you want a trail of blood instead of one

patch,' I tell her, playing through the choreography of this clean-up scene and what we need to do next.

While Esther looks as though she needs to vomit, she manages to hold up Jags's shattered head long enough for me to get a layer of plastic around him. His head is now hooded by layers of takeaway delivery bags.

'I can't do this; whatever it is you're thinking of. Let's call the police, please. It was a moment of insanity or something.'

I breathe.

'No. It was self-defence, protecting your life from being controlled again by him or any man like him. But we're still not going to the police.'

Esther shakes her head, bewildered.

'Do you want your life back? Do you want to have that control over your story you were talking about? A dead actor in your mansion is not how that happens. We are going to deal with this. Like he told us, he's as good as dead to his family, same for his industry, and like me, he doesn't have much in the way of friends. He won't be missed.' I stand up, heaving the top of Jags's body with me.

'Grab his legs,' I tell Esther.

She hesitates, then nods. She seems to guess where we're heading. It's obvious. We slowly shuffle and heave our way out of the living space. Between us, Esther and I use every bit of our energy to get Jags's body through the kitchen, out into the night, down from the veranda and finally to the edge of the lotus pond.

'We need something to weigh him down,' I say, looking about before remembering what I saw in the garage. I run back to the house to grab the key, then yank the lock free.

357

I grab the thirty-pound pipe wrench I once feared Jags might kill me with.

When I join Esther on the bank, I drop the wrench on the bank and signal for her to grab Jags's legs while I take his top half again. With me leading, we drag ourselves deeper into the mud and freezing water, my ex-boyfriend's body a repulsive physical and metaphorical bridge between Esther and me. Then, something shifts. We're in so deep he begins to float, the weight lifting between us. She looks at me and I at her: we're even now; what I did to her with Jackson, and she to me with Jags, those sins are gone. What we are doing right now bonds us even more darkly to each other. It is not mutual revenge that links us anymore, it's mutual protection.

'I'll pull him to the centre. Go back to the bank and get ready to hand me the wrench.'

Esther gives me a shivery nod, while I lead Jags's floating body to the deepest section of the pond. I leave him there and swim back to Esther, all the while pulling through the spent lotus flowers and muddy waters. Shaking, she hands me the pipe wrench.

I struggle back to Jags's body. His form is half-submerged now but will not sink. I tug at his belt, undo his buttons and I shove the impossibly heavy wrench down his jeans.

Jags's body slowly vanishes into the black.

I make my way back to the bank, doing what I can to rearrange the dead lotuses so their pattern on the water's surface does not suggest disruption, Esther watching me from the lawn.

Once I'm out of the water, I search in the mud with my fingers, picking through it until I find the lock of fake hair, the champagne, and pill bottles. Eventually, I join Esther.

We both sit, slumped on the grass in the darkness. 'We'll clean, burn, or bin what we need to tonight. Can you hold off calling your parents and Janine until then? What will you tell them?'

Esther laughs through her nose, a bitter sound, her eyes still trained on the centre of the lotus pond. 'I'll tell them I was testing them, and they failed, and I'll tell them via my lawyer.' Her voice is tight with cold, but her words are slack with resignation. 'I caught the three of them on the CCTV earlier, working out their media lines about the deputyship, figuring out who should get what, regardless of what my will said. They'd only just found out I was dead. I don't know what I did to deserve that.' She looks at me, tears in her eyes. 'I don't know what I did to them to make them treat me that way.' She shakes her head. 'What did you do to make your family hate who you are?'

I think about it a moment. 'Some parents, some siblings, are able to rejoice in their relationship with someone special, someone smart, particularly if it's their sons and brothers who shine. But some families see their children's, especially their daughters', gifts as an affront to their lack of them. Our families both fall into this category.'

'I'm so sorry about all this.' Esther speaks over chattering teeth.

'Let's go inside,' I say.

We help each other up, Esther using my shoulders to steady her, me holding onto her hand to lift me from the ground. We're nearly at the house. The silence between us feels loaded with all we have done to each other and what we have just done to Jags. She feels it too.

359

'April.' Esther's voice is now a childish quiver. 'I feel like this isn't finished. I'm scared.'

I walk on.

When she speaks again, her sweet husk, tightened by shock and cold, makes her sound twenty-one again, like the very first day she came into my life. 'If you were writing the story of what we've done for a film you wanted to get financed, how would you end it?'

I don't have to think about it long.

'For it to really sell, for audiences to properly feel satisfied, I would say a woman has to suffer. There's a general expectation that stories like this need a female victim.'

We climb the steps to the veranda side by side. Esther stops. She touches the side of my arm, so we're almost facing each other.

'Haven't we suffered enough already, April? Let's make a better ending to our story.'

DENOUEMENT

'Consider giving your players a single point of focus in a frame. By giving two central characters a shared, tangible object they both have in their sights, it's possible for you to connect them even more powerfully than if they were looking directly at each other.'

ESTHER'S FILM LECTURE NOTES TRANSCRIPTION

One year later

Esther

I'm a bona fide actress now, but I intend to start directing myself in the next couple of years, as well as producing; put the course I took and all I've learnt from April to use. These are the reasons I get out of bed now.

I don't speak to my parents or my sister unless it's through my lawyers and I don't want to find a man to love, because if I did, I would either have to share what I have done and bring him into my crime, or pretend I didn't fundamentally change the day I did what I did to Jags. I can do neither of these things.

I can't report my father for the rape of April either. I offered to go with her, told her we would do it together so I could be her witness, but, understandably, April is keen we both steer clear of police for as long as we can. On a good day, and these are rare, I imagine I can avoid investigation until for the rest of my life. Until then, the only person with whom I can have a meaningful relationship based on honesty is April. And the only solace I get from being Esther Laycock is when I'm working with her.

We're currently shooting *The Longest Road*, April's rape-revenge thriller that feels like a follow-up to *The Vanished Woman*, though it isn't technically a sequel. I play the woman wronged, and Martin Russo, the grizzled PI I recruit to help track down and then torment the perpetrator. I love every day on set and every moment in character.

But every day, I still wait for the phone to ring, for the journalist to ask the question, for someone who knew the man I killed, whose body has rotted to bone in my lotus pond, to come after me. I deserve living like this, always on high alert, seeing his face every time I look into the water and each time I close my eyes at night. Alone in my grand house that no longer feels like a cocoon, but the thing it perhaps always was from the moment I danced with the devil called fame: a gilded cage I can never leave.

April

Martin is a joy to direct, and he seems to get a kick from being told what to do by his wife. His therapist describes our relationship as a kind of treatment; a mental and emotional reckoning only possible when you stop dating former Victoria's Secret models thirty years your junior and settle into a relationship with someone, physically at least, altogether more average. It's certainly supporting his battle for part-time custody of his children to have a sensible middle-aged woman on his arm rather than some nubile beauty. We divide our lives between the house I chose in Hampstead not too far from Lotus and our home in Los Feliz. I am his third wife, but I believe, his last. None of my family were invited to 'the wedding of the century', but Esther was my maid of honour.

Martin is attached to every project I have in the pipeline, therefore ensuring its success. The day after Esther killed Jags, I pulled out of the first-look deal talks and decided to throw my hat in with a rookie production company whose sole purpose is to bankroll female directors: Lotus Content, Esther's company. There is already Oscar buzz about *The Longest Road* and I do believe Esther will become spectacularly rich on the back of her company. But more than this, she will become powerful. She could continue acting, but I suspect *The Longest Road* may be her last adventure in front of the camera. She'll get behind it, pull strings, be resourceful, deploy her instinctive taste and style and her charm, her shrewdness, and her tenacity to become the super-producer she was destined to be. And one day, she'll direct too, a move I would wholeheartedly support.

Am I happy? I would say my life now is a very enjoyable proxy. Have I finally found true love? I no longer believe that matters. What I do know is that I get to go to bed with Martin Russo every night, and all the world knows it. I like this very much. I also like having the genuine love of my audiences, and the critics. And, of course, my friendship with Esther, the woman who knows all of my secrets; once a source of my deepest pains, now and forever my muse.

Acknowledgements

Thank you Hellie Ogden, Clio Seraphim, Emily Kitchin, Clare Gordon, Ruth Thorpe, Caroline Mitchell, Bernardette Monks-Brown, Joanne Johnson, Bernard Monks, Monica Monks, Helen Nugent, Frances Corrin, Elizabeth Corrin, Victoria Lane, Chloe Leland, Emma Guise, Gurpal Takhar, Gurmail Takhar, Sarah Fountain, and Stuart Gibbon.

Thank you, Mohinder and Zora.

Thank you, Danny.

Nothing Without Me

Helen Monks Takhar

A BOOK CLUB GUIDE

Author's Note

'I'm fed up with the sport-like scrutiny and body shaming that occurs daily. . . . I am an example of the lens through which we, as a society, view our mothers, daughters, sisters, wives, female friends and colleagues. The objectification and scrutiny we put women through is absurd and disturbing,' so wrote Jennifer Aniston for *The Huffington Post* in 2016, and who could be more familiar with the blood sport of female celebrity body objectification than someone who's been subjected to it for three decades.

In my debut, I explored, amongst other themes, the hypervisibility of women in their twenties and the 'midlife cloak of invisibility' slung around the shoulders of women as we age. In my second novel, I examined the high-pressure, performative nature of modern working motherhood and the judgements we are liable to land on ourselves and other women. There is certainly something about female visibility, public performance, and the panorama of judgement womanhood entails that fascinates me, themes in which I could fully immerse myself through a story set in the world of celebrity and the film industry.

'Millions of people are culpable . . . they have their share of blame for pushing me to this point,' says 'dead' Essie at the start of the novel. Every generation creates their celebrity sacrificial lambs. More often than not, these gilded but unfortunate creatures are ewes, women into whom we pour our highest aspirations and deepest insecurities; why else would we consume and generate so much content about the weight they gain; the fortunes, partners and pregnancies they lose? I do not pose this question as an innocent bystander. I have clicked on those stories, responding to the same chum in the water as billions of us trained on the scent of female celebrity failure. April and Essie's story is a place where I could explore why.

Through various stages of my career in journalism, and also working in press for charities, I've been in the distant orbit of famous people. I admit to finding them and the ecosystems that arise around them—the photographers, the assistants, the squads of people facilitating the lives of *The Talent*—utterly compelling. I once watched a young starlet barely able to put a foot in front of the other, so blinded was she by the paparazzi flashes as she left a music awards ceremony. And when I say *young*, she was a teenager. The sheer weirdness and accepted inappropriateness of leagues of middle-aged men braying at her left me deeply disturbed.

I've also been at a post-premiere party where an A-list movie star emanated utter luminosity, such beguiling 'star quality' she seemed herself to be a source of light that energized the air around her. Very famous, profoundly charismatic and beautiful people can leave us simultaneously agog in awe of all they are and mired in dismay at all we are not. Maybe fame is about a human compulsion to elevate some of our number to demigods, but this process leaves the less celestial amongst us frustrated with our lowly fates. This conflict powers us to tear down our idols at the same time as we exult them, perhaps inevitably leaving our human deities churned-up and wounded in the maelstrom.

April's story straddles this tension. She's fascinated by Essie and her charisma; she wants to get close to it; cherish it and use it to elevate both Essie and her own career. But Essie's 'light' leaves April with the darkest feelings. When she's no longer in Essie's life, Essie's *It factor* serves to emphasize her physical lack of exceptionality and heighten the unloveability April has long felt: ' . . . when I was Essie's friend, some of her stardust seemed to settle on me, making me also fated for success, built for love.' For her part, Essie is a woman who never consented to her life and her body being ultra-visible and over-invested by millions, but she's required to navigate all that entails anyway, realizing too late how insincere and ephemeral the love of the masses can be.

A word on female directors and creatives in film. A 2022 report in *Forbes* highlighted how women's employment in top-grossing films remains 'astonishingly low' and while female directors are 'key to getting more women behind the scenes,' a recent study indicates how slow progress is proving. *Inclusion in the Director's Chair: Analysis of Director Gender and Race/Ethnicity Across the 1,600 Top Films from 2007 to 2022* by Dr. Stacy L. Smith, Dr. Katherine Pieper and Sam Wheeler showed more than 80 percent of directors were white men, 14 percent were men from underrepresented groups, 4 percent were white women, and only 1 percent were women from underrepresented groups. This matters not only because

373

diversity in beacon industries like film and TV is the right thing, but because diversity means the best of all of us get to make and tell stories, raising the quality of storytelling and squeezing mediocrity from the mainstream to the margins. More diversity in film and TV gives more of us a chance to see stories that resonate and connect, stories in which we're more likely to recognise ourselves in those on-screen demi-gods.

In one draft of this book, I went along with April's downbeat assertion that spoke to a certain 'sacrificial ewe' imperative: ' . . . for audiences to properly feel satisfied, I would say a woman has to suffer. There's a general expectation that stories like this need a female victim.' However, my female editors created the space for me to write the ending as I have it in the draft you have just read. Our female leads walk off together into an, albeit imperfect, sunset, but at least one where they have the power to give more women the chance to direct their own stories. It would be heartening to imagine this element of the story becomes less the stuff of fiction soon.

Questions and Topics for Discussion

1. Did the novel make you feel differently about the lives of famous women? Do you feel guilty about how you may have felt or spoken about famous women?

2. Why do you think April is so unlikeable to so many people? How do you think being a writer/director makes her feel better about herself?

3. Why is Essie so desperate for her father's approval? Would securing this be enough to make her happy? What do you think would make Essie happy?

4. What did you think of Janine? Did you ever feel sorry for her?

5. Which character do you think has the most power in the novel and why? How does this change as the story develops?

6. Do you think things are any better for women in the film and TV industries post #MeToo? What do you think needs to change to give the real-life Aprils and Essies a fairer shot?

7. At what point did you realise April had engineered Essie's downfall?

8. What do you think the day-to-day reality of being famous is like? Is this the kind of life you would enjoy?

9. What did you think of Jags and April as a couple and how did your feelings change as the story developed?

10. How did the chapters set in the deeper past drive the present-day storyline forward?

11. While Jags is the character who says to April of Essie, 'she'd be nothing with you,' what does the book's title mean to you? Who do you think, 'You'd be nothing without me' is directed at and by which character? Is there more than one character who might say it to another? Or is this something the public should feel entitled to say to famous people?

PHOTO: © SUNFLOWERS PHOTOGRAPHY

HELEN MONKS TAKHAR is the author of the novels *Precious You* and *Such a Good Mother*. She is also joint managing director of the production company Second Generation with her husband, screenwriter and executive producer Danny Takhar. Helen worked as a journalist, copywriter, and magazine editor after graduating from Cambridge University. She began her career writing for financial trade newspapers before contributing to UK national newspapers including *The Times* and *The Observer*. She lives in North London with Danny and their two daughters.

helenmonkstakhar.co.uk
Twitter: @HelenMTakhar
Instagram: @helenmonkstakhar

About the Type

This book was set in Sabon, a typeface designed by the well-known German typographer Jan Tschichold (1902–74). Sabon's design is based upon the original letter forms of sixteenth-century French type designer Claude Garamond and was created specifically to be used for three sources: foundry type for hand composition, Linotype, and Monotype. Tschichold named his typeface for the famous Frankfurt type-founder Jacques Sabon (c. 1520–80).